A Katie Delancey Novel - Volume 3

STRETCHING FOR HOME

J. A. TAYLOR

STRETCHING FOR HOME
Copyright © 2015 by J. A. Taylor

Unless otherwise indicated, all scriptures taken from the Holy Bible, New International Version®, NIV®. Copyright © 1973, 1978, 1984, 2011 by Biblica, Inc.™ Used by permission of Zondervan. All rights reserved worldwide. Scripture taken from The Message. Copyright © 1993, 1994, 1995, 1996, 2000, 2001, 2002. Used by permission of NavPress Publishing Group.

Printed in Canada

ISBN: 978-1-4866-0996-3

Word Alive Press
131 Cordite Road, Winnipeg, MB R3W 1S1
www.wordalivepress.ca

Library and Archives Canada Cataloguing in Publication

Taylor, J. A. (John Alexander), 1956-, author
    Stretching for home / J.A. Taylor.

Issued in print and electronic formats.
ISBN 978-1-4866-0996-3 (paperback).--ISBN 978-1-4866-0997-0 (pdf).--
ISBN 978-1-4866-0998-7 (html).--ISBN 978-1-4866-0999-4 (epub)

    I. Title.

PS8639.A9515S77 2015   jC813'.6   C2015-903861-8
                                                      C2015-903862-6

ACKNOWLEDGMENTS

My thanks to the staff and students of the Rift Valley Academy in Kenya, who were the source of 18 great years; and my thanks to God for his gracious care through many adventures, relationships and experiences that have helped provide the core of what this series is about.

CHAPTER ONE

"**S**top it!"

I set my jaw and clench the bedroom doorknob in a death grip. The thunder in my head doesn't stop. Bizarre auras spring up like northern lights. An invisible drill bores through my left temple and into the core of my eyes. A nerve in my neck corkscrews tighter than a rubber band around a beater on high speed. My gut pretzels and threatens to heave a great quiche all over the tile floor.

My head is caving in and the pounding won't stop. A chill pierces into my jaw and down my spine. I want my bed and a good pillow to put over my head. And I want that incessant banging on the door to quit.

"Stop it!" I yell again.

I stumble to the window, inch the checked drapes open, and squint out. The string of Christmas lights glow faintly along the outside sill. A blurry figure raises a gun butt to my door. The temperature gauge is almost iced over but I can still read it.

Who in their right mind would be out on a minus-twenty Minnesota morning when the sun has barely crawled out of bed?

The thunder erupts again at the door.

Oh God, make it go away.

An entire marching band erupts between my ears. I fall on my knees and press my thumbs into my temples until the vice threatens to crush me.

What in the world is Bruce doing in that shower so long? I need to get back to bed and cover my head with a pillow again. *Stubborn husband!* He's turned up the volume of a country music station so high that he wouldn't know if a train drove through the bathroom. Whoever's at the door is working hard to be heard over that din.

The pounding sounds like it's going to crush in the kitchen door. I pull on a black Rift Academy sweatshirt and some jeans and slouch barefoot across the tile. I refuse to flip on the light switch, but the magic mirror by the door still gets enough light to inform me that I'm currently impersonating a zombie with a blond rat's nest on top.

I need my bed, badly. The sight of a uniform crouching by the kitchen window stops me from going back. The officer cups his hands on the door glass and his beady little eyes look right at me. His nose and mouth form a little frost patch of condensation on the pane, and he looks as freaky as I feel. I look left, out the family room window, at the deep white drifts smothering the landscape, and decide I need slippers.

When I turn my back on him, the lawman pounds on the door again and yells at me to "open up in the name of the law." I ignore the slippers and baby-step my way to the door. I press the heels of my hands against the sides of my head to keep focused. The throbbing is still intense.

I keep it simple. "Who's there?"

"What do you mean, who's there?" The face disappears from the window, but the voice continues. "This is the county sheriff's office. Now, open up this door before I kick it in."

One thing about me, I pick up quick when things are serious. My cellphone begins to play Roger Whittaker's "My Land Is Kenya." My sister Lizzy is checking in on me. Now that's serious.

Bruce turns down the country music blast, opens the door a few inches, and yells from the bathroom. "Katie, honey, before you get that phone can you get me a towel?" Up goes the volume again. The door swings open and the vibrations of endless echoing guitars hit me like a tsunami.

I stand by the kitchen door and yell at the frosted window. "Are you sure you can't come back? We arrived in Minnesota late last night from my sister's and I've got a migraine."

"Ma'am, I don't know who you are or why you're here, but I've got a body frozen in the ditch on the edge of your property and I need some answers—now!"

"Is my horse okay?" I start to pace. "Did you see Lancelot?"

The face appears in the window again. "Ma'am, I don't know anything about your horse. I've got a body and I want to know why."

"You want to know why you have a body?" His freaky face gets fuzzier behind a cloud of frosty breath, and that's all I can see. "You want to know why you have a body?"

I giggle and squeeze my skull as the pain increases. I giggle until the door is nearly smashed off its hinges by the boot of an officer yelling, "Police! Open up now!"

I strangle my blond bedhead into an imitation ponytail and tuck the end of it into the sweatshirt. Lizzy begins her voice message with her usual sisterly affection. Her voice is hardly more than a whisper among the other noises. "Hey, dung beetle, get out of bed. The honeymoon's over."

"Just a minute," I croak as I scoop up the phone from the table and run to kick the bathroom door closed.

My big toe hits the corner of that door. The fire races up my joint and right to my brain. I hop on one foot to the kitchen door, unlock the deadbolt, then collapse into a pretzel. I fold my arms across my chest and howl at the phone. That's how the county sheriff finds me when his boots stop inches from my elbows.

Bruce hops out of the bathroom door to check on my distress and then vanishes back inside. Lizzy screams out of concern at my howling. The sheriff stands over me with his gun pointed at my head. "Welcome to Minnesota, ma'am."

CHAPTER TWO

ooking into the muzzle of a gun is an incredibly clarifying moment. The last few times this happened I didn't believe I'd survive. My double vision continues, but the throbbing in my skull eases. I shut Lizzy's voice off, wrap my arms around my head, and curl up into a ball.

The weapon pokes into my ribs and a gravelly voice says, "If you haven't done anything wrong then you don't have to be afraid." The voice stimulates an image of a Grover Muppet moving its big mouth up and down. I giggle from my gut.

Bruce is yelling above the country music. "Towel! I need a towel. What is going on out there?"

The nuzzle moves along my ribs toward my left shoulder. The Muppet speaks again, "We don't look lightly on druggies in this county, honey." A hand grabs my shoulder, turns me, and presses my chest down into the floor. The tiles are cool against my cheek. The bathroom door is slightly open. The music stops. A knee crunches my spine. "Face down, hands behind your back."

The bathroom door bursts open and a one-legged, six-foot-four, unclothed Special Forces commander takes one hop and attacks my captor. I roll out from beneath the thrashing heavyweights and crawl under the table. The gun skitters across the tile floor and comes to rest against the baseboard nearby.

"Grab it!" Bruce yells.

The gun might as well be a green mamba ready to strike. I refuse to move.

The pounding in my head takes over. I squeeze my eyes shut tight. My stomach lurches and the bile in the back of my throat burns. My breathing is more like short gasps. I wrap my arms around my head again. It doesn't help. I scramble to the toilet and barely make it in time.

The noise of the struggling men goes on and on. And then it stops.

* * *

Two hours pass and my ribs ache from laughter as Bruce recounts again the look on Sheriff Reimer's face. Apparently, naked one-legged men are rare in these parts. The tension of the skirmish is forgotten. The alibi is accepted. The ambulance is gone. So is the sheriff. So is his gun. So is the body from the ditch.

Bruce is dressed. Lizzy is calmer. My migraine medication is working.

A shower would be nice. The golden rat's nest needs taming.

Minnesota is beginning differently than I expected.

* * *

After the shower, I cozy down by the fire with a good book and a cup of tea. Bruce hops to the window and peers through the drapes for several minutes. "Do you think the authorities believe you this time?"

"What do you mean?" I finally have to get up and see what he's looking at. "Are you still hassling me about that dead body?"

Bruce wraps me up in the curtain and swoops me off my feet. "Don't worry," he says. "As long as you're with me they won't suspect you of a thing."

I stiffen like a board until he unwinds me and carries me back to the couch. I stroke a scar on his cheek. "Of course they'd never suspect an Afghan medic who had his leg blown off trying to save someone. They just don't know your secrets like I do."

Life settles down during the days after our introduction to our Minnesota farmhouse. Summers here were part of my former life, but this is a first for winter. Bruce and I walk in the snow, feed and groom Lancelot, race snowmobiles, and cuddle by the fire.

A room full of novels and ugly weather patterns convince me I can put off work for another month or so. Honeymoons were meant to last a while.

* * *

Leaking sinks have got to be a major cause of divorce among newlyweds. Either that, or a CD with a limited number of Christmas carols playing on an endless loop. My head spins from cabin fever, the winter weather suffocating us.

I click off the music and shout out for my new husband as he tinkers under the kitchen sink fixing another drip. "Bruce, I think meteorology is an art in Minnesota, especially in winter."

The flickering fire and lamplight cast just enough glow to let me see a dim reflection in the living room window. The mischievous smirk on my face is obvious. I primp my strawberry blond bangs.

It takes a few seconds, but Bruce's reply echoes out from inside the kitchen cupboard. "How do you figure that, Katie?"

The front window makes a beautiful frame for the falling snow. My Hawaiian lounging pajamas are comfy. The steaming apple cider vibrates warmth through the cup. I don't have any incentive to go out today. I need entertainment.

In southern British Columbia, where I was a year ago, the snowdrops would already be wilted, the crocuses and heather and daffodils in full color. Christmas roses in my grandmom's old garden in Langley would be finished. I probably would have been out jogging or cycling most days if it wasn't raining.

Today, I should have taken Lancelot for a walk. A good horse shouldn't be ignored.

Bruce interrupts my thoughts: "Katie? Are you there?"

The kitchen door window still has a paper heart stuck in the middle of it. The love note is worth a smile.

"Do you know the difference between a Panhandle hook, an Alberta clipper, a Saskatchewan Screamer, a Manitoba Mauler, or just a thunderstorm?" I asked.

Bruce's one foot is flat to the floor and his knee arched. The stump of his other leg stretches out to the knee. He's wearing shorts in winter. It all seems normal.

"Haven't got a clue," he says. "Why are you asking?"

"The computer is predicting all of these this winter. We have to be prepared for everything here."

"So, are you learning all this through correspondence?" His sarcasm reeks.

I ignore the chuckle that accompanies the taunt. "That means not straying too far from home."

"If you didn't notice, I am home."

Ogling that muscular torso, my face breaks into another smile, a different smile. Bruce's t-shirt lays balled up on the counter. "The winds right now are intense. It's a bad time to be vulnerable." I slowly pick up a half-empty glass of cool water from off the counter and pour it completely out on his belly.

Bruce jerks up and smashes his head on the bottom of the sink. He yelps and reaches out to grab my leg. Regret comes quickly.

I backpedal and turn to leave the kitchen, but he propels himself across the floor and latches onto my ankles. I fall hard on my right shoulder and bounce like a bushel bag of sweet potatoes.

My husband drags me to the door, opens it, and slides me out on the porch, just as I am. Even polar bear swims don't hurt like this. The chill air burns when I breathe. The icy deck sizzles my palms and soles. I get up, slip, and fall on my backside. The jerk actually locks me out.

It isn't like I'm some Olympic figure skater doing the splits at center ice to win my gold medal. There's no reward for what I'm facing. The dumb commando didn't even think about the weather when he tossed me out. Last night we had a Panhandle hook dump a ton of snow and now there's a harsh artic chill threatening to turn me into a popsicle.

Sitting outside the kitchen door in freezer-like conditions, the day after my first great Valentine's Day with Bruce, wasn't in the plans. These lounging pajamas aren't for anyone's eyes but Bruce's. Of course, being isolated on a farm, in weather like this, I'm unlikely to be noticed by anyone. Being prone on an icy porch during a Minnesota winter is insane. It's also motivation to move, quick.

I can hardly see the shadow of the barn as the wind swirls snow in endless twisters. My lounging pajamas are already stiff. My elbows are tight against my side. My breath vaporizes and almost visibly drops to the ground.

Pride is stupid. I smash against the door and beg. We have a little routine for apologies and I have no choice but to do my part.

"Bruce, I'm sorry. You and I are like black and white zebra stripes. Please forgive me for getting your belly wet." If it wasn't so cold, I would have been doubled over laughing at my prank. The gusts of wind whip my skin like flying shards of glass. I crouch and wrap my arms around my legs. My knees are blue. There is only silence.

I bang louder. "Bruce, I'm sorry. You and I are like zebra stripes. We belong together. Please forgive me for getting your belly wet." My bare toes are freezing to the door sill. My teeth chatter. My lungs burn. My bladder screams for attention. "Bruce, I'm getting hypothermic out here!"

Three times is my limit and then the joke is over. "Bruce, honey, I'm really, really sorry. You and I belong together like zebra stripes." I take a deeper breath and feel the burn racing to fill my lungs. My hands rise to form a cover over my

7

mouth and nose. "Please forgive me for getting your belly wet. And for banging your head on the sink."

Bruce never makes me go three rounds. I usually have him laughing or salivating or feeling guilty without too much effort.

I grab an old wooden chair sitting by the porch swing and drag it over to the window at the top of the kitchen door. It has several inches of icy snow on it but I step up and peek through the glass. Bruce is sprawled out across the floor with a trickle of red running down his cheek from a gash on his forehead.

I bang on the door and window. He doesn't twitch at all. Without hesitation, I jump off the chair, bang off the snow, and slam the top of it through the small swing-out pane of the dining room window. I reach in and undo the latch, then set the chair in place and step up and onto the sill. After standing on it, I hurdle over the broken glass into the house.

Piercing pain hits me when I land, but that isn't at the top of my priority list at the moment. I step quickly through the scattered glass, and when the pain gets too intense I get down on my hands and knees and crawl over to Bruce.

A small pool of blood near his head is soaking into his black hair, but at least his pulse is healthy. I rise onto my knees, reach for his t-shirt, and soak it in the water still puddled on the floor nearby. I see no noticeable fractures so I flip him over.

I wipe his face with the damp t-shirt, pat his temple, and call him back to consciousness. No response. I slap him and manage to smear more blood on his face. In a few minutes, I can't tell which is his blood and which is mine.

Next I call 911. Forty minutes later, I lie on my bed under a warming blanket while one paramedic picks glass out of my hands, knees, and feet. Another coaches Bruce to relax and keep breathing easy through his oxygen mask. The sheriff tacks up a blanket over the glass hole, sweeps up the fragments, and calls his deputy to bring in some plywood for the window. Someone cleans up the blood.

One day this is going to be a memory. For now, it's just humiliation. *I've been trying so hard to be good all my life. Why is it so hard? I can't ever seem to get it right. I've only been married a few months and now I've probably lost the only man I've let through all my barriers. At least most of them.*

Tears drip off my chin and onto the hand of the paramedic. He assures me that he'll be careful. I can't even begin to tell this guy that my tears have nothing to do with the pain from the embedded glass. It's the pain in my heart which I am not even sure I can feel.

Eventually we get stitched up and revived.

Within the hour, Bruce and I work through our differences and connect again by lounging with a little bit of space between us. He waves off the ambulance and decides to tough it out. The irony is that, because of my foot bandages, Bruce has to fight through his wooziness and serve me.

Our neighbor, attracted by the emergency vehicles, sees our plight and does his best to feed Lancelot. The deputy returns with a carpenter by mid-afternoon and fixes the broken window. The local minister, Pastor Tyson, calls twice and his wife brings by a casserole.

My sister Lizzy and I spend the evening on the phone reminiscing about our double wedding in Kenya. At the stroke of noon the next day, the grocer drops off Bruce's order and my husband tries a few new recipes on me.

On the third day, Bruce seems unconvinced at my helplessness. "Girl, this is twice now since we arrived that you've had the sheriff out here." He leans against the bedroom door cradling a cup of coffee. "And twice you've ended up flat on your back with me serving you."

"The thing is, honey, some days I'm having as much trouble as the sheriff's department trying to figure out who you really are." I set aside the novel I'm reading and sit up in our bed. "Seems they're out here checking your ID more times than a serial killer on probation."

"Oh come on." Bruce adjusts the strap on his prosthetic limb. "The sheriff can see who I am just by looking at me."

I have to smile. "Yes, siree. And he sure got a good look at you his first visit." I tuck the blanket a little tighter under my arms. "You know how to make an impression."

Bruce raises his eyebrows. "Do you think they ever found out how old Sidney got frozen into that ditch?"

"I'm sure they still think it was you trying to drive with that fake leg of yours. Even though they spent hours checking out the Durango and the tire tracks, I don't think they're convinced yet." I pat the flattened space beside me. "I'm sure they think you bumped him off the road and into that ditch. I don't think they trust you."

"Trust me? I think it's you they don't trust." Bruce walks to the window and pushes aside the curtains. He turns his back on me. "Howling like a banshee on the floor and refusing to open the door until they almost break it down. You're no sooner out of your toe cast than you end up having the paramedics here to take glass out of you."

"I don't think the sheriff buys your explanation that putting me out in the freezing cold in my pajamas was a little joke because of another joke I played on you." I grab his pillow and bunch it up. "I think they're going to be watching you like a hawk in this town."

He sips his coffee and turns. "And I suppose you'd play that little abuse card just to blackmail me for some extra attention?"

I hug the pillow. "Would it work?"

"I can't believe you'd even ask." Bruce backs away toward the door. "Do you ever think we should tell the sheriff our real story?"

"Now, that would be asking for trouble." I curl my index finger at him and beckon him toward me. "What do you want to share?"

He smirks. "Everywhere we go, people die. This is more evidence of that."

"It ain't me who ends up getting people killed. It just happens."

"It just happens? Let me see if I can remember." Bruce sets down his coffee mug and begins to count off on his fingers. "First, Tommy Lee, the guy who recruits you into that Firm and Friendly club ends up with a broken neck. Then the Monk, my business partner at the dojo, ends up dead because you steer his van into a ditch. Then Charlie, your counselee, and six others die under mysterious circumstances." He holds up all ten fingers. "Riding bikes over cliffs, jumping motorcycles over rivers, ending up in accidents of one kind or another."

"So are you saying you're a little nervous being out here alone with me?" I kneel up and hoist the pillow to throw. "It sounds like you need to watch yourself. You're not working with the Special Forces in Afghanistan anymore, and you sure aren't being pampered in the Navy or Air Force."

He crouches low and moves around the bed. "So you think I was pampered, do you? Getting my leg blown off? Not being able to connect with you all that time?"

"Are we having a spat? I think it's time to make up."

"Maybe you should get out of that bed and fix supper."

"Maybe you should forget about supper and try out your pillow for a minute."

Bruce gives me the look, but his cellphone plays off the first bars of "Hey Jude." He scans the caller ID and says, "Sheriff."

I launch that pillow square into his shoulder.

CHAPTER FOUR

I t's difficult to establish a routine with Bruce and Lancelot, household chores, and my personal reading. The long hours of darkness are almost depressing.

The sheriff phones or drops by every two or three days. It's impossible to cuddle in the morning as I wait for the inevitable call or visit. It feels like harassment. Bruce seems resigned to it. I'm sure his Special Forces skills are valuable out here, but I figure the lawmen just want to keep tabs on us newcomers. Sometimes it's hard to feel like we belong in our new community.

Everything upstairs needs significant dusting. The toys, clocks, trophies, and fans all leave my washrag black. One of the magical things about my Uncle Jimmy's old farmhouse is that he built the attic with a dozen or more secret rooms. The treasures out in the open allure me first. There's the grandfather clock with paintings of wild geese on the face and gilded gold hands frozen at 3:58. It's nestled against a turn of the century trundle sewing machine, a beige hand-carved sleigh-type wooden couch, and a pair of bluish French Louis XVI armchairs.

Only after cleaning the visible do I explore the hidden spaces. The first of the attic rooms contains mostly old memorabilia from my cousin Billy. There are a few trophies and photographs from the basketball teams he started for. I also find boxes of clothing and shoes and uniforms, a couple of old pellet guns, a hunting rifle, and a few other things I don't bother exploring too much. Billy takes my call and asks me to leave the stuff until he gets around to moving it someday. He also tells me that some of my family's stuff might be up there as well, which motivates me to keep looking.

The second attic room shelters a pile of Aunt Rose's china dishes, cutlery, ceramic dolls, a collection of spoons from around the world, blankets, and a stack of photo albums from the earliest days of my great-grandparents. The photos occupy me for days and get me wondering if this constant moving and looking for home is a bigger dynamic than I imagine. Perhaps it's an inbuilt thing given by God to remind us that no place in this world is really our home, that we are meant to feel restless until we end up one day in the home which he created for us.

The third and fourth attic rooms hold boxes of magazines, books, and information that Uncle Jimmy collected on farming. The mice have enjoyed themselves thoroughly in chewing the edges of these hidden treasures. I don't bother giving the information gold mine more than a few minutes, but one box holds a sheaf of sixty old letters my parents wrote to their supporters from Kenya.

I head for the fireplace to curl up with a cup of chai and a little history. The letters are a fascinating read. Halfway through one missive, Bruce calls me to join him in the attic. "Katie, you won't believe what I found. An old trunk with your family's name on it. I think you're going to want to see this."

The attic stairs are creaky. Bruce is hidden away under the eaves, but I find one of the attic doors open.

"What did you find?" I ask.

Bruce pokes his head out from the doorway and smiles as if he's won the lottery. I squeeze into the small space beside him and a five-foot by two-foot by two-foot steamer trunk. I wipe the dusty label and start sneezing.

"Sneezes Breezes, bless you," Bruce says as he keeps rubbing down the trunk.

The label reads SEWARD TRUNK CO. PETERSBURG, VIRGINIA. The black pine box construction is braced by metal framing which appears almost grey with the dust and dimness in the room. The steamer trunk definitely traveled a lot of miles through the years.

Bruce taps the side where I find another larger label. He wipes it off with his hand to read it: JOHN AND SUSAN DELANCEY, BOX 80, KIJABE, KENYA. Three bigger trunks snuggle at the back of the space, but this is the one Bruce drags out.

The trunk is locked and Bruce attempts to jimmy the metal clasp without success. After a few minutes, he scoots downstairs and returns with his Leatherman knife. He works at the lock and eventually opens it. The fresh scent of age old pine and leather escapes along with an assortment of faint perfumes. Visions of Africa cascade over me as I scan the contents and breathe in the aromas.

The brown-painted lid contains several compartments, a coin box, a lithograph of an old Kikuyu shepherd, a document box, and a tray of some kind.

In the main hold there appears to be a hat box, a section for clothing, and some other secret compartments which don't automatically open at first nudge.

Bruce is intrigued when I sit back in frustration. He begins to play at the corners of the compartments and eventually one of them shifts and opens. Inside is a scribbler with dad's name on the cover.

I grab it. "Dad kept a journal!"

"There's something else in here," Bruce whispers.

He hands me a hardcover album, and when I open it old Africa spreads out before me. Black-and-white photos and drawings on page after page after page.

"Who are the pictures of?" asks Bruce.

The album contains the photographic evidence of all the family faces and experiences I will never see. This history lesson for Bruce becomes a barb in my own heart. I caress each photo and explain the significance. "This is an Arab dhow unloading at the coast of Kenya. The fishermen are holding up a net full of fish which they probably caught for my great-great-grandfather and his group."

"Your great-great-grandfather was in Kenya?"

"Only for short safaris. He went back and forth between America and Britain and Kenya taking photographs of brave souls who were out to conquer the world for Christ."

"Wow, what else is here?" Bruce asks.

One by one I point at the images with an explanation. I remember sitting on my father's lap as a five-year-old looking at this album. I haven't seen it since.

I flip the page and Bruce's phone rings. "Probably the sheriff," I say.

Bruce fishes in his pocket and pulls out his cell. "Hello, Sherriff Reimer. More trouble?" He begins to pace. "Sorry, who did you say this was? Katie? No, she's not available right now... No, she's not looking for a job at the Firm and Friendly... No, she will not be taking out a membership... Goodbye, Mr. Kensington." Bruce turns and holds out the phone in front of him. "Now, that is weird!"

Kensington? Joshua Kensington? What is he doing here? The last time I'd heard about him was from Tommy Lee, the man who moved me into the nightmare of my life.

My owl eyes must give Bruce a clue that something isn't right. I'm hyperventilating, and I can't stop it. My hands clench and I collapse down on the dusty trunk. I hate feeling weak.

Bruce is there in an instant, cradling me and calming me. I tuck my head into his chest and in a minute I'm numb. I remember nothing. I am strong.

CHAPTER FIVE

A bath is all I need. A little lavender aroma therapy, some soft music, some coffee, a lush cotton towel, and an hour to myself.

When I join Bruce back in the attic, it's like the last few hours never happened. I pick up the album. "Here's a picture of a Swahili man with a large mollusc. I loved those seashells." I caress the edges of each picture, smoothing the bent parts. "He's also got a sand dollar which he's trying to sell. Some things never change."

"Katie, aren't we going to debrief that phone call?" interrupts Bruce. "Who is Joshua Kensington and why does he want you to sign up for the Firm and Friendly? I thought that was all past."

My breathing stops and my heart races until I regain control. "Mr. Kensington is nobody I have anything to do with. Let's finish this." I point at a picture of two giant inverted elephant tusks forming an archway over a city street. "My great-great-grandfather is obviously in Mombasa. The island is only about ten miles square." I point at a beach shot. "The place used to be covered in mango, almond, and baobab trees. And look at all the cocoa palms. I think those fat boats in the background might be some of the bagallas from the Persian Gulf."

Bruce reminds me of his international experience. "Those boats have been riding the trade winds up and down the coast since before Solomon. I bet this is where he picked up his ivory and slaves and spices and gold. Probably even a few lions and concubines."

I dig my elbow into his ribs. "Look, buddy, I'm doing the commentary. This is my great-great grandfather who took these pictures."

Bruce mocks me with a half-nod. "Speak on, oh mighty safari guide."

I do. "Here's one of the women in front of the market. They still sell things like guavas and mangoes and Zanzibar oranges and coconuts and bananas. You can get the best limes here for juice."

Bruce does his guy thing and says "Aha, aha" every minute or so.

I continue my tour. "This picture is probably of the government house where the high commissioner lived. I always loved the smell of the bougainvillea and frangipani and jasmine. And look, they've even got some jacaranda and flame trees. Too bad these aren't in color."

Bruce touches the picture and closes his eyes. "I can imagine the color as if I was there just five months ago," he says.

I ignore his obvious reference to our honeymoon in Kenya. "Here's a white hunter with his foot up on an Eland he's bagged. This one has a rhino. Here's one with a zebra. That's a warthog. This one is a leopard."

Maybe it's my monotone that makes Bruce interrupt. "Katie, I know you're an animal lover. You've gone on and on about the poachers. Doesn't it bother you when you see these pictures?"

I answer in a way that perhaps says more than I want to admit. "People have to eat and survive. Sometimes I have to choose not to feel."

"You mean you don't feel anything?" asked Bruce.

"About a month before I met you in Sumas, I had a wasp's nest up under my carport. When they all fell asleep at night I took a can of Raid and sprayed it into the entrance until they started dropping dead. I ran and shut my door to hide from any survivors." I close the book and take his hand. "I felt horrible guilt for days after. The girls who were coming to see me for counselling were afraid of the wasps and I thought I was somehow protecting them by getting rid of the things that scared them." I caress his thumb. "For those wasps, I still feel a lot. For warthogs I didn't kill, no feelings."

I return to my pictures. The familiar jangle of "Oh When the Saints" chimes off from Bruce's cell. We both say it together: "The sheriff!"

Bruce hops up and begins to pace the room from one end of the attic to the other. Considering his height, he has to stay in the center of the floor. He listens and does his guy thing again. "Aha... aha... oh wow... aha. Thanks for letting me know. See you."

He pockets his cell and sits on the beige wood sleigh couch.

"Well?" I say.

"Well what?"

"What did he have to say?"

"He said that old Sidney from our ditch was a former employee of the Firm and Friendly." I grab Bruce's arm as he continues. "He says the body could have been dumped, but they're still investigating."

The house turns incredibly cold for some reason. Bruce insists that I continue my photographic safari, so we huddle by the fireplace. The ice ball in my stomach takes a while to melt away.

"Here's a supply train of camels and donkeys and men loaded with equipment. The guys in the safari hats with the rifles are the British merchants who came along with the missionaries." I turn the page. "Actually, the missionaries wore the same outfits, so you can't really tell them apart. They're all wearing khaki gear with pith helmets."

I point at one titled *Peter Cameron Scott, sister Margaret, and African Inland Mission pioneers, October 1895.* "This one's a treasure. Peter Cameron Scott was the founder of the mission that started the Rift Academy. He launched his mission out of Philadelphia, which is where my great-great-grandfather first met him."

Bruce adjusts the album to see better in the light. "Must have been one passionate guy to give up so much and convince others to go with him."

I touch another picture. "Here's Scott with ten Kenyans marked *Kangundo 1896.* He set up four mission stations in his first year or so and then died of blackwater fever. Most of those with him also died."

Bruce clears his throat. Maybe it's the dust in here. "What a waste," he says.

I look at him as if he's just arrived from another planet. "What are you talking about?"

"To die after such a short time!" He stands up and walks a few steps before turning to me. "How can that be worthwhile?"

I take the bait. "If you stop to think that more than twenty-five million people there say they follow Jesus, I'd say someone had an impact. Jesus didn't have a lot of followers when he died compared to now. I think it's what we're willing to sacrifice that makes the impact."

Bruce looks me full in the face and impales me with his words. "And what are you sacrificing these days to make a difference?"

I focus my glare, penetrating his mind to see how serious he is, but he's as expressionless as I've ever seen him. I decide to ignore his question and turn back to the album.

"Here's a valuable picture: *Baron Delamere and wife (Hugh and Florence), 1906 Naivasha.*" I slip the picture out of its corner tags and check for anything else on the back. "The guy was a dairy farmer and land baron. Our school actually owes him a debt of gratitude." I slip the picture back into place. "We were supposed to have a big tract of land right in Naivasha, and he worked some sleight of hand with the governing authorities to gain ownership of that prime real estate. The mission and school ended up with some property up in the highlands at about seven thousand feet. That saved us from tons of malaria over the years."

Bruce says nothing about my change of topic. "So God can take a situation that may seem unfair and unjust and turn it out for good. He's always in control. Is that what you're trying to say?"

"I'm only saying that this is what happened. I think we should take some time for dinner."

Bruce holds my wrist and applies the slightest pressure. "I want to hear what's really going on with this Kensington guy. Ever since that call, it's like you've become a different person."

I gently pry his hands off my wrist. "I'm going to make dinner. When I know what's going on, I'll tell you."

Between mouthfuls of tuna casserole, we flip through the rest of the pictures without much comment. There are pictures of Maasai warriors decked out in Ostrich feathers, lion's manes, and war paint, plus others with workers pounding in the spikes for the East African Railway as it moved from Mombasa to Nairobi. The photo of a dead lion that had been attacking and killing the workers was labeled *The Ghost in the Darkness*.

I spot a rare shot I hadn't paid much attention to when I was five. "This is my great-great grandfather with George Whitehouse, the builder of the Lunatic Express." I bend up a dog-eared corner. "That's what some people called the six-hundred-mile railroad line because it went through desserts, swamps, volcanic lava flows, vicious tribal wars, man-eating lions, tsetse flies, and malaria just to give the British a stronghold in East Africa. Now, if you're talking about a waste, a lot of people died to make that happen."

A picture of Teddy Roosevelt laying the cornerstone at the Rift Academy's Kiambogo building is labeled *The Honorable T. Roosevelt and Charles Hurlbert, August 9, 1909*. It's highlighted on a page all its own. The stone says "August 4," so I'm not sure why there's a difference.

Pictures of Kenyans with bee hives, others with poison tipped arrows, boys herding cows, women planting corn, and an old Kikuyu man surrounded by sheep show that life hasn't changed a whole lot in the last century for some of the people of the land.

By bedtime, my head is full of images of old-time safaris, stalking lions, and deadly malaria mosquitos buzzing around. They haunt my mind.

The sound of a hunting rifle shakes me out of my restless nightmares.

CHAPTER SIX

Bruce jolts out of bed and catapults himself to the window overlooking the barn. Even without his artificial leg in place, he's quick as a cat. His Special Forces instincts and Tai Kwon Do mastery serve him well.

I begin to pull back the covers so I can join him but he motions me to stillness.

"What is it, Bruce?"

"Shhh. It's a rifle. I'm going out to have a look."

"I'm going with you!"

He silently secures his prosthetic limb into place and dons a tracksuit. I haven't even found my outdoor clothing and he's already slipping out the kitchen door. As I pull on a sweatshirt, I look out the window and glimpse his shadow darting across a five-foot gap between the maple tree and the corral fencing.

I grab a flashlight as another shot rings out.

"Bruce!" I run down the remaining few stairs as quick as I dare and race out the kitchen door toward the place I last saw him, crouching in the shadows. From there I'm not sure where to go. The flashlight stays off so I don't make myself a target.

Lancelot is pacing in his paddock and snorting restlessly. I listen hard, but hear nothing. A long two minutes passes.

Finally, I call out. "Bruce! Are you there? Are you okay?"

A minute later he's by my side. He grabs my hand. "What are you doing here?"

"I told you I was coming." I huddle in tight beside him. "You didn't wait. I was worried. What was that shot?"

"Someone saw me coming." He peers around the corner of the fence where we're hiding. "Don't worry, they missed. Only thing out here is Lancelot, so I'm not sure what they were after. Unfortunately, they got away."

Bruce takes the flashlight from me and leads the way into the barn toward Lancelot's stall. Lancelot is clearly upset. Bruce tries to calm him with a pat, but that seems to irritate the stallion even more. I latch onto a handful of mane and begin to whisper calming words.

"Katie, he's been shot!"

"What?" I look at where my husband is pointing and notice a narrow furrow across his black haunches, bleeding freely. "Who would do this?"

A volcanic fury surges within me, then dissipates like a snowflake on a hot griddle. Darkness begins to suffocate my soul.

"Katie, are you okay? We need to give this guy some first aid. Are you up to it?"

"Hakuna Matata, no problem." I fetch some water, ointment, and rags. *Funny how Swahili sometimes has just the right phrase.*

Within a few minutes the bleeding is staunched and the wound cleaned and covered. Bruce looks around for signs of an intruder and finds a window crowbarred open. Nothing else.

After cleaning up the proud Arabian, Bruce and I cuddle in the hay not far from my horse with a few blankets. Sleep isn't on the agenda.

* * *

Lancelot eats his morning feed and drinks his water without any sign that the trauma of the night before is going to impact him. Bruce uses his tracking skills to follow a set of prints out to the main tarmac. The fresh falling flakes and shifting winds challenge him, but he knows his art. He takes pictures of a tire tread and a shoe impression to give over to the sheriff later on.

I call the sheriff and reach the new deputy in his office. This is the same man who fastened the plywood over our broken window, so I recognize his voice immediately. It only takes a minute to report the shooting and he promises to come within the hour.

While I wait and Bruce is busy outside looking for more clues, I pick up my dad's journal. I stare at the faint ink squiggles put down by my dad to identify himself. Tears come even though all I can feel is emptiness.

I open the journal with an even greater sense of wonder than when I opened my very own first journal. Though I previously saw the photo album for my great-

great grandfather, I've never seen this journal. It feels like forbidden territory and I fight back the guilt. Do good girls sneak into their father's journals and read their secret thoughts?

Regardless, I focus my eyes. Unfortunately, my dad didn't record any dates for his entries. The comments don't necessarily seem to be connected by thought or date.

1870—Collin James Delancey.
1900—Seymour James Delancey.
1930—Franklin James Delancey.
1956—John Douglas Delancey.
Even though I'm the oldest, I somehow missed the family heritage of carrying on the name of James. I don't know why that should matter to me.

There are several more pages which capture my father's journey into missions. I flip through and focus on the last page. My father's final words to me: "Look up. Hold on." Evidently, my dad wasn't a committed journalist. I regret that he didn't write more. Perhaps there are other clues in the letters or in some other secret compartment. I set out to discover them.

I'm still nudging the corners of secret compartments in the black steamer trunk when Bruce calls up that the deputy has arrived. Begrudgingly, I slide the old luggage carrier back into its space and join the men downstairs to describe our ordeal all over again.

I don't like what I hear.

"Likely one of them immigrants," the deputy says. "You know, they can take a fine horse like yours and turn it into a thousand dinners. Use every part, they do."

Bruce is quick to object. "I wouldn't want to jump to any conclusions, deputy. The style of boot and the tire tread of that car doesn't make it look like any desperate restaurant owner, no matter where they came from. Take a look at these pictures on my phone."

The deputy squints at the images and scratches his right temple. "Well, our Swedish and German and Norwegian folks go back over a hundred years in Minnesota. They're well-established, you know. Deep roots, good families. Swedes have been farming this place since the beginning. In fact, this used to be one of those Swedish farms."

Bruce cuts in again. "I'm not trying to accuse any of the Swedes. I'm sure they're all fine folks. We've met some good people in town."

The deputy misses his point. "Well, it isn't the Norwegians. They've been running the lumber business around here almost as long and they don't have any need of horses like yours. The Swiss are running the dairy farms, so all they care about is cows. The Germans have other stuff going on. I tell you, it's the foreigners."

I've heard enough. "Deputy, why does everyone blame the immigrants?"

The deputy reaches for his gun, spins around, and prepares to draw. My approach from behind obviously came as a surprise.

I barge right on over to where Bruce is standing. "They want to make it here as badly as everyone else. Why would they risk their chances with something as stupid as this?"

"Oh, it's the window-breaker," he says with a chuckle. "Don't tell me you're getting all hot and bothered over some wild shooter. Probably some kid hunting illegally."

Instead of the gun, I focus on his name badge. Deputy Wayne Timmons. "What's a hunter trying to break into a barn for?"

"Well, I was telling your husband that it couldn't be the folks who have deep roots here. They watch each other pretty good. The Finns and Slavs are too busy working the mines. The Mexicans and Poles, and some of those other Balkan folks, work over in the meat-packing plants and they value their sleep at night. We've got a good number of blacks and Indians, but they're basically all law-abiding folk. Nothing to worry about."

"So who are you trying to label as suspicious?" Bruce asked.

"Well, all we got left is some of the Hmong, the Vietnamese, the Koreans, the Chinese , and even some Persians. Some of them are running those restaurants and getting creative with the rules around here."

This is too much for me. "How dare you put people into cubby holes, Deputy Timmons, just because of where they were born? How do they let people like you get into enforcing the law? I'm sorry I called for your help." Bruce squeezes my arm, but I'm on a roll. "Please try not to get too creative with the rules when you tell our story to the sheriff."

I stomp off back to the house and leave Bruce to work things out. *Poor guy.*

When Bruce walks into the kitchen, I'm smashing around pots and pans in preparation for lunch. I rip a spaghetti noodle package and the contents scatter on the floor and under the counters. The sauce bubbles on high heat and spits all over the stove.

I can't look at Bruce. I don't know whether to sob or break into a belly laugh. *What's the good thing to do? Who knows? Who cares?*

CHAPTER SEVEN

B ruce wolfs down my spaghetti without stopping to say a word, so I assume everything must be okay. He never mentions the incident. He even cleans up the kitchen so I can spend time with Lancelot. The walk is short as I'm not sure what the crazy hunter might be up to next. When I finish, I forego my foot massage and spend time emailing my best friend Sarah in Seattle.

Subject: Feelings

How does what is happening to someone else impact you so deeply? I have this uncanny ability not to feel what I'm going through while at the same time feeling deeply the emotions of someone else. For example, when I first got back to Canada, I used to watch a show called *Touched by an Angel*. I was in college, but I would identify so strongly with the struggler in every episode that I would end up balling like a schoolgirl. Watching that show was not a good group activity for me. Yet I couldn't not see it. When I watch a live theatrical performance, I become like one of the unseen actresses who enter into the intensity of the moment with everyone else involved. I live my life vicariously. At least, my emotions. I feel like much of my life is locked in the neutral position, as if my emotions are some setting on a washing machine. When I start churning, it's usually because I'm dealing with someone else's dirty laundry. This form of detachment from myself is challenging for my relationships.

Somewhere along my journey I read the life story of John Corcoran. He was a dyslexic, before most people understood how the left side of a brain could continuously misfire and turn the world of reading into a nightmare. John suffered incredible humiliation and bullying at the hands of teachers and students alike. But he learned to fake it and he passed right on through to a college diploma and to a career in teaching without knowing how to read a word. On the way through his school years, he was voted homecoming king, made himself popular with the girls, and even starred on the basketball team.

John married a nurse who was the first one to learn his secret. He couldn't read. She covered for him. He became a millionaire businessman until one day the bottom fell out of his world. At the age of forty-eight, he finally asked for help and a sixty-five-year-old grandmother taught him to read, letter by letter. After many years of hard work, he did the one thing he longed to do: he took out a twenty-five-year-old batch of envelopes and read his wife's love letters for the very first time.

I understand what it's like to fake your way through life. Pretending to feel things you don't. Pretending to understand when you haven't got a clue. Yesterday I spent an hour rereading the email love letters I had stashed in the folder labeled Bruce. I'm still not sure I really know how to love in the way I think others do. Tell me, does God ever heal a heart when it gets numb like this?

I found an old journal my dad started and it didn't say much of anything to me. My horse got shot and I just numbed right up. What's going on? Sometimes I just feel like my inner voice has been choked off and I can't get the words out about what's happening inside.

Bruce and I promised each other that we'd have a date night once a week, but the weather has been so cold outside, and things have been so "hot" inside, that we're saving those date nights for a rainy day. We've started making dinner together at least three times a week and we actually enjoy working together. I'm learning a few chef secrets from Bruce and he's learning a few basics from me. I think.

P.S. How's Keith and the malls out there?

Luv, Katie.

When I finally press send, I write to the other part of our high school trio, Andrea. She was working with the MKs (missionary kids) as a teacher at the Rift Academy as of January. Apparently while she was out in Kenya attending my sister's and my double wedding, she spent time letting herself get recruited as a fill-in dorm parent and Grade Ten biology teacher. The staff sometimes has emergency leaves or shortages and fill-ins to keep the programs flowing. Her commitment perks my own curiosity about going back to the place of my birth in a different capacity.

I press send to Andrea just as Sarah's reply pops up on my screen.

Subject: Numb friend

Nice to hear from you. Keith is busier than ever. Wish you were here so we could take advantage of the malls together. Heard from Andrea. She's back at the Rift. Ever wonder about going back?

I used to watch some of those same shows and I know what you mean. I used up a lot of Kleenex—actually, toilet paper. I haven't watched anything like that since I got married. I don't want Keith watching me melt down in front of him. I know that numbness. Maybe it's an MK thing. You feel rootless. You can connect to people and pick up with them years later as if you've never been apart. You just learn to shut off one part of your life and pick up the next piece, and you kind of stop feeling as you make your transition. You've learned somewhere that the extreme emotions you once felt in all the separations didn't change anything. Maybe it's a survival mechanism. Maybe this is what you once talked about when you said you felt like you were stuck in an eternal now.

Sometimes, I have to admit, I've felt almost paralyzed by the losses that kept piling up. It was too much to feel everything. It was enough to send you into a permanent depression. I'm thankful that Keith does his best to understand me, but I can still tell some days that we're on different planets.

Last year, there was a class reunion and I realized how much all of us had lost on that one last plane ride. I wish you could have been there. I'm sure it would have made it even harder when you didn't graduate with the rest of us. I didn't realize when we were at the Rift how much change everyone had gone through. Some of us were still crying over losing the people and places we knew, all because of some political problem, or a disaster, or tribal unrest, or a completed mission assignment. And then you, and a few others, had to leave because of family health issues. Life is tough for MKs. Of course, there are a lot of great things too.

I found that I had to discover the God who heals. I knew the God who wounds, but I had to know that he keeps his promises completely. I found three verses to hold onto.

Deuteronomy 32:39 says, *"See now that I myself am He! ... I have wounded and I will heal, and no one can deliver out of my hand."* Job 5:18 says, *"For he wounds, but he also binds up; he injures, but his hands also heal."* Hosea 6:1 says, *"Come, let us return to the LORD. He has torn us to pieces but he will heal us; he has injured us but he will bind up our wounds."*

When I understood that God didn't back away from my questions about the pain I felt, but that he actually took responsibility for it and then promised that somehow he would also bring healing, I could relax a little. Before that, I felt that somehow things were out of control. Maybe my parents made a mistake. Maybe it was the boarding school. Maybe I was being punished for something I'd done along the way. Anyway, I don't mean to preach. I just want to say that I know it's hard sometimes.

Finding your dad's journal sounds cool. Maybe you should try reading it again several times until something does click. I'm sure the words are there for a reason. Try putting yourself in his place and reading the words from his perspective.

Maybe you should just keep busy until you get some emotional space in your life. You're just married. You're isolated in the middle of nowhere. Try not to live your whole life in one day.

Lots of love, Sarah

Usually when I get an email from Sarah, I feel warm and cared for. This time my stomach clenches up tight like a pretzel. I leave the computer and walk around the house. I refill my coffee mug and keep on walking.

On my third round, Bruce sounds off. "Katie, what are you doing?"

I stop and glare at him reclining like a king in the living room on his red leather armchair. He has dumped the cross-stitched pillow on the floor beside him. That pillow is the one I got from my mom before she passed away. I have a strong urge to throw my hot coffee all over him.

It isn't even my snarly time of the month and I want to scream. I stare, daring him to press me on what's happening—and then I notice he is reading his Bible. A wave of guilt washes over me as to how unchristian I'm acting toward this man who has done everything he can to get me healed up and on my feet again.

Without a word, I return to the computer to reply to Sarah. This encounter has not happened.

Subject: Busyness

You told me to keep busy. I've just come from almost throwing my hot coffee over Bruce while he was doing his devotions. I think I'm too busy already.

I came across a quote I copied from Chuck Swindoll when I was still in college. I have it taped inside the front cover of my journal. I was feeling alone and unwanted at the time. I couldn't seem to fit in anywhere. Pastor Swindoll's words seemed to help me make sense of what was happening all around me. He said, "Busyness rapes relationships. It substitutes shallow frenzy for deep friendship. It promises satisfying dreams but delivers hollow nightmares. It feeds the ego but starves the inner man. It fills a calendar but fractures a family. It cultivates a program but plows under priorities."[1]

It seemed to be the spiritual word of the day for Christians to answer the question "How are you?" with the word "Busy." As if being "busy" was somehow a sign of special godly achievement. Tell me, how did you survive all these years?

Talking about survival, my blood is frozen in my veins half the time here. At least I haven't had to break out the DEET, Vitamin B, and garlic pills yet to ward off mosquitoes. One nightmare at a time.

The only Bible passage I've related to lately is the story about the woman who comes to Jesus after twelve years of living with her pain. She had a bleeding disease, and I have other issues, but the fact is that no one seemed able to heal it. Reaching out to Jesus made the difference to me. Some days I wonder if I'm just too afraid to reach out in case it doesn't work. I've lived with this numbness so long that I don't know how I'd live without it.

Sending this leaves me feeling strangely disconnected from the real life happening around me. I'm into my fifth month of marriage with an incredible guy and something is still missing.

I mix up a cappuccino. As I pass through the living room again, I notice that Bruce has tucked my mother's cross-stitched pillow under his head and nodded off to sleep. The Message Bible still lays open on his lap.

---

[1] Charles Swindoll, *Growing Strong in the Seasons of Life* (Portland, OR: Multnomah Press, 1983), 377.

It's hard to be angry while looking at him this way. I walk over, pick up the Bible off his lap, and wrap him up in a quilt. He moans with a pleasure, which always makes me melt.

I lay the Bible down on the coffee table and notice that he has underlined a few lines: *"And don't be wishing you were someplace else or with someone else. Where you are right now is God's place for you. Live and obey and love and believe right there. God, not your marital status, defines your life."*[2]

Why did Bruce underline these words? Is he already thinking about someone else? Is he wishing he was somewhere else without me?

Fears have a way of growing their own roots and fruit. What else could possibly come between Bruce and me?

---

[2] 1 Corinthians 7:17, The Message.

CHAPTER EIGHT

Cabin fever consumes me. The Bible passage Bruce underlined niggles at my mind: *"And don't be wishing you were someplace else or with someone else."* Is he wanting to be with someone else? I analyze my words and actions. Did one of his old flames link up with him by email? A few minutes with Lancelot in the barn settles my nerves. The poor horse is down to half a sack of oats. It's the perfect excuse to get away and think.

The banged-up old pickup Bruce bought me has no trouble in the snow and Haley's feedlot is open. Five ranch hands stand around the woodstove drinking coffee and laughing over something they all find humorous. A broad-shouldered gentleman with a prune-skinned forehead nods in my direction and returns my smile and waves. The other four follow suit and stare. I'm still a stranger here.

The store captures that wonderful smell of everything horse. Leather, soap, oats, wool, and so much more. I place my order and, while the clerk is gathering the items, I step up to the counter and glance at the television showing the news. The sound is barely loud enough to hear in the midst of all the chatter going on around me, but my neck and shoulder muscles tighten like a guitar string: millionaire Joshua Kensington and his partner Rita Galinsky are in Duluth and the Twin Cities for the ribbon-cutting on a newly refurbished Firm and Friendly fitness center. Joshua is surrounded by a dozen or so spandex-clad beauty queens. He stands among them with those perfect teeth, that flawless smile, and that practiced wave for the cameras. I swallow back the bile in my throat.

Mr. Kensington should have been a stranger, but when Tommy Lee ran the Firm and Friendly franchise in Bellingham and Seattle he used to brag once in a while about meeting the millionaire at the conventions he went to. Not once did

I assume that the man with the Hollywood smile was connected with something that was now part of my past nightmare.

For some reason, the news inserts a clip of the Bellingham and Seattle franchises for the Firm and Friendly. The cameras pan away from the facility I'm all too familiar with and flashes a headshot of Tommy Lee. The volume of chatter increases around me, and since I miss the commentary I can't follow the reasoning for the change in location. When Tommy Lee introduced me to this whole network, he was pretty confident of his connections—until his neck was broken by Stephen the Monk.

Tommy Lee recruited me during my college days and pulled me into the shadowy world he ran. I was too naïve to understand what was really happening, but it's a world I can't seem to escape. Although I walked away long ago, there seem to be elements who refuse to believe I'm no longer a player.

As the cameras roll back to Joshua preparing to cut the ribbon, five gold rings flash on his right hand. I figure there might be more rings on his other hand. A pulsing throb pushes against my temple and I crush it with my thumb. The store walls seem a lot tighter than when I arrived.

I race out of the store and throw the feed into the back of the pick-up. Bruce is the only man I want right now.

As I turn the key, the sheriff's car turns into the space beside me. Not believing my good fortune, I dismount from the truck cab. As I round the corner of his bumper, I step on some ice and perform an inglorious face-plant in a pile of slush.

The car door opens quickly and footsteps approach. I sense his presence before I see his face. It is Deputy Timmons. "If it isn't Mrs. Southerland showing off the best of Canada."

I'm partway into a half pushup in the parking lot when someone grabs my elbow and jacket and lifts me out of the slush. My feet touch ground and I get spun around like a top. A calloused hand wipes the slush from my face.

I clear my eyelashes. Standing before me is a man who must have been a descendant of Paul Bunyan. His seven-foot frame is outfitted with plaid shirt, overalls and a large axe. He handles me like a rag doll.

His deep bass voice washes over my ears. "You'll have to pardon the deputy, miss. We've had trouble finding gentlemen in this part of the state."

A curly blond beard and close-cropped hair frames the man's gentle face. He has deep blue eyes, the closest I've ever seen to my own shade. "Luke Lapierre at your service, miss. I hear you're from Canada."

His gaze is mesmerizing. Words fumble out of my mouth. "Canada, Kenya, here, there… to tell you the truth, I'm not sure where I'm from. Katie Delancey… I mean Southerland. I just got married and haven't figured out who I am yet."

Heat rushes into my cheeks and ears as my tongue stumbles.

His smile is as big and strong as the rest of him. "Mighty disappointed to hear that someone claimed you first. Lucky man." He takes a step away. "I'm living just over on the Buffalo River. Family's been here since the French trapped these parts some four hundred years ago." He turns toward the deputy. "Survived the English and even the Americans. We've made room for Germans, Swedes, Norwegians and the Swiss." He nods his head slightly toward me. "I assume we have room for a few Canadians. Tell you the truth, I'm probably a mix of all of them. Welcome to Minnesota, ma'am."

The blond giant glares at the deputy, who's still transfixed a few feet away. He turns and walks off down the ice-covered streets as firm footed as if he's strolling on concrete.

Deputy Timmons grunts. "Just ignore the big oaf."

I look down the road at the retreating giant. "Hard to do." I wipe my hands against my jeans and head back to the truck.

My encounter with the deputy and Luke makes me forget completely about the golden-ringed fingers of Joshua Kensington and I'm almost home before the television spot surfaces again in my consciousness.

Bruce meets me on the porch with a loud whoop. "I figured out two more of the secret compartments."

"You don't have to holler in my ear. What did you find?"

"Come and see," he says, grabbing my hand and pulling me indoors. I hardly have the chance to get my snow boots off before he picks me up and carries me toward the stairs. When we reach the stairs, he flips me over his shoulder and starts on up.

"Bruce Daniel Johnston Southerland, I'm not a sack of horse feed."

He doesn't answer and I don't push it as he's working hard to make his prosthetic do its part in bearing my weight. His leg holds up fine. When we reach the top, he deposits me on my feet with the grace and gentleness of a prince.

I give him a peck on the cheek, but he isn't satisfied with that reward. He insists on a full kiss. It's not hard to oblige, but as soon as I get my breath I look for the black steamer trunk. It lies open with a few contents propped up along the edges. I recognize one of the binders immediately. It's the keepsake for the twelve tasks my parents gave me to do in Kenya so I could be declared a woman. On my knees, I pick it up as if it has transformed into a diamond tiara.

Underneath it lies a journal I started when I was thirteen, just before my final climb up Mount Kenya, which marked the completion of my tasks.

I hold the binder giving evidence of my twelve tasks and slowly open the cover of the diary. The first entry is significant and shows that not much has changed.

I feel like becoming an adult is some kind of a game where no one's told me the rules and I just can't seem to win. Every time I'm close to figuring things out, either I change, or the rules change.

Bruce's warm breath caresses my neck as he stoops down over my shoulder. Reading this somehow feels too sacred to share.

I shut the journal and look for his eyes. "I think I'm going to need some time to digest this later. The last time I read my journals from Kenya, it changed my whole life. I'm not ready for anything more right now. I know we were just there, but I still feel like I was a whole different person in a whole different life."

Bruce helps me to my feet and I tuck the binder and journal under my arm and follow him down the stairs. I set them on the nightstand, then head out to unload the truck. Bruce is already halfway there.

He turns and stops as he hears the door shut behind me. "Are you okay, Katie? I'm not always sure what's going to make you happy these days. I thought you'd be excited that I figured out how to unlock those secret compartments."

For such a hulk, the guy still knows how to use those puppy dog eyes on me. I melt. "Bruce. You and me. Zebra stripes. Okay? I'm excited. Just not ready to dance right now."

We work in silence unloading the hay bales, rolled oats, and salt licks. Bruce sets everything in order and I take the time to check on Lancelot's wound.

Seeing that it's healing nicely, I run a dose of conditioner through his mane. When the tangles are removed and the hair is slick, I use his comb to get that hair flowing free and easy. He seems to enjoy it as much as I do. When I'm done the stallion's mane, I stand near his rear shoulder, draw his tail toward me, and begin to work on that hair in the same way I untangled his mane.

Halfway through the process, Bruce steps up behind me and begins to give me a shoulder and neck massage. Lancelot is lucky to get his tail done before I have to follow up on the latest distraction in my life. It's a good thing we don't have any visitors in the barn.

Right after lunch, a sensation of being squeezed by a boa constrictor wraps around my stomach and works its way up into my throat and brain. The snow is blowing sideways, but not coming down. I've been examining the gingham curtains. They just don't fit anymore. The tablecloth isn't my style. The fireplace mantle needs some candles or knickknacks. The walls need some art. The vision of my new home is too big to wait any longer. The road to town is too tempting to resist.

"Bruce, I need something at the mall. Can you hang tight or do you want to come with me?"

For Bruce, walking on fiery coals is preferable to shopping, but I'm always interested to hear his excuses to get out of it.

Sure enough. He is consistent. "Will you be okay on your own? I was hoping to figure out those other two trunks upstairs. Maybe there's more hidden treasure. I promise I won't tell you until you're begging me."

I love his chuckle when he's teasing. I can't help smiling myself. I just need to get out and spend time on my own. Shopping will be great. I'm actually not a great shopper, but sometimes it's therapeutic, even if it's only to walk up and down the aisles to tell myself what I don't need.

The drive into town is worse than usual with the whiteout conditions. Moorhead is the county seat with a population of thirty-eight thousand and it has everything I need. I usually like Bruce to drive when it's this bad, but this may be one of my new tasks for womanhood: conquering a Minnesota country road in the dead of winter.

I can barely see some of the kids out on the pond playing ice hockey as I get to the edge of town. I thank God for His grace every mile of this road, and I question my sanity every half-mile. The doxology is my comfort song until I pull into the Walgreens on Main.

Browsing down the aisles looking for migraine medication, soap, shampoo, and other personal items is mindless distraction. As usual when I shop without a list, I have trouble deciding which items to choose. I blank out, just like that first day back from Kenya when my mom took us to the grocery store and told us to choose one box of cereal each. How do you just choose one when there are a thousand options?

Jasmine perfume goes on easy and I play with my blond hair in a mirror. *Bangs long or short? Pony tail, braids, behind the ears, over the ears?*

A glimpse of glitter flashes behind me. I stop playing and start staring. A young woman I have seen somewhere before is trying out some hand lotion. When she holds up her hands to air-dry them, I notice what caught my attention: she has three large gold rings on her right hand.

Rita Galinsky. This is the girl on the news with Joshua Kensington. She's here, halfway up the same aisle as me. That means Joshua can't be too far away.

I have no reason to fear anything, as the owners of the Firm and Friendly clubs wouldn't know me from anyone else. Still, it seems strange that Rita would be in the same store with me when the weather has kept most other people close to home. Sometimes the coincidences in my life are just too freaky for even me to handle.

I turn away from the mirror and stare straight into the teeth of Joshua Kensington.

CHAPTER NINE

"**A**mazing who you can find in a store like this, on a day like this," says Joshua. He's speaking to Rita, but the message is meant for me.

Looking Joshua in the eyes could prove fatal, so I focus down and mumble "Excuse me" in the best southern drawl I can fake. He's outfitted in an Italian tailored suit that looks like it belongs in a nightclub more than a boardroom. He's definitely a man who likes to make a statement with the ladies.

I step back, slowly move around the millionaire, and move into an aisle that leads straight to the exit. No one tries to stop me. The Tylenol I planned to buy is left with the perfume and I don't even consider going back.

I clear the exit at a run. The whiteout has turned into a full-fledged squall. My cellphone isn't in my purse and my mind flashes a clear picture of the little black box still charging on the kitchen counter. My boots don't make a sound as I hurry through the wall of white toward my truck. Noise has disappeared in this town. The empty parking lot makes it easier to decide which snowbank hides my pickup.

My fingers are like frozen sausages as I search in my jacket pocket for the truck keys. I yank out a Kleenex and see the object of my search perform a perfect arc into the snow a few feet away. It doesn't take long to find the keys, but by then my hands are like blocks of ice, my heart is racing, my breaths are desperate gasps, and my thoughts are a muddled fog. The right key is elusive, but I locate it and attempt to push it toward the door. It doesn't want to fit in the lock. When I finally open the door, I can't figure out what to do next to get out of the snowbank.

I slam the door and pray like never before. My breath slows down, my thinking clears up, and my blood circulation improves. I lock the door and turn on the ignition. The engine fires up without hesitation. The snow is too thick for the windshield wipers to operate.

Setting the car in reverse, I slowly press the accelerator. The truck moves a few inches and then the tires begin to spin. I set it in low and step on the accelerator a little more aggressively. I move about a foot or two forward. Twice more I repeat the process, then finally break free.

A knock on my driver's door window encourages me to intensify my death grip on the steering wheel. The knock unnerves me enough to jolt me into stepping fully on the gas. I slam into an invisible wall of snow. The hope drains out of me. Joshua and Rita and their goons have trapped me.

As I prepare to shift into reverse, I hear several loud voices yelling. I shift into park and slowly open the door. A giant of a man stands side by side with someone hardly up to his shoulder. Even with all this snow, it's easy to recognize his bearded blond face.

"Mrs. Southerland," he calls. "It's me. Luke."

As if I couldn't tell.

"We've come to help you." He holds up his arms, showing his shovel and mitted hands. "This is my friend, Johan."

I glance back toward the entrance to Walgreens. No Joshua or Rita, with their gold rings, coming in my direction.

"Luke, I sure could use a guardian angel."

He steps forward with a smile. "We're just here to help, ma'am. If you'll scrape off your windshield, we'll try to dig you out a little so you can get a running start through the rest of this drift. You might also want to try running the defrost for a bit, just to warm it up inside."

The two men set to work behind the truck while I set to clearing the windows. By the time we're done, the cab is warm and the condensation cleared from inside.

Luke isn't even breathing hard, but I can see Johan is panting from his workout.

I climb into the truck and roll down the window to thank the duo. The bearded giant hunches down to look me in the face. "We'll walk behind you until you get to the main road. If you get stuck, we'll push. It's not the best time to be out. The plows will be through in an hour or two. Why don't we camp out at McDonald's until it's safe?"

I see the glowing golden arches a short distance away and agree to the plan. Somehow, this towering human is an answer to my prayer. For now, I'm not asking how God did it. I'm just breathing easier.

The hour at McDonald's, over hot chocolates, turns into three. Neither Luke nor Johan have cellphones and the public phone is out of order. I try not to think about Bruce worrying about me and focus instead on asking Luke and Johan about their history here.

"What are you two doing out in the middle of a snowstorm?" I ask.

Luke looks down at me across the table. "We might ask you the same thing. I thought you Canadians would know a thing or two about snow."

I smile for the first time in the past hours. "You've got me there. I actually was born and raised in Kenya, and we didn't have a lot of snow to drive in out there."

Johan whistles under his golden beard. "You sure don't look African," he says with a smile.

"My parents were missionaries at a school in Kenya. I was born in a place called Kijabe and spent most of my school life there. I was just over there in October getting married, and now I'm here for a year. My husband is out at the old Olson farm."

Luke seems to be a man of few words, so Johan picks right up. "So you heard all the stories of the Olsons, have you?"

I set him straight. "I really haven't heard any stories of anyone around here. I used to come over in the summers during my college days to ride my Uncle Jimmy's horse. This is the place I came for healing. It was always Uncle Jimmy and Aunt Rose's place. He never told me otherwise."

Johan strokes his beard and stares hard into my face. "Did you hear about that biker who drowned in the creek up there a year or so ago? They never found the body."

I peel the contest sticker off my cup and examine it. "He was chasing me. He has to be dead, but sometimes I still think I see his face in crowds. Why don't you tell me something I don't know about the Olsons?"

Another whistle. "The Olson girl was the one who married Joe DiMaggio. That's what people know her for." Johan examined his own sticker. "Him, being a famous baseball player and all. She was a right good actress in her own day. Passed away in '84 as best as I can recall."

I prodded him for more information. "Anyone famous in your clan?"

"Only my neighbors and friends have famous people in their clans." Johan's beard was golden, like Luke's, but flecked with grey. He stroked that beard in the way of the wise. "Suppose I could have been related to Loni Anderson if I'd met her before Burt Reynolds. She didn't live far from me, you know."

I wait and sip my hot chocolate. I scan the door frequently to see if anyone is coming, but it seems no one's out except the snowplows. I can barely hear them swish by with their eerie beeping and flashing lights.

"Would you call this a Panhandle hook, Alberta Clipper, Saskatchewan Screamer, or Manitoba Mauler?" I ask.

Luke looks at me in his direct way. "I just call it snow, ma'am."

Although I'm used to different forms of respect, being called ma'am by someone old enough to be my uncle bothers me. "Luke, I'd feel much better if you'd call me Katie. All my friends do and I think you've shown your friendship tonight."

Johan ponders this thought and gains energy with his recollections. "You know, I just may be related to some famous people after all."

It was like Luke and I hadn't even spoken.

"Melvin Baldwin knew some of my folk when he went to Congress about 120 years ago," Johan continues. "My daddy said we are descended from Jonathan Carver, who was exploring these parts before the country was born. Of course, James Hill had tea with my great-great-granddaddy when they met about railroad business. He founded the Great Northern railway—James Hill, not my great-great-granddaddy. Course, I was saved from the wrath of God under the preaching of Billy Graham himself when he was just starting out."

That caught my attention. "Really! Billy Graham himself. What was he like in those days?"

Johan faded away to a distant time, stroking that beard. "Right as I recall, he was a little rough around the edges in the early days. I heard him several times over the years. One night he was like a ball of fire and I knew the earth beneath me would swallow me up and drop me straight into the pit of hell if I didn't repent and change my life right then. Been walking the straight and narrow ever since."

I turned to Luke. "What about you, Luke? Anyone famous? Are you walking the straight and narrow?"

Luke pierces me with his gaze. "Ma'am, there is no one who has ever accused me of not walking the straight and narrow."

And somehow I believe him.

By the time darkness is fully on the land the plows have done their work, traffic returns to the streets, and I prepare to say my adieus and take the trip home. I'm standing in the parking lot when our Black Durango eases to a stop at the light across the way. Bruce has come to save me.

I race with abandon across the parking lot and out onto the street, waving like a crazy woman. Bruce sits where he is, even when the light changes, and waits for me to race up. He throws open the door and we stand in the street hugging. I squeal while being hugged.

Bruce shows his protective side right away. "Crazy woman, what have you been doing out here? You had me scared spitless."

This isn't the place for the whole story, so I put it into a nutshell. "I'll tell you everything later. I need you to meet my guardian angels. Pull into the McDonald's."

My prince follows me into the parking lot and I lead him by the hand inside. No one's there except the distracted teen at the counter who's wiping it down with a rag. He looks up. "Take your order, sir."

"Where are the two gentlemen who were here with me a few minutes ago?" I ask. "Big guy, blond beard."

"Sorry, I didn't see them," he said. "I just got here."

I grab Bruce's hand and drag him out to the parking lot. No one's in sight. "Bruce, you just have to meet Luke. He's massive. He and Johan got me out of a snowdrift in the Walgreens parking lot. Saved my life, really."

My husband smiles at me. "Katie, you're so dramatic. I can't wait to hear whatever story you've conjured up sitting here on your own. Let's get you home and then you can tell me all about it."

The thunder in my skull returns with a mind-numbing rumble. If this is what he thinks about me, Bruce isn't going to hear one more word.

CHAPTER TEN

Moping around in a barn with your horse, or shuffling around in an attic looking through old journals, isn't exactly the best way to let your husband know you forgive him for being skeptical about your near-death experiences. Bruce can't understand why my head always hurts. For now, I'm not ready to tell him. I can't seem to overcome this ability to attach and detach quickly. Saying I have a headache seems like the best excuse to maintain an acceptable distance with Bruce right now.

While reading the book of Jonah the other day, I figured out that Jonah might have been an MK like me. By the time the poor guy got to Nineveh, he probably looked a lot like a Ninevite. But what a culture shock in that city. He didn't know the language, didn't share any memories of what had happened during the last disaster, liked different food than everyone else, and didn't even know the names of who was famous and who wasn't. And yet he was supposed to communicate with everyone. No wonder he ran.

Sometimes it seems God can be so hard on his own kids and so easy on everyone else. MKs can be very good at running away from relationships with people they don't think they can attach to. I mean, what options do we have? We can try to become like the people we look like but don't think like. We can throw it all away and join a monastery somewhere. We can try to be the person we learned to be in our boarding school and never get accepted in our new country. Or I guess we could just forget who we were and learn to be someone else completely.

It almost feels like we have to be honest and real, or be loved. You can't have it both ways.

I remember taking part in one of those college re-entry programs during my second year of university. The facilitators gave us a series of tests to check out how well we were doing psychologically and relationally. I was feeling fine at the time. Of course, that was before my dad and brother were killed in a car accident. And before mom got cancer. And before I got involved with Tommy Lee and this insane group from the Firm and Friendly.

If I stayed in Africa I probably would have always been fine. Then again, if I had never been born in Africa and had the chance to grow up here like everyone else, maybe I would have been fine, too. It's this not belonging anywhere that gets to me. Sometimes you can get so lonely that you latch onto anybody who acts like they might like you. Of course, you can also let them go in a heartbeat so you don't have to find out that they might not like you.

The thought of being alone scares me enough to open up and share my feelings. After all, I've been a professional counsellor. I know that sharing deeply with the one you love is the right thing to do. Getting stuck in some emotional childhood shouldn't be so hard at this stage of life. God doesn't always let you get stuck in your own pity party. My own devotional time has massaged my heart into tenderness.

I approach Bruce from behind as he sits in his reclining chair. I put my arms around his neck from behind and nuzzle his neck. I inhale the aroma of Old Spice aftershave.

Placing my hands firmly on his heart, I coo, "You're a good man, Bruce Southerland."

I love making up.

While we're still lying side by side, Bruce gently touches my chin. "Okay, I'm ready," he whispers.

"Ready for what?"

He rolls onto his back and crosses his hands behind his head. "I'm ready for the story you were going to tell me about the heroes who saved you from the snowstorm."

I turn to face him, propping myself up on my elbow. "You sound skeptical. Are you hinting that you think I made this all up?"

"I'm just glad you didn't tell me it was seven dwarves who dug you out."

Although I'm still not convinced Bruce fully believes my story about Joshua Kensington and Rita Galinsky at Walgreens, I give him brownie points for not interrupting. I almost thump him, however, when I try to describe Luke Lapierre and Johan. He actually smirks and tries to tickle me while telling me that I should take up novel-writing. At least I told him everything and one day he'll see for himself. For now, I'm relaxed again with him.

A funny thing happens on my 127th day of marriage. I'm reviewing my journals and reliving some of the intimate times I've had with Bruce. I can't believe the level of passion I can feel at times. Joy is at the top of the charts for us, yet on this day a deep anxiety creeps over my spirit. A dense dark cloud envelopes my mind and the thought persists that I won't have Bruce much longer. My throat constricts and a clear sense of choking causes me to panic. Some days it's like I'm losing my mind.

God has taken away everything I love. My parents, my brother, my friends, my home. This line of irrationality erupts during my early morning daydreams. Bruce is still deep-breathing beside me and I start thinking about my friend Sarah's wedding, but I'm not fixated on the ceremony. I focus on the parents of the bride and groom celebrating with the happy couple. In my dream, I see Bruce and me standing off to the side. Neither of us had our parents at our wedding.

A deep darkness settles into my spirit. The sense of loss and unfairness hit me deep. Or maybe these thoughts have been sparked by a news report about a young bride whose husband was killed by a stray bullet at a Mexican tourist site. Whatever the source, thoughts of intimacy lead to feelings of anxiety. Thoughts of joy lead to feelings of anger. Every muscle in my body hurts and my heart and head feel ready to explode.

I decide to spend some time on the internet surfing for curtain fabric, but I notice an email from Andrea so I check it out.

Subject: I need your brain.

Hey, good lookin'. Hope you're surviving all the snow there. Flowers are gorgeous here. We're past the second term in the school year and it's a good thing. You know how homesick all the staff and kids get at this time of year. It's so hot. The time to go seems so long.

I need your counsellor's brain for a minute. There's a girl in my dorm. One and a half years to go before grad. Been here for ages. She started filling out college application forms and now she's just shutting down. She's gone anorexic on me and the staff here can't seem to help her out. I sure wish you were here. I think you understand girls like this.

One little message, and my whole agenda is changed. I start thinking through all the dorm girls I knew back at the Rift Academy. Wondering how they are doing. Remembering the ways they faced the thought of leaving and not coming back. My stomach knots. My breathing quickens.

I journaled my way through the last years. Somehow trying to capture every minute and thought along the way, I felt like I could keep tomorrow from coming. Or at least I hoped I could always have my world to come back to once I left.

I shut down the computer without answering Andrea's email. I need my horse.

After bundling up in all my winter gear, I step into my boots and trudge out to the barn. I'm so distracted by thoughts of Kenya that I don't even tell Bruce I'm leaving. When I get to the barn, I hold onto Lancelot's neck and weep. He doesn't move or try to push me away.

At some point in my time with him I climb onto the wall of his stall and begin to pat his back. His wound seems to have healed nicely. Without thinking, I slip onto his back and hold his neck as I look desperately for a safe place in my heart. I've only ridden him once before, but the big black Arabian stallion doesn't attempt to move me off. He seems to sense when I need him.

Sitting on the horse pumps life into my soul again. A surge of wildness races through my heart and the lure of riding in the snow pulls at me. I pinch my knees into his sides and push on his satin neck, urging him toward the barn door. He responds with a little hesitation.

The barn door swings open easily and I prompt him into the waist-deep drifts around the barn. He obeys for a minute, then pushes toward the trail Bruce cleared between the barn and the roadway.

I just let him carry me and we don't hurry anywhere. He almost rocks me to sleep as I lay with my head on his mane. His heavy breathing and occasional snorting bring a comforting sense of rightness. The snow heavy on the evergreens is a glorious sight. We soon wander off the road and onto a trail that leads somewhere near Denman's Gulley.

As I lay quietly on Lancelot's back, a large snowy owl launches from a treetop; with powerful, deep wingbeats, he sets up a glide that propels him right onto the back of a small hare. The bird of prey looks like a diving white snowball with yellow eyes and a charcoal bill. His feathered feet reach out and snag the squealing rabbit and in a swoosh he's gone back into the forest.

It all feels ominous and I turn Lancelot around. Darkness is falling quickly and we're a good distance from the farmhouse. I haven't paid much attention to the details of where we were wandering, so I trust the big stallion to take me home. Horses are good for knowing where home is.

When Lancelot stops in the middle of the trail, and even starts to shuffle backward, I sit up and grip tightly to his mane. I can't see anything, but I can hear a low snarl up ahead. Lancelot answers the snarl with his own deep challenge and begins to step forward.

A cougar steps out onto the trail.

I've seen plenty of lions up close, so seeing the cougar from my safe perch doesn't scare me at all. The cat is about six feet long, under three feet high, and is clearly hunting. He was probably tracking a deer when we interrupted him.

What surprises me is the fact that a cougar is here at all. I'd researched the wildlife in this area and the only cat sightings have been bobcats and lynx. Cougar sightings have often been reported, but most proved to be false. They've been hunted down and almost eliminated in this area where the farmers are so protective of their livestock.

The big stallion me regains his composure and begins to stride purposefully toward the mountain lion. The cat snarls but backs off a few feet. Lancelot continues and the cougar makes a small lunge. To my surprise, Lancelot rears up on his haunches and I slip off and fall into the snow. I fall onto the same shoulder that was injured when Anthony hit me with a bat, and when I fell off the motorcycle jumping Denman's Gulley. The pain is intense.

The sky above is pitch dark now, but the snow provides a good backdrop for the silhouetted shadows on the trail ahead. The cat darts away from the horse and into the bush in my direction. I stretch myself tall and protect my throat in case the cat decides to act out of character.

Lancelot seems to sense where the cat is and edges up to stand between me and the forest. He's too tall for me to pull myself up, and with my injured shoulder I don't have the strength. We stand for five minutes before the horse visibly relaxes. I assume the cat has gone.

I hold Lancelot's mane with my good hand and let him lead. We seem to walk for hours without getting anywhere I recognize. Finally we reach a road with a fence. I struggle up onto the fence and then onto the horse, letting him carry me the rest of the way.

The flashing lights are the first thing to get my attention. It's definitely the sheriff and I have a sneaking suspicion he's looking for me. The police car is travelling in my direction about half a mile away. I can see the lights off and on through the clumps of trees that line the edge of our property.

When the lights start coming down my road, I stop and wait for the car to halt. The lights keep flashing. The sheriff's car crunches through the crisp surface of the snow, rolling parallel to where I sit on Lancelot. My worst suspicions prove true.

Deputy Timmons pokes his head out the window and looks up at me. He shines a bright flashlight into my face. "Evening, Mrs. Southerland. Out for a nice ride, are you? Don't suppose you know that half the county is out looking for you. Seems a wife ought to tell her husband what she's up to if she's not up to no good."

I want to defend myself, but he holds up his hand to show me he isn't finished.

"Just to warn you, some crackpot farmer says a cougar took out one of his calves. There ain't no cougar in this county, but them farmers are out hunting, and they just might mistake an unknown movement in the darkness for something dangerous. I'd advise you to let your husband know what you're up to. Evening, ma'am."

He rolls up his window and begins to back his way toward the road and heads toward town.

I don't have a clue what I'll say to Bruce this time as we turn into the driveway and head for the barn.

CHAPTER ELEVEN

I can't even tell you how humiliating the last two weeks have been. Not just with Bruce.

My husband had to accompany me for three trips to the sheriff's office to explain my actions. The operation caused significant expense of manpower and equipment during a needless search and rescue. No one bothered to check if the horse was missing so they could track us. They made assumptions and now take out the consequences of those assumptions on me.

Old accusations surface again about my involvement in illegal activities. The sheriff and several of his deputies take turns questioning me on every detail of my life since I've arrived. Who I've met with and where I've gone. Fortunately, I really haven't gone anywhere and don't have much to say to anyone. I've met a few people at church and during my shopping excursions.

I can't even have Bruce in the room for support. There's no doubt that Deputy Timmons is behind this, even if the questions don't come out of his mouth. When I fail to mention my connection with Luke and Johan, it feels like I'm committing a capital crime. I don't consider them to be significant relationships.

At the post office, we are handed a letter from the U.S. Navy. It's addressed to Commander B. Southerland. Bruce didn't bother to open it until we got home. A lot of our rides are quiet these days.

The letter notifies him that his leave from the Navy is finished and he's being transferred to Naval Base Kitsap, Washington, effective immediately, to assume the post of Executive Officer, Naval Intermediate Maintenance Facility, PACNORWEST.

Bruce is stunned. Both of us were under the assumption that he would have a one-year leave, which is why we leased the farmhouse from Uncle Bob. Somewhere the communication system must have broken down. Bruce contacts his friends in the Navy, but there's nothing they can do to change things for him.

For me, it just means more numbness. I walk to the attic and begin to haul out the suitcases. By now, Bruce has managed to find all the secret compartments on the steamer trunks. The contents lay in the middle of the attic floor. I start packing all the journals, letters, documents, and special papers.

The dresser drawers are half-empty when Bruce walks in and sees me cramming my socks into the corner of a suitcase.

"What in the world are you doing?" He's doing his best not to scream. He still feels the full emotions of transitions; they aren't easy on him. I keep packing until he comes over and physically blocks my access to the dresser. "Katie, what are you doing?"

"I'm packing."

"I can see you're packing, but why?"

"The letter says we have to go to Bremerton. Immediately. We need to pack."

"Katie, there's got to be a mistake." Bruce takes me in his arms and gives me a gentle, restraining hug. "Give me time. I'll work it out. We were supposed to have a year."

I embrace him back, meaning to comfort him. "Life doesn't always work the way you plan. Sometimes you just have to suck it up and say goodbye. I've been doing it all my life."

"Katie, we have a problem." Bruce leads me by my good arm and sits me on the bed. "I have to report by next Monday. They'll sort this out once I get onsite. Katie, my pension rides on my good service record, so I have to go. They say they haven't got living quarters for you there yet. You'll have to find something in the community until you get security clearance."

I have no idea what he's talking about. No place to live? Security clearance? "What do you mean? And what am I going to do with Lancelot?"

Bruce hangs his head. "I don't know. Maybe Uncle Bob can work on that. Or Jimmy. Maybe you can stay with Lizzy and Dean for a few weeks while I find something for us."

Lizzy is more than two hundred miles away in Minneapolis, but with the weather so bad we haven't been taking the chance on the roads. Now it seems like the obvious choice, except for Lancelot.

Since I can smile without feeling anything, I find it easy to reassure Bruce. I even hold his hand. "You just go on ahead. I'll take care of things here." This is insane. Why is my leg jumpy? "I'm sure Luke and Johan can help me if there's anything heavy to deal with." I'll probably be arrested by that deputy. "I'll call Lizzy. She and Dean might be able to come down for the weekend and help with the little things." I stand up and face him. "And you're right. Uncle Bob probably knows exactly what I need to do with a stallion in the middle of winter." So much for the wedding vows about protecting and providing. "Don't worry about a thing. Just remember, you're a good man."

Unbelievably, my so-called prince buys the whole act. "Really? I'll make sure I keep things moving from the other side. We'll be back together in no time." With that, he gets up and starts searching the closet for his uniform and other Navy wear.

I want to harpoon the guy. Where is my protector, my warrior, my knight in shining armor? We've only been married five months and the guy is ready to abandon me again for some work issue. Am I enough for him, or am I too much? Do all my adventures scare him away? For a Special Forces veteran and Tai Kwon Do master, he's not scoring very many points at home right now.

We continue through the motions of marriage, and while the intimacy is there, the anxiety spikes so high that it almost shuts me down. Bruce loads up the Durango after church on Sunday and drives off with Pastor Tyson to the Moorhead municipal airport. From there he's going to catch a flight to Minneapolis and then somehow get over to Seattle.

I flip on the computer and notice an email from Harmony Cooper. She's the youngest daughter of our old next-door neighbors at the station at Kijabe in Kenya. She loved to come by our house and feed my dad's tortoises. I haven't heard from her since our family left thirteen years ago. She must have been about six years. It shocks me to realize she has graduated by now. I scan her email carefully.

Subject: Hello from Harmony.

I don't know if you remember me, but I grew up next door to you. I loved your dad's tortoises. I got your email from the mission head office. They thought I should connect with you.

When I first got to the States, I was psyched to try everything I'd missed out on. All our family members and friends in New York were more than willing to take us. I hit every fast food outlet I could get to. I hit the theme parks. I hit the malls bigtime. I tried to catch up on all the movies and music I'd been missing out on.

That lasted about a month. Then I just got sick of all the shallowness and emptiness. I was putting on weight faster than I could take it off. People were nice to me, but no one really wanted to hear about my life, who I was, and what I'd experienced.

I ended up with giardia for some reason and the doctor didn't really know what to do for me. The weather was a shock to my system. And the kids my age at school and church already seemed to have all their friends in place.

I decided to transfer schools to see if things were better in California. I loved the beach so much that I had trouble getting my schoolwork done. The people I got to know at the beach didn't seem to know the people I met at school, and neither group knew the people at church. After a few months, I felt like a pinball bouncing around from place to place without getting to know anyone.

Besides, the guys all seemed to have their mind on one thing. I wasn't sure who hated me most. The guys hated me because I kept refusing their charm and ruining their reputations. The girls hated me because the guys they liked seemed distracted by me. Besides, while everyone in New York seemed fixated on Broadway, in California they seemed fixated on Hollywood. Everything seemed just as superficial.

I started missing my family and friends in New York. It seemed that I'd spend hours every day on email, Skype, chatting, or on the phone with people far away. I really wasn't doing that well at school. And I really got overwhelmed by all the freedom. No one seemed to care what I wanted to do.

Next semester, I'm wondering about whether to join some of my MK friends in Texas or just head back to New York and try and get it right this time. Any advice? Harmony

With the pain from Bruce still fresh on my heart, I'm not ready to advise anyone. I shut down the computer and head out to the barn.

Lancelot isn't very responsive to my attempts to convince him to go for another ride. He's probably had enough adventures with me around. I comb out his mane and tail, then wander up to the attic again. Bruce has everything neatly laid out for me to look at.

Some of my old Rift Academy Yearbooks catch my attention. I've forgotten these treasures. I quickly scan the covers with their buffalo crests. I notice that the records of my third and eighth grades are missing. Those were the years I was back with my grandparents in Langley.

I pick up my tenth grade yearbook and look at the pictures of my friends. Tenth grade was my last year. There is Andrea and Sarah, friends forever. There's Chelsea. We got to be friends that year when she was stuck in the dorm with a migraine and the dorm mom wouldn't believe her.

Chelsea was studying for her British O levels and trying to keep up with her American courses at the same time. We'd seen her stressed out for weeks and none of us could make it easier. I was looking for Sarah one day, but when I walked by Chelsea's door I heard her groaning. I walked in on her and asked what was wrong. She said her brain was ready to pound right out of her skull. She needed a bucket quick because she was ready to lose her breakfast. She needed the blinds drawn shut because the light hurt her eyes. She said she couldn't move the right side of her body and her whole insides seemed to be tremoring out of control.

I thought Chelsea might be dying. When I flew into Aunt Nancy's room, I told her so. Chelsea's dorm mom assured me that it was probably just stress and that I should go on to class and let the girl rest a few minutes. I skipped classes and spent the time stroking Chelsea's hair and rubbing her back. She finally was able to go up to the infirmary.

By staying there with Chelsea, I got my first and only demerits from skipping class with an unexcused absence. Chelsea got one, too, but that was withdrawn after the investigation and I was able to get Aunt Nancy to verify that I had reported the situation to her.

My dad, as the chaplain, didn't know at first whether to be ashamed of me for getting a demerit or proud of me for putting the needs of someone else above my own. We went for a walk after supper around the mile circuit road. The fact that he kept me in a side hug most of the way, while talking to me about how to make wise choices, made me think he was more proud than ashamed.

Next to Chelsea's picture in the yearbook is Belinda. I got to be friends with Belinda after a drama practice when we were invited to Miss Carly's to do some baking. Together we made the best cinnamon rolls with raisins. We shared them with a couple of the junior guys from the rugby team and I'm sure some deep and lasting relationships could have happened for me if I hadn't had to leave.

I flip to the back cover to read the comments from my friends, but I'm interrupted by a loud knock on the kitchen door downstairs. I realize that Pastor

Tyson is probably returning the Durango. The aroma of freshly baked chocolate chip cookies fills my nostrils as I move through the kitchen. I made them as a thank-you gift for the pastor and I step quickly to let him know that they'll be ready in just a minute.

I move aside the drapes in the living room to look outside, and the only vehicle in the yard is the sheriff's car. I stroll over to the door and open it a few inches. Deputy Wayne Timmons stands there with a grim look on his face.

CHAPTER TWELVE

I anchor the door firmly with my foot and move my head a little into the opening. "Yes, deputy, may I help you?"

The deputy shifts from one foot to the other and looks over his shoulder toward the barn. "Mrs. Southerland, I just came to check on your horse. Is your horse safe in the barn? You haven't been out riding this morning have you?"

I open the door a few more inches. "Deputy, I've been in church like I always am Sunday mornings. I fed Lancelot early this morning and he was doing fine. I'd appreciate it if you didn't harass me right now."

Deputy Timmons flips open a small notebook he withdrew from his vest pocket. "Ma'am, do you happen to know Barney Kostonopoulos?"

I'm sure my irritation is starting to show through in my response. "Is there a point to this questioning, deputy? How would I know whoever that is?"

"Poor guy died in a suspicious fire in his home yesterday, ma'am. He's been here less than a year. He was trying to set up a fitness club in the Twin Cities area. Your name came up as a possible connection."

"I've never heard of the man. I really have to go."

Before I can close the door, the deputy puts his foot forward and blocks it from shutting. "Ma'am. I'd appreciate it if you could accompany me to your barn to check on the horse. We've had reports of a horse shot just a few miles from here. It sounds a lot like the one I saw you riding the other night. I just want to check, ma'am."

The door is wide open now. "If this is some kind of trick, deputy, I'll have you know that the Pastor Tyson will be here any minute."

The deputy touches the tip of his hat and backs off a step. "Perhaps it would be just as good to wait for him, ma'am. You may be needing his prayers."

When the deputy drops those words, I can't wait another minute. I slip on my boots, grab a jacket, and slush my way toward the barn. Twenty feet from the barn I begin to call for Lancelot.

"Lancelot! Lancelot! Lancelot!"

Usually he responds, but not today. I open the door to the barn. No sound. I quickly step off the twenty feet to his stall and look inside. No horse.

It's like someone has turned off the oxygen. Things aren't making sense anymore. Bruce is gone and now Lancelot is gone. *Gone, okay... but, shot? No way.*

I race out to the deputy and slush over to where he's still standing by his car. His look tells me that he knows what I've found.

"Ma'am, would you mind if I looked for myself to see if we have any tracks to follow?"

I'm not sure to say, but I sense him walking by me toward the barn and circling the area for a while. I sit on the porch chair, slumped over, when he stops at the bottom of the stairs.

"Appears he's gone, ma'am. His tracks lead out to the road. Doesn't appear to be anyone with him, ma'am. Did you leave the door and the gate open? Maybe he was trying to follow you to church."

If the deputy wasn't been so calm and compassionate I would rip him apart for such a stupid comment. I follow him back to the barn and along the tracks that lead to the road. Twenty yards down the road, the tracks end.

"Horse trailer tracks," he says. "Someone took him."

"He would have fought all the way. They couldn't have forced him out. Not unless they drugged him and blinkered him."

"I'll take you to him, ma'am."

I nod, and am just about to get into the car when Pastor Tyson drives in through the gate and up to the house. I step out of the deputy's car and move over to our Durango.

The pastor hands me the keys and assures me that Bruce has gotten through the security queue and baggage check without complications. He asks if I would mind dropping him off at home. Deputy Timmons steps up behind me and intrudes to assure me that he can drop both us off if we'll come for a short ride first.

Pastor Tyson's quizzical look prompts me to fill him in about Lancelot's disappearance. "Lancelot's missing and someone said there's a horse that looks like him shot close to here."

Tyson takes the keys from my hand and turns to the deputy. "I'll drive. You lead. I think I need to spend this time with Katie."

The deputy takes us around and around in circles, among the farmhouses, for half an hour before pulling over. Tyson pulls in behind him. I'm a wreck by now, looking in vain for Lancelot lying on the side of the road somewhere.

Deputy Timmons strolls back to the Durango, where we wait. The pastor rolls down his window.

"Looks like a mistaken report," the deputy says. "I was sure the horse was right back there. Either someone has hauled him away or faked the whole thing. Strange thing that your horse would be missing at the same time."

My spine tingles with terror as the deputy ambles back to his car. The pastor looks at me as I begin to curl up into a semi-fetal position. "Katie, are you okay?"

"It was a trick," I stutter. "They took Lancelot so they could get to me. Deputy Timmons is in on this with Joshua and Rita. They just won't leave me alone."

"Katie, what are you trying to say? It's just a mistake. The horse isn't here."

I look at him and decide I can't trust anyone. "Never mind. Let me drop you off and I'll get back home. He's probably found his way back home by now."

Pastor Tyson is definitely a shepherd. He pats my shoulder and prays. After his amen, he says, "Katie, you're in no condition to drive home. Let me take you to my place for a while."

It takes a cup of tea and another round of prayer, but I'm soon ready to head back home.

Marie Tyson stands arm in arm with her husband as I drive out of the driveway. She might be married to a good pastor, but neither she nor her husband understand how evil a world they live in.

The darkness descends too quickly and my headlights hardly chase the shadows from the edge of the road as I crawl home looking desperately for any sign of my horse. When I drive through the gate, there he stands, near the house. Side by side with Luke.

I almost forget to put the SUV in park before racing out the door. I can feel my anger boiling up like a volcano. The words are out of my mouth before I realize what I'm saying: "You horse thief. You lowlife, freak of nature, thieving horse-snatcher. How dare you steal my horse! How dare you pretend to be a friend and then steal my horse!"

I'm not sure whether to pound my fists into the giant's chest or throw my arms around Lancelot's neck. Both of them stand still in front of me. Hugging my horse seems like a safer choice.

When Lancelot gets restless, I finally release my hold on him and step around to Luke. He hasn't moved since I arrived. I stare him down. "Well, what have you got to say for yourself?"

"I found him on the other side of town and brought him home." With that short statement, he turns and starts walking toward the gate.

"Wait a minute!" I yell. "You can't just walk away like that. What do you mean, you found my horse on the other side of town?"

Luke turns and takes a few steps toward me. "Your horse was in someone else's trailer sitting in a parking lot. I knew you wouldn't let him go, so I freed him and walked him home."

"You freed my horse from someone else's trailer? Who would take my horse and leave him in a parking lot? This doesn't make sense."

"Whether it makes sense or not, Mrs. Southerland, that is what happened. I'd be more careful with my horse if I were you. There are some evil minds working around here these days."

With that, the giant leaves, crunching the snow as he walks.

The night is bitterly cold, but there's no way I'm leaving Lancelot. I just have to make a few calls first before I can settle down. Bruce is still en route, so he's out of reach. There's no way I'm calling the sheriff's office. I call the vet but get the answering machine, so I leave a message. I decide to call Lizzy to see if she and Dean can lend some support, but they both have to work in the morning; she assures me she will try to come down Tuesday.

Pastor Tyson is my only hope and he immediately comes by with his wife. The pastor sits in the barn with the horse while his wife Marie purposefully works in the kitchen assembling coffee and snacks. I gather blankets and pillows, and even a heater, and head to the barn to set up for the night. The three of us huddle and talk about the strange events happening in our little county. If only Lancelot could talk.

Pastor Tyson reports that the horse seems restless and that he has looked at Lancelot's eyes. They look glazed. "Probably from when they tranquilized him to get him to the trailer," he surmises. "Doc Goertzen will check him out in the morning."

Lancelot is becoming increasingly restless and I try to get him to eat or drink without success. Usually I can calm him down with my voice, but something isn't right. I finally have to lie down and get some rest.

Two hours later, Lancelot falls over with a thud that cracks the sideboards on his stall. I scream and scramble to find out what has happened. His breathing is shallow and rough. His nostrils are flared. His eyes have a look of panic I've never seen before. His belly is distended and his muscles are twitching. He is solid and stiff.

"Bring a blanket," I yell. "Bring the heater. Call the vet. Bring some water."

While he fights for life, I cry and urge him to hang on. He gasps valiantly for breath. I stand back and nearly lose my own.

Half an hour later, it's all over. Lancelot is gone. I turn and walk away without a tear. My heart is broken. My world is finished. I am lost.

CHAPTER THIRTEEN

D r. Goertzen arrives from the barn after doing an autopsy. His broad shoulders are hunched and his gum boots shuffle slowly through the slush. He peels off his examination gloves and tucks them into a bag which he shoves into his pocket. His snow-white bushy moustache and goatee move in tandem as he speaks. "Ma'am, what I see here is impossible."

"What do you mean?"

"Your horse has been poisoned, but it isn't natural."

"What do you mean?" I ask again.

"Looks like a couple of substances are registering." He pulls out a clipboard from under his armpit and scans it before continuing. "Copperheads don't come this far north, so their venom is impossible—and doubly impossible in the dead of winter. Besides, it would take a hundred bites to get this much venom into him." He points halfway down the list. "Looks like a good amount of botulinum toxins got into his feed as well. Even traces of rat poison." He waves the clipboard. "It's my professional opinion, ma'am, that someone did your horse in. I think you better call the sheriff."

Doc Goertzen, Sheriff Reimer, and Pastor Tyson do their best to comfort me. Bruce finally calls and gets the full brunt of my heartache. Lizzy assures me she will be down in the evening.

Shamefully, I put the blame, and vent the full fury of my verbal anger, on Luke and Deputy Timmons. I even accuse Joshua and Rita. All the pieces come together in my mind to confirm their guilt over this tragedy. My tale probably sounds like a farfetched conspiracy to the doctor, sheriff, and pastor.

"It's their way of intimidating me," I say. "Joshua and Rita saw me in town. They think I'm still part of some international trafficking ring they're setting up." I walk around, flapping my arms like a wild turkey. "I'm sure they took Lancelot as bait and were trying to get the deputy to lure me into a trap." I spin and point at the pastor. "If Pastor Tyson hadn't come along at just the right time, I'd be gone by now. When they couldn't get me, they took it out on my horse." I tuck my elbows in tight to my hips and clench my fists. "I don't know how Luke Lapierre is involved, but he was with my horse last. He either poisoned the horse or he knows who did."

The sheriff shifts uncomfortably as the other two men lean against the stall railing. "Fact is, ma'am, I sent Deputy Timmons out to pick up Mr. Lapierrre and we haven't been able to locate the man." He steps toward me with his hands up near his shoulders in a gesture of surrender. "We're assuming he is armed and dangerous. Deputy Timmons is just doing his job." He takes another step as I back away. "I believe he's been out to your place several times in the past weeks helping you out. I have to admit, Mrs. Southerland, that most of what happens has a clear explanation."

I'm not ready to let it go yet. "First, my horse gets shot and now he's poisoned. Do you think that's just a coincidence?" I walk to the porch and wrap my arm around the post by the stairs. "And why was Luke there at just the time Joshua and Rita saw me? And why did he just disappear from the McDonald's when my husband came into town that night? How does he just happen to always be there when I'm in trouble?"

The radio dispatcher signals the sheriff through his car and the lawman walks over, opens the door, and picks up his receiver. "Sheriff Reimer."

It's Timmons. "Sheriff, been talking to this Johan fellow. Friend of Luke's. Said Luke is out trapping for a few days. Does Mrs. Southerland have any evidence to prove he was really there? I'd hate to go chasing an innocent man. And where is Mr. Southerland? He never seems to be aware of what his wife is up to."

The deputy doesn't realize I can hear everything he says. The sheriff looks over his shoulder at me, then gets into his car and shuts the door. I can still hear him. "I'm with Mrs. Southerland. Doc Goertzen says the horse was poisoned."

Pastor Tyson takes this interruption as his cue to gently grip me by the elbow and lead me off on a walk. Doc Goertzen goes back to tending Lancelot so he can be transported out of here.

The crisp air bites at my nostrils. The intensifying wind strains to suck the warmth out of the hands, which I have tucked up under my armpits. Silence is a welcome friend as we walk.

"Katie, I can't imagine how you're feeling right now," Tyson says.

"Neither can I."

More silence. "I can't imagine the questions that must be whirling around in your mind. The memories you've shared with Lancelot."

"I don't think the thoughts and words have even figured out how to turn into questions yet."

He stops walking and turns toward me. "What support do you have to help you through this?"

"My sister is coming in tonight. Bruce is calling me in a couple of hours. I've got friends I can call if I need to."

"Katie, by what I hear you saying, I'm not sure you feel safe here. Would you be willing to let us put you and your sister up for a few days until things get sorted out?"

"Pastor, I haven't got a lot of time before I have to leave this place." I turn back toward the farmhouse and make a decision. "I've got packing to do. The sheriff thinks this is all in my head. If you can send some of the men over to help me move some stuff tomorrow, that would be great. I guess it's too late to ask you to pray for my horse."

I don't even watch them load Lancelot's body. I just sit in the attic and pack away the memories of another life, one that Lancelot helped me heal from. It strikes me as strange that I've worked so hard to help others heal and yet I'm not even sure how healing can happen for me. How do people persevere through relentless pressure?

Lizzy flies into the Moorhead Municipal Airfield and catches a taxi out to the farm. I don't dare go out on the roads on my own and I'm too proud to ask for help. Besides, I want to sit in the middle of Lancelot's stall and feel whatever presence might be left. I want to think through the memories of our races together. And I want to try to pray again.

I'm slumped on a half-chewed bale of hay in the corner of Lancelot's stall when I hear the car drive up to the farmhouse. By the time I get to the barn door, Lizzy is knocking frantically at the kitchen door. I call to her as the taxi slowly slushes its way through the melting snow and down the gravel driveway. A lot of traffic has been through here lately.

Lizzy abandons her suitcase on the porch and walks quickly across the yard to where I stand. We hug and cry. I don't know for what. Just for everything we've ever loved and lost.

My cellphone rings as we walk through the door. I realize that I forgot Bruce was going to call. He's a little intense when I answer.

"Katie, are you okay? What's happening?"

I assure him that Lizzy is with me, but he's ready to book a ticket back to be with me when I tell him that Lancelot has been poisoned. At least he gets brownie points for trying. I let him off the hook. Besides, I'm sure the Navy probably has some rule about abandoning ship on the same day you report for duty.

"Bruce, I'm almost packed. There's nothing for me to do. I just need you to call Uncle Bob and explain what's going on. I can't deal with whatever happens next here."

He assures me he'll do whatever he can and then asks a loaded question: "So where will you go now?"

The answer seems obvious. "I thought I'd stay with Lizzy for a few days, then come and be with you."

I hear that throat clearing thing he does. Sure enough. "I've got a problem."

"What's that?"

"They've booked me for sea trials starting next Monday on a nuclear submarine that's just been commissioned. After that I'm supposed to be on standby for a new aircraft carrier that's heading for Japan."

"What does that mean?"

"I'll be out of contact for the next several weeks. I can't even tell you how long."

Internally, I turn to jelly. "Bruce, you have to tell them this isn't going to work. Your wife needs you right now."

"Honey, there's nothing I can do. This is the Navy."

Again, numbness. "Okay, call me when you get home."

That's it. I hang up, and I don't answer when the phone starts ringing again. Call me passive aggressive, but I need all my energy just to keep myself safe. I have no emotional energy left to argue over the phone with someone whose heart is like a rock.

Lizzy's phone rings next and I beg her not to answer it. She tells me this isn't the way marriage problems get sorted out, but she sees how distressed I am and holds me instead. It takes my husband ten minutes to realize how stubborn I can be before he gives up trying anymore.

CHAPTER FOURTEEN

L izzy and I start packing. We don't finish until the first slivers of light poke their way through the pine trees. Busy is good right now. Everything's stacked throughout the living room with name labels, but no address. I have no clue where this stuff is going.

Lizzy puts together some waffles and fruit while I shower and change. The warm water soothes my spirit and eases my mind. I keep turning it hotter until it burns me red. I scrub and scrub and finally feel clean.

When I get downstairs, Dean is there in an embrace with Lizzy. I don't even hesitate about walking in and thwacking Dean on the back of the head. "You're in public, Gonzo," I say. "What are you doing here, making out in my kitchen?"

The two of them separate and laugh.

"Lizzy called me last night," says Dean. "Told me to get here quick. She said it would be good if I could drive the Durango back to Minnie for you."

Lizzy shrugs. "I didn't want to have to load this all myself. Besides, Dean says he knows a good storage unit less than a mile from our place."

I straddle the kitchen chair backwards, bow my head in a brief grace, and start gorging on the waffles and fruit. We're almost out of maple syrup anyway, so I guess it's a good time for a move.

Lizzy and Dean sit across from me, hold hands, whisper a brief grace, then join in the refueling process. As I scoop up my fruit, I picture Bruce all decked out in his commander's uniform. Four gold bars covering the wrists of his dark jacket. Cap proudly perched on his head. Back straight. Eyes front. Proudly serving his country. Shamelessly abandoning his wife.

Dean works out the details of moving my stuff. A moving company is supposed to come and clear everything out by noon. I call to tell Pastor Tyson that we're heading out. He gives his farewells and best wishes. Uncle Bob calls to say that Bruce let him know what's happening and he's very sad about the horse. He'll be by later in the week to clean up the place and take care of selling it.

Sarah phones to say that Bruce called her and that she's devastated by my loss. She can't wait for me to get out to Washington so we can see each other again. Andrea leaves me a text message saying that the girl's counsellor at Rift Academy had to leave with cerebral malaria and they need badly a replacement. She asks if I know anyone who could fill in for at least three months?

I take one last walk to the barn to say farewell to the memory of Lancelot. It doesn't take long. I stand in his stall, close my eyes, and breathe in the smell of the barn. Woodchips, hay, dust, damp grain, and something that doesn't quite fit. I realize that this is where Doc Goertzen did his autopsy. Ammonia? Other fluids I don't want to think about. It's time to go.

As I reach the barn door facing the house, I see the sheriff driving in. I pull back and wait in the shadows as he gets out of the car and makes his way to the porch. He stands knocking, then turns to survey the yard. I slip back and shelter myself in Lancelot's old stall.

When I emerge from my hiding place in the stall, I see Luke standing in the shadows by the entrance to the barn. Exactly where I had been standing.

I want to feel anger, but I don't. I want to feel terrified, but I don't. I want to feel anything, but I don't. I just wait for whatever happens next. I have nothing to lose.

The blond-bearded giant takes one step forward and stops. He speaks hesitantly. "Mrs. Southerland, I am truly sorry about your horse. He was one of the finest animals I've known. You have no reason to believe me, but I had nothing to do with his poisoning, ma'am." He looks around toward the sheriff, then leans toward me. "I saw a woman with gold rings on her fingers leaving the diner. She got in the truck that hauled the trailer. I don't know anything about her except that she's up to no good. It's a good thing you're leaving, ma'am."

His words hardly register. "Why did you come back here?"

He answers without hesitation. "Truth is, ma'am, the deputy has it out for me. He's making it look like I had something to do with this." The blond giant glances over his shoulder again. "I'm not sure if they'll let me live through this one. I wanted you to know I loved your horse. That I had nothing to do with this horrible thing." He backs away. "You need to know who your friends are. I'm truly sorry for your loss."

He bows his head briefly and turns to go.

"Wait." He hesitates and slowly faces me. The words aren't hard to say. "Thank you for everything."

Dean and Lizzy direct the moving truck into place when I emerge from the barn. They don't mention anything about Luke, so I assume they didn't notice him. Dean loads some of my personal items into the Durango, then we head out and leave the rest to the professionals. A quick trip down Highway 75 and then the 52 gives us a direct route toward Minneapolis and my new home.

When we drive past the Municipal Airport, I almost ask Dean to drop me off so I can head back to Seattle. But Bruce isn't even there. He's off sailing some nuclear submarine. I shut my mouth and we keep going. The land of ten thousand lakes isn't going to have one lake more from my tears.

Although the chat starts superficially, as usual, it doesn't last. Dean isn't that kind of a guy. One minute we're talking about why Highway 52 is the same as Interstate 94 and how confusing that might be for visitors. The next minute we're talking about how MKs must be a lot like that—carrying both local traffic and outside traffic that's just passing through.

Lizzy comments from her perch behind the wheel. "Dean, that's why us MKs are so confused. We're in the same place as everyone else, but we're not sure whether we're Highway 52 or Interstate 94. Do we belong local or are we just passing through?"

I chirp in. "As some MK once said, 'I'm neither blue nor yellow—I'm green.' I guess we're a mix of both and not always sure which one should count most."

"So, tell me ten advantages you two have had because you're MKs," Dean asks.

Lizzy responds first. "Most of us know how to get by in more than one language." She raises her index finger above her head. "I think that makes us sensitive to people coming here and learning our language. We grew up with a really close family and added a ton of aunts and uncles and brothers and sisters."

I add a couple of things while Lizzy keeps track on her fingers. "A lot of MKs have a bigger worldview, a greater understanding of political and social and religious issues that might be in the news. They tend to have a stronger sense of where countries are located and what might be happening in those places. "

Lizzy continues the list. "I think we make great observers. We see things from a different perspective than others who have only grown up in one place. We're adaptable and tolerant and we usually like to get involved in helping people, especially if they come from other countries. We also get to do things most of our friends here haven't, like helping in surgeries, or preaching, or building, or travelling to exotic places or tasting amazing foods."

I finish off. "I'm not sure how many advantages that is, but I think we can say that most MKs have seen God work firsthand in some miraculous ways. We learn somehow that there's much more to our world than what everyone sees."

A golden retriever has its head out the window of the pickup passing us. Its tongue flops in the breeze.

I miss my Kijabe pup.

"A lot of the basic truths of our faith have been nailed down, so we can deal with bigger issues," I say. "We've often had some strong boundaries modelled and explained to us."

With Lizzy driving and in control, Dean reaches inside his jacket and pulls out a sheet of paper he'd prepared for this moment. We still have over two hundred miles to go and it looks like it might be a long ride.

Dean usually has a lot of wisdom and wit, so I wait for his sermon on my recent losses. Instead he moves the conversation in a different direction. "Katie, Andrea's been sending emails from the Rift Academy about the need for a counsellor there. You'd probably be good at that kind of stuff. But let me ask you something first."

"About what?"

"I was sitting in the church library last week, waiting for Lizzy to finish up her women's meeting, when I saw a book written by an evangelical author. It seemed to imply that growing up in a Christian home could be dangerous. I took it down and opened it up at random. I copied a few quotes and came up with a few questions for you."

"Wait a minute, Dean," I say. "Are you trying to tell me that you were eavesdropping on a women's meeting?"

"No, it was our date night and the meeting was running over. I was just trying to make good use of my time. When I saw the title, I was surprised to think it might have been dangerous to grow up in a Christian home." He raises the paper and clears his throat. "It seems this guy thinks it's not just MKs who could be warped. Aren't you flattered that I thought of you enough to write down these quotes?"

"Dean, don't forget I'm getting to know you. I know you have an alternate motive, but go ahead. Read your quotes."

Dean smirks and smooths his paper. "Okay, the first question has to do with the fact that the way parents live out their faith on a daily basis has a lot more impact on the kids than any religious practices they might have." He looks over his shoulder at me. "I wonder, is this part of what MKs deal with? Not having their parents around for daily living?" He turns back and looks out the side window. "Since there's a whole book on this, could it be that MKs are just facing the same issues as all Christian kids, except more, since they don't have their parents all the time?"

My brother-in-law doesn't get the reaction he's probably looking for. I look out the window for a few more seconds. A mom and her little girl are walking hand in hand into a country store.

I miss Mom.

"I wouldn't know, Dean," I say in my best monotone. "Mom and Dad treated Lizzy and I pretty good. Both of us had a rough time when we transitioned."

I miss Dad, too.

"Robert seemed to be the only one who came through unscathed."

I really miss my big brother.

"Maybe it has something to do with birth order, or personality, or cultural expectation, or preparation for your experiences of separation. Not everybody seems to go through the experiences in the same way."

Dean isn't ready to back off. "Another thing I saw in this book is that so many parents quote scriptures and tell their kids that God is watching them, but they only do it to get their kids to be good." He raps his knuckles in a rhythm on the passenger window. "The kids are controlled and manipulated and the parents don't take responsibility for proper teaching and modeling. Doesn't this mean Christians everywhere are creating huge guilt trips and warping their kids by trying to make them good?"

I can see a little of the trap ahead. "Dean, it's the way you use scripture and God. The Christian life is about learning to live in grace and love and forgiveness and hope." I reach into my purse for a stick of gum. The cherry burst over my tongue is like a taste of summer. "Some people use God and scripture as weapons to manipulate obedience. When they do this, they don't help anyone to love God, or to love a neighbor, which is the whole point of being God's child."

Dean straightens out his paper and waits as a double trailer truck pulls past us and rocks our vehicle in its wake. Lizzy eases up and lets the semi change lanes in front of us.

Dean picks up where he left off. "Katie, God put each of us into a single package. Our personalities, our feelings, our faith, our mind. It's easy to get warped if you get exposed to the wrong influence or authority." He looks back over his shoulder at me. "I've heard some great Christian family therapists say that boarding schools warp kids. Do you think missionary parents are warping their kids by forcing them into boarding schools?"

CHAPTER FIFTEEN

L izzy breaks into the conversation. "Let's play license plate alphabet. I see an A and a B!"

My little sister has never been one for tension, but Dean and I are quite fine with it.

My brother-in-law ignores the game. "I see a lot of C. A chicken Christian counsellor choking in a car."

Dean almost has me with that one. I feel the spark ignite, but I douse it in time. I don't even look at him in the front seat.

Lizzy takes her hand off the wheel and gives Dean a backhanded smack on his chest. "You take that back, Dean. This isn't the time to be teasing Katie."

I smile in response to his groan. It's my turn to jump in, and I try to do it as calmly as I can. "I'm okay, Lizzy. I know these gorillas need a beatdown every once in a while. I'll answer him."

Lizzy gives Dean a sideways glare. "This can wait, Katie."

I shift and look up toward Dean, trying to be slow and deliberate. "Most godly parents choose the best options they have and trust God with the outcome." I spot a flock of crows landing on a grove of trees by the highway. They seem carefree. "None of the parents dropping off their sons or daughters at boarding school looked like they were intentionally trying to warp their kids. God can use even our hardest experiences to shape us." *Haven't I been learning this the hard way?* "Hard experiences come to kids in boarding schools and to kids outside boarding schools. They come to kids in Christian families and to kids outside Christian families."

Dean knows he's getting close to my vulnerable spot, so he tries again. "This book talked about emotionally struggling Christians who are stuck in their adolescence. Because they were brought up in an environment of submission, they never learned to question the things they'd been taught by their parents or the church." He turns his paper over and scans it for something. "It said that if a young person never has the chance to question successfully, they'll get stuck in fear, guilt, or perpetual submission. Do you see this happening in yourself or in other MKs?"

Despite his insensitivity to my loss, I play his game one more time. "Dean, I'll tell it like I see it. MKs just walk a different path than a lot of their peers. It can be confusing for them." The sun bursts through a break in the dark clouds overhead. It's a sign of hope. "Not just for them, but for their parents, their relatives, and their classmates in college. They see life differently because they've experienced life differently." The clouds close the gap and a shadow drops over the land again. "When their teen years drop them into the stage of figuring out who they are, they don't always have the same playground, the same parameters, the same limitations and freedoms their counterparts in Boston, Los Angeles, Vancouver, Toronto, or London might have."

"Or Langley," Lizzy pipes up. We exchange smiles through the rear-view mirror.

"In these past few years, technology and freedom of travel is changing a lot of this, but not all of it," I say, trying to be honest and vulnerable with Dean. "Today's youth are growing up with a certain sense of entitlement, which creates its own issues, regardless of where they grow up." *If they grow up.* "So many confusing signals come at youth from so many voices. Sometimes they get stuck before they get to the crisis of young adulthood, which is intimacy versus isolation."

Lizzy jumps in again. "Katie, don't give us all that psychology stuff. I just need to know that some of us are normal. MKs are getting analyzed to death. I've filled out tons of those tests." She hits her fist lightly on the top of the steering wheel. "I know I have issues, but you should hear the issues from the women in our women's group. Some days I think we're all just struggling in different ways." She lifts her fist off the wheel and makes a jerking motion toward Dean with her thumb. "At least we're not as messed up as Dean is."

Dean gives Lizzy a playful shoulder punch and the two grab hands, beginning to wrestle until the Durango swerves.

"Whoa! Enough," Lizzy says as she settles back in to concentrate.

Dean turns toward me again. "Actually, I did study something about that. Wasn't it Erikson who came up with those eight stages of human development?"

I smile. "Someone was paying attention. Yes, back in 1959, Erikson formulated eight psychosocial stages of human development."

Lizzy pops in again. "Katie, if we have to go through this, can you talk human so the rest of us can understand it?"

"Stop me if it gets too hard. There are eight stages. The first is called trust versus mistrust. It means we either learn to trust others in our world or get stuck in mistrust." I check to see if Dean is paying attention. "We have to answer the question for ourselves: is my world safe enough? It doesn't take much to realize this has a huge impact on our relationships."

"I think this is where Lizzy and I are stuck," Dean breaks in. "Every time I say something, she punches me. My world just isn't safe."

Lizzy reaches over and thwacks him backhanded into the stomach.

He groans. "See! I don't have a chance. What's next?"

"We try to move toward autonomy or independence. If we get stuck here, we end up feeling a lot of shame or doubt. By the time we're three or four, we start asserting ourselves more and working to take initiative in the world. If this doesn't prove successful, we can slip into a stream of guilt."

Lizzy speaks up again. "I think half the women I know are stuck there. They feel like they're under this incredible cloud of guilt. I think that's what Dean was hinting at with his quotes about Christian homes being so dangerous to grow up in."

Dean reaches over and rubs the back of Lizzy's hair. "I'm impressed, woman. Are you telling me that none of my guilt trips on you have been working?"

He's in a perfectly vulnerable position and Lizzy thwacks him again in the chest. I suddenly have a huge ache in my gut for Bruce. I miss our own version of horseplay. The ache becomes a physical pain, so I ignore Dean's groans and keep talking.

"I hope this makes some sense. The value of elementary school is that it helps us move through a phase where we learn new skills and develop new competencies. We learn to succeed or sink back into a sense of inferiority and failure."

Lizzy pipes up to make another attempt at wit. "See, Dean? You have a reason for all those feelings of inferiority and failure. You had a lousy elementary school experience. Maybe some night school could help you with that."

The acceleration of the SUV in the next lane isn't alarming, but I instinctively push back into the seat when the car suddenly brakes and matches our speed. Dean and Lizzy are too engaged with each other to notice.

The SUV's rear passenger window slides down and a camera pokes out in our direction. I reach up and tap Dean.

"What is it, Katie? Feeling left out?"

"That SUV beside us. They're taking pictures of us."

Lizzy almost creates an accident by braking quickly. The SUV shoots ahead of us without slowing.

Dean watches the vehicle for a few minutes. When it turns off toward a small tourist attraction, he laughs. "Katie, they're tourists. Not everything has to be a major drama."

Lizzy giggles. "Dean, Katie can't live life if there isn't something mysterious and suspicious going on."

I feel like a third wheel as Dean smiles at her. In a few seconds, he takes care of that by engaging with me again. "So what's next if we get out of elementary school?"

"Identity," I say, playing along. "It's the stage of adolescence that makes us finally figure out who we are. This means aligning ourselves with a faith or political affiliation." I look out the back window to see if the SUV is following us. I don't see it. "It means settling on a gender identity and role. It also means focusing on a future occupation or dream that's ours. Sometimes what and who you're exposed to can make all the difference in your aspirations and understanding of who you are, and who you could be."

"Whoa, now you're losing me," said Dean. "Am I right in saying that teenage MKs are especially vulnerable because at the very time they're trying to figure out who they are, they're being shuffled back and forth between two or more cultures?"

"Well done! You see, each culture has its own signals to tell us whether we're making it or not." A silvery-grey BMW falls in behind us when it could easily have passed. My neck is stiff and my jaw sore. "When you get several sets of conflicting signals, it can get you stuck. But that can happen all in a single place, too. Just imagine what happens to a teen's sense of who he is if he's hearing different sets of values from his parents, his school, his church, his friends, and then the media."

Lizzy adds her thoughts. "None of this works out in real life like it works out on paper."

I agree. "Nothing is as simple as it seems on paper, even in the stage of intimacy or isolation. MKs can graduate overseas and be naïve about what their words or actions communicate to members of the opposite sex." The BMW passes us and a little girl in the back seat waves at me. "Their peers may be hitting this stage at full speed, if they haven't been in it already for a few years, whereas the MKs are just peeking in the door. Or maybe they're running into peers who have no interest in anything but video games, sexual conquest, and expressing a value system which is foreign to the MK. A lot of people get stuck somewhere along the line. The key is finding the right mentors or advisors to prod them through the crisis. That's enough for now."

Lizzy takes her opportunity to say something. "Katie, I found this great fitness center that opened up down the street. You wouldn't believe the stuff they have. Elliptical trainers, bikes, rowers, steppers, treadmills, all kinds of weights and circuits. I could work out for hours and hardly cover half of it."

"What's it called?" I ask without thinking much.

"The Firm and Friendly," she says with a smile. "Same as the one you used to work with. I figured you probably had a lifetime membership, and this would be a great way to work out your stress. This girl, Rita, gave me a great deal when I told her you were my sister."

If it wasn't for the seatbelt that holds me in place, I would have reached up through the seat and grabbed the steering wheel.

"Stop the car!" I say. "Stop the car! They got Lancelot and now they're trying to get you. Stop the car."

CHAPTER SIXTEEN

I'm sure Lizzy and Dean think I'm losing it. The claustrophobia is intense and I'm flailing away in the back seat before I realize the seatbelt is holding me back. I unbuckle the belt as Lizzy brings the Durango to a stop in the Holiday Inn parking lot. We're in Alexandria, only halfway to that Firm and Friendly franchise in Minneapolis, but I still find myself hyperventilating.

Dean has to talk me down. The man who stole my sister's heart helps me get out into the fresh air and walks with me to make sure I don't slip and fall. I'm embarrassed at his attention by the time we get back to the Durango.

Lizzy breaks in to lighten the atmosphere. "How about if we stop for a really early supper here? If we just get salads we won't have to use that fitness center." She looks my way and shrugs." The movers have the key to the storage locker and they can drop it off with our neighbor when they're done."

"Lizzy, she's scared," Dean whispers to her. "Give her a minute."

My sister is a really caring soul and usually understands my emotional limits. My brother-in-law, on the other hand, knows how to ground me. He endures my sister's chatter until she waits just a tad too long between comments.

"Katie, you didn't answer my questions about the dangers of growing up in a Christian home and how it relates to MKs. Was that intentional or did I just give you a soapbox for some pet peeve of yours?"

Lizzy jumps to my defense. "Dean, she's just lost her husband and her horse. Give her a break."

I calm my breathing. I need to finish this conversation. "Dean, I'm sorry for freaking out on you. There's a lot more I need to talk to you two about when we get settled. It's good for me to think about something else. Let's go eat and I'll answer your questions."

The little café we settle on has a bit a fifties theme going on. The front half of a maroon '57 Chevy protrudes from the wall above the entrance. The jukebox has all the old rock and roll favorites my dad used to love. The gumball machine still takes dimes for the massive rainbow-colored treats. The speckled arborite diner tables and red leather barstools look like the original décor.

The waitresses have a strange combination of bobby socks and scarlet red pencil skirts. I've seen a picture of my grandmother in one of these outfits back in her college days. These skirts, with their high and tight-pleated waists, formfitting hugs, and slight tapering through to the knee, were once considered fashionably sexy. Nowadays they seem quite conservative.

Pictures of roadsters and cars line the walls, along with autographed photographs of several dozen rock artists, sports heroes, and movie stars. Elvis Presley, Bill Haley, Jerry Lee Lewis, Frank Sinatra, Nat King Cole, and Perry Como are featured at their best. James Dean, John Wayne, Marlon Brandon, Paul Newman, Audrey Hepburn, Ava Gardner, Kim Novak, and Marilyn Munroe form their own gallery of famous faces. Even Billy Graham has his serious features framed. Lucille Ball, Doris Day, and Elizabeth Taylor are included at the back outside the women's washroom.

Hunger is a distant dream, but I order a bowl of broccoli cheese soup. When the soup comes, I get back to Dean's question. "Dean, you asked me if growing up in a Christian home, especially a missionary home, has a significant impact on a kid's development." I savor a spoonful of the goopy broth. "Development is a journey. It's a marathon, not a sprint. The roads and signposts and milestones aren't the same everywhere."

I see the child who waved at me from the BMW. She's licking an ice cream at the counter.

It's winter, I think as I turn back to Dean. "When a child is transplanted from one place to another, or from one culture to another in the middle of the journey, the signs can be confusing. Especially if you don't have anyone familiar to explain the new signs to you."

"With the way people move around these days, I think all of us must be confused," interrupts Dean.

"Things might be different for a person depending on their ethnicity and the view of the culture where they live. It may be different if their country of birth is different than their parents' country of birth." I dip my bun into the soup and chew on the soggy treat. "It might be different if their socioeconomic status in North America is different than the country of their temporary residence. It might be different if their level of education, or the education of their parents, is at a different level than others around them."

"Are you saying there's no real normal?"

"I'm just learning to listen to MKs. As I do, I learn more about myself and my own journey." The little girl's mother wipes a smear of ice cream off her face, then takes her hand and walks her into the washroom. "We may have had some tough times, but most of us wouldn't trade them. If we did, we'd feel like we were losing part of who we are. This understanding seems almost impossible to explain to someone who has grown up in only one place or one culture."

Lizzy puts her hand on my elbow. "Are you okay? You seem distracted."

I look away from the washroom where the little girl has gone. "Some of us have learned to let go of people and places so quickly that we hardly feel a thing when a move or relationship ending looks inevitable. In fact, sometimes we assume things are done and walk away just to get it over with." I sop up the last of my soup with my bun. "It's the numbness inside that's confusing. We're supposed to feel something deep and painful."

"So that's why Lizzy needs to go on so many walks by herself?" Dean asks.

Lizzy raises her eyebrows and gives her head a slight shake. "Ignore him."

Dean finishes off his clubhouse sandwich with a smirk.

"Every child is on a unique journey which a parent has to be sensitive to," I say. "The preparation and support around any boarding school has a lot to do with how children do there. Of course, sending your child away to boarding school isn't ideal." The little girl emerges from the washroom and walks confidently ahead of her mother. "In my counselling with families in North America, I rarely see a situation which is ideal from start to finish. Part of the struggle of humanity is that we're all broken people on lifelong journeys. We will inevitably mess up ourselves and others along the way. Some will do better than others early and some will do better than others late."

Dean is thoughtful for a moment. The silence is wonderful as darkness creeps over the landscape.

Finally, he speaks. "I noticed you haven't mentioned God in all your comments."

I let the silence sit a few minutes. "I'll deal with that once we get driving again. We need to go. I know Lizzy has to clear up the guest room and change the sheets, and she has to get to work early tomorrow. I just need to take this all in bite-sized pieces. And please, let's not talk about the fitness center again until I can fill you in on my past."

Dean pays the bill on our way out of the restaurant. We fill up with gas, pick up bottled water, and settle in for stage two of the drive. The faint reddish bellies of clouds catch the last of the sunset. The darkness all around is actually comforting, as long as I don't have to think about my last few nights at Uncle Jimmy's farm with Lancelot.

Lizzy gets our conversation back on track now that Dean has taken over the driving. "Katie, you were going to answer Dean's question about where God was in the middle of this whole Christian MK experience."

I swallow, focus, and let the words flow. "God is probably the only stable thing MKs have, no matter where they go. If they can develop a personal relationship with him as a help in their trouble, instead of seeing him as the cause of their trouble, they will gain a strong faith that will continue to stabilize them in turbulence." Someone still has their Christmas lights up at a house at the edge of town. It's a comforting sight during March. "MKs never really feel like they fit, and this is a challenge for some of them. They know someone is responsible, but who do they blame? Being good, they don't want to blame God or their parents. Who's left?"

"Us!" said Lizzy. "MKs, one and all."

"They think they fit best with people like themselves, who are looking for roots and wings in a single package. If you find people like yourself, no matter where you are, it gives you a sense of belonging. It helps you feel normal." The oncoming car lights sweep over us endlessly, like a river of luminescence. I close my eyes and lay my head back. "When MKs disperse after finishing boarding school, it isn't always the easiest thing to find people who share their experience and values and worldview."

"It's hard to find people who share my worldview even here," says Dean. "How are MKs different?"

"Some MKs take a while to get settled inside and figure out they really are. Some spend a lifetime wrestling with confusion. Some always feel lonely and empty."

"Is it different for girls and guys?" asks Lizzy.

"Adolescent girls can stay quiet and disconnected no matter their background, and if they're insecure they may put up a false self to gain acceptance. It's strange, but girls find out who they are through relationships. If those relationships are disrupted, it can leave them stuck in uncertainty."

"You're making me wonder about ever having kids," says Lizzy. "How do parents stand a chance?"

"The way I see it, from my experience, like most Christians, missionary parents do the best they can in whatever situation they find themselves. I figure Erikson's stages don't only work for human relationships; they work also in our relationship with God." *If that's true, where am I with God?* "Sometimes we get stuck at mistrust, or shame and doubt. Sometimes we get bogged down in guilt or inferiority." I search blindly in my purse for another piece of gum. "Sometimes we forget who we are and whose we are. If you make it this far with God, you just have to keep on keeping on so you don't get stagnant and fall into despair."

Dean reaches back with his right fist and opens it as if to shake my hand. "Congratulations. You've got the job."

I look at his face in the rearview mirror to see if he's mocking me, but his smile seems genuine.

He must have noticed my confusion, because he finally fills me in. "We've got a few MKs at our church who need someone to help them with their transition back here. Lizzy said you'd be perfect, but we could never think of a way to get you here." He shifts in his seat so he can look back at me for a second. "Then there's this position Andrea's talking about at the Rift. You're obviously perfect for that as well." He turns away and focuses back on the road. "With Bruce away for a while, this might be a good time for you to do something you've been dreaming about. Something you've obviously got a passion for."

Before Dean realizes what's happening, a five-ton truck barrels toward us through an intersection. It's headlights are off; it just leaps out of the darkness like a ghost bent on devouring us.

My scream startles Dean enough that he yanks the wheel hard right and puts us into a spin. The larger vehicle clips the front bumper as it speeds by, and I can almost feel the tearing of the Durango's fiberglass. The contact accelerates our spin and we don't stop until we plow sideways into a snowbank on the side of the road. I instinctively wrap my arms around my head and feel a dull thud as I'm thrown toward the side window. The air bags deploy, pinning us to our seats. If our vehicle wasn't so solid, I'm sure we would have been crushed.

The five-ton aggressor doesn't even slow down to see if we're all right. My mind whirlpools, and then my hyper vigilance kicks in.

"That wasn't an accident," I say.

The On-star system connects us with an operator who assures us that help is on the way. Without that contact, I'm not sure how we would have freed ourselves. I can hear Lizzy crying quietly up front. Dean assures her that everything is okay. We are safe, or are we? For the first time, as I lie pinned in the back of that battered Durango, I question whether the accident that killed my dad and brother was really an accident.

When I hear sirens in the distance I begin to relax a little. We are going to be okay. If Joshua and Rita are trying to scare me, they have accomplished all they need to do. The one thing they may not have thought about was how passionate I can be when they mess with my horse and my sister.

CHAPTER SEVENTEEN

L izzy and I spend less than five hours in emergency before we're released. We're hurting bad, but the X-rays show nothing broken.

"They're keeping Dean overnight," Lizzy informs me. "He's got some head trauma from banging his head against the window during the accident."

Bruce doesn't answer his cell, so I leave a message about the accident. He loves his Durango and now it's a write-off.

Two female officers take our statements.

"Tell me what happened," one of them asks me.

"That truck driver intentionally targeted us," I say. "There's an international group of human traffickers trying to take me out."

She pauses from her writing. "I see. Did you get a license number?"

"I was just trying to stay alive."

"I see. Thank you for your help."

Both Lizzy and Dean are questioned in more depth and their words seem to be recorded in some detail.

My sister doesn't want to leave Dean, but she knows she can't leave me alone either, so she accompanies me home. We sip tea, chat, and sleep.

Dean is discharged Wednesday. Lizzy brings him home to rest in his own space.

Both Dean and Lizzy book time off work so we play Scrabble, look through Lizzy's old scrapbook photos of our adventures in Kenya, read, and relax. By Friday, I'm ready to get moving and start hobbling around the neighborhood.

The Durango's demise gives Lizzy the chance to rent a classy black SUV to ferry us around for the next few days until Dean can help her find a new ride. "I want something solid," she tells me as she pats the steering wheel and smiles. She always loves to get the best, if she can.

On Sunday, Lizzy and I attend the local community church where Lizzy sets up a meeting for me with four MK girls who recently attended the Rift. "They need some re-entry help," she says.

The service is upbeat and relevant to most of us. It deals with our identity in Christ in a world that tries to press us into a pseudo-identity we aren't made to accept. The four girls—Steph, Mindy, Jazz, and Carly—find us within a minute after the benediction and we talk like long-lost friends within moments.

Steph's bleach blond hair flows over her shoulders and stops halfway between her shoulders and her elbows. She has piercing indigo eyes. She's stylish in her black pleated skirt and sky-blue blouse. The tennis shoes are an interesting touch.

Mindy sports a tight black braid pinned up like a crown on her head. She constantly touches the braid, repins, pats, smooths, and ensures it stays in place. Her hazel eyes are constantly scanning the room. She's outfitted in navy slacks, black pumps, and a flowery top.

Jazz's brunette coiffure is a neat bob cut around her ears. Her dark, Asian eyes continually focus on her fingers as she moves them slowly together and apart like a drawbridge dealing with boat traffic. She wears well-worn jeans, a sweater vest, and a pair of tennis shoes. Definitely the most relaxed of the four.

Carly's shoulder length hair is mousy brown and well used to a brush. Her long-sleeved denim top and black jeans fit well with her short heels and slim figure. She scans the visitor card and uses it to fan herself.

When the pastor comes by to shake hands, we look around and realize we're the last people in the sanctuary. We arrange lunch plans, then head for the vehicles to reach our destination. Lizzy drops me off at the eatery and heads back home to see Dean.

The deli is a quiet country-western style setup. We each find our selections at the counter and sit in a corner for some privacy. For the next while, we likely would not have noticed if the world imploded.

The four girls all graduated within the last three years and are finishing their college degrees in the Twin Cities. Steph, Jazz, and Carly all have family members here and Mindy has a potential long-term relationship which her to Minnesota.

Steph's family lived in Tanzania in an isolated location. Boarding school was a reluctant choice for them. As the oldest of three girls, she never really got to know her two homeschooled sisters.

Jazz has three brothers who also attended the Rift. Although her parents had wanted her to stay a little longer with them in Uganda, she was begging by the time she was eight to join her brothers in Kenya. She still isn't sure whether she made a good decision.

Carly is the lastborn of three girls, but she has a brother five years younger. She mothered her little brother during his first traumatic experiences at the Rift. After watching her mother sob when her two older sisters went off to school, she determined that she was going to be good and never give her mother cause for concern when it was her turn. Carly knew she would have to go if she was going to reach her dreams of becoming a doctor.

Mindy was the daughter of a staff member and always felt close to her family. She did struggle some days with having to share her parents with so many others, but she also had so many positive experiences. She didn't know if she was being ungrateful when she felt like she wanted to just go her own way and make her own decisions for once. Everything on campus was tightly regulated during term, and even during vacation, because her parents had to keep up both their reputation and the reputation of the school.

I work hard to keep my ears open and my mouth shut during their introductions and short histories. Finally, I sense it's my turn to probe. "So, if you had to summarize your experience in Kenya in just a few words, what words would you use?"

The words come quickly. Mindy: "Phenomenal, heart-changing." Carly: "Bonding, the best." Jazz: "Faith-building. It gave me a worldview I don't regret." Steph: "Once in a lifetime experiences, top-quality education, lifetime friendships." Carly again: "It made me closer to my family." Jazz: "I'd add beautiful and adventurous to my collection."

During a brief pause, I chip in again. "How did boarding school fit into all of these words?"

Jazz speaks first. "Almost all of those words happened at boarding school. It was a huge part of our life. It's what we knew. It helped define who we became."

"How were you impacted emotionally by your school experience?" I ask.

Carly sets down her ham and pineapple pizza slice and looks me straight in the eyes. "I'm an emotional survivor. The memory of watching my mom cry when my older sisters left for school still grabs me." She pushes her hair behind her ears and twirls one of her heart-shaped earrings. "One of my sisters is on her third marriage. My other sister married one of her classmates. He's a pastor and they're doing great." She looks away toward the large front windows. "My younger brother has already decided he wants nothing to do with Christianity anymore." She looks back at me. "Don't get me wrong. I did great at school. I had great teachers and I aced my classes. I did well in music and sports. On the outside I did great, because that's where I learned to live."

Jazz swallows her mouthful of cranberry juice and changes direction. "I remember the birds. I marked the number 205 in my bird book by the time I left." She stands up, lifts her arms overhead, and begins to pace around the table. "They were so free. I once saw a Secretary bird stalking a snake. The crest on its head was right up like a halo and its long legs were just marching, marching right after that little reptile." Several patrons watch as she sits again with a smile. "It must have been three and a half feet tall, and grey as charcoal with those four black tail feathers just sweeping along behind it. It got that snake and slurped him up just like a noodle. I always liked the days when we got spaghetti or hamburgers in the cafeteria. Solomon the cook always smiled at me."

Steph picks up the conversation. "Since I've been back here, I realize that those were probably the best years of my life. The dorm girls were like sisters to me. We were a family. The guys were my brothers." She brushes her long hair off her shoulders. "I learned more about God and the Bible and real faith because we got to put it into practice in the community." She pops a fry into her mouth and talks around it. "The outreach days were awesome. I understood why my parents were out there. I had the most incredible national friends. I could share anything."

"It was the stars." Jazz lifts her hands up like a drama queen. "I used to lie out on the upper field or at our mission station and just stare up at those stars. They were like friends. The country could be in chaos, the crops might be failing, my classes and relationships may not be doing the best, but those stars were just steady. It was like God put them there day after day to say, 'Jazz, I'm still here.'"

Mindy takes the last lap. "The hard thing for me to process is that there are so many good things and so many hard things. Doing the transitions for the home assignments and having to leave friends there, and then make friends here, and then leave friends here, and then go back and try to catch up on what I missed there." She sips her caramel latte. "By the time I graduated, I was sure I was two people. The hardest thing was trying to figure out whether I had to be a third person with my parents." She grabs a fry from Steph and pops it into her mouth. "Don't get me wrong. I wouldn't trade my life for the world. It's just that I was so self-reliant and independent that I felt I didn't need anyone. I knew I'd be perfectly fine if everyone walked away from me. Maybe that's what scares me most."

Jazz asks me if she can talk about a personal issue, since I'm a counsellor and all.

"I'm no one's Savior," I tell her.

She nods. "It's just that my boss is so aggressive. He makes decisions so quickly and expects me to do the same. He doesn't seem to take anyone else's feelings into consideration."

With the help of the other girls, we spend time reflecting on how culture impacts our way of interpreting our relational experiences. There are cultures which are shame-based, fear-based, and guilt-based. Within each culture are personalities, positions, and processes which impact the way decisions are made and carried out. It's fun to interact on something that matters.

Steph confides that she's part of a group of third-culture kids who meet once a month to share their experiences with transition. "My trust level is so low that I went to the group for six months and didn't do anything more than share my name. I kept thinking the others were going to think this was all pointless and drop out. I wasn't going to share my life with people who were just going to leave again. But everyone except two stayed, and I finally took the chance and talked about my fears and questions. It's been great and I almost believe I can survive in this place."

My cellphone vibrates. Lizzy's warning me that my time is almost passed. Why won't Bruce give me a call? I excuse myself and assure my sister that I'll be ready in a minute.

I thank the girls for taking the time and ask if I can pray for them. By the time I'm done, I notice that three of the girls have tears running down their cheeks.

"My dorm mom used to pray for us like that," Steph says. "You'd make a really good dorm mom."

We hug and are still chatting when Lizzy comes through the door. I limp out after her and climb into the SUV. It does feel solid, and it sure draws the attention of onlookers.

A billboard along the side of the road almost gives me whiplash. The ad features a twenty-foot-tall image of Joshua Kensington and Rita Galinsky offering special membership rates at the Firm and Friendly.

Lizzy doesn't even seem to notice. No matter where I go, those two sets of eyes seem to be looking down on me and warning me to watch out.

CHAPTER EIGHTEEN

I meet Simone at the Franklin Community Library on East Franklin. The brick structure, with its high-arched white-framed windows, stands proudly in the middle of the first clear green lawn I've seen this spring. The building is one of my favorite places to be these days, and Simone has found similar comfort within the stacks of books inside.

Since 1914, new immigrants have been huddling over pages of learning here. In the early years, the Scandinavians were the most familiar with the call to knowledge. Nowadays the neighborhood is filled with Somali and Spanish families, and there are book sections inside to cater to these groups.

I find Simone chatting quietly with a Somali girl near the children's center. Simone has only seen me once before, at Lizzy's church, but she recognizes me and introduces me to the girl, Hannah.

Simone is a shy, diminutive Ethiopian nursing student who has come to upgrade her skills in America. She previously worked with Samaritan's Purse and knows several former Rift students who have become part of that organization.

"I sure wouldn't want to be out there now," Simone says. "Not with Al-Shabab shooting up malls and universities and hotels and sports events. These terrorists have no sense of God. I cry for the victims and their families, for all the people who live in fear of those terrorists. I'm just glad we made our memories when it was still safe and peaceful."

We share a few memories of our times in Africa, and then Simone bids Hannah farewell and asks me to join her for coffee. I still limp from the accident, so she walks slowly.

Once we're seated, the next three hours fly by as she unfolds her life. She says that she never has a place she can call home, but she has a lot of friends who make her feel at home. She's hardly into her thirties, a few years older than I am, but she's working on her third marriage. She cannot seem to connect with people, and as a result she experiences a lot of lonely and empty times. Shallow relationships are the order of the day. She's called on several men to fill the void inside, but they've been unable to understand the depth inside her. She has given herself too readily without making them dig down to find the gold.

The pain is intense a lot of times, and very few see behind her masks. The medication and alcohol. Giving away her body without giving her mind or soul. The grief and loss. Talking and talking and spinning a personality she hardly recognizes. Putting the past in a locked box and making sure she throws away the key. Fighting to see if there's life behind the fortress surrounding her heart. Always pushing others away before they push her away. Longing for security and hope and love. Wondering, morning after morning, whether life is worth trying one more day.

At some points, I sense deeply that she's telling my own story. Tears stream down my face. She sees me crying and wiping my tears on my sleeve. She finally hands me a napkin.

"Don't cry," she says. "I quit years ago. It didn't help."

I do the best I can to reframe her life story and give her tips on coping and growing through the pain. She seems to appreciate it and gives me a genuine embrace as we part.

She looks back at the library down the block. "Don't you ever wish you came from a place with a little bit of history and mystery?"

"Oh, but I do," I say. "Sir Francis Drake was carrying on secret expeditions and claiming territory along the west coast of Canada way back in 1579. That's forty years before the pilgrims landed at Plymouth Rock. Drake charted the coastline and deliberately left some things out to throw off the competing Spanish, Russian, and French explorers looking for the Northwest Passage." I point northward. "Jacques Cartier had already charted the St. Lawrence River in 1534. Canada's history is filled with intrigue, if anyone is willing to check it out."

She looks at me closely as she hands me her contact information. "So you think you're Canadian now? How can you be from a place where you weren't even born?"

She gives me a smile and a wave, and walks away.

Since I still have a few hours to spare, I wander back into the library to look at a mural I saw in my brief time there. There are so many historical artifacts to appreciate. Almost every place has a history and mystery waiting to be uncovered and explored.

The computer section is a wonderful upgrade to this heritage building and I linger near it. I notice the back of a man who seems familiar. He's just a bit taller than my five-foot-seven and his curly blond hair hangs generously over the back collar of his plaid shirt. He stands, looking over the shoulder of another rather large man. Then it hits me. These two live near Uncle Jimmy's farm in Moorhead. Johan and Luke.

As I turn to go, Johan spins around and smiles with pleasure. He walks over to me, firmly grasps my hand, and pulls me toward Luke Lapierre.

"Come, come," he says as he pats my hand.

When Luke turns around, his broad smile shows his pleasure at the chance meeting. If this is a chance meeting.

"What are you two doing here?" I whisper in as controlled a manner as I can manage.

"We're doing research," Luke whispers back as if we're in some conspiracy.

"On what?"

"Joshua Kensington and Rita Galinsky," says Johan from behind my right shoulder. "We think they had something to do with the death of your horse. Luke here saw that lady when he tried to rescue Lancelot. The deputy's been spreading news around Moorhead about you running off with some guy, and he's saying that Luke poisoned your horse."

"I'm trying to clear my name by finding out what's really going on with those Firm and Friendly owners." Luke glances back at the computer. "I know they're up to no good, but nobody really knows them over in Moorhead."

"How do I know you're the good guys?" I ask. "How do I know you aren't making this all up and that you're not really working for Joshua? How do I know you aren't following me? You seem to be everywhere I go."

Luke looks me in the eyes. "How do we know you're who you say you are? We aren't asking you to get involved in this. We're just trying to put some distance between ourselves and the deputy. Johan has a brother in Minneapolis and we're staying with him. He works down at city hall. That's the only reason we're here. The fact that we keep showing up in your life may be the grace of God, if you're lucky."

"Okay," I say. "Do you know what you're looking for online?"

Johan and Luke look at each other and smile.

"We're kind of new at this," Johan says. "Any chance you can help us out?"

For the next forty minutes, I surf the net and find out more information than I really want to know. Half of the articles are publicity pieces about some glitzy event Joshua and Rita are attending or hosting or planning. Some focus on charities they helped sponsor. The bulk of recent articles are about introducing Firm and Friendly franchises in different parts of the eastern and midwestern states. From what we can see in our brief research, seventeen franchises are now under their control.

Johan holds up several articles he has managed to print. "The strange thing I see is that in almost every one of the places where Joshua and Rita open up a new outlet, there's a prominent murder in the community. I find that more than strange."

I take the articles from him and scan them. "I find this frightening."

"Look at the gold rings in these pictures," Luke says, pointing at several images on the computer.

I look again at the articles. "This doesn't look good. What do you think makes sense from all these clippings?"

Johan shrugs and Luke groans.

In the latest article, the gold rings are so prominently displayed on their hands that I wonder if there may be other rings which are not being displayed. My personal fear is that a group of these people all have rings and someone is orchestrating some nationwide deadly game. The game seems to be to take over as many franchises as possible. I don't want to believe it, but after dealing with Tommy Lee, the Monk, and others from the Firm and Friendly group, it seems that Joshua and Rita have formed a partnership to enhance their stake in the game. There are huge gaps in my suspicions, but I feel a sense of déjà vu from my days with Tommy Lee.

Although Luke and Johan don't understand everything they're seeing in the words and pictures, I learn enough to know that if Joshua and Rita think I'm part of the competition, they'll be ruthless. My mind is in hyperdrive as to what Joshua and Rita might be planning next and I don't want anyone else I care about to get hurt. I need to find a way to convince these people that I'm not in this game of theirs.

I thank Luke and Johan, explain that I need to go, and make arrangements to meet them back in the library in two days.

Lizzy confirms arrangements for me to meet with one more MK in the evening, and I need to get emotionally and mentally prepared.

Feona is a wonderful young woman. She was in her first term at the Rift, and only eight years old, when I left the school just after my sixteenth birthday. I try to remember a little redhead who might have crossed my path during the big-sister, little-sister events. She became Andrea's little sister in the year after I left. The two are still in touch.

If MKs are all impacted through their experience, this is one girl who thinks she hides it well. Feona brims with confidence on the outside and shares an easy humor.

"Katie," she says, "have you ever noticed something? During the months before we get ready to come here, we're all sneaking around looking at magazines and peaking on the internet to see what the latest fashions are so we can fit in." She gestures at a fashion magazine sitting on the coffee table. "Almost everyone ends up wearing the same jeans. The things I told my dad not to wear are the things my best friends think are the best. One day, I was sitting in a study group at school talking about fashion. One Latino guy had one of those old shoestring ties on a polo shirt, untied Nike shoes, and baggy jeans. A Jamaican friend had a six-inch flowered tie from who-knows-when with an Armani suit. One of my Asian friends wore tangerine platform shoes with a goth hairstyle and black lipstick." She pulls her hair up above her head to demonstrate. "Another was wearing leather sandals, a cardigan sweater, and she'd shaved herself bald and put a tattoo on the back of her head. The group leader always wore a porkpie hat. We were supposed to be answering the question, 'What does it mean to be American?' We couldn't do it. I stopped worrying whether I fit in after that."

She repeatedly tucks her red hair behind her ears, using both her hands in perfect unity to accentuate a point. I register the act as a coping mechanism and try to ignore it. She leans forward on her elbows as we sit in Lizzy's living room.

"Andrea talks about you constantly," she says at the end of our introductions. "She always tells me about the great adventures you used to have. How you saved her life at the falls. How you used to race against the leopards and the zebras on your motorcycle. You were a legend at the Rift."

The heat fills my cheeks. "Andrea has an incredible imagination. She's the best friend anyone could ever have. I still have days when I miss her."

Feona flips her hair back around her ears again. Twice. Three times. She leans in another inch. "Andrea says you might be coming out to the Rift. Those girls could really use someone who understands what it's like to grow up out there." She flips her hair again. "You really should do it, you know. Even if it's for a little while."

Sidestepping her comment is challenging, but I haven't been in this business all these years for nothing. I share a few more of my adventures and then get her to fill me in on those last two years when she connected with Andrea. Andrea had been a major athletic star on the girl's teams in volleyball, soccer, and field hockey.

When I ask Feona for an update on her recent life, she says that she decided to drop out of college to take up a new job at a fitness center that's offering special benefits and job security. The muscles in my neck and shoulders tense up.

"And what's the name of this place?"

"The Firm and Friendly. The owners are incredibly friendly. When they found out I'd been in Africa, they hired me immediately. They said they really needed young women with international experience."

I take her hand as calmly as I can. "Feona, I worked for the Firm and Friendly during college. This looks promising, but it's dangerous. You have to quit and get back to school. This is one road you really don't want to go down."

She pats my hand. "Don't worry, Katie. I know what I'm doing. I know what I'm doing. I've met the bosses and there's nothing dangerous. It's just an exercise place and the owners want it to go national. Don't worry. If I notice anything suspicious, I'll quit."

I walk her to the door and watch out the window. Feona is still waving at me when a silver-grey Mercedes lurches away from the curb and drives right toward her.

CHAPTER NINETEEN

My scream drowns out any noise Feona makes. She jumps out of the way of the Mercedes and lands on her hands and knees between two parked cars. A few seconds later, she pops up, brushes off her pants, shrugs her shoulders, and waves goodbye.

The driver was talking on a cellphone and probably didn't even see her.

People often say that curiosity killed the cat. Well, I've learned from personal experience that curiosity almost killed the Kat. Kat was my granddaddy's nickname for me when I was young. It was also the name Anthony, my almost assassin, used to call me when he was playing coy.

For a week I'm almost angelic about making sure I take my daily walks in any direction but south. That's where the Firm and Friendly is located, just a block and a half from Lizzy and Dean's.

On Tuesday, during one of my forty-five-minute powerwalks around the suburb where we live, I chance upon the street that runs right in front of the forbidden zone. I'm deep in thought about the opportunity to go to the Rift Academy without Bruce. I've called him every night, leaving messages, and now his inbox is full. I call Sarah and she lets me know that Bruce has already shipped out. My loneliness is strong.

When the flash of the Firm and Friendly sign first catches my attention, it doesn't register clearly. The presentation is a lot flashier and more confrontational than the signs Tommy Lee used to set up when I worked with him. Times have changed.

I decide to get a coffee in the Starbucks right across the street. Feona's well-being is on my mind. I order a grande half-sweet vanilla latte. No one's expecting me anywhere right now, so I sit for thirty minutes watching perfect strangers walk in and out.

Spotting the fitness trainers isn't hard. They all look the same. Perfect Barbies in super tights. Shoulder-length hair perfectly scrunched into pony tails. They walk the same. Strong and confident. I really want to talk to one of these insiders and find out what it's really like under Joshua and Rita.

The personal specialists are also easy to spot. Young Asian girls looking like they're barely into their teens. Petite. Compliant. Ready to please.

At last I see what I'm looking for: two young fitness trainers finishing their shifts and heading over for a coffee. One blond like me. One brunette. The two glide through the coffee shop door, held open by some businessman who still knows his manners. The two young women get caught up in ordering and talking about their day and never give me a second glance. While they're busy, I strategically relocate myself to a central table, trying to hear the differences in their voices. The brunette is a little more tonal and the blond a little breathy. Their speech is frothy, forced and artificial as though they're still on a job where every little effort is worth a gold medal cheer.

The place isn't huge, so I'm not surprised when they settle down right behind me and keep up the chatter. It doesn't take long for their conversation to catch my interest.

"Next time Joshua calls me over in front of all those guys, I'm seriously thinking of just walking right out the door," the blond says.

Brunette is quick to respond. "Mel, how many times do you say that a week? You know you can't walk away from Joshua. Why do you think Rita keeps reminding us about Linda every time we complain? Mind you, if the big guy didn't have the cops paid off, I'd probably join you."

The two of them carry on about the different men they've been training that day. The positives and negatives of each guy. Definitely not family talk. When they're done, the brunette slips into the washroom and the blond exits.

I nonchalantly mosey into the ladies room and start washing my hands at the sink. The brunette finally emerges from her stall.

"Do I know you?" I ask.

The brunette looks at me and scrunches up her eyebrows as if searching her memory. "Have you ever been to the Firm and Friendly? My name's Jen. I work across the street."

"You must know Linda."

Jen's eyes get wide and she looks left and right quickly. "How do you know Linda?"

I oblige her by leaning a little closer. "I used to work for the Firm and

Friendly. Rita is always going on about Linda and what can happen if you walk away from Joshua."

Jen stands up straight. "And you did it? You walked away from Joshua and lived to tell about it?"

I join in her conspiratorial talk and move to stand with my back to the washroom door. "I worked for a colleague. Joshua's in another league. He's got a long reach. If you leave, you need to move fast and quick and far."

Jen's fear is obvious. "I'm not leaving. If Rita sent you, I'm not going anywhere."

"Relax. I'm not with them. If you and Mel ever get serious about leaving, go to Canada and talk to the RCMP. They know all about this and they can't be bought."

She moves a step closer to me and starts rubbing her eyebrow with her right knuckle. "Are you the black queen?"

"Pardon me?"

Her eyebrows furrow. "The black queen! If you know Linda, you must know about the black queen."

"Yes, but you asked if I *was* the black queen."

"Well, you almost seem like her." She reaches for my hand, but I pull away. She moves a step closer. "Linda told me she overheard Joshua and Rita talking about the black queen."

She motions me away from the door.

I keep one hand on the door and step toward her. "What are you trying to tell me?"

She holds her forefinger up near her lips. "They think they're the white queen and king and that this is all some kind of a chess match. They say the black queen doesn't play fair because she doesn't wear the rings." She points at my hands. "They say she's got nine lives, like a cat, and no one seems to get through her to find out where the black king is hiding."

"So?"

"You admitted you're in the game, but on a different team than Joshua. I heard the black queen has blond hair just like you. And you're not wearing any rings."

All kinds of puzzle pieces fall into place. It's time to leave. "It doesn't matter who I am. I'm just letting you know how to get out of the game if it gets tough."

When I slip out of the coffee shop, Jen is still in the washroom. My mind is almost made up. If Joshua and Rita create as much fear in their girls as Tommy

Lee created in me, then this isn't a good place for me to stay. They obviously think I'm still a player in their game. If being with Bruce isn't an option, the next step is clear. I almost skip home.

The silver-grey Mercedes hesitates a little too long at the stop sign. It gets my attention the first time it passes me. It looks a lot like the Mercedes that almost ran down Feona. That seemed like an accident, but my senses are on high alert. When the car comes by a second time, it's too much to be coincidence. As the driver turns at the next corner, I jog down an alley, through a parking lot, across a children's playground, and into the back entrance at Lizzy's. There are freaks everywhere.

I change from my tracksuit into jeans.

Lizzy walks in from her work at the chiropractic clinic. She's apologetic almost immediately. "Katie, I don't know how you survive here. You must be so bored. I'm sorry I have to be gone so much. I guess you've had plenty of time to think through your Kenya option."

There's no way I'm involving Lizzy in my crazy scheme. "I actually just got back from a walk. I stopped off for coffee. I've had plenty of things to keep me busy. I think I'm ready to go."

Lizzy flops down on the couch and looks up at me. "Go? Go where?"

I slip my left foot onto the loveseat and sit down. "I'm going to Kenya. Being here without being able to contact Bruce is driving me crazy. Maybe God is giving me a chance to do some healing and put some pieces back together. And maybe I can help a few others while I'm at it."

"Aren't you worried about Al-Shabab and those terrorists? I know we had our weddings and enjoyed Mombasa, but you have to admit that what those people are doing is scary."

Ever since being asked to return to Kenya, I've been hiding the depth of my fear. "I know Dad had terrorists in his day, and they'll always be around. Somehow love has to be stronger than fear."

Lizzy pulls her hair around and examines it for split ends. "It'll be different without Bruce. I can't imagine doing it without Dean now that we're married."

CHAPTER TWENTY

Luke and Johan are already huddled over the computer monitor when I walk into the Franklin Library on Wednesday morning at ten-thirty. They don't notice me until I tap Johan on the back. He jumps noticeably.

Luke does a shoulder check. "We found you on here," he says quietly. "You're pretty famous out west."

I have no trouble responding. "The price of my kind of fame isn't worth it."

Johan breaks in. "Some of these writers seem to think you're a part of this whole thing. Bringing in underage Asian girls to service clients at fitness clubs."

"They are so wrong. Reports like that are getting Joshua and Rita all worked up. I was just here to ride my horse and finish my honeymoon. Now I've got neither."

Luke turns to face me. "Katie, we've seen enough to think you're not safe here. We've found seventy-three of these clubs around the country and there are mysterious deaths in every place they set up. I can't believe the FBI, or someone like them, hasn't stepped in yet."

"I need to find out one more thing before I go," I say. "There's a woman named Linda who used to help manage the Firm and Friendly here. She's disappeared and it's scaring some of the fitness trainers." I point at the computer screen. "See if you can find out who she is and find a way to warn the girls that what they're into isn't good."

Johan steps closer. "The only person we know here is Luke's brother. How are we supposed to do what you're asking?"

I turn back to Luke. "Didn't you say your brother worked at city hall?" He nods slightly. "Ask him to look through some of the business records. Or the housing records." By habit, I scan the room for anyone listening. "Linda had to work and live somewhere. Pay taxes somehow. He can cross-reference the employees list for the Firm and Friendly."

I arrange to meet the men in another two days, but I don't have to wait for them to find the information. In Thursday's paper, page three, I read that Linda Davenforth was discovered still in her car in a water-filled ditch thirty miles out of town. No one has to tell me that she once worked for the Firm and Friendly.

The local evening news has a quick note on the story and a sound bite from Joshua, saying how saddened he is to have lost one of his best employees. I can see Rita in the background fixing her hair in front of one of the workout mirrors. I bolt for the washroom, feeling like I have to vomit.

Within the hour, I call Andrea in Kenya. She's ten hours ahead of me and is just getting out of bed when her phone rings. She's ecstatic to hear that I'm seriously considering her request to come. I tell her I just have to clear things with Bruce and a few others.

Within the next twenty minutes, she promises to work out all the arrangements for housing and job assignments with the school superintendent. I'm sure to get a call from the mission, the school, and from a local representative to help with paperwork. They'll need me from August through at least November.

What gets to me most is Andrea's passion for her dorm girls. One girl, born in Korea, spent her first year of school in California, switched to Montreal while her parents did language training over two years, and then was raised in North Africa until she arrived at the Rift Academy. Another was born in Germany, raised in a small Tanzanian village, attended a local national school, and then transferred to the Rift in ninth grade. She learned English from the King James Bible and had to learn quickly not to use *thee* and *thou* in her speech. Every girl was a mosaic of nations in a single body.

I have four months to figure out how I'm going to get Bruce's okay, find the finances to make the trip happen, and get myself mentally and emotionally in shape for what's ahead.

The phone call Friday afternoon from the mission headquarters catches me off-guard. They tell me that because of my immigration status, my paperwork and processing would go more smoothly through the Canadian office. Since I'm supposed to be raising my financial and prayer support, it would work better to do that from a base where people know me well. That means a trip back to the Pacific Northwest. A place no less safe than where I am now, trying to lie low. I almost give up on the idea of going to Kenya.

Lizzy holds me while I cry. Dean helps me process how God sees a much bigger picture than we do. I share a few more hidden details of my past—things even Lizzy didn't know, experiences that once filled me with shame and terror, choices that reaped near-deadly consequences and are still threatening to catch up with me.

We talk through how this will impact my desire to counsel MKs in Kenya. Dean suggests it will be therapeutic in dealing with my own issues and suggests we stop by the church to see what help is available for short-term missionaries.

Their pastor promises to consider me for at least a love offering, if not support. The MKs I've spoken with cheer me on and offer their prayers. Luke and Johan promise to do what they can to warn the girls at the Firm and Friendly about the danger they're in. And Bruce is nowhere to be found.

Six months after my wedding, I'm on the move again. Sarah invites me for a visit to Seattle. Keith and Sarah have some contacts I can talk to before checking out my friends in Bellingham, Sumas, and Vancouver. And hopefully— sometime, somewhere—I will connect with Bruce. I send him detailed emails every single day except one and nothing comes back.

Lizzy and I both cry at the airport. I think I cry as much for leaving my place of healing, and for losing my horse, as I do for leaving my sister. Lizzy hangs onto me like she'll never see me again. This is our usual airport ritual. We live with that emptiness inside until we numb up and get on with whatever's next.

Sarah and Keith meet me at Sea-Tac airport and Keith surprises me with a sheaf of letters which have come from Bruce. Keith is a doctor who knows a doctor who works for PACNORWEST and the crew that services the Trident submarines. Bruce somehow slipped him the letters and Keith picked them up just yesterday. This confirms what I'll be doing this evening after the visiting is done.

Spring is in the air everywhere and the flowers are everything I remember them to be. The mist in the air keeps things chilly, but it really does feel like I'm halfway to Hawaii after experiencing a Minnesota winter. I shrug off my down winter jacket and don a navy blazer and white sweater combination. My sister once told me, on vacation here, that you can smell the difference in the air this close to the coast, and she's right.

Once I bring Sarah and Keith up to speed with what Bruce and I have been going through in the past six months, they do their best to comfort and encourage me in my future options. Sarah and I share chai in front of her artificial fireplace while Keith wanders off to cover his rounds in the ER at the local hospital.

I can tell Sarah still doesn't understand how serious a situation I might be in.

"Katie, you've always lived such a wild, adventurous life." She cuts a piece of Nanaimo bar to go with our tea. "You can find trouble where no one has found it before. It's a good thing you're out here now where you're safe again."

She rearranges the flower vase, curls up in her recliner, and wraps her hands around the cup.

"Maybe going to Kenya is even safer for you," she says. "I can't believe anyone would think you were into all this crazy stuff with trafficking little girls."

Her past experiences with me has dulled her to how serious the current situation is. The day has been long and tiring. I'm not prepared to put out the energy needed to let her know that the little bit I told her is more than just another adventure in my life.

Sarah suggests I take a bubble bath to unwind and I take her up on it. I carry in a dozen of Bruce's letters and settle back to soak and enjoy the words of the husband who loved me and left me.

Bruce's first letter is typical of him.

Katie, I'm so sorry you won't get this letter until some day in the future but I want to let you know that I'll be thinking about you every day and writing you when I can. All correspondence is previewed before dispatch for security purposes so don't expect much pillow talk. Maybe after I return I'll get set up on the email here.

I can't tell you where I'll be on any given day, but during my training time I'll be moving between the subs and aircraft carriers, and if we're not at sea I'll be in Bangor or Boston or San Diego or Japan. Of course, they could be creative and send me other places as well. Tomorrow, I'll be writing you from the bottom of the Pacific somewhere.

This has got to be one of the largest U.S. Navy bases in the world and we're getting drilled from early morning until late at night. The place has been here in some form since 1891. The mission at the nearby base is "One Team Getting the Job Done," and they're doing it. The vision is for us to be "Navy leaders in safety, environmental stewardship, innovation, and delivering first-time quality on time, every time." There's more I have to spout off from memory, but I don't want to overwhelm you in the first letters.

I'm fairly sure we're the only shipyard that designs, builds, operates, and recycles nuclear-powered ships. And we're environmentally friendly while we do it. That's shoptalk. They've consolidated a lot of separate operations into coordinated efforts in the last several decades and you learn a lot of initials quick around here. Everything is focused around Bangor, Bremerton, and Everett, so if you find a place locally, I'll never be far from work.

I'm not allowed to say much about the leadership team here but three of the four men are from the east coast. They've had a ton of international experience on the Navy ships we service. They've all seen active duty in our recent clashes, so we have a lot in common. These guys have more gold bars on their uniforms than I've seen for a long time. It's a privilege to learn from them.

There's more detail about his interaction with some of the men and a little mush at the end, but that is it. When I read the other letters, they are summaries of his days, followed by sentences letting me know I am not alone. Once in a while, Bruce scrawls in a Bible verse or a truth he thinks might encourage me. I just want him to come home. I have a good cry in the tub.

When I climb out, dry off, and settle into a fluffy white bathrobe, I slip into the guest room and power up my laptop. Among the sixty-three emails there is one near the top of the list from Andrea. I click onto it immediately.

Subject: I can't wait.
Oh, Katie. I can't wait until you come. I'm discovering a whole side of Africa I didn't experience as a student here. I just got back from volunteering up in Northern Kenya for a week. My heart was shattered by what I saw. Let me share just a small entry from my journal:

Without rain there was no hope.
There is huge pressure on the Kenyan government from the one million or more refugees who have struggled into Dadaab from the famine and civil war in Somalia. The Horn of Africa has become a wasteland and the sixty miles set aside for the feeble plastic lean-to shelters is hardly the center of hope that these refugees expected. More than ten million people have needed help in this part of the world.
Despite the wasteland surrounding the survivors, there seems to be no more space, no more food, no more water, no

more safety, and no more escape. Hyenas lurk on the outskirts of the camp waiting to sneak in for an attack on the unwary little ones who have not yet been buried or discarded. Robbers and rapists hover like vultures along the route, ready to prey on travelers.

Little waifs of bone held together by baggy skin retch their stomach contents onto the desert sand as their weary caregivers look on helplessly. They're all malnourished. Some stand in pools of diarrhea unable to keep the little nourishment they have. The international team of nonprofits tasked with solving this disaster is understaffed, undersupplied, and underrated. Death is everywhere. We have to stop feeling just to keep going.

Plastic water containers lay on their sides by the bare feet of those tasked with waiting in endless lines for a small sample of life. The flies seem as numerous as the grains of sand whirling about in the cruel gusts of scorching winds that threaten to dismantle the flimsy homes of the destitute.

When I think of how much I have, just a few hundred miles south of here, I ache inside.

Katie, I can't believe I was writing and living that just last week. My heart is still recovering, if that's possible. I'm not attaching pictures, as that would be too unfair for anyone not having been there to feel, and to smell, and to hear death, all around. Tell Sarah happy birthday for me.

Love and prayers, Andrea.

I finish absorbing Bruce's letters and Andrea's email. A nanosecond later, the phone on the night table shatters the silence.

CHAPTER TWENTY-ONE

Sarah knocks loudly on my door. "Katie, come quick! Katie, hurry, it's for you."

I scramble to my feet, knocking the chair over backward. I hurdle over it and lunge for the door. My first thought is of Bruce.

Sarah stands outside the bedroom door holding the phone at arm's length. "It's Lizzy. Something terrible has happened. She needs you."

I grab the phone and fearfully raise it to my ear. "Hello, Lizzy? Don't tell me this has something to do with Bruce."

The silence only adds to my fears. Finally, a voice. "Katie, is that you?"

"Yes, who's this?"

"Katie, it's Jen. I'm at your sister's place." The girl is clearly hysterical. "They got Mel. She tried to run and they got her."

"Who has her?"

"Joshua or Rita or someone who works for them. We were in the washroom at the bus depot. She was buying a ticket to Canada. I was in a stall and I heard her scream. I opened the door an inch and saw them putting her in a duffle bag. She was unconscious. I couldn't do a thing."

"What happened next?"

"I waited a minute and then followed them outside. They put the bag into the trunk of a silver-grey Mercedes. I didn't get the license plate, but I've seen Joshua in it before."

"Did you call the police? 911?"

"I couldn't."

"Why not?"

"There was a note on the bathroom door saying, 'Tell the black queen that we will take out anyone we see her talking to, including you.' You're the only one outside the Firm and Friendly that Mel has talked to. I didn't want to die."

"How did you get my number here?"

"I followed you the last time we talked and I saw where you went in. It didn't take much to find out that Lizzy was your sister." There's silence and I wave to let Sarah know things are okay. "I can't stay here, but I had to warn you. Whether you're the black queen or not, Joshua and Rita think you are." Another silence. "Watch your back. Linda told me they plan to control coast to coast."

The line goes dead, and I stand there looking at it.

A minute later I call Lizzy. She answers after six rings. "Are you safe?" I ask.

"Of course! Why wouldn't I be?"

"Didn't you just have a girl named Jen using your phone to call me?"

"No. Dean and I are here, sleeping." Several seconds pass. I assume she's leaving the bedroom so she can talk. "Katie, are you okay? Hey, thanks for calling to tell me you made it. Do you know what time it is here?"

"Yeah, fine, sorry. Just thought I'd call." Not wanting to trouble my sister any longer, I hang up. Now I need to run. I just don't know where.

I end the call.

"Wrong number," I say.

"But she said she was your sister, and that it was an emergency," Sarah says. "And why would you talk to a wrong number so long?"

Sarah's husband Keith knocks gently, and then steps into the doorway when Sarah waves him in.

"Katie got a suspicious phone call," says Sarah.

"We need to take this seriously, with all the other trouble you've had out here," says Keith. "Who do you think the call was from? And why do you think they're calling at this time of night?"

"It was a girl I met in Minneapolis. She works for the Firm and Friendly. I tried to warn her to get out. She told me that the owners kidnapped one of the girls I talked to. She wanted to warn me that I was in trouble."

Keith takes charge. "Call that sergeant friend of yours. Sergeant James. We need to get you into hiding."

I stare him down and then pace back and forth alongside the bed. "I don't want to be locked up again. I'm not the criminal. I'd rather go to Canada."

Keith turns to Sarah. "Get her packed. I'll get the car ready and alert the

RCMP that Katie is on her way north. Katie, get dressed. You're going home."

I do have a really strong urge to go home, the problem being that I just don't know where home is anymore.

"What about Bruce?" I ask.

"We'll deal with Bruce when he surfaces," says Keith, and that's that.

I settle for my navy capris and a double-knit white cardigan to ward off the night chill. I borrow a pillow and blanket to be as comfortable as possible.

I'm sleeping when we hit the Peace Arch border crossing. Usually I cross at Sumas, where I lived for six years during my college and post-grad days. Sarah gets me coherent enough to hand over my passport and smile when the flashlight shines into my eyes. With Keith's credentials, we don't have any problem, even when he says the purpose of our visit is to take me home.

Keith must have spouted off more than he told me because the RCMP are waiting at the first Tim Horton's doughnut shop across the line. When Sarah and I emerge from the washroom after using the facilities, soaking our faces, two big officers stand outside the door.

Constable Baminder Sall wears a scarlet tunic, navy breeches with a yellow stripe down each side, and a pair of almost knee-high Strathcona boots. His brown gloves and hat sit on the counter beside him. His partner is in plainclothes.

Sall was prominent in guarding me the last time I was in Vancouver, trying to escape from a Russian gang of human traffickers who's mistaken me for competition. His familiar face makes it easier to breathe.

I almost give him a hug, but I resist. "Wow, you went all out," I say.

The constable gives a mocking half-salute. "I'm subbing on the motorcycle drill team this morning and didn't have time to change before they told me to come and meet you. This is constable Dosanjh. He'll be taking your statement when we get in. I'm just your escort for now."

I assure Constable Sall that I can ride to the station with Keith and Sarah, but my reputation is well-known up here and he insists that I accompany him so we can set up some parameters before we reach the station.

The location where we stop is one I haven't been to before. It looks like a warehouse tucked into a smattering of four-story apartment buildings. There are no obvious markers or logos outside the building. The entrance is a little more discreet and the security inside the front door seems obvious. Little moving cameras with flashing red lights hover at half a dozen locations below ceiling level. Someone knows I've arrived.

Constable Dosanjh brings me coffee, then asks Keith and Sarah to enjoy the cafeteria for a while. "The security desk will update you on Ms. Delancey's progress and expected time of release."

It doesn't take long for me to realize this man needs some sensitivity training. First, he has to leave to get Kleenex. Then he leaves to get a mirror and wet cloth so I can fix my mascara. Then I need a coffee refill. Somehow, in the middle of all that, he hears about Lancelot and Joshua and Rita and Jen and Mel and Johan and Luke and Deputy Timmons. I don't tell him anything about the MKs.

When he leaves for consultations, I snuggle down with my head on my arm.

Sometime later, I feel a persistent nudge. I look up into a pair of eyes I know all too well. "Sergeant Richardson? What are you doing here?"

James Richardson tries to look stern. Being six-foot four, and somewhere around two-hundred and fifty pounds, he doesn't have to try hard. His voice is gentle thunder. "I think they call it penance. Last time I lost you. This time there's no chance of that happening."

I follow him out into the corridor where we meet Keith and Sarah.

Near the entrance, the sergeant's cellphone vibrates just enough to stop him in his stride. During the brief conversation, he stares me down and nods. At the end of it, he replaces his phone and reaches for his handcuffs. There's no question who he intends to use them on.

CHAPTER TWENTY-TWO

Richardson's steel-grey eyes never leave me. He walks up to me and bends slightly to whisper in my ear. "This is for your own protection. Would you please turn around and just do as I ask? You'll have to trust me."

Keith makes an effort to interrupt when he sees Richardson's intent, and I have to back him off.

"It's okay," I tell him. "Let it be."

For some reason, I do trust Sergeant Richardson. Something in the phone call he received changed things.

The four of us reverse our direction and walk toward the front entrance. Three more officers join us and we march straight to a police van. One of the new officers is a woman around my height and build. She joins me in the back. I look out the window at Keith and Sarah, scrambling to get in their car and follow behind us.

The female constable undoes my handcuffs and issues instructions. "We've got five minutes to change clothing. We understand you're being followed and we need to get you to a safe place. I'm going to be your decoy. You'll wear my uniform and go with Sergeant Richardson. Unfortunately, we can't warn your friends. I'll explain things to them once we get to a safe place."

I have to trust the men up front to respect our modesty. I don't hesitate to exchange my white cardigan for a police shirt. Exchanging my capris for her slacks is a little more challenging in the tight space, but we manage. Our feet are close to the same size, so exchanging shoes isn't so awkward. Somewhere in our verbal niceties I find out that the officer's name is Monica Jorgensen. She has darker hair than me but someone would have to look fairly close to notice she isn't me.

Monica hands me the handcuffs, puts her hands behind her back, and has me snap them shut on her. This is one of the strangest experiences I've ever had.

When the vehicle stops and Richardson opens the side door, I follow Monica out. Richardson takes her by the arm and leads her into another police car, which car leaves in a hurry, with lights flashing. I casually join Richardson in another police vehicle. We drive down into a nearby parkade, circle for a few minutes, then emerge at another exit.

Fifteen minutes later, we're being served coffee inside a safe house just off Kingsway in Burnaby. Our chitchat is meant to be idle but purposeful. Richardson reviews the conversations I had with Constable Dosanjh and Monica. The RCMP are looking for something specific, but I'm not sure what it is yet.

Richardson excuses himself. A minute later, a beautiful young redhead pops in. I recognize her as well. Constable Connie O'Brien first met me during one of my hospital stays.

She plays it straight with me. "I need you to come with me."

She leads me to a smaller room fashioned after some of the interrogation rooms I've seen on television shows: one-way mirrors, a single table in the middle, two chairs. It looks strange to see myself in a police uniform reflected in that mirror. It isn't a perfect fit, but it does the job.

O'Brien points at the chair, then stands and crosses her arms. She wastes little time in her comments. "Katie, it seems there's a lot of chaos wherever you go. People die. Power vacuums get created. Our informants seem to give us conflicting information about whether you're in this game or not. Your competition definitely thinks you're in."

I look her in the eye and try to be as straightforward as possible. "Connie, you know my past inside and out. I told the others about Joshua and Rita. They're setting up this game, saying they're the white king and white queen and I'm the black queen hiding a black king, somewhere." I search her face for empathy and can't interpret what I see. She'd be great at poker. "You and I both know that these fitness clubs are just a front for trafficking and a lot of other stuff that's going on. I'm just trying to stay out of the way and let you do your job."

O'Brien paces back and forth on her side of the table. "We think someone is using you as a cover. There may be a black king." He stops and stares at me. "Someone who is maneuvering unseen in your shadow. We'd like to move you out of this picture as far as possible for a while."

"How about Africa?" I say. "I was hoping to go back and counsel at the boarding school I grew up at in Kenya."

106

The officer stops midstride, squints as she ponders my thought, and then smiles. "Give me a minute."

She leaves the room. The minute turns into at least fifteen before she's back with Richardson.

"Explain this Africa thing," he says.

It only takes me five minutes to give the basics. I wait for his response as three officers huddle up in the corner.

Finally he turns and sits across from me. His hands are folded. "We think it can work, but we'll need to keep here for a month before we let you go. You'll need to be busy, with a high profile."

I try to read O'Brien's face, but she looks down at the floor.

Richardson stands up. "We'll have your back every minute. We need to see what happens in specific situations." He runs his fingers through his hair and looks toward the mirror. "It will be a little like being a chess piece moved around the board. We want to see who's watching you, reacting to you, looking for you. In return, we will help you resource your trip."

Right then, I'm convinced God is the most creative person I know. Who could imagine having the police as my main supporters for my mission trip? As long as God keeps me safe, I can do this.

"What about my husband?"

Richardson looks sideways at O'Brien, who nods.

"Commander Southerland is being taken care of," she says. "Someone from the FBI is briefing him when he gets back into port. Both of you are in the best possible situation for us to work this deal. Unless Bruce is the black king. Is he?"

I spring to my feet. "What are you talking about?"

I'm not usually loud and aggressive, but when O'Brien reaches for her holster it's clear that I've pushed my limits. I slouch back down and put my head on my arms on the table.

I talk with my face to the ground. "Last September, just before I got married, I saw a few of the 9/11 widows talking about what it was like to have a gaping hole in their life that would never close." These shoes don't fit that well. I hope I get mine back. "I told myself that if Bruce and I really did get married, I would never complain again about having to be apart from the man I loved. I know this man as much as anyone. Bruce is not the black king."

Richardson speaks in a low rumble. "We need to check everything. It's odd that your husband is the one man who's close to you while all these things are happening. He's got the ability to make things happen. Someone is counting on us thinking that way. If both of you are out of the picture for a while, it'll force the real players to give themselves away."

O'Brien brings me some takeout Chinese food and a can of Coke and apologizes for her actions earlier. We chat a bit about Bruce and Africa and being on the run. Somewhere everything I'm saying will be cross-referenced with other conversations for consistency and intelligence. Nothing in this building, with these people, happens casually.

An hour after I'm left in a waiting room to shuffle through some outdated magazines, Constable Dosanjh walks in with my suitcase, duffle bag and laptop.

"Good afternoon, stranger. Keith and Sarah are heading back home." He drops the suitcase at my feet. "They understand the situation and will keep it confidential. They say goodbye. Keep in touch when you can." He moves toward the exit. "Monica put your clothes and shoes in that bag. She says you can leave her uniform at the front desk. Any last messages you want to pass on?"

There's always that effort to get a little bit more information.

When Dosanjh leaves, I assume I'm free to change. I use the facilities, wash up, change, and try to make my face look as presentable as possible.

CHAPTER TWENTY-THREE

ometimes it's hard to know what you're saying yes to when you're asked. Richardson, Sall, O'Brien, and three other officers hover around a table stacked with files and photos when Dosanjh escorts me into the room. Whiteboards line two sides of the room. Three laptops sit open on the table. Giant monitors fill the wall.

Once again, Richardson walks me through the last twelve years of my life. To do so, he uses the whiteboards to draw a neatly constructed chart like a family tree. I recognize several of the pictures: Tommy Lee, Steven "the Monk" Anderson, Sebastian St. Jean (alias Anthony DeSuza), Natalia Sarakova (Alexis), Pavel Ivanovich Putin (Ivan the Terrible, alias Damian Harding), Barney "the Greek" Kostonopolous, and Linda Davenforth all have large X's beside their photos.

As I mention each name in my story, Richardson places another small X beside the first X. When I finish, he taps the board with his erasable marker. "Don't you find it interesting that you're either directly or indirectly responsible for the death of each of these leaders in the Firm and Friendly clubs?"

I examine the board while the group watches my every facial response.

"Tommy Lee recruits you and trains you in the Firm and Friendly clubs. Your husband's partner, the Monk, breaks Tommy's neck. Then you crash the van that kills the Monk."

I look around the room at the faces looking my way. "None of that had anything to do with my part in the Firm and Friendly," I point out.

Richardson raises his right hand for silence and points back at the board. "Three others try to take over the human trafficking through the Firm and

Friendly clubs. You're the one who delivers Alexis to the two men who eliminate her. You're the one who takes Damian down Whistler mountain on a mountain bike and over a cliff. You're the one who's out racing motorcycles and jumping rivers in a way that gets Anthony killed." I raise my hand to speak, but he waves me down. "And strangely, while you're in Minnesota, within a few hundred miles of you, Barney the Greek dies in an arson fire, Sidney Bartoli is found outside your farm in a ditch, and Linda Davenforth also ends up in a ditch."

"I'm not a part of the Firm and Friendly, Sergeant!"

Another fifteen photos appear on the monitors. I'm not surprised to see Joshua Kensington and Rita Galinsky there with the words *white king* and *white queen*. Bruce Southerland is there with the notation *black king*, followed by a question mark. The picture was taken before our wedding. My picture is there as well. Not the best one I've seen. I don't even get a question mark, but the words *black queen* and *Kat* are obvious beside the name Katrina Joy Delancey.

I recognize a few of the other faces from past encounters with Tommy Lee and his friends. Two are familiar through newscasts. Five of them I have never seen before.

"You can see why you're of interest to us, Mrs. Southerland," says Richadson. "You're born in Africa, hence the black queen. If both the good guys and the bad guys are fingering you, and targeting you, that makes you hard to ignore."

I turn to the group and address them as calmly as I can under the circumstances. "So what's the plan to flush out the real black king and queen?"

I see the looks on the faces of the three who don't know me. They seem to be in disbelief that I wouldn't cave under the evidence. Those who know me step closer to the table. Richardson begins to lay out my part in the next steps.

Getting my hair dyed a little darker than my current platinum blond is the easy part. Getting the right outfit to convey the impression of power and confidence is the fun part, especially when the department is paying the tab. Getting the words and actions down for a carefully planned encounter is the challenging part.

Monica, wearing a wig, is going to partner with me. She'll be my protection, and my protégé, as she'll take my place once my first stunt is done. For three days we practice, until we have the sound and feel right, even on the videotape. Our two coaches stand and applaud on our final run-through.

The sting is set for Monday morning and I'm free to relax over the weekend. That is, if you can relax in a small condo guarded by three officers round the clock.

The Firm and Friendly in Vancouver is a new setup, so the police consider it a great target for the operation. It's close to the Olympic Village where a significant number of health-conscious people live. All I have to do is to accomplish two things. First: convince the manager who I am. Second: convince the manager that I want to own her business, immediately.

Looking at my outfit in the mirror isn't a comfortable experience. The black dress, designed by Yves St. Laurent, hugs me close and is cut just above the knee. Short, for me. The neckline is a little too daring. A discreet pin will fix that. I don't expect Armani, but this look is a far step from the sharp-cornered shantung pantsuits I think of as power-dressing. It looks professional yet feminine. The brooch and pearls are a nice touch with my auburn coiffure. A set of petite dangling earrings complete the look.

The Cartier gold watch is a late addition. I don't usually wear Prada heels, but with practice I get the walk down. The whole outfit makes me look like I'm heading out for a gala dinner rather than a dangerous encounter with someone determined to win a game of life and death.

As a bonus for my cooperation, the group brings in a professional makeup and spa team to do everything they can to enhance my features and make me feel confident. They need to apply the makeup to me and Monica in such a way that we can be mistaken for each other in the weeks to come. Monica sits in the next chair having her features blurred for this run-through. Even my legs and arms and face are treated to look like I've just come from a week in Hawaii or Rio.

At 8:00 a.m. sharp, just after the first group of eager fitness buffs vacate the premises, I step out of a leased BMW and onto the curb in front of the Firm and Friendly. The damp air makes me wish for a warm coat, but I'm too committed to stop now. I tug my skirt into place, wait for Monica to secure the car, then begin the walk. My heart is racing so fast I'm sure I will give us away.

The breathing exercises Bruce taught me during our Tae Kwon Do lessons come back to help me now. I push through the door and walk confidently up to the front desk.

Monica begins the drama. "Please let the manager know we need to see her."

The surprised receptionist begins what she has been trained to do. "Are you members here? May I help you first?"

I step in, look quickly at her nametag, and continue. "Milly, just tell Ms. Barghozi that Katrina is here to talk business."

The receptionist stands slowly, examines me, looks through the window at our BMW, and calmly walks to a back area down the hall. Monica quickly scans the counter, positions her iPhone, and discreetly takes pictures of whatever's laying there.

Ms. Barghozi is supposedly from Kazakhstan, according to her police profile. She's fit and confident but still in the old school with her dark pantsuit. I don't have to worry at all about her. I just have to deliver my lines and leave the rest to the police.

She extends her hand in my direction. I don't bother to shake her hand or nod my head. I notice she has two gold rings.

"The white queen and white king would like to have your franchise," I say. "I'm prepared to offer you more right now. Name your price."

The franchise owner is startled at my revelation and takes a step back. Her right hand, with her gold rings, moves discreetly behind her back. She clears her throat quietly. "The franchise open only few months. Not selling."

I hand her a fake business card made by the police. "You have until tomorrow to begin negotiations."

With that, my part is done. I turn and walk out. Monica opens the door for me, turns to take a picture of the startled owner still standing in the entrance. Once we're in the car again, Monica settles herself behind the wheel, grinning like she's won the lottery.

The smiling constable drives us back to an underground parking area where she drops me off with another police escort. Fifteen minutes later, the officer driving receives a call which I overhear. The message is brief: "Tell your passenger, 'Well done, the bees are already buzzing.' She must have whacked the hive a good one."

CHAPTER TWENTY-FOUR

The next three weeks are a mysterious game of hide and seek. The police dress me up, send me out with Monica for brief little interactions which are carefully choreographed, and then whisk me away into hiding again. The department has done its best to cover the smell of the newly painted suite by installing air fresheners, but it definitely isn't an easy experience for my sinuses. Give me a garden any day. Especially with lavender or jasmine.

I'm under a complete communication blackout when it comes to people I know. Mostly I just sit and read books on healing, look at Bible passages about Jesus healing people, and wonder what else I need to do to heal. One of these days I'm going to have to reread my dad's short journal entries to see if I can find some hidden meanings.

Apparently Monica is much busier than I am during the times between our escapades. My outings are designed to whack a hive, as one of the officers said, and Monica has to dodge the reactions of the human traffickers and their bodyguards, pretending to be me until the police clean up the mess.

Five days before my assignment is supposed to finish, Monica meets me in my dining room, which sometimes doubles as an interrogation and debriefing room. She dresses me up as a cleaning made and secrets me down to the real interrogation room at RCMP headquarters. Richardson meets me there. He's smiling, his right arm is folded over his chest, and in his hand he waves a CD of some kind. He tosses it on the table in front of me.

I assume he wants me to see it, so I pick it up. There on the cover is a picture of me. Underneath are the words "THE BLACK QUEEN."

My questioning look prompts him to begin. "Katie, this is working. Three hits have been put out on you. Monica has had two attempts on her while posing as you. We've picked up five guys and two women so far. As quietly as we can."

Nausea grips my gut. "Does Bruce know?"

"The word on the street is that the black queen is still successfully claiming her rings. We actually did find one gold ring on one of the men. He was from Chile. This is a worldwide game these guys have set up. We're estimating there are over five thousand Asian girls being trafficked through this network."

I pace on one side of the table while the sergeant paces on the other. "I'm not sure I can do this anymore."

"Four of the people we suspected of masterminding some of the female trafficking in this area have been taken out by newcomers making a move. The newcomers are definitely operating under the cover of your name." He places his phone on the table and slides it toward me. "They've got a website, with Facebook, Twitter, and other traffic flowing in and out. They're fairly mobile, but we're closing in on their pattern of movement."

I slide the CD and phone back across the table. He's standing in front of the one-way mirror with his back to the wall.

"Does this mean you're done with me now?" I ask.

He sits in the chair across the table. "It means we can loosen the strings on schedule. We'll be letting you access your laptop for emails. There are 317 at the moment and we think most of them are safe. The ones from Luke Lapierre and Johan are interesting."

He examines my face closely for a reaction. He gets one.

"Don't you have any invasion of privacy laws here?" I ask. "Luke and Johan are friends from Minnesota. They've helped me out a few times when I was in need. Right now, they're finding out who killed my horse."

Richardson scratches his chair forward. "Are you sure that's all they're doing? Do you know what the police are saying in Moorhead and Minneapolis?"

My back stiffens. I stand as straight and tall as possible, set my chin, and glare. "How would I know what anyone is up to or what anyone is saying? I've been locked in your little rooms, dressing up like a puppet, and doing the dance you stage for me. I see no one, hear from no one. Not even my husband."

The big man pushes back from the table and walks toward the door. "Constable O'Brien will see to it that you're moved to a better location and given access to your emails." He turns toward me as he grips the doorknob. "Just so you know, we're having copies of your emails channeled to us until we complete this investigation."

I step toward him and he doesn't budge. "How can you do that?"

He turns the knob and opens the door an inch. "Our officers are discreet, but I thought you should know. If you see anything suspicious or out of line, just highlight it and forward it to us. We'll follow up." He nods across the room toward a camera mounted high on the wall. "You used the letters MK and TCK a lot in your emails. My officers spent a lot of time before they figured out that you were talking about missionary kids and third-culture kids." He looks me in the eye. "You don't seem like what I imagine for a missionary kid or a third-culture kid. You almost scared us when we saw how many individuals you could mobilize if you were the black queen."

O'Brien escorts me to a different two-bedroom condominium overlooking the thousand acres of Stanley Park. The view here is even better. The North Shore Mountains, with their dense snowcaps glittering in the spring sunshine, tower over the park. The twin peaks of the Lions are especially prominent against the grey-blue skyline. Tumbling clouds play in the wind overhead.

I'm on the twenty-first floor and nicely hidden. I spend the first hours watching the sea plane traffic on the harbor flit in and out like Canada geese. The sea bus ferries faithfully thread back and forth between sail boats, tugs hauling massive barges, millionaire yachts cruising serenely toward the Lion's Gate Bridge, and various fishing boats and powerboats doing their business.

One of my first tasks, after tearing myself away from the view, is to power up my laptop. 326 emails now. I count five in total from Luke and Johan, but deliberately resist looking at them in case the police are monitoring my connection there. None from Bruce. A lot from Sarah and Lizzy. I delete about a hundred emails that are worthless junk. I decide to take the rest from top to bottom.

The first is from Jazz.

Subject: Strange experience.
Katie, I had the strangest experience. I met a Muslim guy whose dad was a banker in Europe. This guy was born in Holland and felt he didn't belong there. His family moved to Belgium, and to France, before he came to the U.S. for college. Even though he had a different religion, different family background, different country of birth and education, somehow I felt like I had more in common with him than I did with some of the American girls in my college classes. Is this normal?

I told Steph about my experience and she said that she had felt something similar with the son of a Korean businessman who had been born in Nigeria, studied in England, and then come to the States. She also had a little flavor of it when she heard a Navy recruiting officer talking to some of her friends about how he never felt at home in any port since he had travelled so much with his parents.

I replied the best I can.

Subject: Normal

Jazz, I've been away for a bit. Thanks for connecting. What you're seeing in common is called the third-culture kid experience. I'm constantly struggling through the consequences of this myself. You probably heard this term at the re-entry or transition seminars you went through at the Rift.

My dad used to work with a man named Dave Pollock on this kind of thing. Third-culture kids refer to anyone who has spent a significant part of their developmental years outside the parents' culture. That's how I remember it. It means you've grown up in a place different than what your parents call home, and when they say that you're going home it doesn't have the same emotional connection for you as it does for them. It's like you're living on a hang-glider moving from cliff to cliff, unsure if you'll ever find your feet on solid ground.

As you've seen, it's not just missionary kids. Children of businessmen, military, diplomats, and others go through this. You try to become a part of everything and find out that you aren't really all there anyplace you live. There are a lot of good sides to this if you can see life from God's perspective. It's good to remember that this world is not our home. We're just passing through. Keep in touch. Love, Katie.

The next email is from Diedre, an MK I haven't heard from in years. Somehow Andrea had put her onto me. She's a bit nostalgic as she pushes me toward thinking of the Rift Academy.

Subject: You may not remember me.

You probably don't remember me. We left the Rift at the same time but I was two years ahead of you in your brother's class. You and I played soccer and volleyball together a bit the year before we left. Even though I was leaving because of graduation, I remember thinking how hard it must be to have to leave without graduating. Your brother used to ask us to pray for you and your sister. I think of you often, especially since Robert and your dad died. Now I hear your mom is gone. You've lost a lot.

Diedre is pushing all my buttons. I put myself on lockdown. I almost decide to only scroll through the rest and avoid the pain. Somehow I manage not to quit.

The girls you're about to care for at the Rift are incredible jewels. They are the treasures of heaven being cut and polished by their Abba. They are children needing a family to love them and not every family knows how to do that when they're separated. You need to help the parents learn and you need to learn from the kids how to best care for them. Allow me to share my memories.

Mom used to write my sister and brother and me every week without fail. We knew a letter would come and it always did, somehow. We had pictures of Mom and Dad above our beds, and they had pictures of us three above their bed. Every night we would pray for each other, and almost every night I would cry. The crying helped me to realize I could still feel. We would get valentines and birthday cards and just-because cards. Sometimes I cried for the kids who didn't get anything.

I started boarding school in Grade Three. During my first years at school, Mom would come and put on a birthday party for me with the whole dorm. When I graduated, some of my classmates told me those were the only birthday parties they had in those days. Two friends even told me they considered my birthday as their real birthday.

I was glad when Mom came by the school because when we were home there was never a chance just for us as a family. Our home was always full of missionaries or nationals and Dad was always busy with the ministry. Only on the first night when we came home from boarding school did Mom and Dad make sure they were both available and the house was empty just for us. Mom made our favorite meals and we could just relax and talk. And they would listen.

Being in the community at home was sometimes strange. I loved having freedom from the school schedule and I loved the joy of the people who had almost nothing compared to us. I didn't always know what to do in my relationships.

When we first came home from school, the children and adults would all have to run their fingers through my hair as if they hadn't done it the last time I was there. I could tell this bothered my mother because some of them had snotty noses they'd wiped with their hands or they had been playing in the mud. We would sit through three or four-hour church services not understanding much of anything, even when Dad talked, and the people behind us would be constantly grabbing my hair. Sometimes Mom would hold me in front of her and that was great until my sister started complaining about her hair getting pulled as well.

The rest of the vacation, I would follow Mom or Dad, doing whatever needed to be done. Mostly I'd follow Dad, since I never saw him much during the term. The people loved him and he loved the people. Since hardly anyone else had cars, our old Toyota would be the ambulance, the hearse, the wedding car, the taxi, the crop carrier, the safari tour bus for visitors, and the armored car for bank deposits.

My dad was always the driver. Sometimes the people would surround our car and press their faces against the windows looking at me. I felt like an animal in a cage. I don't think Dad ever understood why I was scared to travel to new places with him. Once a year we'd go on vacation to the coast or to a game park. That was a highlight of my life. Being alone together.

Even though it was hard to be apart in Africa, it was better there than in America. All the churches expected Dad to come and tell them about the work and Mom knew that we had to stay in one place for school and for our sanity. Dad was gone so much, but wow did we celebrate when he came home. Life is hard for missionary families on both sides of the ocean. That's why it has to be a calling. Talk to the parents as well as the kids. Being a family, as much as possible, is important. Blessings, Diedre.

Tears stream down my face as I read. I'm ready for a break already, but I give a quick reply.

Subject: Thanks

Thank you for reminding me that there are challenges for parents, and kids, in the boarding school experience. I think the school has started a parent orientation program to try and help with this. Things have changed a lot for the better since you and I went to the school. I remember listening to one of the graduates, in his last week, standing by my dad's office with his father and my father. The boy's father was telling him that he would be fine. Thousands of Rift grads had gone through this transition experience and done fine. I'll never forget that young man's words: "But Dad, I'm going through this for the first time. I've never done this before, and I don't know anyone over there."

There have been a lot of research studies on MKs and what helps them adjust to transitions. You can't avoid the loss experience. It's learning to grow from it, and through it, that can set us MKs apart.

I'm glad you learned to keep feeling. That's a really healthy way to live. I haven't always done so well, but I'm learning to heal. I think my own personal struggles will make me a stronger person when it comes to being sensitive to the needs of those I will be counselling. I appreciate your subtle advice and the memories that remind me of who you are. Please keep in touch. Love and prayers, Katie.

I don't capture the pain which accompanies my writing, but I jot words down and send them. Even small steps are victories.

Those few emails are all I can handle for now. I set aside the rest of the evening for catching up on the international news. I then have a long soak in a hot tub of bubbles, surrounded by lavender candles, tea lights, and some easy-on-the-ears instrumental music. Sleep is going to be a welcome friend.

That is, until the phone rings.

CHAPTER TWENTY-FIVE

The incessant ringing feeds my imagination with all kinds of wild thoughts until I realize that the police are the only ones who have this number. I step out of the tub, dripping wet, half-covered in bubbles, and make my way into the living room. Half my hair is soaked. I grab a tea towel as I answer the call.

"Katie, thank you for answering. This is Constable Dosanjh. I hope you're doing well this evening."

"I was, Constable. Anything I can do for you?"

The tea towel isn't going to get me dry, so I traipse back to the bathroom for a real towel. I grab another towel to wipe up the floor with my foot while I talk.

"Katie, I know you remember the sting we pulled with you and Monica at the Firm and Friendly, with that Barghozi woman." Images of the strong, confident woman from Khazikstan come quickly to mind. "You'll remember leaving a card with her, giving her a number to call with her response to your offer."

He waits for my response and I oblige with a brief "Uh-huh."

"Monica has been monitoring the calls to that number. Most of them have been things you don't have to deal with. But two days ago, there was a call from a cleaning woman named Hanan." He lapses into silence, but I don't react so he continues. "She said that she'd seen your number on a desk at the Firm and Friendly, where she was cleaning, and that she had been a former client of yours. She needed to be in touch as soon as possible. We need to know who Hanan is."

My gut twists at the thought of Hanan getting caught up in the middle of this. I take a few seconds to slip into a calf-length white cotton bathrobe and rest against the dresser as I finish drying off. "Hanan is a refugee who was part of the New Hope welcome homes where I volunteered. She was also a counselling client at my office in Langley."

"How well do you really know her?"

"She helped me out a lot when I was on the run from Anthony, Alexis, and Ivan in the last round of these Firm and Friendly wars. The RCMP hid me out on Bowen Island for a while and in a condo not too far from where I am now. She was my caregiver while I was healing up from an accident."

Dosanjh takes a minute, I assume to make some notations even though this is all being recorded. "Could she be in real trouble or do you think she could have been turned by Barghozi to work for the other side? Can we trust her or do you think this might be a set up to flush you out into the open?"

I unwrap and suck on a cherry Tootsie Pop. I take a few seconds to twirl it around my mouth and embrace the flavor.

"Hanan is a trusting soul," I say. "She may have been fooled to call me by someone else. She would never want to harm me from her own side." I think through my words. "We have a good relationship. I think if Monica spent a few minutes alone with her, you'd be able to find out what's happening."

"Okay."

"Just don't tell her you're the police. Have Monica tell her that she's a friend of mine, coming on my behalf. I'm not available at the moment, but I would like to know how I can help her."

"How do we gain her trust?"

I share a few things. "Tell her that I've given you three things to help gain her trust. Tell her that while travelling on the ferry from Bowen Island to Horseshoe Bay we saw the mountains and realized that the Creator of the hills is the one we can call to for help."

"You preached to her? Isn't she a Muslim?"

"Constable, I'm helping you gain her trust. She believes in the Creator, just like I do. If you trusted him right now, this would be a whole lot easier." I bend over, reach into the bubble bath, and pull the plug to drain it.

I snuggle my feet into some sheepskin slippers I brought back with me from Kenya.

"Fine, anything else we need to know?"

"Let her know that I had trouble with the man who sailed with us at Cultus Lake during our New Hope retreat. Let her know that there will be no more secret messages from Alexis. Everything is okay now." I swish out the tub's soapsuds with the hose. "And let her know that I've finished my honeymoon and have a wonderful husband. Thank her for the great care she gave."

The constable repeats my words. "That's all? What can we expect in response?"

"Just let Monica get her trust. Then ask Hanan what she knows about the Firm and Friendly."

"One more thing. Do you have a contact number for Hanan?"

I remember stuffing my old address book into the corner of my duffle bag as I cleaned up my things from Uncle Jimmy's farmhouse. Although I brought the duffle bag on the plane to Sarah's, and then again up to Vancouver, I haven't opened it. The police have been generous in budgeting for my wardrobe, so my old stock hasn't had the same appeal.

But now I need that address book. It has Hanan's cellphone number in it. I ask Constable Dosanjh to hold on for a minute as I shuffle to the hall closet and drag out the duffle bag. Trying to hold the mobile phone between my head and shoulder while hauling out a fifty-pound duffle bag wedged securely into the back of a closet isn't easy. In fact, the bag drags onto the back hem of my bathrobe and anchors it enough that I lose traction with my slippers and almost fall out of my robe. The phone slips off my shoulder and crashes to the floor.

Dosanjh yells through the phone, but when I pull the bag toward me I pull it on top of my legs. I fall and the phone slips across the floor out of reach. My cherry Tootsie Pop shatters. It takes me a few seconds to get out from under the bag and get my bathrobe into place. By then, the constable on duty outside my door is knocking.

There's no way I'm answering the door looking like this.

I pick up the phone. "Constable Dosanjh, tell your man I'm fine. I just fell trying to get the phone number."

"Ma'am, are you alone? Are you safe?"

"I'm perfectly fine. I'll give you a minute to call your man off before he breaks down my door. Then I'll let you know the number."

Three undercover police in the building take turns disguising themselves as various maintenance, security, and delivery people. Sometimes they even pretend to be residents or staff. Whoever's banging doesn't want to create enough disturbance to draw attention to this suite. It doesn't take long before the constable makes contact with them and the knocking stops.

By that time, I've unzipped the old blue denim duffle bag, dumped half the contents on the floor, and discovered not only my address book but my mom's old Bible and my dad's journal as well.

I flip open the address book, give Dosanjh the number, and hang up.

Within five minutes, he calls again. Getting a call this late is ridiculous. "Yes, Constable?"

"Sorry to disturb you," Dosanjh replies. "I forgot to tell you that a Deputy Wayne Timmons from Moorhead has scheduled a meeting with Sergeant Richardson and yourself tomorrow morning, in regard to the situation with your horse. The meeting is at 8:00 a.m. wherever you feel comfortable."

I stand still, watching myself in the bathroom mirror. My jaw drops open. "I'd rather not meet with that man," I stammer.

"I'm just the messenger, ma'am," he replies calmly. "And one more question, Ms. Southerland. Do you know the whereabouts of either Joshua Kensington or Rita Galinsky?"

I hang up on him again.

I'm too wired to sleep. The bathroom is a mess, the hallway is a mess, and I'm a mess. I resist the urge to cry and instead just do what I have to do.

As I transfer the contents of the duffle bag into the dresser drawers in the bedroom, I set aside Dad's old journal for future reference. Sarah had suggested I look at those words in more depth and I determine to do that. I turn on the gas fireplace, make myself some nice hot Kenyan chai tea, and try to calm myself down.

Since sleep is no longer in the immediate plans, I put on my sky-blue frilly pajamas and grab my dad's journal. The first part is history and gives me a sense of roots.

CHAPTER TWENTY-SIX

I'd seen these writings before in the attic of the farmhouse when I first discovered my dad's brief journal in the secret compartment of that old black steamer trunk. I determine to read slowly and reflectively. The first section is simply a genealogy of sorts.

1870—Collin James Delancey.
1900—Seymour James Delancey.
1930—Franklin James Delancey.
1956—John Douglas Delancey.
Even though I'm the oldest, I somehow missed the family heritage of carrying on the name of James. I don't know why that should matter to me.

This short section sets up a huge ache in my heart. There's so much I didn't know about my dad and now we'll never get the chance to talk it out. I never knew that he struggled with his sense of identity just like I'm struggling. Just because he wasn't named James, my dad spent his whole life feeling a disconnection with all those who had gone before him. He spent his whole life trying to find connection points. Maybe that's the trait of every one of us humans.

I go back to the journal.

Sometimes God gives you a chance to heal through your children. Sometimes he gives you a chance to feel the pain you ignored the first time round. My grandfather spent a lot of my early life away from home setting up his business. He spent the last few good years of his life away in the war. He was never the same when he got back. His body was there but his mind wasn't. I didn't want to be that kind of a dad. Neither did my father.

My father wanted to capture the imagination of us kids by challenging us with the world. He invested his life in us. He tried to recapture the adventures of my great-grandfather, who travelled and photographed the world in action. I think his favorite adventures were in Kenya. I always hoped to follow in those footsteps, if God allowed.

Several things hit me as I read this, including a strange yearning to have a child. Bruce and I have talked about it casually, but not to this level of desire. With that yearning comes a question: *Do I have to wait to have a child before I can know healing? Is it impossible to be healed on my own?*

Before I have time to process that, the angst of Bruce's military career hits me. Dad's grandfather came back from the war, present in body but not in mind. Will that happen to Bruce? Will I be left with a mindless robot in uniform? Left to raise my children alone?

And there's that happy, painful thought. It was my own grandfather's love of Kenya that drew my dad back there, under God's calling, to minister his acts of healing and compassion. I finish reading the last entries.

When we knew God was calling us to missions, we wanted our kids to be close enough so they knew we cared. It's one thing to trust God yourself when you're apart and another to have your kids trust God.

One of my problems, right from the start, was trying to understand how to deal with all the demands of so many people who seemed to have so few options to turn to. I knew that somehow my kids were going to get caught in the middle of the hurricane. I can say without hesitation that I depended on the community to help raise our children.

My father's last words to me: "Look up. Hold on."

I wanted to be one of those who healed others... not one of those who hurt them.

I wished I had practiced Isaiah 61 all my life.

This last comment hits me as highly coincidental. I had opened my Bible this morning, needing to talk to the God who heals. I opened up the Bible to Isaiah 61 and read the first four verses:

The Spirit of the Sovereign LORD is on me, because the LORD has anointed me to preach good news to the poor. He has sent me to bind up the brokenhearted, to proclaim freedom for the captives and release from darkness for the prisoners, to proclaim the year of the LORD's favor and the day of vengeance of our God, to comfort all who mourn, and provide for those who grieve in Zion—to bestow on them a crown of beauty instead of ashes, the oil of gladness instead of mourning, and a garment of praise instead of a spirit of despair. They will be called oaks of righteousness, a planting of the LORD for the display of his splendor. They will rebuild the ancient ruins and restore the places long devastated; they will renew the ruined cities that have been devastated for generations.

This is the very same passage my dad wished he had practiced all his life.

I have so little from him. How much have I missed? In his few words I can hear the pain and regret and desires of a man who has learned to care from a personal knowledge of having been disappointed and hurt. His healing didn't come from some magic disappearance of pain; it came from using that hurt to practice compassion for others in the middle of their pain.

One thought niggles at my mind: healing happens as you give of yourself. This is the secret Jesus and his followers knew. This is the secret dad wished he had always practiced.

As I'm about to close the journal, I notice a tiny sliver of paper sticking out two-thirds of the way through the journal. I carefully open the book to the page and see a few words carefully written:

We may soon be surrounded by Mau Mau. Chipps, the lone guardsman onsite, has requested support, but there are no reserves available for the missionary children. We have gone to prayer.

I realize right away that these words were penned by one of the six staff right before the planned Mau Mau attack on Saturday, March 28, 1953. I have no idea how my father came into possession of this paper, but it seems authentic. One trained guardsman was onsite when the missionaries and their children went to prayer. When the attackers advanced, they were made to see an overwhelming number of fully armed defenders surrounding the school. God had protected his children once again. Terrorists or not, fear can't win. The thought gives me great courage.

In that instant, I decide. It can't wait until morning. I speed through Luke and Johan's emails, then march to the closet and set about deciding what I will wear. I have to be convincing.

CHAPTER TWENTY-SEVEN

When I look away from the mirror and examine my choice of outfits, the red digital numbers on the alarm clock catch my attention. 4:17. Dawn seems forever away. I haven't slept in almost twenty-four hours, but now is not the time.

I look back into the mirror. My ensemble, which I first wore to the Firm and Friendly in the sting with Ms. Barghozi, seems even more absurd at this time of morning. Bruce would have loved the way my platinum blond hair contrasts with the shimmering black dress. The matching pearl necklace and earrings are a solid combination. The Cartier gold watch and Prada heels mark me as a woman of distinction. I hope. For now, it will all be covered up with a calf-length leather coat.

Constable Sall has the responsibility of escorting me to Richardson's second office at Starbucks. The tall Indo-Canadian drew the night shift. While he listens to my request and looks at his watch, his facial expression suggest that he thinks I'm a bit over the edge. He refuses to call the sergeant before six.

A few bleary-eyed Starbucks patrons seem to wake up a bit when I enter. My lungs appreciate the full aroma of ground coffee beans. Only then do I move to the counter to order. Coffee aficionados everywhere crave this moment of choice: does the occasion call for straight and dark or sweet and frothy? The two teens behind the counter seem bored enough and look prepared for any challenge I might throw their way. I don't make it too difficult.

The pastry selections entice me as I wait for my order. I've spent a lot of hours in shops like this in years past, mostly studying for exams. There's even free WiFi now. Everything seems just a little bit more convenient, a little bit more pleasurable.

That's about to change.

I take my grande half-sweet vanilla latte and set up for my own sting. By the time Richardson strolls in with Dosanjh, there are only twenty-five minutes before Deputy Timmons arrives. I nurse my drink until it's barely luke-warm, sketching out the scenario and twice reworking parts that my unwilling allies may be too reluctant to participate in.

Finally, with five minutes to go, we have enough agreement to move ahead. I saunter toward the women's washroom and wait just outside it.

Deputy Timmons comes in eight minutes late. He's clearly frustrated as he scans the tables. Seeing the small group of police in the back corner of the busy shop, he threads his way by the other customers and flops down in the chair indicated by Sergeant Richardson.

"We usually try to run on time here," Richardson says.

Timmons stares him down, and then sinks back when it's clear the sergeant is in control.

"This is my third coffee shop," Timmons says. "Seems your assistant wasn't sure exactly which coffee shop Ms. Southerland chose. She kept giving me alternatives. I don't usually have to use a GPS to get my coffee. Besides, this traffic is a little heavier than I'm used to in Moorhead, and these rental cars don't come with lights and sirens."

Richardson doesn't let up. "Blaming others for your issues isn't going to be helpful, deputy."

The unnerved deputy ignores the comment and tries to take the offensive. "Where's Ms. Southerland? I thought we agreed to have her with us."

I look carefully to Timmons' right hand. Sure enough, he's wearing three gold rings he didn't have before. The email leads are proving true. It's time to act.

Constable Sall confirms with a signal that I should come over. With that, I remove my coat, straighten my black dress, check my pearls, and head for the vacant chair opposite Timmons. It's clear that a lot more than just the men at the table notices my entrance. Timmons, who has rarely seen me in anything but jeans, is transfixed.

As we rehearsed, I take the lead. "Deputy Timmons, what brings you all the way from Moorhead? I hope you're enjoying our Canadian weather and hospitality." His eyes follow my movements as I run my fingers through my blond hair and fix it behind my ears. "Or are you just here for the scenery?"

He seems to have a hard time finding words. "Yes, ma'am."

"What's the matter, deputy?" Richardson asks. "Don't you have any beautiful women down south? Or do you just think all women are scenery?"

Timmons is caught in a verbal vice. He's already answered "Yes, sir. No, sir" before I can tell that he isn't sure what he's saying.

I take the lead again. "Deputy, what have you found out about the couple that poisoned my horse? Have you charged Joshua and Rita yet?"

I grab a blue manila folder sitting in front of Corporal Sall and withdraw the five emails I received from Luke and Johan. I hold the batch toward him. The flash on his fingers is unmistakable as he reaches out for the documents. I can see from his gold rings that he has other motives in recent days. And I'm sure he's up here to see me for something more than an interview. I pull back the documents and leave him clutching air.

Timmons focuses back on me and makes a valiant effort to look me in the eyes. I can see he's captivated by both the file folder and my dress. He's having a hard time concentrating. I stand up to make it a little harder for him.

He fights to gather his thoughts. As soon as he stands, he points across the table at me. "What are you doing? I'm here to interrogate you. Sit down, you stupid Canadian! Listen for once!"

By now, the entire shop is looking in our direction and Richardson has to intervene. He stands up and I sit down. I look around. While half the men crowded into this place were likely born outside the country, they're now proudly Canadian. Several take a step toward our table.

Timmons has his back to the group, and it takes him a minute before he senses the trouble he's in. He reaches for his gun, then seems to remember that he was relieved of his weapon at customs and immigration. I see a sense of panic in his eyes.

Richardson turns and waves back the group. "It's under control, gentlemen. Thanks for your patriotic concern. We'll handle it from here."

And he does. The deputy is taken back to a safe house where he's confronted with the contents of the emails from Luke and Johan. Contents that prove his links with Joshua and Rita in smuggling young Asian girls through Canada and down into the Firm and Friendly Fitness Centers in Minnesota and beyond. Emails that reveal a tidy little profit he gained for himself. Emails that include scanned newspaper headlines which clear up the mystery as to why Joshua and Rita have become invisible in the media lately. Tuesday's Minneapolis paper heralded Deputy Wayne Timmons as a hero for his breakup of a major human trafficking ring in Moorhead and Minneapolis. Wednesday's headline, on page three, mourned the loss of two upstanding citizens, Joshua Kensington and Rita Galinsky, gunned down by unknown assailants outside the newest Firm and Friendly club. Thursday's paper announced that further clues emerged in the death of Linda Davenforth and that the car accident is being ruled suspicious.

I don't get to see the deputy's face when the handcuffs are put on him, but it sure would have been a great joy. Canadian law has gotten a lot harder on human trafficking and this is going to be a tough knot for the greedy lawman to untangle. Minnesota doesn't have the death penalty, so I assume this case will be in courts north and south of the border for some time to come.

For me, Lancelot's killers are dealing with their own justice, both before God and before man. Perhaps those who killed my brother and dad have also been brought to justice. Others will be scrambling to replace the white king and queen in this deadly game of control, and perhaps somewhere, hidden in the shadows, there really is a black king and queen who are just as serious about eliminating the opposition.

For now, I need to move on with my life.

CHAPTER TWENTY-EIGHT

I take a walk in the gardens at Queen Elizabeth Park in Vancouver ten days before my scheduled flight to Kenya. Looking up at the small bridge near the conservatory, I have the distinct impression that a man with binoculars is focused on me. I have two plainclothes police escorts, but somehow I don't feel safe.

I fidget with my sunglasses and mention the observer to Constable Sall. He turns to the place I indicate, but by the time he focuses in the right direction the man has moved on. We all pass it off as a coincidence. I'm leaving soon to join the counselling department at the Rift Academy in Kenya and I only have two depositions to endure in the FBI's intended case to shut down all the Firm and Friendly clubs in the country. The RCMP are helping facilitate the investigation on this side of the border.

My interviews with the mission representatives proceed well. Tim and Eileen sort out my orientation details and a week of evenings focused on paperwork clear that channel as well. Normally, like other missionaries, I would spend considerable time sending letters and travelling in order to raise financial support. Fortunately, for me, the police honor their word and find backers for my five-month commitment.

I'm behind in my correspondence, so I spend my last Monday night catching up on emails. One of the messages is from Gayle, the outgoing dean of women at the Rift, now safely tucked away in Texas.

Subject: Hope this helps.
Greetings in the name of Jesus. I hear you're about to take over the girls' counselling at the Rift for the next few months. You're a Godsend and

I thank you. I was asked by the superintendent to pass on a few tips to help you streamline into what's happening here. A few alerts. Elections are happening in several countries where the families of our students are working, including this one. Elections are always unsettling times since parents and children are separated and can't control the outcomes.

Several of the countries have tribal conflict or religious tension with radical religious groups, and that is also unsettling and distracting for students. Famine is impacting large parts of Africa, and that means refugees and a lot of international aid. Several of the missionary kids have experienced robberies, assaults of various forms, carjackings, and serious illnesses. They've all experienced significant losses. They're dealing with all the normal issues kids their ages deal with. They're a resilient group but learn to hear what is happening in their lives behind the smiles. The realities they aren't smiling about. Most of them have learned to appear independent even if some of them cry themselves to sleep at night.

Those without parents nearby may have to deal with some relational inadequacy. Watch for codependency. Most MKs will try to be good to avoid disrupting their parents' ministries. They carry heavy weights of expectation. They grow up quick and need a nurturing acceptance when away from home. So much of a boarding school focuses on performance, and those who perform get the strokes they look for. Self-acceptance and self-esteem are all wrapped up in the package. Watch for those who aren't in the choir, the team, the drama, the outreach and service positions.

Go for walks on your own during the big events and see the child with a book sitting alone on the swings. Scan the dining room to see who isn't being included in the conversations. Spend time in the library to see who might be a little too concerned about their marks and not concerned enough with their relationships. Learn to see what others are missing. Look harder at the ones who are a little too obvious to see, but don't overanalyze. Just be aware.

The school has done a solid job in creating a positive environment of social interaction, personal skill development, and community outreach. It isn't usually what's here that is the problem. It's usually what isn't here. Take time to find out what that is for each student you spend time with. Affirm who they are. Model the love and compassion and grace of God for them. Affirm their families and encourage them to be honest with their feelings and with their family members.

Consistent values and support will provide some of the stability and security they need. Encourage the girls who come to see you to build strong support networks in their peer group, but also to get involved in activities and situations where they can get to know others from a variety of cultures and age groups. If they have siblings at the school, encourage them to keep that relationship strong and active.

Gently monitor the girls to see if they are getting the healthy hugs and supportive touches they need. Keep them talking and expressing their true emotions. If you get the chance to be involved with parents, encourage them to keep in regular contact with their children. Honest and regular connection will help establish an inner sense of well-being for the parents and the children.

For some of the students, there will always be a stigma attached to asking you for help. Some of the MKs won't even realize they need someone to help them. If they have struggles, they may feel afraid that their parents' ministries will be jeopardized. They may be afraid of being labelled or of being inadequate or weak. It takes time to build and nurture a culture of being accepted for who you are.

You are never going to be a parent to these students, so be careful how you present yourself. You are never going to do the work in their lives that only God can do. Relax, and walk the few steps of their journey that God privileges you to have. You are becoming part of a great team of caregivers. Don't try to make things happen. They're already happening. Just do your part.

Please make sure you don't let your issues become their issues. Every single person walks their own unique path. But you know this.

Please feel free to email me with any specific student issues once you get underway. I'll be travelling but will take the time if you need me. I'll be praying for you. The Rift family is worldwide and someone is within reach if you only ask.

Love and prayers, through his grace, Gayle

I reread the email twice, then copy it to tuck into my Bible to take with me. My heart and my head are spinning. *Did anyone think of all this when I was a student?* All I can reply is "Thanks. Katie."

I email Andrea.

Subject: One week.
One week, girl, and then I'll be with you. I just got the most amazing email from Gayle. She just dumped her heart all over. I know we had counsellors when we went to the Rift, but somehow I didn't realize how important it was to sit down and let go of all the stuff I was carrying. I'm still dealing with stuff from back then and the choices I made because I didn't sort it out when I could. I have a feeling God wants to do some healing in me as well as in others. I'm praying for a new heart and new eyes to see. Get some rest while you can, because I'm on my way. Love always, Katie.

Three minutes later, I get a reply.

Subject: Can't wait.
Your email just popped up while I was on here with Sarah. She was freaking out about all you've been through. Hope you're still okay. They had some kind of break-in at their apartment while they were up in Canada but only lost a laptop and a bit of jewelry. These addicts hardly make it safe for anyone. I'm off to Northern Kenya to help with the Somali refugees this next week. I'll be getting back about the same time you do. Maybe we'll meet at the airport. See you soon. Luv, Andrea.

Throughout the week, I pay close attention to the news as the enforcement agencies in the United States and Canada work to thwart the escape of the owners and operators of the Firm and Friendly. While details are sketchy, it's clear that nothing is going to be the same anymore. A lot of the young Asian girls, intimidated into some of the shadowy services, have been picked up and channeled into the proper immigration processes.

Monica continues to be my chief contact with the RCMP, but there isn't much for me to do once I give my testimony. I let her know about the annoying vandalism done to my rental car on Thursday night. The rear passenger window and trunk lock were both broken. Fortunately, I didn't have anything valuable in the car except for a small digital camera I used back in Minnesota. Leaving the car at the repair shop is going to save me from rushing over to the rental place on my last day.

Luke and Johan celebrate the incredible police action over email and assure me that they'll keep in touch as I spend these months away. They meet with

Uncle Bob, and Luke is thinking seriously of purchasing the farm so he can be closer to his brother in Moorhead. I would be welcome anytime if I return.

I manage to leave a voice message for Hanan, expressing my regrets that I haven't been able to get together with her or any of the other New Hope refugees. I assure her that upon my return she will be one of the first people I take out for lunch.

Between packing and catching up on my correspondence, I barely notice that the calendar is advancing rapidly. What's worse, I begin to hardly notice that Bruce is no longer part of my routine.

I say my farewells to Dean and Lizzy, along with Sarah and Keith. They assure me that they'll pass along the bundle of cards and love notes I leave for Bruce.

Saturday afternoon arrives. I'm just about to call a taxi when Monica calls. Her comments are brief: "Don't go anywhere. Don't answer the door or your phone. We're on our way."

Five minutes after Monica's call, the phone rings again. I ignore it. My curiosity is incredibly high. I should be on my way to the airport by now. Security line ups these days are getting longer, especially for international flights. I double-check my carry-on to make sure I don't have any oversize liquid containers or sharp objects inside. One last application of lipstick.

Two minutes later, there's a knock on my door. I almost move to the door, thinking it's Monica, but then I stop and wait. The peephole is there for my security, but my instincts hold me back. The security chain dangles and sways slightly. I hadn't set it in place. My feet freeze.

The knock repeats several times before someone works on the door lock. Tension grips my shoulders and neck. I head for the bathroom and lock the door. No more than thirty seconds later, I hear the bathroom door being tried. I sink back behind the shower curtain.

I hear drawers and doors being opened and shut in the bedroom and hallway. I set the extra secure latch installed by Richardson on the inside of the bathroom door and kneel down into the tub. Once again, the bathroom door is tried and a heavy shoulder budges it. I haven't even thought to bring my cellphone. All I can do is to pray.

A few seconds later, I hear the sounds of sirens. The pressure against the door becomes more intense and the frame starts to give way. I pray, and less than two minutes later I hear Constable Sall's voice through the door. "Katie, are you here? RCMP. This is Constable Sall. Open up. Are you okay?"

It takes me a minute to unwind, but I finally kneel up in the tub and announce my presence. "I'm here, Constable. I'm okay. Just give me a minute."

I'm not sure what to do, since Monica told me she was coming and that I shouldn't open for anyone. I can't believe my trust level is so low.

I flush the toilet to continue my stall and then run the water in the sink. "Is Monica with you?" I call out.

The constable seems a little irritated. "She's down at the station filling out some paperwork. She sends her farewells."

I move toward the door and reach up to release the latch, but then my hackles of suspicion rise up. If Monica is down at the station filling out paperwork, why did she tell me to wait for her here? I decide to hold out a little longer.

The constable clearly doesn't appreciate having to wait. "Katie, we've got to hurry. I'm supposed to have you down at the airport early. They've got some extra security right now."

I don't move. The door handle turns and the door is pressured again.

Sall's voice becomes intense now. "Katie, I'm assuming you're in some form of trouble. I will kick down this door to get to you. If you're okay, open up!"

I move back to the tub and kneel down inside again. The door begins to fracture—and then the shouts come.

"Police! Move away from that door. Drop your weapon. Now!"

I recognize Monica's voice at high volume. The sound of a skirmish and other noises mingle together.

Then Sergeant Richardson's voice. "Don't move!" More scuffling and grunting. "You almost did it, Baminder. Jorgensen, take Constable Sall back for booking and read him his rights."

"One minute, Sarge," Monica speaks up. I hear a light knock at the door. "Katie, are you there? Are you okay? It's Monica. It's all clear now."

I release the safety latch and tug hard to get the door open since the frame is significantly broken. When I get it open, Richardson is standing over a kneeling Constable Sall. The constable is in handcuffs. My luggage lies strewn across the floor.

Monica steps forward and hugs me. I'm still not sure what's happening.

Two Vancouver police officers walk into the room and take over from Richardson. They yank Sall to his feet. His eyes focus downward and his face seems expressionless. Richardson reaches into the constable's shirt pocket and pulls out a flash drive. I recognize it as mine.

Monica moves with me toward the mess on the floor and begins to gather everything together. The police take Sall into the kitchen to search him before moving him out. I search through my laptop and document bag, but everything seems to be in place. Of course, it's clear now that Sall saw the details of my flight information.

Once all my luggage is back in order, Monica takes me by the arm and leads me out of the room.

"I thought we might be too late," she whispers once we're in the elevator. She's actually crying. "I should have seen it coming. He had me completely fooled until today. At first he kept insisting you were the black queen, and then he kept lobbying me to let him escort you. I never suspected a thing. We need to get you to the airport."

As the elevator door opens to the ground floor, I give Monica a thank-you hug. "What happened?

Monica wipes her eyes with her sleeve. "I'll tell you in the car. Let's go!"

One hour later, I'm through customs at the airport. I stand and stare at the giant tropical aquarium on my way to international departures. The pieces of Monica's story dart back and forth in my mind, just like the fish in the aquatic display.

Constable Sall had apparently been an old classmate of Tommy Lee's. Monica had been double-checking all the contact numbers in a discarded cellphone when she realized there were calls to the Bellingham Firm and Friendly and others to the Vancouver Police Department. From the same phone.

Through a forensic investigation going back several years, she tracked down any overlap between members of the Vancouver police, the Firm and Friendly, and Tommy Lee. Two names came up: Baminder Sall and Carmen Shaw. Shaw had been lost last summer when her brakes failed and she went over a two-hundred-foot cliff on a windy road in the remote interior regions of British Columbia. Her car wasn't found for a week.

Besides being a classmate of Tommy Lee, Baminder Sall was a shareholder in the Firm and Friendly. His application and acceptance to the RCMP had come a year after his exceptional performance on the gang taskforce with the city police. He had an uncanny knack for being able to identify and track down members of two specific gangs. A warrant to trace the constable's cellphone records linked him with Joshua Kensington. Why he was still targeting me isn't known. The investigation is just beginning and I'll be back from Kenya long before it gets underway.

In the meantime, I have a plane to catch and MKs to counsel.

In the departure lounge, I power up my laptop and make note of the sixty-seven emails I've accumulated. Twenty-seven are deletable. Half the rest are labelled farewell. The first unusual one that catches my eye is from Steph.

Subject: You know what I miss?

You know what I miss about Africa? The drumbeats in those tiny little village churches as they vibrate through my chest cavity. The smell of cows and chickens and goats and mud and charcoal smoke around the village homes. The gecko lizards running across the ceiling above my bed. The friendly chatter I hardly understand as I sat for hours with Dad around fires, in dark places, listening to the laughter and stories of new friends. The unknown foods and sweet chai and warm Cokes that would stop the rumbling in your tummy after a four-hour service. Being welcomed wherever I went, by everyone I met. Looking up at night and seeing stars that went on forever. Hearing elephants munching on sisal plants so close I could hit them with a stone if I dared. Listening to hippos tearing up the grass outside my tent. Finding another new bird to check off. Walking on winding trails that seemed to go nowhere, forever. Watching sunsets in colors impossible to describe. Always trying to fit one more into our car. Coming home after being away at school. Getting back to see my friends at school after being away. Getting the chance to do things that none of my peers in North America could do. There are a hundred other things I could list. I just wanted to say, I envy you right now. Throw a kiss to the skies for me when you arrive. Shed a tear for me. Hug someone for me. And if you get the chance, do a dance of joy if you feel like you're home.

So much seems to happen in Africa in one lifetime. Nothing unusual ever seems to happen here.

All the best, keep in touch. Steph

These images of Africa grip me, but I can't help shaking my head at her closing remark that nothing ever seems to happen here. For me, too much is happening here. I've lost my place of healing and the horse that helped me heal. I've been left behind by the man I thought God provided for me to heal with. I've lost the family who could nurture and encourage me in my healing. I've run into so many hurting people that healing seems like a mirage.

The boarding call sounds. I shut down my laptop, secure my carry-on, pull out my boarding pass, and ignore the man staring at the tears running down my face.

CHAPTER THIRTY

One of Monica's great gifts to me is an aisle seat. She knows me. I get claustrophobic if stuck in the middle seat too long.

The flight through London is going to be almost nine hours, and those nine hours are going to need some distraction. It doesn't take me long to find out that God is sending that distraction in the form of a chatty twenty-three-year-old Kenyan woman named Valerie Njoroge. She's an extremely extroverted and self-confident graduate, six years younger than me.

Before we leave the tarmac and vault into the clouds, I learn she was born in Limuru, Kenya, fifteen miles or so from where I was born. Her parents came to work for the Bible Society in Canada when she was seven. Valerie just finished university, studying community development, and is heading out on a short-term summer mission trip.

But first she's going to stay with her Uncle Timothy Kamau in Nairobi to get to know the rest of her clan. Her Uncle Timothy is involved in security somehow, and he's extra busy with the elections coming up. Before that, she's meeting an aunt in London for a three-day layover, so she can see all the sights.

Her dad has been out to see family in Kenya several times, but this is her first trip back and she's doing it alone. Valerie has been away from her country for sixteen years, but still feels like it is home. She has been praying that God would give her someone safe to talk to on the way. To think God gave her someone like me, born only fifteen miles away.

Somewhere over the Rocky Mountains, we experience a bit of turbulence. Valerie puts a death grip on her armrests. Her jaw is set and her eyes get big. God put me next to her for a reason.

I speak calmly as the seatbelt signs continue to flash. "Valerie, how powerful do you think God is?"

No response. The turbulence calms down for a minute and then starts up again.

I engage again by being open. "Valerie, these pilots have flown through rough weather so much that it's like a ride at the fairground for them. These planes are so safe they can almost fly themselves if anything happens."

Still no response. I try distraction.

"Valerie, I was sixteen when I left Kenya and came to Canada. I was scared of everything. I learned a verse which God keeps giving back to me. It's from Philippians 4:4. Can you help me remember it? *Rejoice in the Lord always. I will say it again: Rejoice! Let your gentleness be evident to all.*"[3]

Her face looks like it's frozen in time.

I put my hand over hers and she stirs. "Valerie, do you remember the next part of the verse?"

She turns to face me as if she's never seen me before. She visibly relaxes. "The Lord is near."

I squeeze her hand. "That's right. Even now. Even here. Let's say the rest together."

And we do. *"Do not be anxious about anything, but in everything, by prayer and petition, with thanksgiving, present your requests to God. And the peace of God, which transcends all understanding, will guard your hearts and your minds in Christ Jesus."*[4]

We look each other in the mouth, trying to synchronize our words.

She gets stuck when we finish verse seven, so I finish the last verse for her: *"Finally, brothers, whatever is true, whatever is noble, whatever is right, whatever is pure, whatever is lovely, whatever is admirable—if anything is excellent or praiseworthy—think about such things."*[5]

A sense of peace comes over me. "Valerie, this is the verse God gave for my healing. It's meant to heal my anxiety and fear. It's meant to heal my thinking patterns. It's meant to heal my relationships. It's meant to heal my rollercoaster mood swings. I think we should pray."

And we pray. Right there, in our seats. The plane settles down sometime in that prayer, but they are settled for Valerie and I even before. Our own friendship is cemented in that time of trouble

[3] Philippians 4:4–5.

[4] Philippians 4:6–7.

[5] Philippians 4:8.

Just before London, Valerie hands me her contact information in Nairobi and invites me to connect when I can.

As the seatbelt sign flashes off, Valerie is back to her confident extroverted self. "Stick with your Bible verses," she says with a smile.

We part ways with a hug and I trudge on toward the endless lines that will take me toward my connection.

I settle into the lounge at Heathrow with a decaf coffee, my Bible, and a notebook. Valerie's encouragement to stick with my Bible verses focuses me on the healings of Jesus. I pray that I'll be able to see MKs as they really are. For some reason, the story of Jesus healing the blind man pops into my mind. When I flip to my concordance there are five different healings of blind men. Can their stories help me with mine?

There's the story of the two blind men who follow Jesus calling out for him to have mercy on them. He goes indoors and they follow him inside without any apparent invitation. He asks if they believe that he's able to make them see. They say, "Yes, Lord." Jesus says, "Because you believe, so be it." And they see.

Can I believe that Jesus can open my eyes to see what I can't yet see? Do I honestly have the faith to believe like these men? Maybe I need to prove myself a little more persistent in following after Jesus and calling out for mercy.

There's another story of a blind man who is also mute and demon-possessed. Blindness is a side-effect of a deeper issue. Jesus deals with his blindness and muteness first. His healing results in some people wondering if Jesus could be the one they've all been wishing for. Others who saw the event claimed he was empowered by Satan.

Do I need Jesus to take care of other issues in my life besides blindness? I identify with this blind man, since all kinds of controversy seem to get stirred up just because he shows up and lets Jesus do something in his life.

Then there's the story of the two blind men sitting by the road near Jericho who call out for Jesus. Some of the people tell them to be quiet, but they work even harder to be heard. Jesus stops and asks them what they want. "We want to see," they say. Jesus touches their eyes and they immediately receive their sight.

Will my voice and desire for healing get drowned out by others who think they know better than Jesus what I want and need? Will I find my voice to call out louder and more persistently? And if Jesus asks me, will I know exactly what I want from him?

There's a story in Mark 8 of a blind man who is brought to Jesus by some friends. They want Jesus to heal him. Jesus takes him outside the village and spits on his eyes. He touches the man and asks him if he sees anything. The man sees people walking around like trees. Jesus touches the man a second time. This time the man sees clearly.

Do I need a second touch to see clearly? Maybe everything is fuzzy. My marriage, my relationships, my past, my family. Maybe even coming to Kenya for four months without my husband is part of my fuzziness. Or maybe it's part of my second touch.

Should I head for a plane back to Seattle, where I can be close to Bruce, or continue on to Kenya, where I can work on my healing? There are still three hours until boarding and I'm suddenly unsure of everything. I turn to the last passage to see if there's anything more for me to see.

Before I turn away from Mark 8, I notice Jesus' instructions for the man not to go back to the village, but to go home. The thought impresses itself on me so strongly that I read it twice more. Don't go back. Go home. I take this to mean that I should press ahead. A surge of joy washes over me.

I turn to the fifth and final blind man story. Jesus' disciples notice a man who's blind, and they want to know whose fault it is. Is it because of his parents' sin or his own sin that he is the way he is? And then this glorious word: "Neither." Jesus spits on the ground, makes mud, applies it to the man's eyes, and then tells him to go wash in the pool. The healing creates quite a stir. When the authorities investigate, all he can say is "I once was blind but now I see."

Not being able to see isn't because of the choices my parents made or the choices I made. God set this up to display his own glory in my life. God is reminding me that he's taking full responsibility for my inability to see so that I can depend on him to bring glory to God when he does help me to see. One day I want this testimony to be able to say that once I was blind but now I can see.

The issue has never been about how I was or wasn't wounded as an MK. It isn't whether I was or wasn't wounded by a boarding school experience. It isn't whether I did or didn't fully work through all the psychosocial stages in their proper order along with everyone else. It isn't even whether I feel at home somewhere or not. God set my life in a place to keep me desperately dependent on him in the same way he is doing it with every other person on the planet. We're here to remind each other of that, to give him glory for his healing and show our faith while we wait for his touch in the areas where we aren't healed yet.

Someone once told me that I can't take my clients down the path of healing any farther than I have gone. I'm still not completely convinced. For me, healing is like going on a plane trip. It could be a Cessna, an executive jet, or a 747.

Once I buckle myself in, my control is very limited. Things change all around me whether I want them to or not. If I buckle myself into the journey of healing, I have a pilot who knows where I need to go. Right now that journey is taking me home.

I spend some time in prayer and soon hear the garbled boarding call announcing my flight to Nairobi. I pack away my Bible and race toward my next lineup. The young woman dragging her carry-on and running behind me step for step seems like just one more passenger trying not to be left behind.

CHAPTER THIRTY-ONE

From the moment I step into the departure lounge at Heathrow I see, smell, hear, and feel home. Colorful kitange cloths flutter like butterflies on so many surfaces. Swahili words tickle my ears like the freshest of breezes. Tired children sprawl on the floor at the feet of tired parents, bringing a smile to my heart.

Images tug at the corners of my mind. First, Bruce laughing, Lancelot running, motorcycles jumping, golden rings flashing, Luke and Johan waving. Then Lizzy dancing in her wedding dress alongside a Maasai warrior, dad's tortoises, a breathtaking sunset over Mount Longonot, a baobab tree. It feels like I'm morphing from one dream world into another.

I shuffle my way into a corner seat and notice that the young woman who had been running right behind me settles two seats over. Her blond hair, style of dress, and fine features make her appear as if she could be a sister of mine. She looks my way without hesitation and says in a slight southern drawl, "Whew, I thought we weren't going to make it."

I smile and introduce myself. "Katrina Joy Delancey."

She looks startled but introduces herself as well. "Emily Fisher."

Emily shakes my hand firmly and then asks if I could watch her things while she uses the women's room. I tell her I will. Five minutes later, she's back. She offers me an extra bottled water she bought to say thanks.

I get the urge, too, so I ask Emily to watch my things while I visit the washroom. While there, I set the bottle of water down on the sink counter for just a minute. I'm almost back to the departure lounge when I realize that I'm thirsty. A picture of the unopened bottle in the washroom flashes into my mind and I realize I left it behind. I don't want to offend Emily, so I return to the washroom. The bottle is already gone. I stop by a dispensing machine to buy another one so Emily won't wonder what I've done with her gift. I even open it and drink some before I get back into the lounge.

I thank her for the water and keep sipping it. Tiredness from sitting so much leaves me feeling like a deflated balloon. I set the water bottle on the floor, thread my arm and hand around the bags on the seat next to me, and lie my head down for a minute.

I pick my head up briefly at the siren of an emergency vehicle. There's a scurry of footsteps in the hall outside but all is quiet in a few minutes. I look up to see if Emily is aware of what's happening but she has disappeared. I hope she's okay. I reach down for my water, but for some reason it's gone. I lie down again.

Then I hear my name. "Mrs. Katie Southerland… Would Mrs. Katie Southerland please report to the check-in counter?"

I gather up my laptop, carry-on, jacket, and camera case, and negotiate my way through legs and luggage to get to the counter. I finally get the attention of one of the men standing there by waving my boarding card and passport.

"I'm Katie Southerland," I announce.

The man nods and waves at one of the security guards. A deep gnawing in my gut creeps over me as the stern looking British official marches closer. More than anything, I want to run, but there's nowhere to run. I'm so close to home.

"Passport, please," the guard says. I surrender my passport and boarding pass. The gentleman examines the documents, and scans my face. "Come with me!"

I follow his quick pace as best I can, all the while dragging my carry-on, squeezing my jacket under my arm, keeping my camera bag on my shoulder, and lugging my overloaded laptop case. I can see my passport held securely in his white-gloved hand. I'm not about to lose my ticket to home.

We leave the departure lounge and wind our way through several hallways until we arrive at a security office. The official opens the door, then steps aside and waves me in. All this without another word.

I gather my courage and finally speak. "Would you please tell me what this is about? I have a plane to catch."

Just as I finish speaking, another official carrying a file folder steps through the door and waves the first man out. "Mrs. Katie Southerland, I presume, or is it Katrina Joy Delancey?"

I'm not sure how to reply. "Both!"

J.A. Taylor

"Both?" His grey walrus moustache waggles back and forth as he ponders my response. His left eyebrow dips a bit as he waits for more.

"Katrina Joy Delancey is my maiden name. Mrs. Katie Southerland is my married name."

He seems satisfied and sits down on an upholstered chair by the desk. "Please have a seat," he says, pointing at two black plastic chairs.

In my confusion, I can't make a decision about which one to sit in. I stay standing. "I need to catch my plane."

"They're holding it. Sit!" More moustache waggle.

I put my laptop and camera bag on the left chair and flump down onto the right chair. My jacket and carry-on lay stranded in the middle of the room. Tears flood to the surface quickly. "What's happening?"

"Don't you know?" Seeing my stunned look, or teary eyes, he must assume I don't. "We have two people checked in with your name. Half of your paperwork is signed with one name and half with another. We also received a call from the Canadian RCMP asking us to detain you for a security check."

This is too much. I bend over my laptop and sob. The man sets down a Kleenex box near my head. I hear the official making a call.

Two minutes later, a woman's voice whispers into my ear. "Mrs. Southerland, all will be well. This is for your security."

I sit up and look at her through my blurry vision. I wipe my eyes. A compassionate face comes into clarity and tries to calm me down. I choke out a few words. "What's happening?"

The woman reaches for a cellphone being held by the first senior official. She holds it out. "Please, speak to the RCMP officer."

I take the phone. "Hello?"

The voice on the other end is familiar. "Katie? This is Sergeant Richardson in Vancouver. Are you safe?"

With my mind having started to switch worlds, I find myself unsure how to respond. "I guess. Why?"

He speaks rapidly. "We've intercepted a message saying that the black queen will not be reaching her destination. From what we understand, a double is supposed to take her place. We checked your paperwork and found out an alternate ticket with your married name. The ticket we bought was cancelled. When we tried to get the security there to double-check, they had one set of papers with Mrs. Katie Southerland and another set with Katrina Joy Delancey."

I have no idea what could have happened.

Richardson ignores my silence. "Did you meet anyone who tried to get close to you? Did anyone try to get any personal information from you?"

All I can think of is Valerie Njoroge on my last flight. Then the face of Emily Fisher flashes before me. I tell him about both women and he seems satisfied. He wants to speak to the security official, so I hand the phone back to the man patiently waiting in his upholstered chair.

After a brief conversation, the senior official closes the cellphone and sets it on the desk. "Come with me. Leave your things." I notice his moustache is quite still.

We walk down another set of hallways and then stop outside a room with a large shuttered window.

The officer stops. "One of our security officers is speaking with a woman inside this room. I will turn on this speaker and you will tell me if you recognize her voice."

He turns a small knob on the wall and I hear a familiar voice with its distinctive southern drawl. She's explaining to someone that she's a teacher going to Kenya to fill in at a mission's school. He turns the knob again and the voice disappears.

"I think it may be Emily Fisher," I say.

"Who is Emily Fisher?"

I look at him and feel my eyebrows arch. "How should I know? She's a passenger. I just met her in the departure lounge."

"And you've never known her, met with her, or talked with her before today?"

"Never!"

He turns toward the shuttered window. "I'm going to open these shutters. I'm sure you've heard of this. You can see the woman, but the woman can't see you. Please tell me if this is the woman you say is Emily Fisher."

He opens the shutters and I instinctively duck when Emily seems to look in my direction.

"Yes, that's Emily."

The shutters close.

"You may go back and board your plane," the official announces. "And you may thank your RCMP for their alertness."

Another official leads me to the original room where I find my belongings opened and spread around the room. This is getting all too familiar. I stand with my mouth open at the door. The compassionate woman sits by the desk.

"Come in. We apologize for any inconvenience. We've had a lot of excitement in the past hour. One woman was poisoned with a water bottle. She's in hospital. Claims she found it in a bathroom. There are four sets of prints on that bottle. One of them is yours." She holds up her hand before I can speak. "There's more. The RCMP called about some concern for your safety. We picked up the ticket switch. Documents for you have been filed with two different names." With this news, she holds up a ticket and flight documents. "In the front pouch of your laptop we discovered a ticket for another flight to Cairo in the name of Dorothy Hemingway."

I walk over and take the ticket and paperwork from her. It definitely isn't mine. I walk over to the laptop. It definitely is mine. I look around at all the scattered things. All mine. Nothing makes sense. I walk back to the desk and give the paperwork back. My brain is working overtime.

"The only thing I remember," I start, "is that Emily sat near me in the departure lounge and asked me to watch her things. She came back a few minutes later with a water bottle, and then I had her watch my things when I went to the washroom. I forgot the water bottle in the washroom, and when I went back it was gone. I bought another one so Emily wouldn't think I didn't appreciate her gift. I drank it and then put my head down to rest on my laptop. I heard the emergency vehicle, but Emily was gone and so was my water bottle. I have no idea how the ticket got into my laptop."

"This is brilliant," said the officer. "Your Emily Fisher was travelling under the name of Dorothy Hemingway, yet her papers mysteriously appear in your laptop case. So, someone you've never met switched documents with you for some reason we're still trying to settle. She apparently tried to poison you. Someone signed your documents with the name Katrina Joy Delancey."

"I guess that's how I introduced myself to Emily. I'm a bit foggy. I guess sometimes, without my husband around, I forget I'm married."

"Well, Mrs. Southerland, we've had to send your flight on without you. Is there anyone we need to notify about your delay?"

CHAPTER THIRTY-TWO

My two days in a London suite, somewhere under police supervision, didn't make it to my list of all-time favorite memories. I can't sort out my thoughts and feelings. I'm just numb. On the second night, I hallucinated that my brother Robert and my parents were standing around my bed. It was frightening enough to keep me on my feet until dawn.

Endless conversations with different inspectors, who undoubtedly double-check every word, remind me that the police everywhere in the western world use the same techniques to try and get information. But I have to remember that there are a lot of countries where interviews are a nightmare instead of an inconvenience.

Eventually my truth is established and I'm sent back to the airport under escort. I'm handed a large manila folder as I leave the police precinct for the last time. I store it in with my laptop without looking at the contents.

A female undercover officer sits with me right through to my boarding, then nods to me as I disappear down the tunnel toward the plane. I've been given an upgraded seat near the front of business class. I finally feel like the worst is behind me.

On this trip, I'm not taking any chances. I put on the eye-blinders, put in earplugs, tuck the pillow under my neck, and cover myself with a blanket. I stay that way for at least half the flight until the person next to me nudges my shoulder. She needed a washroom break, or at least a chance to stretch her legs.

I take off my blanket and my blinders and move into the aisle. As I turn toward the back of the plane, I come face to face with Valerie Njoroge. Her smiling black face is enough to make me whoop out loud. I give her a hug. She's as surprised as I am but returns the hug.

While my seatmate is away, Valerie slips into the row and tells me that London is the most incredible place she has ever seen. "But why are you here? I thought you told me you were booked straight on to Nairobi."

When I start to answer her question, she smiles and says, "It's okay, Katie. You don't know me. You don't have to tell me your whole life."

I sigh and realize that no one in their right mind would believe my story. Sarah was right when she said I could create trouble in places by just showing up.

I decide to summarize everything for Valerie. "There was a mix-up with my paperwork and I was asked to delay my flight. I got to see places in London I've never seen before."

Valerie seems delighted at our reconnection and jumps back into the conversation with descriptions of her visits to Buckingham Palace, Big Ben, Parliament, and a boat trip down the Thames. She's just beginning to describe her side trip to Oxford and Cambridge when my seatmate returns and we bid farewell until Nairobi.

As I settle into my seat again, I remember the manila folder I was given. I stand up in the aisle, take down my laptop, unzip the case, and withdraw my prize. Inside are numerous pieces of paper. Almost all of them have familiar handwriting on them. I feel an inner smile threatening to burst my heart open.

Five of the letters are from Bruce. I devour them several times each. Even the mundane seems amazing. I am not forgotten. I am missed. I am loved. I am even longed for. One line especially sticks out for me:

I'm so happy you're getting to make a dream come true. I'd love to be out there to celebrate our anniversary and make another dream come true. Pray.

I hate to move on, but I take the time to read two more typed letters from Lizzy, one from Sarah, and a memo from Sergeant Richardson thanking me officially on behalf of the RCMP for helping in their investigation. His last paragraph is a request asking me to report to him in January after my return.

The rest of the trip is uneventful. I don't see the Mediterranean through the windows. I don't see the Sahara desert. But when the seat monitor in front of me shows that we've crossed into Kenyan airspace, I rise and look out a window at the back near the washrooms. Within ten minutes we are instructed to return to our seats, return things to our stewardesses, and buckle in for descent. The landing is flawless, but I miss seeing the ostriches I often see as I land.

Valerie finds me in the passport visa line. "It seems strange coming back to the place where I was born with a passport from somewhere else," she says as she holds up her Canadian passport.

"Tell me about it." I hold mine up next to hers. "I'm not sure where home is anymore."

As we move up the line, Valerie and I switch over into Swahili. I'm surprised to find out that her fluency isn't much better than mine. At first we're both embarrassed by our stumbling efforts, especially as others look back at us. Once we start laughing, helping each other, and taking helpful hints from a guard who tries to move Valerie to the line for national Kenyans, we feel the flow of the language start to live in us.

Our passports are stamped without problem and we skip down the stairs, pretending to kiss the ground when we get near the baggage carrousel. I see people smiling all around.

One of the security officials comes over to ask how he can assist us. When we tell him briefly about our homecoming, he calls over one of the baggage handlers and tells him to take good care of us. We sail through customs and give each other a final hug as we near the exit.

Valerie abandons her cart to run into the arms of a well-fed woman. I assume it's her aunt. As I watch this reunion, I'm crushed by a hug of my own. Andrea has found me.

She is ecstatic as she holds me at arm's length. "Girl, you look terrible. Does everything in your life have to be an adventure?"

"You know me. I hate to be boring and I hate to be bored."

Andrea is Korean by birth, but her recent week in the refugee camps in Northern Kenya has bronzed her even more. It leaves her full of life. Her dark eyes sparkle.

"I can't believe we get to be together for five months," she says as she hugs me again.

This makes me miss Bruce more than ever. I would give anything for a hug from the man I love with all my heart.

The Rift Academy van is loaded with my luggage, plus a few supplies Solomon, our driver, picks up in town. He begins negotiating the clogged traffic arteries. Even though I was here less than a year ago, the choked streets look almost worse. Solomon keeps up his cheery stream of Swahili banter with me and Andrea and with the other drivers and pedestrians traveling at the pace of slugs. When we take our final roundabout and emerge from the bumper-to-bumper, exhaust-puffing, music-blaring streets of Nairobi, Solomon settles into the drive home and leaves me and Andrea to our own conversation.

Andrea finally asks the inevitable about my hold-up in London. I tell her basically the same thing I told Valerie. My paperwork got mixed up in London and I was delayed. She doesn't believe me for a second.

"Katie, don't even try to go there on our first day together. I grew up with you. I know you found trouble of some kind. Now spill. What happened?"

I start by telling her about meeting up with Valerie Njoroge in Vancouver and how I helped keep her calm. Andrea knows I'm stalling and she lets me hear it. I tell her about getting to the departure lounge and meeting Emily Fisher. I tell her about the problem with the poisoned water and the paperwork mess-up. I tell her about the various security officers, and especially the man with the grey walrus moustache which wiggled as he thought. I tell her how the RCMP helped alert everyone to what was happening.

Andrea can't wait for more. "What are you doing mixed up with the Royal Canadian Mounted Police?"

That leads to more details about Joshua Kensington and Rita Galinsky and my sting operation with the Firm and Friendly. I can tell Andrea is impressed, so I end up telling her about Lancelot and Luke and Johan and some of the MKs I talked to. There's nothing like a friend to open up those hidden areas of one's life.

Before I notice, we crest the top of the escarpment and the whole Rift Valley lays spread out below me. I never get tired of this sight. This tear in the earth's crust extending from Israel all the way south of here is a wonderland of exotic life. I crane my neck for the first glance of the volcanoes, Suswa and Longonot. These are my markers of home.

I notice with some concern that huge swaths of the forested areas along the highway have been clear-cut for farms and small settlements. Just the last year has seen enormous loss. Andrea notices what I'm looking at and speaks up.

"You noticed how many trees have been massacred. We're going to be in crisis mode soon. The school is going to be in trouble for water in just a couple of years. Charcoal burners are taking it all. They're trying to make a living today without realizing that there may not be anything left to live on within a few years. The rains are shrinking. We really need to pray."

The devastation is obvious until we turn down the steep hill toward the school. My ears pop from dropping from 9,200 feet to 7,500 feet. I yawn to clear my hearing. I'm still yawning as we swoop through the gate and pass the upper field.

A few seconds later, Solomon begins honking his horn.

CHAPTER THIRTY-THREE

orn-honking is a Rift tradition to announce a victorious return for teams who have won games or tournaments. Everyone listens for that horn, especially when there are significant varsity games at stake. Victory for the Buffalos is a campus-wide celebration, not just a team celebration. Solomon is honking because of my victorious return.

We creep over the speedbumps, past the first staff homes and student dormitories, and around the maintenance and chapel buildings. The sight of Centennial Hall, where Dad used to preach as the chaplain here, chokes me up. I miss my dad's reassuring presence, but the van keeps driving and honking. To my left, the new clock tower rises near the kitchen and dining rooms. A lot of changes have been made since the days when I lined up behind the old dining hall to pick up pasteurized milk for my family.

Curious looks flow our way from workers and students as Andrea leans out the window screaming. Solomon continues to lean on that horn. Fortunately, classes are finished and fist pumps and smiles are the most common response to our loud entry. Andrea pulls back into the van and wraps her arms around me in joy.

Some of Andrea's students wave. She squeezes her head and arm out the window, waving madly and screaming again. "She's here. She's here."

Even though I visited these grounds just eight months ago, before my wedding, it feels like forever, and it feels like yesterday. We circle past the science building and take the final bend by the tennis courts, then ease up in front of the library and park in front of the flagpoles guarding the main building, Kiambogo.

This building has been standing since Teddy Roosevelt laid the cornerstone in 1909. Many students have secret histories of their own in the rooms and passageways and porches of this monument. Even I have a history here, holding hands with my heartthrob Jason as we watched the sun set over Longonot one Saturday night, just months before I thought I was leaving for good.

My heart races. I'm back to my first day here, ready for an adventure, fearful that I might fail. Hoping to be a source of help and healing. Anxious that no one will overcome the barriers of a closed community to the point of trusting me.

Questions fill my mind. Why did I come here? How can I have left Bruce? Am I so selfish that I would pursue my own healing at the expense of loyalty to my husband? How am I going to relate with kids so young? Will the staff accept me? Why would anyone think I am the black queen?

By the time I open the van door, several students and staff surge forward to see what all the excitement is about. Andrea crawls up onto the side ladder of the van and introduces me.

"This is my best friend, Katie. A Rift legend. She races leopards and giraffes in her spare time here. Tames wild stallions and cougars in her spare time in America. Give her a great Rift welcome!"

And they do. More fist pumps and hoots and hollers. Even a few hugs from some of the women and girls. There's nothing like a friend with a foggy memory of your past to set you up. Because of my crazy past in America, I now have five months to see what God will do in Africa.

One of the biggest hugs comes from Chelsea Hobbis, the girl whose migraine helped me earn my first demerits. She's filling in at the infirmary for the year. I knew one day we'd have to catch up with each other.

Graduation is in six weeks. The seniors are anxiously preparing to finish up exams, play their final tournaments, head out on their final safari celebration as a class, and get through their re-entry weekend. This is all supposed to help them get ready to leave a big part of their lives behind. Some, permanently.

The faces around me blur into unknown youth and I try to discern which ones might be seniors. Are there clear signs in their eyes? Is there anxiety in their body language? Is there excitement in their chatter? Do I have what they need?

My next six weeks will be spent experiencing this land and preparing staff, families, and students for the next steps of their journeys. My final three months will be dealing with the everyday realities of MKs and their caregivers. And if Bruce can make my dreams come true, I'll be celebrating my first anniversary with him right here at the end of October in the middle of it all.

Andrea takes me up to the offices and helps me sort out paperwork and introductions and welcomes. The rest of Friday becomes a blur of faces and movement as my journey catches up with me. Sports and student activities are happening all over campus but they hardly faze me. My eyes begin to droop with jet lag as Andrea talks on and on. I work hard to keep my head up, but eventually the battle is too much.

I'm aware of Andrea building a fire in the apartment on the side of the single's duplex which I've been given to live in. She hands me a cup of warm chai and I breathe in that sweet blend of boiled milk, tea, and sugar. Somehow I get into bed, because that's where I find myself when someone's rooster crows.

Dawn in Kenya arrives like clockwork, even on Saturdays. Somewhere around 6:00, give or take half an hour, the blazing monarch of the sky catapults up over the escarpment hills like a daredevil stuntman attempting to hurdle the huge valley below. The brilliant ball shoots its streams of life down onto the hills and plains where life stirs, and responds, and sometimes withers.

Since Kijabe sits so close to the equator, there isn't much change over the year. For a good portion of twelve months you get twelve hours of sunshine. Twelve hours to wrestle with the dirt, to claim your space, to make your mark, to share your life. Twelve hours to trust God for crops, or water, or food, or shelter.

I'm a creature of habit no matter where I am. When my eyes finally fight through all the forces that work to keep them closed, when my internal urges motivate me to move out of my comfort zone, when I finally get my first foot out of bed, then I'm focused. Usually, a shower is at the top of the list. Before coffee, before anything. Today, something beats out the shower. I need to brush my teeth and clear out the grunge taste of days of travel and snacking.

I'm still standing in my towel, staring at my open suitcase, when I hear a knock at the door. I can't imagine why someone is here so early. Then I hear the friendly Kikuyu chatter of the ladies who bring vegetables every Wednesday and Saturday. My mom always handled this in the past, and now this mantle of womanhood has passed to me. I have to choose my own onions, potatoes, pineapples, carrots, and greens. But first I have to get dressed.

The knocks persist as I throw on a pair of blue capris, a green sweatshirt, and my sheepskin slippers. My hair lies wet, tangled, and plastered around half my face. I don't have a scale to weigh things, and I don't have any shillings to pay, but I have this inbuilt urge not to insult the ladies who lug their hundred-pound loads up to my door.

I throw open the door and launch off with my best "Wimwega Muno" (greetings). Instead of the smiling black faces of my vegetable ladies, I'm face to shoulder with a man. A white man, built like a fullback. Broad shoulders, strong jawline, reddy-brown goatee, full lips, an aquiline nose, and the deepest pools of amber I've ever seen in someone's eyes.

One moment I'm moving forward with all the enthusiasm I can manufacture. The next, I jump back and start to slam the door out of embarrassment.

I can hear laughter in the background as a nearby group of ladies sees my reaction. It's the same full-bellied laughter that overflows from them when someone falls off their bicycle or when someone gets butted by their own goat. This had been a great practical joke.

Staring at someone you don't know when you're looking like a drowned rat isn't the best way to start your day. The intrusive oaf swings a huge potato sack of vegetables down off his shoulder in front of my feet and puts out his hand. "Jambo, Katie. I heard you were here. Remember me? Jason Miller."

Now I really want to slam the door in his face. This is the biggest embarrassment of my life. Well, maybe not the biggest, but certainly one of them.

Jason Miller was the tenth-grader I held hands with on Kiambogo Porch, watching that sunset over Longonot almost fourteen years ago. Jason was my first heartthrob. Someone I'd said goodbye to forever ago. Someone I never wrote back to even when he sent me dozens of letters.

I'm sure he sees the horror on my face. He backs off a few steps and apologizes. "Obviously not exactly who you expected to see. I was just out for a jog and couldn't resist stopping off at the dukas and picking you up a few things. It looks like you're busy. I'll call you later. Sorry to surprise you like this." He lifts up his hand in a wave and begins to jog away.

And I can't say a word. The knowing looks of the ladies aren't even filtered. As Jason disappears around the bougainvillea bush, they step forward with their own gifts.

Just then, the door to the other half of the duplex opens and a kindly middle-aged woman pokes her head out the door.

"Atiriri, Muriega," she calls.

The ladies all answer, "Eh, Turiega."

The middle-aged woman steps off her concrete stoop and walks over to me with her hand extended. "Janey Simpson, your neighbor. I know, you're Katie Southerland. Welcome. Missed you yesterday. Let me help you get your vegetables. I see you met the doctor."

At first, I think she's commenting on my appearance. Perhaps blue capris and this shade of green sweatshirt, crowned with dripping wet hair, has something to do with the hospital. By the time I shake Janey's hand and watch her joke around with the ladies, it dawns on me. Jason must be the doctor.

Now I'm really baffled. His eyes were familiar. The setting is familiar. But a doctor? How did a tenth-grader I once cared about become a doctor?

In the next few minutes the ladies unload potatoes, onions, carrots, lettuce, hard pears, and zucchini at my feet. All of this has come from their gardens, or else the duka (shop), as a welcome gift. When I ask Janey about the vegetable ladies I'd been expecting, she smiles and lets me know that in the good old days, the ladies used to come door to door twice a week. Now, if you want vegetables, you have to go to their stalls at the duka. That's where the doctor had bought mine.

I'm still not sure what else Janey says to me before she disappears back behind her door. My mind is foggy with jet lag and surprise. I pick up the produce and set it on the counter. It all has to be bleached.

It's time to call Andrea and find out why she hasn't told me about Jason before now.

CHAPTER THIRTY-FOUR

ndrea brings a splendiferous fruit salad half an hour later as a peace offering. At least that's what she says when she plunks it down in front of me and I ask her about Jason. Apparently Jason arrived three weeks ago to fill in for a pediatric specialist who went back to Florida for a one-year home assignment. Andrea had been too busy to find out the details and she'd only seen him three days earlier.

I forgive her, but I have a hard time believing her. Those sweet mangoes are awesome, however, and the pineapple is the best I've had in years. The loquats, gooseberries, watermelon, papaya, and strawberries make me wonder why it has taken me so long to get back here.

I use my time after talking about Jason and Janey to change into a pair of jeans with a cardigan the color of jade. The skies are a little overcast, so I put on socks and tennis shoes. The rainy season is erratic these days. I start putting my strawberry blond hair up into a ponytail but finally decide to blow-dry it instead and let it move freely in the wind.

Andrea and I eventually get around to the inevitable.

"Is he married?" I ask.

My Korean friend looks at me with eyes wide. "What does it matter? You are!"

The heat in my face is instantly obvious. "Sorry, my life has been so crazy dealing with gold rings that I try not to look anymore."

She backs off. "He's been doing med school, residency, and a specialty in pediatrics," she said. "He really hasn't had time for women."

"That makes two of you," I say, trying to turn the tables. "Maybe God has set up this little rendezvous for something more than you can imagine."

Andrea ropes her long dark hair into a side braid as she picks up the verbal jousting, just like old times. "Jason and me? Yeah right! Why is he coming to your door so early if he's interested in me?"

I wink at her. "Come on, girl. Who else besides me knows your innermost, darkest secrets? And who besides you knows hospitals and doctors better than anyone else? How long have you really known about him coming here?"

She blushes at my dig, and that's amazing to see with her complexion.

Andrea was a Korean orphan adopted by an American doctor in Florida. Her dad was a surgeon at the station hospital right next to the Children's Care Center where Jason is now practicing. So she knows hospitals. She assisted in her first surgery when she was in ninth grade. There are a lot of things you can do out here that would be impossible in most other places.

When Andrea, Sarah, and I used to hang out together as best friends, we were the most unlikely trio. Andrea had straight midnight black hair down to her waist. She used to be five-foot-four, but now she's about even with me at five-foot-seven. She's always been the smartest person I know, except for Jason.

One of her weaknesses is her guilt complex. I've taken advantage of that so many times, which almost makes me feel guilty. One of the good things about her is that she's one of the few people who can honestly read my heart, and maybe even my mind. I don't have to say a word. She'll suddenly be there to listen and say what I need to hear.

I'm sure people used to think of us as strange friends. Sarah was so much taller. She had short curly black hair compared to my shoulder-length blond curls and Andrea's long black braids. In our school days, Sarah lived four hours away where her dad taught at a training school for Kenyan pastors. She was from California and as American as anyone there, but since she's black, the local people always assumed she was as Kenyan as they were.

Time melts when Andrea is around. We talk and walk and connect without trying. In those high school years, whether we were bird-watching, collecting tortoises for my dad, or just reading back to back, we could also spend hours in silence together.

So I know her. And this blush catches me off-guard. Not only because of what happens to her, but because of what happens to me. I almost feel jealous. In fact, I do feel jealous—and that shocks me because I'm a married woman completely committed to Bruce.

161

Things get worse because Andrea knows what's happening inside me and she, in turn, looks shocked. This is an incredibly difficult start to my time of healing.

Andrea flops down on my loveseat, stares at me, shakes her head slowly, then drops her forehead to her knees.

I have to deal with things straight on. "Bruce and I are happily married. Seeing Jason after fourteen years is a shock. I was a mess. He doesn't look like the boy I remember. I'm happy for him, and for you, if things happen. I just don't know how you talk to your first heartthrob after so many years. I'm as surprised as you are at these feelings."

"It's going to get awkward sometimes here, Katie. Let's face it. Things have changed." Andrea pushes up from the loveseat and stretches. "It's time for senior store. The juniors are on duty this third term, but I'm a senior sponsor and I've got to get the grill organized and show them how everything works. Why don't you come and help? You can get some of those famous doughnuts you've always loved."

The Rift Academy senior store contains a full-out cafe run by the graduating class to raise funds for a final farewell trip to the coast. They have a full menu including hamburgers, hotdogs, taco salads, Philly cheese steaks, sandwiches, grilled chicken burgers, doughnuts, and whatever sodas are in stock. Everything is made fresh, and this takes significant human effort. Every volunteer is welcome, and today that invitation to help is mine.

As I walk out the door for the senior store, I notice the diamond on my wedding ring catch the glint of the morning sun. I think of all that dough and icing getting caught up in the ring, and with reluctance I take it off while apologizing out loud to Bruce. I tuck it away in the back of my sock drawer for safekeeping and head out.

Andrea tasks me with turning over pieces of grilled chicken and I soon get into the chatter of teens intent on having fun during their work. The doughnuts have definitely changed recipes, but they still have that fresh fried taste and a distinctive smell.

Just before noon, Andrea sends me up to the kitchen with a pile of dirty metal trays the chicken has been kept on. She introduces me to a junior girl. "Shelly, this is my friend, Dr. Southerland—or Aunt Katie, as she'll probably be called around here."

Most of the younger staff or dorm parents get the Auntie or Uncle label at an MK school. All three of us walk quickly together to my next assignment. I'm hoping to get a conversation started while we wash up.

Apparently Shelly is one of the popular girls because she greets a constant stream of passersby along the way.

Without intending to, I move into one of my deeper analysis moods, tracking her body language and speech patterns. I'm so intent on watching her that when we turn into the kitchen, I collide with someone pushing a trolley of doughnuts. The metal trays I'm carrying slide out of my arms and crash with an incredible clatter onto the concrete floor.

As I turn to apologize, I find myself staring into the same shoulder I'd seen earlier this morning. Only now Jason has on a white apron sprinkled with flour. Again I'm speechless. Again Jason takes the lead.

"Fancy running into you here, Katie." He crouches down and scoops up several of the scattered trays.

Shelly picks up others and I stand like a dolt, mesmerized.

Jason rises and looks me in the eyes. He keeps talking like nothing happened. "They sure recruited you in a hurry. It took me a week to get on as a sponsor. This sure brings back memories."

I missed my year for doughnut-making and chicken-grilling and a lot of other things because I left early.

The incident doesn't seem to faze Jason at all. He's too busy remembering his own experiences. I take the trays from his hands and finally get my first words out. "Thanks. Asante. Thank you."

As I move toward the sink, Jason calls after me. "Katie, good job with your hair."

And he's off pushing his trolley of doughnuts.

When I finally dump the metal trays into the huge kitchen sink, Shelly starts to analyze me. "Something tells me you two had something going on. What's happening, Aunt Katie?"

Her familiarity throws me for a second as I try to adjust my mental focus. I came here to clear up my past, not recreate it. I take a deep breath and sigh. I look this popular young girl in the eyes and try to get the words out of my mouth. If I expect others to talk about their realities, I better start with my own.

"Once upon a time, Dr. Miller and I were students here," I say. "We watched the sunsets over Longonot together when we were younger than you. We were kids, but we sure liked each other."

"So what happened?"

I scrub at a stubborn spot on a tray, rinse it, take another breath, and continue. "My dad was the chaplain. He got really sick and we all had to leave after my tenth grade year. It was probably the hardest thing I've ever done."

She takes the tray from my hand and sets it up on a drying rack. "Did you stay in touch? You and Dr. Miller?"

I work at another tray, smiling wistfully. "He was certainly no doctor back then, and I really wasn't in a good space when I left the Rift. Everything I knew and loved was here."

Shelly sets her towel down and leans against the draining table. "So how did you make it until now?"

"Shelly, I made some terrible decisions along the way. One of them might have been never answering any of the letters Dr. Miller sent me. I got into some terrible relationships. I've lost some people I loved with all my heart, including my mom, my dad, and my brother. If God didn't work his grace and get me an incredible man, I don't know how I would have made it."

"Are you talking about Dr. Miller?" Shelly asks.

I don't connect with her question at first and give her a confused look.

"The incredible man," she clarifies. "Are you talking about Dr. Miller?"

I answer quickly. "No. Yes. Yes, Dr. Miller is incredible, but I married someone else who is incredible."

"Is he here?"

"No, he's working for the Navy." I pile another tray on the growing stack that Shelly is ignoring. "No, he's not here."

She finally picks up her towel and a tray. "Then why are you here?"

CHAPTER THIRTY-FIVE

B efore I answer, Jason returns with a load of dirty dishes from the doughnut-makers. These bowls are covered in rich chocolate and vanilla icing used to smother the special treats.

"Beep-beep, party animals," he says. "Mind if I add to your workload?"

Shelly pierces me with a questioning look and reaches for another metal tray. She looks over at the energetic young doctor. "Dr. Miller, Aunt Katie was just telling me about the incredible sunsets you saw together."

A stab of betrayal hits my gut and the kitchen suddenly gets hotter than I remember it. My face is burning up. I have nowhere to look but down into the sink as the icing bowls tumble into the water. The avalanche of dishes splash the soapy water up onto me and I jump back to get out of the way.

In the worst scenario possible, I slip and fall right into Jason's strong hands. He quickly lifts me up and sets me on my feet. At that second, Jason earns all my admiration.

"Shelly, Katie and I used to practice this move a hundred times a week just to get people talking. We saw some incredible sunsets in our day and we'll probably see some more while we're working out here. All those sunsets just keep reminding us of how good God is."

Shelly isn't ready to let go of this yet. "Don't you two still feel a spark? Even I can see the way you look at each other."

Jason doesn't back away. "Shelly, there's no one around here I feel closer to than Mrs. Southerland. If my looks at her give you the wrong impression of our friendship, then I stand corrected. I'll do my best not to betray her husband. I don't know if you have someone you haven't seen for a long time. Someone who used to be your best friend. Mrs. Southerland was once my best friend and I'm happy to see her again. Maybe too happy."

With that, he walks away.

I must have looked like a whipped puppy because Shelly sets aside her towel and walks over to give me a strong hug. As I slump into the arms of an eleventh grade girl, I begin to sob for the friendships I lost when I left so long ago. Friendships like Jason's.

The young woman strokes my hair and whispers into my ear, "Don't worry, Mrs. Southerland. Your secret is safe with me."

By the time I clean up the dishes, finish watching the volleyball tournaments, and share a dinner with several of the dorm moms, I notice a subtle change happening inside me. I'm being accepted as an adult here—a professional who has a place. The little girl I left behind will have to heal in her own free time.

I decide it's time to explore the office where I'll be counselling these girls. On the way, I notice a monstrous new tower rising near the chapel.

"What is the tower for?" I ask a passing student.

He glances briefly at where I'm pointing. "Oh, that's the siren in case of terrorist attacks. Don't worry. We've already done the drill for this term. You won't hear it again. We haven't had trouble since the last elections." He nods in my direction and moves on.

The terrorist siren wasn't here when I went to school. How do these kids handle these pressures as if it is all normal? I run down a double flight of stairs and turn the corner into the alumni court.

Posted on the wall as I enter the brightly colored office is a plaque featuring Proverbs 12:18: *"Reckless words pierce like a sword, but the tongue of the wise brings healing."* The words take me back to my dad's journal and his desire to be a source of healing. In some ways, my profession is actually helping his dream come true.

Sitting on the shelf in the counselling office is a copy of *The Happy Room*, by Catherine Palmer. It's the story of Peter, Julia, and Debbie Mossman, who are taken to Africa and left at this very boarding school by their parents. Mom and Dad Mossman are focused on sharing the gospel with the Maasai and anyone else who will listen. Feeling as though they're constantly abandoned at school, the children are impacted by long-term psychological consequences. The story is a tapestry of tragedy and hope for missionary families.

I remember being a fourteen-year-old, cuddling up on the family room couch with my arms around my knees and listening in on Mom and Dad talking with anxious parents at the dining room table. The visiting parents were filled with dread and guilt after reading that book, thinking that somehow the very act of leaving their children at boarding school was an act of abandonment that would wreak permanent harm on the children they loved. I knew those kids and they looked fine to me. But what did I know back then? I was just a kid.

The first time I read this book as an adult, I nearly threw it across the room. Of course, my love for books and my sense of goodness kept me from doing it, but I came close. This school has been my home from birth; any attack on it would feel like an attack on me, my family, and my faith. I made myself read it through for professional reasons, then put it on the shelf for five years.

The second time I read it, on a snowy Minnesota morning, Bruce found me at least five or six times curled up on the couch sobbing. I became one of those Mossman kids, feeling the agonies of their confusion and loss. Issues of attachment, grief, fear, anger, and insecurity tore at my soul. I couldn't stop reading it. This time through, my husband was the one tempted to throw the book across the room. The Mossman family story touched me deeply. My Special Forces protector thought that perhaps I was being impacted too deeply.

The loss of a sibling in that book reminds me of how much I miss my own brother Robert, and my dad as well. Their death left me emotionally paralyzed with guilt and grief.

One soul-impacting part of *The Happy Room* is a story about an old deranged Mau Mau warrior who traps the three children in the family Land Rover while the parents are in the market shopping. The old Kikuyu man is painted all in white and wears only a trench coat. He terrifies the trio of children, but the brother's quick wit make him a hero. He saves the day and the parents never do understand the terror of the experience for the children. In fact, the parents never seem to understand what's really happening for their children at any time.

Remembering the story now, as I reach for the book, reminds me of my own encounters with the young sorceress in the cow skin who often crossed my path during my final year of school. What ever became of her? With the threat of terrorists around, it seems likely that no one is worried about a sorceress.

Sleeping through the night on Saturday doesn't work very well, although I do feel physically, mentally, and emotionally exhausted.

Sunday morning arrives too early. Andrea invites me to join her as she leads a junior high girls Sunday School class. They are studying great women of the Bible and it's a good chance to get to know a different group of girls.

When we finish teaching, feeding, and saying goodbye to the twelve girls, we rush off to Centennial Hall for a morning service. The ache inside me grows incredibly as I sit near the back. This is where Dad usually was on days like this. Preaching his heart out. Making us laugh. Reminding us that God is with us no matter how we feel. No matter how far away our family is. No matter what might happen in our relationships.

Andrea lets me know that a father of one of the senior students is speaking today. He's a doctor who she met working up in the refugee camp. She doesn't tell me that Jason is going to be part of the service.

My curiosity rises when Jason stands with a guitar at the far right of the platform. After we've sung several songs and choruses, the chaplain introduces him as our special music. He has an incredible voice. What else did I miss out on with this man? He seems to make a point of intentionally not looking in my direction. I understand, and his choice doesn't spoil the message of the song.

But he isn't finished when his song is done. Jason talks briefly about how much he learned from the God who heals and how it's a privilege to work with this healing God. He calls up six of the small children he works with at the Care Center and explains how each little one needs specific healing. A cleft palate, a heart valve, club feet, complications from polio, a few limb deformities. Then the good doctor asks some of the senior students to step forward, put their hands on these children, and pray for God's healing. Others of us will pray in our seats.

Something in my heart cries out, wishing that I was one of those children being prayed for. And in some strange way, I am. I put myself in that group of needy little ones and let the prayers of eight hundred people wash over me.

Dr. Fletcher preaches on the touch of Jesus in our lives. His message is filled with real life examples from his own time at the refugee camps and around East Africa. It's also filled with a focus on the touch of Jesus on those he healed. When others recoil, Jesus moves toward. When others withdrew their hands, Jesus reaches out and touches. He touches us right where we are. He touches us where we hurt.

As though in a flash of lightning, everything becomes clear. I need to go to each of the places where I've felt wounded—if not in body, at least in my mind. I need to let Jesus touch the places that hurt.

Andrea books me in for lunch with the administrative staff, including the superintendent and his wife. Introductions are briefly made and then it's open season on the new counsellor. The questions are fairly straightforward from a team dedicated to making sure their charges are well cared for. My previous email from Gayle, the dean of women, prepared me for much of the territory the group wants to focus on. I leave, comfortable with the leadership. By the smiles on their faces, they have enough level of comfort with me to drop me into the deep end.

We decide that I will introduce myself to all the students in chapel the next day. Then, after chapel, to the rest of the staff. At staff meeting, I'll present my philosophy of counselling, and after a shortened period day on Wednesday I will talk to any parents who might be available. I'll begin to visit one girls dorm per evening until I've made my rounds. We all hope that this quick face-to-face exposure will allow trust to start developing.

Each day I do my best at breaks and meal times to circulate with the students. During class times, I schedule myself with the boys' counsellor, the chaplain, with dorm parents, the dean of men, and with the infirmary staff to get a clear picture of what's happening behind the scenes. I also make myself available to parents and teachers who need some coaching in dealing with teens.

The last task I'm given to do is join the team responsible for setting up the re-entry seminar for the seniors. My background and fresh experience in North America could be helpful to those preparing to leave in a short time.

If my start with Shelly is any validation of my ability to help students, I'll have to spend some significant time begging God for wisdom. Some days I still feel like I'm a little girl in big girl's clothing.

Night is a welcome relief from all the words and faces coming at my weary mind. I nestle down and don't wake up until a piercing siren rattles the windows of my house.

CHAPTER THIRTY-SIX

The sound is so penetrating that I cover my ears and curl into a fetal position with my pillow over my head. I was deep in a dream about going into a nuclear submarine with Bruce.

Is this part of my dream? Are we being attacked? Are we diving? What's happening?

Through the intermittent wailing, I hear muffled shouts. I finally remember that I'm in Kijabe, not in a submarine with Bruce. The station lights turn off and it's pitch black. All I can think of are terrorists—and this can't be a drill, because the drill was already done.

Someone bangs on my door and shouts in a language I don't understand. Maybe it's Kikuyu. Every muscle in my body feels as tight as an old bedspring. My bladder screams for attention. It hurts to unfold myself. The pounding continues and I crawl under the bed, pulling in a blanket to cover myself. I leave a narrow opening for my eyes.

The siren stops and the silence is deafening. Someone fits a key into my outside door and slowly opens it. I stop breathing.

"Memsup? Memsup?"

A flashlight beam plays over the bed and around the living room. I see two tire-sandaled feet and a machete blade. I also see a dozen large cockroaches scrambling to escape the light by scurrying into the darkness right where I'm hiding.

The feet turn and take the light with them. There's pounding on Janey's door, but she's already gone to the airport for her home assignment. I hope all is okay in town. Whether I've just been visited by a guard or a terrorist, I no longer feel safe knowing someone has a key to my door. My prayer life suddenly takes on a deeper meaning.

I don't move from under the bed all night, even when voices and laughter echo in the courtyard. My door is open and the moonlight streams in. It's bright enough to silhouette a small shimmery snake that slips over the sill and into my kitchen. As long as it isn't a momba or a cobra, I'll be okay. Still, having the door open is unnerving because I don't know what other night life might be visiting.

Soon after the sun comes up, I crawl out from under the bed and shut the door. I latch it. I want to phone Andrea, but it seems early. A shower is my best solution, and in the shower I remember that I'm supposed to speak at chapel this morning.

Chapel goes fine. I just tell my story and give a brief devotional.

I decide not to say anything about my night of terror. No one needs to feel guilty for my problems. Andrea is too busy to even ask.

The superintendent lets us know that the siren was set off accidently by a guard who didn't tell anyone it was accidental. They're looking into the incident. He's glad everyone is safe and that they followed drill proceedings and got to their safe space in good time. Finding out this drill procedure is now high on my priority list.

In both the staff meeting and the parent meeting, I try to imitate the superintendent. I'm not sure if it's for my benefit, but he clearly sets down his modus operandi. After greetings and general introductions, he launches right into it.

"There are three basic truths I operate from. First, God is sovereignly in control of bringing together the members of this community to experience his grace and learn to love him and love each other more. The staff, students, administrators, families, and workers are not here by accident. God wants to accomplish something in each of us that's greater than we could ask or imagine. And each person here is an important part of that happening.

"Second, while we aren't a church, per se, we are all part of an interdependent community and need each other. Each person is gifted for the sake of the others in this group. Each person brings life and experience and love and strength that others rely on. It is more blessed to give than to receive, but if we don't receive in this community, someone else won't get the blessing of giving.

"Third, every person in this community is equal before God. Your family background, financial status, denominational foundation, personal education, and accomplishments may have marked you somewhere else. Here, we are equals on a team, for one purpose: nurturing, guiding, guarding, and releasing competent and confident Christian young men and women who know how to love God and to love others.

"Education is one part of the holistic care we offer here. One of our former students, Dr. Katrina Southerland, is here to help us with our counselling for girls. I'm going to ask her to let you in on what she hopes to accomplish with the daughters of this community."

I get up as confidently as I can. "Good afternoon, everyone. You can call me Katie. I'm pleased to be back where I grew up and learned to love God, this beautiful land, and its people. I even learned to love MKs here.

"There are three basic areas I'm checking out when I meet with these girls, your daughters. First, I want to find out how well they're dealing with the stress, challenges, and issues of life. What are they facing and what kinds of judgments and choices are they making? What are they thinking and feeling?" I scan the room and the mothers are especially attentive. "What kinds of inner resources do they have in place to help them through this stage of growth? How does each girl deal with her own self-care and aspirations?

"Secondly, I want to find out what kinds of networks and support systems are in place. How flexible and compassionate and tolerant are these girls toward others who let them down?"

My mind fills with the image of a Grade Seven classmate who lost her temper and escaped campus for an afternoon. She caused a lot of panic. She was so mad when a staff member found her wandering the train tracks. The dispute was over a boy. I reign in my mind and focus back on the parents.

"I want to find out how forgiving and gracious your daughters are to those who hurt them? How trusting? How successful are they in repairing and restoring relationships?" I scan the concerned looks of a few new moms and press on. "How open are they to new friendships? How long do they keep their relationships? How do they handle the losses of relationship?

"Thirdly, I want to find out how responsive and giving this young woman is in her relationships. With her family? With her peers, guys and girls?" Even the fathers are paying attention. "With other adults in her own culture and with those from another culture? Does she accept the help and nurture she might need, or does she always try to stay in control by nurturing others?"

A short question and answer time follows, but I've made some strong connections, especially with those who have previous Rift relationships.

When Saturday rolls around again, I realize that life has been so busy that I haven't even unpacked everything yet. I haul my duffle bag out of the closet and set it on the bed, right beside my half-unpacked suitcase. I open the dresser drawers and begin transferring clothes from one location to the other. When I get to the sparkling black dress I wore on the police sting, I can't imagine what I was thinking when I packed it.

Just for my own little dream world, I put on the dress and shoes and jewelry and primp up in front of the mirror. I imagine myself at the coast with Bruce, dancing on our anniversary, palm trees swaying, African drums beating in rhythm with our hearts. I picture the two of us back in his home in Virginia, before we were engaged, dancing in front of that large fireplace mirror.

Then the knocking starts. I almost lock myself in the bathroom before I realize that the knocking is for a women's Bible study next door. Images of Jason Miller standing at my door start to surface and the thought of him seeing me in this dress drives me quickly to action. I stuff the dress in a bag, along with the pearl necklace and earrings, and the Prada shoes. The only reason it doesn't all go in the trash is because all the trash is sorted and I don't want anyone in the community questioning my reputation, or my father's. Not even Andrea is going to see this little number.

I settle for jeans, a rainbow-striped cotton t-shirt, and tennis shoes before my cellphone starts vibrating. This is my first call and it takes me a few seconds to identify the sound. I'm as transfixed as if watching a cobra.

As the phone nears the edge of the kitchen counter, I grab it with the quickness of a snake handler. It's Andrea.

"Morning, sister," I say.

"Morning, Katie. I know you've been up for hours wondering how to spend your day. I've got the perfect option. Check your email in five minutes."

She hangs up.

Andrea took time on Monday to help me get set up with a cellphone plan and my email. Apart from a dozen messages sent out by the administration to all the staff, I haven't had anything personal sent to my email. Mind you, last night was the first time I had the chance to send out a mass email to about twenty of my connections back in North America.

When my new email account fills the screen, I see that there are seventeen messages in the inbox. I scroll down the list and Andrea's name pops onto the screen. Below her, apart from administrative messages, are two from Lizzy, one from Sarah, one from Shelly, four from staff members, one from Jason—and one from Bruce.

CHAPTER THIRTY-SEVEN

When I look at his email, I'm not disappointed:

Great to get your contact info. We're in port for a week. I've put in a request for our anniversary. Keep your lips fresh.

I'm still typing my reply to Bruce twenty minutes later when the cellphone buzzes again. I pick it up but don't answer. It's Andrea. I want to finish writing to Bruce, so I ignore it.

Five minutes later, the phone buzzes again. I want to hide it under my pillow for a while. I keep typing. I have so much to tell Bruce about my last two weeks. I've lived on old notes and love letters long enough. I need to connect with him. Skype, phone, a personal visit. I don't care. I just need to know how to get hold of him.

A few minutes later, there's a loud knock on my door. Andrea makes sure I hear her. "Katie! Katie! Open up. Are you okay in there?"

I quickly sign off with Bruce and press send.

When I open the door, the look on Andrea's face, and the tone in her voice, tells me she is not amused. "Why aren't you answering me? Oh wait, don't tell me. You were busy with Jason."

If Andrea wasn't one of my best friends, I might have slapped her. The accusation is unbelievable with Jason and I having worked so hard to be discreet. I haven't seen him since the Sunday service. There's something going on that I don't understand.

"Whoa, hot mama!" I say as I step back into my space. "For your information, I was busy writing to Bruce. I haven't seen Jason since Sunday."

Andrea seems to relax. She examines my face, sloughs her shoes, slinks over to the loveseat, and lies down on it with her feet on the arm. "Katie, I need an appointment. I'm going crazy."

I pull over one of my three dining room chairs, set the back toward her, and straddle the chair with my arms across the back so that my chin rests on my wrists. "The doctor is in."

"You need to pull up my email. I can't believe that I pour out my heart to you and you're off busy with your husband who's half a world away."

I know my friend's heart and voice. I let her words slide like sand through my fingers. I click onto her email and read her heart.

There are three things. One, she needed to talk immediately. Two, her dad has suffered a heart attack and is in the hospital and she isn't sure whether to fly back to be with him. Three, the lead couple on the piki (motorcycle) interim had to drop out due to personal issues with their junior high daughter, and since the interim is next week, the school needs immediate replacements. Interim is a week-long cultural experience where students in the upper two grades take their learning out of the school grounds. Under the supervision of sponsoring staff members, the students choose from options like aviation, camel, piki, coastal exploration, game parks, and many more. Andrea has suggested that I be allowed to serve as a replacement for the lead couple who had to drop out, and the administration is willing to let me, under the circumstances.

I turn to her after reading the email. "Piki interim? I'd be happy to go. That was one of the interims I wanted to go on anyway if I'd stayed here my last two years." This is already an exciting and a painful discussion. "Your dad? Call him, talk to him, and find out what he needs from you." I look back at the email. "Okay, so you need to talk. Go ahead."

"Aren't you supposed to use some kind of Rogerian, indirect prompting to get me to come up with my own solutions?" Andrea asks, mocking me. "We still have a problem."

I squint down at her. "What do you mean, we have a problem?"

She covers her eyes with her left forearm and I almost dread listening. I wait long enough for her to explain. "I don't want you to go on the piki interim and I don't want to go climbing Mount Kilimanjaro anymore."

"Okay, so I won't go."

"But you have to!"

175

"Why?"

"Because Shelly Winston has been dreaming about this interim for the past three years. She's the only girl in the group, and the only way she can go is if there's a female staff member also riding. And I told her that you'd be going."

"I've met Shelly," I say. "I don't see the problem. Except that you're making my decisions for me before I know that I'm supposed to make them. Is there a problem with Shelly?"

"The problem's not with Shelly," Andrea says as she unwinds herself and sits up on the edge of the loveseat with her hands clamped down firmly by her sides.

"Who is the problem with?" I ask patiently.

"The problem's with me."

"Okay, we're back at the beginning. Please explain." I stand up and retrieve a glass of water. I look at Andrea, but she shakes her head and declines. For some reason I have a feeling I'm going to need something to calm my stomach.

"I'm not pregnant."

"Were you worried you might be?" I ask in my best Rogerian voice.

"I'm just foolin' wit' ya, girl," she says, smiling. "Of course not. Me and the virgin Mary are like twins. I'm just jealous."

I haven't been in close personal contact with Andrea since the wedding last year and her comments aren't making sense to me. "I don't understand. Who or what are you jealous of?"

She looks at me in mock disbelief. "I'm jealous of you, Dr. Katrina Joy Delancey Southerland, that's who."

"Why?"

"Because I wish I was going on that piki safari. This is the very last year they're going to include that option." She gets up and walks into the kitchen. She puts her hands on the edge of the sink and looks out the window. "All those times you kept asking me to stay over the break and ride pikis with you, I'd come back after a month away and hear about you riding with the giraffe and zebra and the leopard. I just needed to be with my family. Do you understand?"

"Of course," I assure her. "I was fine. I had my brother and my dad and other station kids to ride with."

"You're missing my point! I want to go on this piki interim, but because I never learned to ride, I can't go. Remember dreaming about going on interim together? Now this is our only chance."

I try to let her know that I'll be fine. "If you're concerned about me with all those guys, don't worry. I can handle them. And if you're worried about Shelly, I promise I'll try to watch out for her."

"You're still missing my point! I'm not worried about you or Shelly. Of course you'll be fine."

"Then who are you worried about?"

"You and Jason."

"What are you talking about?" I'm sure there's fire in my eyes now. "Jason and I have worked real hard to make sure nothing inappropriate happens between us. I'm happily married to Bruce and he'll be here to celebrate our first anniversary in October. Please don't ruin my time here by creating more problems than I already have."

I need a walk badly. I open the door and head out to the mile-long road circuit. A few seconds later I hear Andrea's footsteps pounding down behind me.

"Wait up, girl! Just because you have your doctorate doesn't mean I can't share how I'm feeling."

We walk over half of the circuit without saying anything. Of course, I have to smile and wave at everyone out enjoying the freedom and the scenery. Always have to keep up the reputation. And now that I'm a professional, with a doctorate, I have to try all the harder. My only compensation is that Andrea is working hard to keep up with me, and she has to smile and wave as much as I do.

Somewhere around the half-mile mark, the adrenalin wears off and the altitude kicks in. I start panting hard. I've forgotten how hard it is to breathe the first few months at 7,200 feet. I've been experiencing it the first week, but I've been strolling and pacing myself. Now my true lack of conditioning shows itself.

I move to the side of the road as a van comes by and negotiates the security gates. I walk through the gates and move to the embankment below the gym. Instead of continuing to gasp like a fish out of water, I sit on the edge of the grass and put my head onto my knees. Andrea stands over me and shadows me from the sun.

Finally she speaks. "Do you even know what I'm talking about?"

I keep my head down. "I get it. You like Jason and you want me to keep my hands off, my eyes shut, and my mouth closed."

Andrea puts her hand on my right shoulder. "I don't even know whether I like Jason or not. I hardly know the guy. I just remember that I used to like Vern a long time ago. Remember Vern? I dreamed of going on interim with him, but no. We ended up in different groups both years. I know you and Jason always wanted to go on the piki interim together. That's why I'm jealous."

I look up and shield my eyes in case the sunlight gets past her sheltering body. "But I wasn't even here for interims. I never got to go on interim with anyone."

"I know, and that's what makes this so amazing. It's also why I'm so jealous."

I finally stand up and look her in the eyes. I speak as straightforwardly as I can. "Andrea, I haven't got a clue what you're talking about."

She looks back at me and a light seems to dawn in her eyes. "You mean you really don't know?"

"I don't even know what I don't know."

She takes on the look of a patient teacher. "Do you remember me telling you a few minutes ago that a couple dropped out of the piki interim and that I had recommended you to be there for Shelly?"

I nod with no clue where this is going.

Andrea continues. "You going on the interim means that there is still one space left. Don't you read your emails at all? Last night, the assistant superintendent asked Jason to be the other substitute and he said yes. He sent out an email this morning saying this was his dream come true. That means you and Jason are going together and your dream will come true. That's why I'm jealous. Hardly any of my dreams come true."

The energy drains right out of my legs and I collapse. "This is not a dream come true. This is a nightmare waiting to happen." I need to talk with Bruce more than ever.

Just as I finish my thought about Bruce, Jason jogs around the corner toward us.

CHAPTER THIRTY-EIGHT

In wide open spaces, there's just nowhere to hide. Jason slows his jog as he gets close to me and Andrea. No way am I going to invite him to talk, but Andrea is so social and she hates being rude. She calls him over and tells him how happy she is that he's going to get to have his dream come true.

I let the two of them chitchat about the junior-senior store transition and about how things have gone. Andrea compliments him on his singing at the service and gushes about how wonderful his work is with handicapped children. He seems comfortable talking with her until there's a lull in the conversation. Then he looks past Andrea and catches my eye.

"Katie—or should I say, Dr. Southerland—I just heard twenty minutes ago that you've been okayed to go on the piki interim. Not sure if you got my email this morning, but I didn't know at the time that you would be going. Do we need to talk? If this is going to be too awkward, we should sort it out sooner than later. I'm willing to back out if that would make it easier on you. Anyway, just thought I'd let you know. Get in touch if you want to."

With that, the good doctor is off to finish his jog. I never used to be this tongue-tied around him when we were younger.

I'm almost home when Shelly sees me near the field and comes running over. "I've been looking for you." She throws her arms around me and whoops. "I heard you're coming on piki interim just so I can still so. Asante sana. You're incredible. I hope we get to race some of those leopards."

She high-fives me and dashes away to tell all her friends.

When I reach the house, after an emotional debrief with Andrea, my email from Bruce is waiting. A phone number is attached to his note and I dial it without considering the time difference. He answers on the third ring.

I needed the verbal connection to get my head and heart back into focus again. Commander Southerland still knows how to make my heart skip a beat, make me laugh, and make me feel safe and wanted. I explain the piki safari situation to him and he tells me to pray about it. As far as he's concerned, we're in a group of Christians, in a controlled setting, and he trusts me. I love the guy more than ever and am determined not to let him down.

My prayer time doesn't bring up any strong convictions from God on this.

Jason and I finally talk after the Sunday service. I actually approach him and invite him to walk the mile with me. He raises his eyebrows in question but doesn't hesitate to say yes.

It takes almost all afternoon, but we catch up on each other's lives and talk things out around how this piki safari is going to work in such a way that neither of us will be put into an awkward situation. He fully understands my relationship with Bruce and expresses his happiness for me.

When it's clear that the conversation is winding down, Jason makes one last request. "Can we pray before we go? I have to admit that I didn't know why God was working out this trip for me. I didn't realize how strong my feelings were for you until I heard you were here." He runs both hands through his hair and interlocks his fingers behind his head. "I've been so busy all these years with becoming a doctor and helping others that I haven't had time to think of myself. I think God needed to bring me here to heal me in part so I could let go and move on." He turns and looks me in the eyes. "Thanks for being part of my healing. You're really good at what you do."

I almost reach for his hand as we prepare for prayer but realize that would only intensify the complications. I also realize this is an important moment for my healing.

"Jason, you never forget your first love." My tongue feels awkward. "I didn't realize how powerful those feelings were in me either, and I too have been brought here by God in part for my own healing. And you've been a part of that." I stare at his face even though the heat burns my cheeks. "So, thanks. I'll try harder to be a friend without making things awkward. Thanks for understanding. I'd love to come down to the Care Center sometime and see what you do."

Jason smiles at me and the twinkle in his amber eyes is back. "Let's get through the piki safari first. After that, we can take it a step at a time."

He prays long and I pray short. Then, like the gentleman he always was, he walks me back to my door and says his farewells briefly.

That night, I review my notes from the week. During my times around the dorms, and in the informal discussions during breaks, I've come to realize that the girls today aren't much different than the girls I went to school with over a decade ago. The one thing I have to guard against is the assumption that I know exactly what they're thinking and feeling just because I've done this before.

I try to summarize it all in an email to Bruce. It feels heavy, but I'm not sure how else to let my husband know what I'm dealing with.

Subject: MKs are real people too.

Dear Bruce, I can't believe how much I miss you. I wish I could share every sunset and sunrise with you. Our wedding seems so long ago. I'll sweet talk you some more in our next phone call. For now, I just wanted to let you in on a secret. MKs are real people too and I might be more normal than you thought. I've just reviewed my notes from the week and here are a few things I recorded.

My needs as an MK: I needed loving parents who were accessible. I also needed consistent values that I understood and could live out without being humiliated. I needed friends who would be available, a strong sense of personal safety and wellbeing, and the necessary information and knowledge for what I faced. I needed the freedom to be independent and move where I needed to go, plus a strong sense of self and who God made me to be. I also needed an environment with reliable affirmation and hope for a future worth living. If I had a cause to fight for, all the better. I'm not sure if all MKs need all of these things. I realized again that I needed these things and most of the kids I've talked to this week seem to be consistent in needing these things as well.

Let me get a little professional and drop a few other things on you, just so you know I'm doing more than just having a holiday out here.

Identity issues seem to be a major factor among these MKs. I once saw a quote from Wendell Berry that said, "If you don't know where you're from, it's hard to know who you are." One of the hardest questions for MKs is "Where are you from?" Do you remember us having that discussion?

Some of the girls have expressed fears about violent deaths of family members or friends. They've been through some fairly horrific experiences. With elections just a few months away, even in this normally stable environment, things are intense and these kids have an instinct for feeling the faces and emotions of the people around them.

Some of the girls are trying to cope with their lack of control in a restricted setting by reducing all the complex issues down to one: weight. I think, so far, that I have more anorexics than bulimics, but that's hard to discern.

With so much technology here, and so many gadgets, these teens are much more in touch with the wider world than I ever was. Their exposure to music alone gives them a vehicle to move them into a wide world of strange and exotic ideas beyond the scope of this global village. Their natural interdependence on their peer group gives them strength and helps them through their explorations of faith.

In some ways, these girls could be a part of any multicultural community. There are so many nationalities represented in the student body that when the group goes to the Model United Nations forums in Nairobi they look as if they could be the genuine assembly.

When I overhear conversations, it sounds like discussions at any school, except with a touch more compassion in most cases. There are endless details about interactions that happen in the dorms, in classes, or during breaks, including constant analysis of the reactions of other girls. But especially the guys. Most of the guys and girls have grown up like brothers and sisters and there's a lot of wholesome physical contact and expression. This is the area where they'll create confusion when hitting the university scene.

Bruce, I honestly am wondering if we might come back here sometime in the future. I feel like I'm a part of this family, but I'd feel so much more a part of it if you were with me.

From my past experience, I know that some of the newer students take a while to reframe their mindset so they can understand what's happening between those who have lived in this scene for years. Not every new student immediately feels welcome in this tightknit family or the little groups that make it up.

There are usually girls in a community like this who try to cope by targeting others through teasing, shunning, or intimidation. Smart girls, confident girls, pretty girls, and fringe girls are often the targets of these attacks. I can't pick up the pattern or the perpetrators yet. It may be a dorm thing if it's going on. I expect normal and often get better results than expected.

Many of the new students arrive with the latest fads and designer labels, and this always creates a mild interest by the veterans. It often passes after making a mild impression on the overall culture of the school, but then the informal uniform of jeans takes over again. In a conservative climate like this, there's always the issue of acceptable clothing styles, tattoos, piercings, hairstyles, makeup levels, and the obvious behavioral issues.

I'm just glad I'm passed most of this. No comment, please. These kids are just normal.

When you're trying to figure out who you are, it's not unusual to test the boundaries and adjust to the new standards in a new community. Girls are going to face different values and standards here, just like they're going to face other values and standards when they leave. For now, I have to realize that I'm not a parent, a friend, or a judge.

I think you've had enough to help you sleep for the next week. I love you, Katie.

P.S. You help me live in reality.

I hope that reality isn't going to be put to the test when Jason and I leave on the piki interim Monday morning.

CHAPTER THIRTY-NINE

Saturday is a busy day of preparation. I call Bruce early to get him at a reasonable time in Washington. He'll be pulling out in eight hours for the test run of a new Nimitz-class aircraft carrier. We enjoy our freedom to communicate while he's in port. We know this is going to be at least a four-month hiatus and we want to make the most of it.

Our piki interim group has one last meeting and then rides at ten, so I shut down with Bruce at 9:30. I scarf down a few chocolate peanut butter banana muffins on my way out the door and head over to pick up the motorcycle that will carry me across some pretty wild and rugged terrain.

The bike is being lent to me by the wife of the couple who can't go on the trip. Pat and Brian are a wonderfully generous couple to trust me and Jason with their prized possessions. My dad lent his new piki to a student on one interim and it didn't come back looking so good.

When I arrive, Jason is already helmeted and ready to start up. He's paying careful attention to the instructions from Brian and doesn't notice me arrive. Pat greets me with a hug and takes me over to her bike, which is all ready to go. Brian and Jason wander over as Pat gives me instructions. When she finishes, Brian affirms her great job and then adds a few small details in bike care.

The bikes are both Yamaha XT250s and are designed for road and off-road purposes. The four-stroke engine roars out power. The five-speed transmission will do the job for sure with all the different places we'll be going. The bike is off-white with purplish trim.

The helmet has a full visor and is a great fit, but I hate to think what my hair is going to look like at the end of each day. I'm going to bring a few scarfs for that very reason.

Jason and I say our thank-yous and farewells to Pat and Brian, then high-five each other and settle in for the ride to our meeting place at Kiambogo.

I outwardly smile as much as the others, but butterflies are doing cartwheels inside. While I probably have more experience than most of the other riders, Andrea has been pumping up my reputation as a wild woman and the teen guys on this trip are already talking about who will get closest to the leopard we might end up racing.

Even though it's been fourteen years since I've ridden around Kijabe, I have more experience than Jason. Since one staff member has to be in front and another behind, we decide that I will lead on the way out and he will lead on the way home. This is going to be a slow ride to test the skills of our riders. If Jason and I think one of the students doesn't have the needed control of their bike, we can still deny them the chance to dream with us.

We say a short prayer before revving up our engines. A crowd of spectators surrounds us and cheers us off as we begin. The posse of bikers flows down the muram road until we reach the tarmac that twists its way down to the valley floor. The forests I was once so proud of have been raped down to scattered groves. The resultant landslides almost make it seem like I'm riding in a completely unfamiliar world.

When we reach the valley floor, we head out to where I used to ride with the giraffe and zebra. With the incredible expansion of Kikuyu farmers building houses across the valley floor, the natural wild herds have moved quite a distance away. Apart from a few zebras, the wildest thing we see are Maasai cattle.

In four hours of riding, we pick up two flat tires between all of us. Our support vehicle helps with repairs. Despite Andrea's earlier effort to promote me as a wild woman, and despite the students' expectations, my reputation tames down quite a bit before we get back to the station.

By the time we clean up the bikes, make some small adjustments in equipment, and review our supply list and travel route, it's suppertime. I shower quick, switch into my white capris and scarlet cardigan, and slip on my short-sleeved jean jacket. I stroll down with a group of students, and Andrea, to Mama Chiku's duka for some stew and chapattis. This was always one of my favorite meals.

This evening, a drama production is scheduled in Downing Hall. With the consistent high quality on the stage at this school, I'm not going to miss it. When I join the queue entering the hall, I notice that I'm three people behind someone I recognize. I try willing her to turn around, and eventually she does. I catch her look.

"Valerie," I call.

I move forward and give her a hug.

The students standing immediately in front of me start razzing me and threatening to turn me in for a demerit for cutting in line. I smile and pull Valerie out of the line for a minute to talk. Apparently her cousin, Timothy Kamau, is in the play and she had come out to get some seats for herself and her aunt and uncle, who still haven't arrived. She was looking for them when she saw me.

I assure her that I can help her set aside some seats once we get inside, and I can stay there while she steps out to make sure her aunt and uncle find us. Valerie tells me that she's been having a great time and that the rest of her mission team will be here in a week. Her uncle has been incredibly busy with security concerns surrounding the upcoming election.

We stand to sing the Kenyan national anthem, as we do at the beginning of any official event. Valerie then steps back into the auditorium with a rather imposing man and his wife. It doesn't take much to see that this broad-shouldered, self-confident, well-dressed Kenyan leader is used to being heard.

The music leader stands with his arm raised for the opening of the anthem. He drops his arm and two unwary flautists chirp off a note before silence descends on the auditorium. We all stand still as statues while the trio of new arrivals is seated near the front, right beside me. While Valerie's uncle isn't the president, it's clear this is a special occasion and the national anthem is sung with special energy.

Valerie introduces me in the moments before the curtain opens and I shake hands with both of the Kamaus. Mr. Kamau leans over to me and whispers rather loudly, "Valerie tells us you helped her survive her flights and gave her courage at a very important time in her journey. We are grateful. You must visit us in Nairobi soon."

I assure him I would like to visit them, and that's the end of our conversation. The curtains open and the enchantment begins.

At the break, other staff come forward to talk with the Kamaus and Valerie. I slip away to purchase a few of the ice cream treats being sold by the sophomore class as they coach the freshmen on fundraising for their senior safari.

We're just beginning the last act when someone's cellphone rudely sounds off nearby. We were given clear instructions not to bring our cellphones, so there is immediate tension in the room. Mr. Kamau calmly reaches into his pocket, takes out his phone, looks at the number, and takes the call.

Right in the middle of the action, he speaks up: "Hello, why are you calling me now?" He listens for a minute. "I am coming now. Meet me in twenty minutes."

He doesn't seem to recognize that the entire production has come to a halt. He simply stands up, waves at the audience, and announces, "It is a matter of national security. Please do not leave this station tonight. Thank you." He then looks toward the actors on the platform. "Well done! Please continue."

Of course, this causes a huge commotion in the audience. Almost every student will be wondering if the crisis involves their families.

I move out into the aisle so he can leave. He motions for his wife to follow and Valerie makes a move to join them. Mr. Kamau waves her back. "Stay," is all he says. The two walk out and the superintendent follows.

It often takes us forty minutes to an hour to reach Nairobi, so if Mr. Kamau is meeting someone in twenty minutes, they will be moving quickly, likely with sirens blaring.

I lean over to Valerie as she sits down with confusion on her face.

"I guess you're staying at my place tonight," I say.

She smiles gratefully and then refocuses on the actors who are trying to regain their concentration and finish their scene. The sixty students involved in the production deserve the standing ovation they get, but as we move to congratulate individual actors I can't help wonder what this matter of national security might be about.

CHAPTER FORTY

Valerie slips out to congratulate her cousin Timothy on his fine performance, but we agree to meet up again in fifteen minutes.

Andrea grabs hold of my arm and asks me if I know what the national security issue might be about. I'm about to ask her how I would know when the superintendent steps out onto the stage with a microphone.

"Greetings, everyone. That was a great performance tonight and the applause is well-deserved. We're always so proud of the students here. I'm sure you couldn't help notice that Mr. Kamau had to leave early." Several students move closer to the stage. "Mr. Kamau requested that no one leave the campus this evening until things are resolved. At this point we've been told that there have been bombings in Nairobi, and perhaps an attempted coup." The superintendent holds up his hands for silence as the crowd noise escalates. "There's no reason to think that we are in danger. For those who need to find accommodation tonight, please join me at the front. Others who can help provide accommodation, please come up onto the platform."

By the time Valerie and I finish catching up, it's past midnight. I loan her some night ware and we work carefully to sleep in the same double bed. I'm one of those sleepers who needs my bedroom to be absolutely still and dark. I need to have the right temperature and the right weight of blankets on top of me. I need the right kind of pillow. Marriage to Bruce has been a huge adjustment. Between sharing my bed, recovering from the jarring rough roads, and recent events, it's not a good night for sleep.

Valerie calls her aunt in the morning to check on their well-being. Mr. Kamau has still not returned, but he is taking care of a situation at the university and he'll be home later that day. All appears calm in Nairobi, although the army is moving everywhere and there are a lot of rallies in the parks. She hopes that most people end up going to church today. Mrs. Kamau asks Valerie to wait until after lunch before trying to come into town.

Valerie isn't sure she has anything appropriate for the dress code at the church. I tell her to go ahead and look through my clothes while I'm showering to see if anything fits.

As I blow dry my hair, I hear a knock. It's Valerie. "I like the black dress and pearls. I bet they look great on you."

The heat creeps up into my ears. I have no words.

"But they're probably not good for church," Valerie continues. "I'm wearing the blue-and-white skirt and blouse. Thanks. It fits almost perfectly."

When Valerie goes into the washroom, I discreetly tuck the black dress and pearls even further into hiding. Neither one of us mentions the item again that day.

Today's service is at the local African Inland Church building. The place is packed as congregants hope to hear some news of the day's events. Many of the local students are listening to small radios on the outskirts of the building. The Rift students aren't supposed to bring these items with them to church.

We sing the usual hymns, listen to a Kijabe hospital choir, watch a Kijabe girls school drama group, observe some local boy scout troop showing us their marching maneuvers, then sing some more. Finally, when the pastor gets up to preach, we hear the news. There may have been an assassination attempt on the president. Nairobi is under curfew and all large assemblies are banned for the next week.

The administration has an emergency meeting in the afternoon to consider what to do about the interims. One year while I was in junior high, all the interims were cancelled because of political unrest. The tension is considerable right now for students whose parents work in Nairobi.

Valerie has no choice but to stay with me. We eat some chicken fajitas over at Andrea's and then head for the student worship meeting. Half of the meeting is singing and the other half is given over to prayer for the country, the families of students, and for the administration as they make decisions.

At the end of the meeting, the deputy superintendent steps up to the front. "Thank you for your prayers. As you know, we've been monitoring the situation in Nairobi closely. It appears that all your families are safe and doing well. In light of the situation, we've had to make the following changes to our interim program.

For those who are impacted, we will be looking at alternatives. The aviation interim, which has our students attending flight school, and then flying around the country out of Wilson Airport, will have to be cancelled." There are significant groans. "The interim scheduled for Kibera slums is also cancelled. The piki interim will be permitted to continue as long as we reroute everything to the west of Kijabe." I hear Shelly screech joyfully somewhere near the back of the hall. "The other interims will also continue, but any routes that take you through Nairobi will have to be adjusted. For those of you who are impacted, please see me. Once your leaders have cleared their new plans with me, you can leave tomorrow."

I have to call up Jason and work out the changes before morning, but it's getting late. I'm not sure whether he goes to bed early. I inform Valerie that I have to make a call and we leave.

I'm still nervous when I dial Jason's number, even though we have worked things out between us. I hear the phone pick up and a woman's voice answers. "Hello, Vicki here."

I'm confused. "Ah, sorry, I was trying to call someone else."

The young woman responds without hesitation. "Were you wanting Jason? I'll get him."

I hear her call Jason and within a minute he answers. I really don't know how to move forward at this point, except as straightforwardly as I can. "Jason, I need to see you tonight."

He hesitates a moment. "Katie, is this you? I'm not sure right now is such a good time."

I can't back off. "Jason, there have been some problems in Nairobi and the interim director says we need to get some new travel plans to him tonight if we hope to leave tomorrow."

"I'm afraid you'll have to take care of it. I'll go along with whatever you come up with." He clears his throat. "I'll explain things when we have time to talk. I need to go now. Thanks for doing this. I owe you."

He hangs up.

Valerie must have seen the look on my face because she moves to my side. "What's wrong, Katie? Is everyone okay? Is something else happening in Nairobi?"

My mind is in a different space, trying not to imagine the man I respect entertaining a woman in his apartment at this time of evening. I assure Valerie that the issue is just a personal one for our piki route tomorrow. I pull out a map of Kenya from my interim leadership folder and ask Valerie to help me plan out a few changes so we can avoid Nairobi.

It's two o'clock by the time we finish detailing the trip and this is going to mean a lot of calling to hosts to change things. Once again, my mind is too active to rest. I'm afraid my tossing and turning keep Valerie up as well. I finally take a blanket and slouch into the loveseat in the living room.

My thoughts of Jason are bad enough, but they have my mind wondering about Bruce. How is Bruce dealing with the women in his world when he's all alone? I want to call him right now, but he's out of communication range for six more weeks. My trust level in men is sinking quickly. I've seen too much of the dark side and now the place of my innocence, Africa, feels tainted.

Emotions shouldn't be the standard for reality, but I'm fully into girl mode now. I reanalyze my entire Sunday conversation with Jason. I replay all our interactions and think again about the looks he gave me. One week ago, he told me of his deep feelings for me. Now, a week later, he's entertaining some other woman in his apartment instead of doing his duty. I don't appreciate having everything dumped on me like this.

My teenage years are long past, but right now my emotional state is surfacing. I'm standing in the bathroom at four in the morning, looking in the mirror and playing with my hair, when Valerie walks in on me. I see the hesitant look in her eyes.

"Katie, like I told you on the plane, we hardly know each other and your life is your life. But something is definitely bothering you. Neither one of us is sleeping. Do you need to talk?"

Tears stream down my face and I turn and hug her. Exhaustion, shock, disillusionment, fear, doubt, anger. A kaleidoscope of emotions play in my heart and I hang on for the ride while Valerie holds me.

For the next two hours, we sip chai and I pour out my life to my new friend. She sits with her back to the fire and listens. At the end, she simply says, "Wow, God is sure trying to do a lot in your life in a hurry."

I appreciate her refusal to pass judgment on me.

CHAPTER FORTY-ONE

The phone rings at seven o'clock. I uncurl from my comfortable perch on the upholstered chair and grab the receiver. "Hello."

The voice is distinctive. "Is this Valerie Njoroge?"

"No, this is Katie Southerland. I will give the phone to Valerie." In Swahili, I tell her to wait a little please: "Ngoja kidogo, taffadali." I hand the phone to Valerie and leave to shower and change for the day ahead.

I absorb the wonderful warmth of the shower before a loud knock sounds on the bathroom door. Reluctantly, I turn off the water.

"Katie, my aunt says all is well now in Nairobi and they sent a taxi for me. I'm going to wash my face at the kitchen sink and then change. The taxi may be here in five minutes so. If I don't see you, thanks for sharing your life with me. I'll be praying for you on this trip. My aunt set up a time for you to meet with us in two weeks. I think you should wear the black dress."

I get out of the shower, dry myself, and get covered. The thought of that black dress makes me very uncomfortable.

I spend the next several minutes on the phone clearing our new route with the assistant superintendent, adjusting our host for one night and cancelling another who happens to be too close to Nairobi. Everyone understands.

The taxi takes another half an hour to arrive, so I'm packed up and ready to go by the time Valerie leaves. The distinctive sound of Jason's bike revs up my driveway and I determine that his business is his business. I will not ask him anything personal. I'm a married woman and have no right to control who he sees or doesn't see. I'm just concerned for his reputation. At least, that's what I tell myself.

My duffle bag of clothing and other goodies was dumped into the support vehicle last night, so all I have is a backpack in addition to my riding gear. Jason pops open his visor and gives me a childlike smile as if he really is getting his dream come true. I nod his way, pop on my helmet, make sure my gloves are snug, and start up my Yamaha XT250. This bike is one nice ride.

By the time we find our space in the gaggle of bikes, we see there's only one bike left to arrive. Shelly's. We toss all extra supplies, including extra wheels, gas, food, tents, and personal gear, onto the support pickup. I trace the new route and schedule for the group, and still Shelly isn't there.

We talk about the tension in the country and ask the guys to be especially careful about doing anything that might get bystanders upset. When we ride through residential areas, we'll need to be especially respectful of what might scare the children or upset the adults. A large group of bikes like ours isn't a common sight here.

I call up Shelly's dorm mom and am told to wait a few minutes. Eventually Shelly answers. I try to be calm. "Shelly, are you still coming? We were supposed to be on the road ten minutes ago."

Shelly gets defensive. "I was told we weren't going until everything got approved. No one called me. I'm trying to put on my makeup."

I try to ease the tension. "Shelly, Shelly… relax. I'm sorry you got missed. I guess we all assumed we would be departing at the same time unless told otherwise. And about the makeup, hey, I understand. As someone said, Helen of Troy didn't launch a thousand ships because she was a hard worker."

"It's not easy being a woman. I'm coming, don't leave. One suggestion, off the record. Please make sure you wear your wedding ring this time."

Fifteen minutes later, we hear Shelly's motorcycle cautiously making its way around the upper field toward us. I warn the guys about the situation and they do well not to overdo their razzing of our late arrival.

When Shelly stops, I tell her to fall in beside me and I'll explain the rest of the day at our first rest stop outside Lake Naivasha. We're going to take it easy on the first day and make one-hour rides the norm. Shelly hands over an extra backpack to the support team driver and then turns and falls into line. We say a short prayer and head out.

Every hour, Jason and I will switch from leader to tail and back again. Everyone else tries to pair up. Shelly rides with me for the first several hours, but as she gets to know some of the guys during the breaks, she begins to change her riding partners. There are inevitable stops to use the facilities in little shops, use bushes at the side of the road, or shelter behind our bikes for as much modesty as possible when nature calls. Somehow we make it work and finish the first three days without incident.

Each day consists of three to four hours of riding, with two or three cultural experiences scattered throughout. We visit carvers and find out about their craft and their home lives. We visit flower growers, a police post, an army barracks, a Dorobo village, a national missionary training facility, and an orphanage.

Most of what we do is build relationships and share love. On the fourth day, we're supposed to stop at noon and help repair a mud and dung hut for a widow who's trying to raise five grandchildren on her own. For some reason, no one informed the widow we were coming. I stop on the edge of the settlement to keep things calm for the people ahead and the guys immediately follow my lead and stop as well. We can see that there are good-sized holes in the side of the crudely built shelter.

Shelly, who has been travelling slightly ahead of me, rides right up to the widow's home. A little boy no more than three years old shrieks in terror and the old woman emerges swinging her machete panga, advancing toward Shelly. The poor teen is so unnerved that she attempts to get off her bike without shutting it down. The bike lurches forward and crashes into the side of the house, creating even more damage, shouts, and swinging from the widow.

One of the guys who knows the language calls out to the woman. The familiar greeting in her own tongue distracts her enough to let Shelly find her feet and run behind me. We all shut down our engines, take off our helmets, and get off the bikes. The young man, who now represents us, steps slowly forward and crouches down with a candy in his hand for the frightened boy.

The boy hesitantly moves toward the reassuring voice of the young man and takes the candy before running back to hide behind the rags his grandmother is wearing for clothing. The old woman sets down her panga and talks. Somehow the young man explains that we're here to help fix up her house. Apparently, some church elders were supposed to have set everything up for us and someone missed this important part of the communication with the widow.

The support vehicle with the two staff members, Jim and Les, leaves in search of the elders and any others supplies we might need for this mission.

Several of the senior guys have been involved in the school's community outreach activities since they were young, so this type of activity is old hat for them. They know all about what to do to get the mud and dung and water mixed and molded and patted into place. Even I remember doing this with my dad fifteen years ago.

In this country, things change very slowly. There might be concrete block houses with mbate (corrugated tin roofing) on most of the plots of land around here, but there are still people who can't provide the basics of a safe shelter, reasonable clothing, and sufficient food so the children can prosper. This grandmother is one of those few. Her only possessions include five large burlap sacks, one to mark the bed of each child. She shares one of those bags. When the three oldest children return home after a day of begging in the village market, we see that their rags are little better than the old woman's.

The widow never offers the children anything to eat. What they gained at the market is what they survive on. The oldest child is around nine years old and this girl brings a small plastic bag of fruit scraps and chapatti pieces to her grandmother and the youngest boy. The grandmother immediately offers them to us.

We've been working hard in the sun, drinking and snacking and looking after the need we thought was obvious: the house. Now we see the larger need. Tears run down my face because of this woman's generous hospitality. All of us empty snacks from our backpacks and dislodge water bottles from our bikes. Together we share a rare moment.

Jason and I have a quick discussion, and then take one of the guys into the village to see what they can find while the boys continue to work. I call Shelly to join me and we sing songs and play games with the five little kids while the widow supervises and shares her advice on the repairs being made to her home.

Jim and Les left us with a five-gallon plastic jerry can filled with water to quench our thirst. This is the only water we have for our mud-dung mix, so it's used sparingly with the dried cow manure and reddish clay the guys bring back to us. The cow herd is less than a mile away and the bikes make quick ferries to transport needed materials.

Although the children look up in wide-eyed wonder, each time the bikes roar back, there's no more screaming. When the nine-year-old girl accepts the offer of a ride, there's no stopping the rest of them. Only the old widow declines to hop on and go for a spin.

The next fascination is looking into the mirrors and cameras each of us have. The children have never seen themselves in a picture before, so we put hats on one child in the group so he can identify himself. Then we switch the hat to someone else until all five can recognize their own images. The grandmother is amazed at this magic we produce.

The support vehicle arrives back with the church elders at about the same time Jason arrives with one of the children still holding onto his waist all her might. We all pitch in to unload the supplies from the vehicle and place them in front of the widow. She begins to dance and singing in the middle of the dirt. The elders join with her and we all have a small revival service in the middle of the dirt and barren patch of land she calls home.

We set down a tarp as the new floor for her home and bring in long-lasting plaster to coat the inside walls. We lay out sacks of fruits, vegetables, rice, and even a few good chunks of beef. We give the widow a Coleman camping cooler to store the food and protect it from nearby scavenging dogs and the merciless heat.

There is some discussion as to whether we should buy the woman a metal jiko (portable heating place) to cook her food over. The elders advise against it, as in this small space a child might get burned. It might also bring violence against the family if someone is jealous and wants to steal it. There's some strange protection in having less than others.

The four of us staff members agree that we will come back during the month-long break between school terms, with others, and try to build this family a proper home of concrete block and tin, so things like a jiko will no longer be an issue.

We finish our work by firelight and flashlight, then decide to pitch our tents around the widow's home. Jim and Les take the elders back home and join us after ten. I'm exhausted, but as team leader I have to make sure everyone is in their tents and that everything is safe. As I bid goodnight to Jason and turn away toward my tent, I'm frozen in place by a snarl like one I heard more than a dozen years ago.

CHAPTER FORTY-TWO

My immediate reaction is to shine my flashlight at the glowing eyes that reflect the dying light of the fire. The hyenas have probably been attracted by the smell of the beef we brought. They are hungry predators, with jaws capable of crushing flesh and bone with ease.

Jason moves immediately to my side with his light and joins me in trying to find out how many nocturnal hunters are in this pack. Several high-pitched staccato sounds and barks emanate from the group. The grunts, giggles, and groans seem to show some sign of distress and discomfort with our lights.

"Aunt Katie, what is that?" Shelly calls out from the tent we're sharing. "Where are you?"

I try to respond as softly as I can. "Shelly. Guys. If you can hear me, stay still. It's hyenas just checking us out. We're handling it. Just pray."

Jason speaks quietly. "I studied these guys during my senior year here at the Rift. They're crafty survivors. Some people think they're scavengers, but they prefer to kill their prey and eat it fresh. The sounds they're making mean they're excited. They know there's something good here, but they're not sure how to get it."

A few loud whoops in the distance announce the approach of others. The tones modulate up and down as the newcomers get closer. Jim creeps toward the support vehicle parked several hundred feet away. When two hyenas appear from underneath it, he backs off and joins Jason and me in a tight circle.

My heart races and my throat feels dry. I lick my lips and whisper to Jason. "Since you know so much about these guys, do you have any ideas on how to get us out of this mess?"

"Don't back down. Don't back up. They're uncomfortable with our lights. Get the other guys with us. Back the pack off by proving the size of our pack. Use the pikis, if we can get to them. They won't know how to handle the noise and lights."

Jim calls to his partner who's still in their tent. "Les, get the big mag light and bring the rest of the guys with you. We have ourselves a situation."

I hear the whimpering of the widow's grandchildren, which seems to draw the interest and attention of the pack as they slowly move in that direction. The volume of their groaning noises increases.

Jason grabs me by the hand and pulls me toward the widow's home. Jim follows close behind. Les begins arousing the guys, and each of them brings their lights along. Shelly is the last to be encouraged out of her tent. She immediately makes her way to my side and stays close. I let go of Jason and take her hand instead.

Five of the guys move with Les toward the pikis and start their engines on a coordinated signal. The children inside the widow's home scream in terror as the bikes rev and move in the direction of the pack. The lead animals immediately back off and scurry several hundred yards away. When the hyenas close ranks, the boys begin to deliberately move forward at a slow pace.

The widow's machete panga lies a few feet from the edge of her home and I pick it up. As the bikes move farther away from us and into the surrounding area, the guys begin to slowly walk in the direction the bikes are taking. Shelly and I are left together near the widow's home.

Jason trails the group, but turns toward me as he goes. Suddenly, he shouts, "Katie, watch out!"

My martial arts training kicks in instinctively and I rotate in time to see a hyena charging toward me. I duck low, swirl, and jab upward with the panga. A loud yelp lets me know that I struck my target. The wounded beast's deadly jaws snap wildly as it turns on me. Shelly is actually closer at this point and the hyena lunges in her direction.

As Shelly screams in terror, I instinctively speed across the few yards of dirt and drive the panga up to the hilt into its throat. The animal writhes in the dirt as I reach over and pull Shelly away.

Jason grabs us both and pulls us away. "Wow!"

The guys who aren't on the pikis had turned in time to see the drama and they surround the dying animal to ensure no more harm is done. The teens on the motorcycles make a quick turnaround after they hear Shelly's screams.

When the group reassembles, and it's clear that the attacking hyena is dead, one of the teens uses his Leatherman knife to cut off the hyena's ear as a trophy for me. I refuse it, but Jason keeps it to provide evidence to anyone who won't believe our story.

With that one simple act, my legendary status at the Rift is secured again. I'm trouble and I attract it. We all circle up to thank God for his deliverance and post guards to sit awake in the support vehicle throughout the rest of the night. Every hour, the guards will change. We're so wired now that it's unlikely any of us are going to sleep. All I want is a hug from Bruce.

Around fifteen of the local villagers join the patrol and keep watch through the night. They assure us that this is very unusual behavior for these hyenas. Some of them hike out into the bushland to drop off the carcass as a warning for any other predators who come this way. The vultures will probably have it picked clean by noon.

Shelly won't stop talking about how I saved her life. Jason sits outside with his back near the door of the widow's home. He keeps with him the young man who knew the language, and this teen is able to bring calm again to the widow's family.

The sun seems to take forever to come up, yet it comes up far too soon for my weary eyes.

After Jim and Les leave to alert the church elders about our adventure, the rest of us hold a group conference over breakfast and decide that we've had enough excitement for one interim. We'll cut out one day of travel.

When the support vehicle gets back with a couple of the elders, we unload the unneeded bulk of our supplies and give our final hugs and prayers to the widow and her children. Through the elders, we promise to return when we can. Final prayers and sermonettes are shared, and then we depart. We wave goodbye at the one hundred or more people gathered to see the newcomers who created so much chaos in their community overnight. In a slowly rising cloud of red dust, we ease our way out of the village and back toward home.

During our lunch break, I call the missionaries at our next stop. That's when we learn of God's providence in providing the hyenas to turn us around.

CHAPTER FORTY-THREE

Tribal warfare broke out early that morning between two groups at just the time we would have been travelling through the area. AK-47s were used the previous evening by cattle raiders and five herdsmen were killed defending their herd. The villagers went on the rampage to exact revenge. Houses were burned, cars and vehicles hijacked, and people put on the run.

The four of us on staff hold another brief conference to consider our options. We call the school to make sure the coast is clear ahead and the superintendent informs us that political disturbances have erupted in Nakuru, where we are scheduled to stop next. We're advised to find an alternate way home and stay overnight somewhere if necessary.

We alert the students and then gather in a circle to hold hands and pray to God for his safekeeping.

Jason asks us to give him time, and then he withdraws to make a call. He waves us over in a few minutes and tells us that he knows someone at a nursing clinic who can set us up for the night while we chart our next moves. It's only an hour and a half away. Another meeting with the students confirms the plan.

Jason smiles. "I'll call Vicki and tell her. She'll be so happy to see me so soon."

Shelly catches the questioning in my eyes as Jason turns away. When I move in her direction, she gives me a very intentional stare. She lifts up her hand and points toward her ring finger. What she's saying is clear, but she has the wrong impression.

I retreat to the women's washroom to wash up. Shelly follows me there.

I stand at the sink washing my hands as she makes her entrance. "Aunt Katie, this must be harder than I think."

"I'm happily married." I point at my wedding ring for emphasis. "Dr. Miller is my friend. I'm just curious at how he's had time to meet some nurse here when he's always so busy."

She doesn't say anymore. We leave together and join the rest of the posse. It takes over two hours of riding across washboard roads and winding pathways, but we do make it to a clinic nestled on a piece of land next to Lake Bagoria.

The woman who meets us there could have stepped out of a modeling magazine. She's modestly dressed in a jean skirt and flowered blouse. She has no ring on her finger. Her face beams with a joy I rarely see. Is it because of Jason?

The good doctor is the first to reach her and he gives her an enthusiastic hug. I catch Shelly looking at me and manage to keep myself busy with something in my backpack while the rest of the crew shakes her hand and thanks her for having us.

I'm bent over inspecting the valve on my rear tire when I hear footsteps behind me.

"Katie, I'd like you to meet Vicki," Jason says.

I turn around and stand up to shake her hand.

"Vicki, this is Katie. The girl I told you about way back in tenth grade. This interim was always one of our dreams."

Vicki's handshake is strong and warm. Her smile is of genuine welcome.

"Come on in," she says. "Jason has been raving about your wild adventures. I'm sure you have more to tell me about this trip. There's some Coke just inside the door over here."

I'm the best professional you've ever seen. Even Shelly has nothing to fault me over. I don't have to say anything about my exploits because the guys exaggerate it all for me.

Just before supper, Vicki gets a radio call from headquarters in Nairobi. She lets us know that it will be safe to get back to Kijabe in the morning via some backroads that crisscross through a lot of tea plantations and coffee fields. We spread out our sleeping bags on the concrete floor and through the rooms of her modest home nearby. She feeds us what she has and we pitch in with the last of our supplies.

With the hard floors, I don't sleep all that well, again. I have fitful thoughts of a wedding, but it isn't mine. I try to pray the images away.

By dawn, most of us are up and ready to get home before the rooster in the yard quits crowing.

We make three stops on our journey back, don't have one flat tire, and coast home just after noon. We honk our feeble horns and cheer as loudly as we can. Most of the students are still in class, so our reception isn't anything memorable.

All the way home I work hard to tell myself that this is a great relationship for Jason. No one needs to talk about us anymore. We don't have to think about old feelings. Times have changed and we can move on freely. I even sing praise choruses to get myself in a good mood.

We meet at Kiambogo one last time to pray and thank God. Jason lifts up the hyena ear in one last sign of God's protection over us, and then we part. I need to wash down the bike, myself, and my thoughts. When all is done, I'm completely at peace. I fulfilled a dream without any compromise. I only wish Bruce was available to talk with.

By the time I return the motorcycle to Pat and Brian, fill them in briefly on God's care for us, and then wander down to the student center, the exaggerated exploits on the trip are taking on proportions I can't even fathom. The younger students drink in every word from the older students.

When I get home, just after ten o'clock, I have no problem falling into bed and sleeping the night away.

* * *

The phone rings way too early. I look at the clock and it isn't even 8:30. I can't get myself to answer. Another ring sounds just before 9:00. And another ring at 9:15.

I finally pick it up. It's Shelly. "Aunt Katie, your problems aren't over."

I have no clue what she's trying to tell me. "Shelly, can this wait?"

"Of course it can wait. I just thought you need to know that she's his cousin. I'll talk to you later." And she hangs up.

CHAPTER FORTY-FOUR

At 9:30, the phone rings again. I refuse to be baited into another conversation with Shelly until my shower is done. I hear two more calls before I finish dressing. I have to get an answering machine. I hadn't thought of one as a necessity when I came to Kenya.

At eleven o'clock, I answer the phone expecting to hear Shelly. It's Chelsea from the infirmary.

"Is everyone okay?" I ask her as soon as she identifies herself.

"Everyone but me. I need to talk when you have time. You were there for me a long time ago. I need you again. I'm finished here in a month and I need to leave well this time."

We make arrangements to meet near the Kedong girls dorms right after lunch. We walk the hall in our two hours together, stopping at the doors to her old rooms and reliving some of her memories in this space. This bright cheery personality hugs me and cries in the laundry room. We step outside and sit on the grassy bank near the basketball court, looking at this imposing structure that's housed thousands of girls over the years.

"I still get so angry sometimes. I need to let go of this. The situation with my dorm mom ignoring my migraine happened ages ago." She rubs her stomach slowly. "I still feel the nausea and pain of hearing her call me about one of her sick girls. I ask God, 'Why didn't someone care for me like that?'" She turns toward me. "Of course, you cared, and maybe you were his angel at the time. I'm realizing that I became a nurse and came back here to try and make sure healing happened everywhere, but I haven't got the strength or energy to heal everyone." She nods at a passing student. "Not when I'm so raw inside. God is reminding me over and over again that he alone is the Healer. Especially of those wounds I can't even see. Wounds of the heart and spirit."

I just listen, my arm around her shoulders as she pours out her heart. The girls who walk by give us a respectful distance and understand that serious heart issues are being dealt with.

Near the end of our time, Chelsea says, "Some days, we missed Mom and Dad more than we can say. And some days, other staff and students didn't know how to fill that void." She wipes away a tear. "God honestly used my wound for so much good. So many good things happened at this school. I used to find it strange that I'd focus on the hard things. Then I realized that those wounds were the places where God wanted to meet me, work with me, make me stronger. I came here to help heal others. I didn't realize that the major impact would be on me."

We pray together, cry together, and then part ways. Somehow the memory of a moment that drew us together for a brief instant, so long ago, came back into our lives to help us with our healing now. God's sense of timing intrigues me.

When I return to my little duplex apartment, Shelly is sitting on the concrete stoop, patting my neighbor's cat.

She looks up as I approach. "This is Simba, if Aunt Janey didn't tell you yet. He's the first kitten I held, on my second day at the Rift, after my Mom and Dad dropped me off. I was only eight back then. He seems so old now."

The young woman examines my face to get a read on my response to her, and somehow I must have passed her test.

"Simba has had quite a few different owners," she continues, "but we've been here for each other. Next year is my last year here and I wonder how he's going to last." She stands up and cradles the cat in her arm as she walks toward me. "Pat him. He loves to purr."

I hold out my hand and pat the grey tabby cat. This is part of the trust test.

Shelly picks up her story. "My favorite place to pat old Simba is over on the titchie swings. I'm too big for them now, but everything just feels right when I'm patting the cat there."

I put my hand on Shelly's shoulder, look the young woman in the eyes, and wait. Tears roll down her face. Right there, she pours out her story of pain and confusion. Her feelings of abandonment, of loss, of dreams she didn't dare to reach for. The façade of trying to be popular around campus. The helplessness at being taken advantage of by an older student while back in Chicago. The pain of being taken advantage of by a male babysitter from her parents' own church while her two younger brothers watched a special movie in the next room. The feelings of worthlessness, dirtiness, guilt, ugliness, and shame that threatened to overwhelm her when she sat alone in the darkness of her room. Emptiness.

"Some days, I just feel like my heart is buried in concrete," she summarizes. "I want to love and be loved more than anything. I'm just afraid to try. I'm not sure I can handle the pain of being rejected anymore."

The cat squirms to get down and I take Shelly in my arms and hug her. In many ways, I relate with how she feels. I join her in releasing the years of pain that bury a wounded heart. It isn't professional, but it is healing.

We move inside for chai and cookies and talk through each of the significant pains. At one point she looks at me and says, "I didn't think anyone would ever be strong enough to handle my pain. I didn't think anyone could care enough to help me with it. But when you killed that hyena, as it was trying to get to me, I knew God had sent me someone strong enough who could help me." She sips her chai. "I've been crying through the past two nights and I couldn't wait any longer. Thanks for being here. I love you."

I hand her more Kleenex and sit back in my chair. I speak slowly and gently. "Girl, you are one of the most courageous young women I know. Sharing this is as brave as anything I've ever done."

She blots her tears away.

"In our weakest areas, God breaks us and builds his strength. That's what he's done in me." I pat her hand. "That's what he's doing in you. He just wants you to remember that you're never alone. But remember what I've learned through my own pain. There is only one Savior, and it isn't me."

We talk well into the evening, after I call her dorm mom for permission. Both of us take significant strides in our walk with God and with each other. Shelly wants to know more about my relationship with Bruce, and I'm happy to tell her all the good parts of what it's like to be loved by a man that God sets apart for you.

While we're curled up on pillows, sipping chai near the fireplace, Shelly dares to broach the subject of Jason and me again. "Aunt Katie, it really helps me to understand that you are so in love with your husband. I haven't had to sort out the 'first love' feelings you talk about between you and Dr. Miller. It seems strange that you react so strongly if there's nothing still there."

The heat in my cheeks isn't from the chai or the fireplace. "It's strange for me, too, Shelly. I left this place with so many unresolved feelings, and they all seem to be coming to the surface at the same time. I'm not sure which feeling belongs to which experience. I came back partly to heal, but healing is much messier than I imagined."

Shelly sips her chai and looks into the dancing flames. "Why did you react so strongly to Vicki?"

I stand up, close the curtains, and fill a glass of water. "I was confused. I thought Dr. Miller was a good man. When I called him, he had a woman I didn't know in his apartment late at night. I let myself think the worst."

"But she's his cousin."

"You told me that Vicki was his cousin, but neither Dr. Miller or Vicki told me that. And I can't figure out why. I've doubted the meaning of our friendship. I've questioned my own integrity. I don't even know anything about her."

Shelly stretches out and sets her cup on the floor. "She's three years younger than he is. She attended here and graduated after you left, so you never met her. She's been serving at her clinic for a year." She moves into a cross-legged position. "She's the one who alerted Dr. Miller to the pediatric opportunity at the medical center. She came to meet her cousin for the first time at the drama, and then had to stay overnight when the national security issue arose. She is beautiful, though, isn't she?"

I nod. "That she is. Like a model. It's funny how unmet fantasies creep out of your heart when you least expect them. I guess I need to talk this out and let it go."

The rest of the week is an interesting mix of meeting mostly senior girls. They present problems like how to set standards with their boyfriends at the senior safari in Mombasa the following week, how to forgive friends who steal their boyfriends, how to fit in at college in the coming year, how to deal with spiritual warfare, how to deal with sexual identity confusion, and how to help parents to let them grow up when they have to go back to living with them for longer periods of time.

Toward the end of the week, I notice a trend toward other, deeper concerns. How to deal with anger toward the Muslims who trapped one girl's parents and two young brothers inside a bathroom and burned the house down. How to trust God when your favorite national playmate is beaten to death by the police in his town. How to let go of all your childhood memories when your parents have to flee during tribal clashes and you never go home again. How to deal with being raped by a group of young men in your tribal area, when you never tell your parents. How to understand God's love after spending an entire vacation working in a refugee camp where most of the people, including children, are starving to death. How to deal with your home church in the States when they drop your family's support due to their own economic situation.

Needless to say, I'm emotionally, mentally, spiritually, and physically drained by the time the weekend rolls around. The seniors are heading off on safari to the Southern Palms Hotel near Mombasa. Administrators stay in constant touch with Mr. Kamau to assess the security situation in case this trip of a lifetime has to be cancelled. The buses leave on schedule for the coast, with Andrea yelling like a maniac out the window.

Senior safari is one event I dreamed of experiencing until the day I left the Rift at the age of sixteen. This is Andrea's second chance, and I'm jealous. There's still more healing to deal with.

My task for the coming week is to meet with the staff and visiting consultants who will be putting on the senior re-entry seminar in another two weeks. Someone has to keep the programs running on campus while others are carrying out their duties from a distance. This is a team of over one hundred dedicated staff committed to caring for the needs of some five hundred students, most of whom are sons and daughters of missionaries.

The Saturday when the seniors are away is dedicated to one last outreach. I join the Naivasha prison ministry team, which does manicures and pedicures for the residents of the women's prison. Even the male guards want to have their hands and feet done. It's clear that these ladies aren't used to being pampered like this.

Others are involved in the men's prison. There's singing, volleyball, and testimonies, and the influx of students seems to provide some good merriment for those locked in these dreary enclosures. Several of the prisoners become believers through a chaplain who works there. Our visit seems to remind them that they are not forgotten.

Dozens of other outreach teams move in small groups to impact the community with practical helps so that the love of Jesus is not only verbalized, but lived out in real life as well. During this day of watching God move in the hearts of tough individuals, I realize again how good God is. I take daily walks to thank him for his goodness to me.

On one of my solitary walks, thinking through the issues of the week, planning for the re-entry seminar, and birdwatching, my senses grip me. I'm being watched and followed. At a bend on the isolated muram-covered Kijabe town road, I turn quickly and see a long forgotten figure advancing quickly in my direction.

CHAPTER FORTY-FIVE

Every time I saw this sorceress in the cow skin dress, she appeared at ominous times of trouble. She was hovering overhead on a fallen tree when Andrea broke her arm at the falls. She was there just before a major rainstorm almost washed our family car away, while we were visiting at Kariuki's, in Kijabe town. She was in Mai Maihu, the town right below our station on the valley floor, after horrendous tribal clashes forced the creation of a displacement camp. When she was young, her aunt ordained her for succession with powerful dark powers. A leopard, a rooster, and a snake were all part of that ceremony. And now, in the middle of the road, a rooster sits calmly on her head. I'm sure the snake and leopard travel nearby.

When I was sixteen, I remembered her as someone who was my age or younger. Now she appears older, wizened, thin, an adult with the life sucked out of her. But I'll never forget those eyes.

As she approaches me, I realize there is no one else nearby. Never before has she appeared and stayed. Always, when seen, she ran. Probably, most wise people turned and ran as her power grew. But I stay.

When she's ten feet away, she stops and looks into my eyes. I feel a strange stirring in my spirit, but I'm completely at peace. There is only darkness through her enlarged pupils.

Suddenly, I feel a shift and her pupils constrict to normal size. She smiles. "Atiriri, Wimwega."

I have never heard her speak before.

I respond, "Eh, dimwega muno."

She takes the rooster from off her head as if it were a hat. She drops it onto the ground and shoos it away with her foot. It runs off into the bush.

"Greetings to the one who rides with leopards." She speaks good English.

"Greetings to the one who walks with leopards."

She seems to ponder that for a moment. "You have big power. You have been gone many days."

"How is your aunt? The one who chose you."

She looks puzzled. "She was long ago eaten by the leopard. I am alone. I must soon choose a successor. The leopard is hungry again."

My mind begins to fit the puzzle pieces together. I have to ask. "Do you mean that you must choose a successor so that you can be eaten by the leopard?"

"It is the way of life. The powers demand it. I have come to choose you as my successor. The leopard and the snake and the rooster are waiting."

Although my heart races, I still feel inner peace. Somehow I know how to respond. "The power inside me is greater than the power inside you. This power will not accept what you offer."

For a second, the woman's eyes reveal a flicker of childlike hope. "It is truth then. In my first days, I tried many times to use the powers against you and the others. Even in these last days we have not been successful." She looks toward the bush and speaks quickly. "Give me this power and release me from mine."

We both hear the menacing snarl deep in the bush, less than a hundred yards away. I see the fear come back into her eyes. I grab her hand, turn her away from the bush, and tell her to speak the name "Jesus" quickly.

The snarl grows louder, and closer, and I urge her again. "Speak it. Jesus!"

Her lips move slowly as she considers the consequences of my command.

The snarl suddenly explodes from the edge of the road and she screams out the name as one falling from a great height: "Jeeesuuuus!"

I hold her and pray, not daring to take my eyes away from the bush. The slithering form of the snake passes along the edge of the grass and moves back into the bush. The snarl of the leopard diminishes to a low growl. I assume that the faint fluttering in the trees is the rooster.

I continue to pray as I hold the hand of the woman wrapped in cow skin. I stand between her and the bush as we walk along the road toward the school campus. I pray out loud, frequently calling on Jesus for his deliverance. Although we hear frequent noises in the bushes, we make it to the gates without a problem.

When the security guards see who I'm with, they back away, urging me to run. The leopard smells their fear and snarls viciously. The woman tenses up but continues to move forward as she obeys my commands.

I tell the gatekeepers to call the church elders and the pastors, and to tell them to come to my home immediately. The cow skin dress this girl has been wearing for the past fourteen or fifteen years is starting to disintegrate under my touch. I hear groans and whimpering from her as she walks.

By the time we reach my apartment, the garment is in tatters. I move her inside quickly and lead her into the bathroom. She probably hasn't bathed in all these years, and in a closed space it smells like it. She stands quietly as I set the temperature and pressure for the shower. I tell her to remove the shreds of her garment and stand under the water; she does so without thought of embarrassment. I hand her a bar of soap and instruct her to rub it all over her skin and then to rinse it off under the water.

I walk outside the bathroom and leave her on her own. She continues to do what I asked for the next ten minutes, and in that time she begins to find her voice of joy. I'm not sure I would call it singing, but there's definitely a change in what I hear.

I finally knock on the door, open it, and try to ignore the flooded floor that greets me. I reach over and shut off the tap. She looks disappointed, but moves to the next phase of this new ritual. I hand her a towel and tell her to dry all the water off her body. Again I withdraw, this time to find some clothing that might fit.

The former sorceress emerges from the bathroom in all her glory, just as I'm returning with a sweatshirt and skirt. I tell her to put them on, but she holds out her hands and says that I must first pray a prayer to her new master. Many pastors and missionaries have prayed spiritual warfare prayers against this sorceress, so I'm not sure exactly how this is all happening. No one has given me instructions, but I pray and ask Jesus to take control of his new servant.

When I'm done, she insists that I must put on her garments, so I do. I sit her down and prepare some chai and bread with butter. She eats hungrily. As we prepare to refill our cups, a knock at the door signals the arrival of the pastors and elders.

CHAPTER FORTY-SIX

The next three hours are an education for us all. The pastors and elders move from a high level of suspicion and doubt about the woman's story, to telling a stream of stories about all this woman has done to bring evil in this community, to expressing praise toward me, and finally to a time of prayer and thanks toward God.

The greatest thing for me is to see the increased faith in men of God as they realize how strong the healing power of God really is. For me, it confirms that the good work God began in me a long time ago is a work he will bring to completion in his own time, and in his own way, no matter what the circumstances look like at any given moment.

The glowing woman agrees to accompany the elders to meet with a group of ladies who will care for her needs. I'm grateful for this Kenyan community which so willingly displays the love of Christ for their new sister. I can't imagine how complicated my life would have been if I was left to deal with the consequences of my encounter with this woman who used to walk with leopards.

Although I'm free from the primary responsibility of care for this woman, our lives have not been disentangled yet.

That night, I have strange dreams about a hungry black leopard looking for its next meal. When it can't get the woman, it starts to deliberately move in my direction. Twice I find myself rising up to pray for peace of mind and heart and for protection. When the morning comes, I'm grateful that the One in me is greater than the one who is in the world.

The return of the senior students is a noisy affair. Andrea drops by to let me know that she used a jet ski for the first time. She has also been wind surfing. She's picked up a slight burn from too many hours snorkeling and playing beach volleyball. And she stuffed herself at every buffet, since the hospitality package included full board, everything except ice cream included.

Just before leaving, my good friend borrows some scissors and cuts off the wristband which gave her all the privileges at the hotel.

"The best thing about safari," she tells me, "is that I had so many chances to talk to the seniors. These young adults are going to be world-changers. I can't wait to hear how God lives out his love through them."

She leaves, still smiling, and I'm able to release her to her joy. We each have a separate journey to fulfill.

The first of the exams begins and most of the week involves younger students concerned about upcoming family issues that they want to talk through before going home.

Senior Sunday is the last church service of the year, and it's only weeks away. It features some of the incredible giftings of the Grade Twelve students, including music, speaking, drama, and a photo slideshow of their greatest moments. I celebrate with the group in the cafeteria and enjoy some great lasagna. I realize again the incredible magic that happens in this kitchen to produce between four and five hundred meals three times a day.

Bruce finally comes through with an email that afternoon. I'm opening it when I hear a knock at the door. The back of my neck tightens. I'm consumed by irritation that I can't even have a moment to enjoy time with my husband.

I open the door and Pastor Jeremiah , the leader of the local community church, steps back from the porch. "Memsap, come quickly. It is the girl you brought to us. We must hurry."

I recognize that if this pastor invites me, without the traditional greetings, we're in for something challenging. I slip on my tennis shoes and begin to pray silently as we move into a slow jog.

Shelly sees me jogging and rushes out to join me. "What's happening?" she asks as calmly as if we are out for a stroll.

"I don't know," I huff. "The pastor told me to come. I think there's an emergency with a sorceress who just came to Jesus. Tell Aunt Andrea I may be missing the Sunday night fellowship tonight."

Shelly tells me she'll be praying and then drops out of our run.

Pastor Jeremiah and I move past the field, past the Centennial Hall, past the final dorms and staff homes, and then through the gates and over to the local church. I can smell the acrid odor of smoke before I see the grey curling plume beside the worship center.

My legs are turning to rubber and my lungs giving out as we slow our pace. I'm glad that I've had some time to adjust to the 7500-foot altitude here, but somehow I need more oxygen right now. God is keeping me desperately dependent on him in every way I can imagine.

A large crowd of several hundred people are expressing themselves at high volume. Screeches and howls pierce through the chants and singing, adding to the chaos. Pastor Jeremiah doesn't let up until we reach the outskirts of the group. He begins to shout and push his way through the group. I huddle in behind and try to squeeze through the wake he creates.

When we emerge at the front, I see the old, wizened former sorceress—except now she appears as young as I am. Though she was once bound by the leopard, snake, and rooster, she's dancing around a fire and waving her hands wildly in the air. She doesn't even seem to notice my arrival.

Several other women have tossed things into the fire and are now writhing on the ground. Immediately a group of believers gather around them and pray out in loud desperation. In minutes these women are pulled to their feet; they join the former leopard woman in a dance of joy and ululation. Salvation here is a lot more chaotic than anything I've ever witnessed before.

Pastor Jeremiah turns to me. "The leopard sorceress is burning all her images and has called on the community of women to burn theirs as well. Many are coming and the demons are screeching and leaving the figurines where they've been hiding. It is like the book of Acts. She told me that you must be here to pray over the people, because the power in you is greater than hers. She also is asking for baptism and she wants you to give her a new name."

The two of us stand side by side for another twenty minutes as the former sorceress dances around the fire and others cast their amulets, charms, potions, and carved figures into the flames. As if by some unseen signal, the former sorceress freezes in mid-step, stops, and turns in my direction. A huge smile spreads across her face and she trots over to me, enveloping me in a hug. She grabs my hand and starts skipping around the fire, pulling me along. She waves at everyone as loud applause spreads spontaneously through the group.

Others step forward and grab our hands, and soon a large circle is moving slowly but deliberately around the fire. Pastor Jeremiah finally steps into the middle of the circle near the dying inferno and calls for our attention. He announces in Swahili, Kikuyu, and English that the baptism is ready. The crowd drops their hands and move around to the other side of the worship center. After a twenty-minute message, and a series of prayers by a few elders, the beaming new believer is called forward. Ten others line up behind her.

When her immersion is completed, I'm called forward and asked to pronounce her new name. I've been praying desperately for the past ten minutes, and the only name that comes to mind is Miriam.

When I announce my choice, the young woman who used to walk with leopards raises her hands to the heavens and shouts, "I am Miriam." The believers around her cheer as we hug and celebrate. I almost feel sorry for the other ten who are being baptized without the same reception.

As all of us dance, the rain begins to fall ever so lightly.

The crowd cheers again, because rain is always a sign of God's blessing. For the past years, the rain has not been good. The dust is deep on the fields and roads. The pattering on the tin roof nearby is a rhythm of hope for a weary people. The sprinkling lasts only fifteen minutes, but the timing is significant.

As the ululations and cheering quiet, Miriam turns to me and warns me clearly: "The leopard has been waiting many years for me and for you. He is very hungry. We cannot sleep lightly or walk blindly." She looks over my shoulder into the forest. I hear a distinct and angry snarl. It sends shivers down my spine. I look into Miriam's eyes, and she's smiling. "Inside you is greater."

Dozens of women begin to shuffle food out of the church's stone-block kitchen. The celebration lasts until the sun dives for the crater of Mount Longonot. Dazzling pinks, purples, oranges, and blues blend across the sky. It seems that God is displaying his glory in every way he can.

* * *

The experience with Miriam is further proof that life in community out here can be unpredictable. I finally get another email from Bruce, but his letter ends up being a single sentence telling me to read the attachment, since he'll be away for five days. When I look for an attachment, I find nothing.

This last half of the graduating students' final term seems a washout with interim, safari, and now re-entry coming up. Complications in second term pushed several of these events and activities to third term, and now the crunch is on with exams and graduation just around the corner. The coming weekend will feature re-entry seminars, the following will be senior Sunday, and then the last will be graduation. I begin to realize how quickly time is passing.

I'm walking the mile with Andrea when I finally have to clear the air. I tell it to her straight: "No one ever told me how hard the staff work at this place to try and make sure students are ready for their next steps. What am I going to do for this retreat?"

"I'm sure there's a folder from the past years," she says. "It didn't seem like that big a deal when I went through it. What do you know so far?"

I stop to tie my shoelace. "We're going to the Southern Baptist Retreat Center at Limuru."

"Sounds good so far." She slowly backpedals as she waits for me. "Have you ever done one of these before?"

"Yes." I resume my pace. "But it was over a week and we did these major tests and individual counseling sessions. We dealt with all the grief and loss and identity stuff."

Two friendly Jack Russell terriers rush to the edge of the road, barking and bouncing and wagging for all they're worth. I take a moment to scratch behind their ears before continuing.

"I've got two days. If I do this wrong, I could mess everyone up."

Andrea points out a hawk circling high overhead. "I assume you still believe in God."

"Of course, but what does God have to do with this?"

"Ah, there's the rub."

After I finished the circuit with Andrea, I do another circuit with God.

* * *

The weekend goes fine. I lead one session on grief and loss and another on developing realistic expectations around values, behaviors, and everyday life. Andrea leads a few sessions that involve narrative therapy; we talk about anger, identity, depression, finding a church, finances, and sexuality. And God is in the middle of it all.

At one point, we break the students into small groups and deal with the issue of what it means to be home. What does home feel like? What does it look like? What does it smell like? Who is there at home? This is a lot harder than it seems on paper and I find myself choked up trying to be part of the discussion group. We also do a session on examining what kind of unseen luggage we're carrying onto the plane with us. That, too, proves to be a little emotional. This is the kind of interaction that probably would have been helpful when I left at sixteen. Then again, maybe I wouldn't have been ready to hear it back then.

Repatriation to the parents' passport culture, or to an alternate culture, is a significant process. The seniors are a tired bunch and I'm not sure how well they understand the importance of the information they're getting. One day, the notes and ideas we're planting will come to life.

Other staff members have a lot of group participation activities to help socialize everyone toward their upcoming college experience. It takes a team effort to make the weekend work and I think we're all sufficiently exhausted by the time we get back to the Rift campus late Sunday afternoon.

The first thing I do upon reaching the relative tranquility of my apartment is to check my email. Bruce has finally responded to my alert that there was no attachment on his last message. This time, the attachment pops right up. I can't believe what I read.

Subject: I'm coming.
Since you didn't get my attachment last time, this might be a bigger surprise than I thought.

Last Saturday, I sat down for a review with the other commanders. I've done all that I've been asked and had some great experiences, but I can feel in my heart that I'm done here. The big brass have agreed to recognize me for my combat experience and to allow me to retire with honors. I'm going to be put on a leave of absence for a year, but I can leave immediately. I plan to be on a plane coming in your direction within the month. Hope you can find a place and an assignment for me. I've contacted the mission and they say there is a one-term opening for a biology and physical education teacher. They could also use a soccer coach. All of this is right up my alley. God is good.

CHAPTER FORTY-SEVEN

The rest is all the usual mush, which Bruce is becoming increasingly sophisticated at. He has my heart thumping as fast as if I just sprinted around the mile.

I'm flying high the rest of the week and hardly notice the goodbyes I'm saying. The one that does get through to me is Shelly, but I'll see her next term, so we both shrug off the separation with a hug and dry eyes.

The last Friday of term is a night dedicated to the graduating students showing off their talents to parents and family members who have come in for the graduation ceremonies on Saturday. It's a late night full of laughs and good memories. It's also a painful night, with all the reminders of what I missed in my final years here.

I haven't had any time to interact with Jason in the past ten days, so I'm pleasantly surprised when he sits down beside me when the evening starts. I can tell fairly quickly that his choice to sit with me is intentional.

"Katie, I have to talk with you sometime soon," he says.

I shift myself around to look into his face a little easier. "Okay, what's up?"

He looks me in the eyes and then turns away. He rubs his hands together as if he's nervous. It's like he's that tenth-grade boy I once knew, not a confident professional surgeon saving the lives of children.

"Can you take a quick walk with me at the break?" he asks.

The hesitancy in his voice alerts me that something deeper is going on. I, on the other hand, don't hesitate to say yes. My curiosity builds through the first half of the program.

When the first break is announced, we make our way outside and stroll through the old elementary school playground. The stars are out in full majesty.

The full moon is about to roll up into the sky. The slight breeze swishes through the leaves in the treetops and bushes. The faint smell of jasmine lingers. It's a perfect night.

"Katie, I've already told you how much I missed you," Jason starts. "When you didn't respond to my letters, I felt like my heart had been ripped out. I didn't want to go to junior or senior banquet with anyone else." He looks up at the moon and then turns to stare into my eyes. "On senior night, they flashed a picture of you and me on Kiambogo Porch looking out at a sunset and I nearly got up and ran. In fact, I walked right up here to the tire swing and sat on the tree limb over there. It was the first time I really cried."

I reach over and take his hand. "I'm so sorry."

I pull him over to a bench and we sit. Jason looks down at our hands together and puts his other hand on top.

"I thought I was over you. I realize that I need to be. I know you're happily married. I just need to have this part of me healed up." He eases his hand out of mine and puts it over his heart. "Please tell me why you never wrote back. I need to know. I thought we had something special."

My heart agonizes at how I hurt my friend. I reach out and cradle his hand in both of mine. "Jason, of all the guys at school, I cared about you the most. It was something special." I can see him searching my eyes for words of life. "Of all my regrets, not writing you back has been near the top. When I left the Rift, I was angry and sad and so focused on what I was losing that I didn't stop to think about what others might be losing." I stand up and put my hand on his shoulder. "When my mom dropped your letters off on my bed, I could feel my heart tearing in two. I hate to admit this, but I never even opened them. I knew it would hurt too much."

Jason's wince nearly chokes me into silence, but I have to explain myself, for his sake and mine.

"For a while, I didn't read anything from Sarah, Andrea, or anyone else. I didn't open up an email account for a year because I thought I couldn't handle hearing about all the good times you were having without me." I sat down beside him again and try to look back at him. "I was mad at God, at my parents, at the world. By the time I surfaced again, I had made some really poor decisions in my relationships."

Now I look at him for life and grace. He's looking down at his feet.

"God was gracious in giving me Bruce to help me through some really dark days," I finish. "I really am sorry about hurting you."

The good doctor turns toward me and squeezes my hand. "So it wasn't anything I did or said that turned you off?"

"Of course not. You were the kind of guy I always dreamed of loving. Life just didn't let it happen." I do my best to smile. "There must be a million girls with racing hearts whenever you walk by. You're charming, caring, witty, good-looking, and in your profession you will always be wanted."

Jason lets go of my hand and stands. I join him face to face but take a step back.

"So here's the million-dollar question," he says. "If you were still single, would you consider me?"

"In a heartbeat."

"That's all I need to know," he says with a smile. "Let's go back and finish this night. I think I can live again."

The rest of the program has us laughing and smiling. Something has definitely cleared between us. One of the seniors has the hyena ear and uses his gifts of storytelling and exaggeration to draw too much attention to me. Jason elbows me gently in the ribs as the story continues and I put in a dig that he'll remember. I hear him chuckling beside me and I breathe easier again.

Instead of going home, I stay up talking with a group of girls and end up sleeping at Andrea's dorm overnight. I hear the rains begin to fall a little harder.

I slip out of Andrea's dorm at dawn without even taking a shower. The cotton mist has embedded itself in the forested hills and refuses to let the sun through. The foggy blanket embraces Mount Longonot and shrouds its majestic crater from those who daily scan its rocky crags. The chill-bearing cloud hovers over a Rift Valley still filled with withered maize, wilted beans, and endless dust.

* * *

Mid-July is here and the elements show no mercy on the departing pilgrims longing for one last glimpse of their beloved countryside. Shivering and weeping through their final hugs and farewells gives no strength to the waning sun that once freely scorched the land without restraint.

An auger buzzard with a five-foot wingspan hovers watchfully overhead, then plunges futilely after a darting sparrow. The Kenyan guards pass cheery greetings as they hunch by their gates. The season of the reaping has come, ushering in the chill harvester of death. The reaper claims the sick and the elderly. Churches will be filled with weeping survivors. Fresh mounds of earth will be created while drums pound out the message of sorrow in an endless rhythm. Yet for those who feel the death of eighteen years of effort and commitment, there will be no drums. There is only the releasing of clasping hands, the tearing of blended hearts.

I push through the mists across an empty rugby field. A lone figure, my hummed songs accompany tears streaming down my puffy cheeks and quivering lips. A commandeered swing provides a restful pendulum for my desperate heart.

Outside, this day is designed to be filled with celebration. Inside, there will be numbness and pain. There will be no release from the step to come. Strength is an illusion. Comfort is a dream. The end of a journey has begun.

Permanently leaving a place is like facing one's own execution. You move toward your destiny in numb shuffles, controlled by external forces you feel powerless to stop. I'm just glad it isn't me leaving today.

My neighbor Janey stops me outside my door. "Did you hear about the excitement here last night? When I got home from senior night, I saw a black shadow in the hedges, moving quickly." She points at the hedges twenty feet from my front step. "I got in my door fast and called the guards. They came with two dogs and chased off a leopard. I can't imagine why a leopard would be here on campus with so many people around."

I remember Miriam's warning about the hungry leopard and pray hard for God's ongoing protection. There's no point in trying to tell Janey a whole lot of my story. She's leaving tonight for her year-long home assignment. The story of the leopard girl in the cow skin sounds farfetched even to me. If I hadn't lived it, I would have dismissed it as the blithering of an overactive imagination.

I thank her, shower, and prepare myself for graduation. I choose a new white skirt and black cardigan to go with my pearl earrings and necklace. I blow-dry and brush out my blond hair and am satisfied by the resulting ensemble.

Andrea confirms my choice the moment we meet. "Katie, you are so adorable. If I didn't know better, I'd say Bruce was showing up today."

Andrea looks over at Jason and her tongue is about to engage. I hold up my hand to her mouth.

"Don't you dare," I say. She raises her eyebrows and attempts to back away from my hand. "Yes, Bruce is on his way."

This stops her cold, and from then until the ceremony starts we rattle on about Bruce and what this might mean for us and for the school.

During the ceremony, we weep together through the songs "I Miss the Rains Down in Africa" and "Mayibuye." We swell with pride at the future world-changers who stride across the stage. We listen hard to try and apply the message.

Some of these grads are heading off to Harvard, Yale, Cornell, Stamford, and MIT, while others are heading off to Bible colleges and universities and colleges closer to where their families and friends are anchored. Some are repatriating to their family homes in Korea, Congo, Kenya, England, Europe, and even Australia for other educational and vocational options.

A deep knot forms in my heart as these idyllic teens launch out. God is only just beginning to refine them in the crucible of life. The pains ahead will be soul-crushing for many of them. More than anything I want to reach out and protect this next generation from all the pain ahead, but that isn't my role. For many relationships, we are only here for a season.

My chest is tight and shoulder muscles sore as families come together after graduation. Sobbing goodbyes mix with hugs and pictures, tears and waves. It all grows blurry as tears blot out my vision and convulsions shake me to the core.

I'm standing on Kiambogo Porch watching the sunset over Mount Longonot when I hear footsteps behind me. I know whose they are without looking. "It's another A+ sunset," I say.

"So it is," Jason responds.

CHAPTER FORTY-EIGHT

There must be twenty minutes of silence as the two of us watch the last of the colors drain from the sky. The faint kisses of air brush our cheeks and dissipate. A few swallows dart up and down, stitching the night to the horizon, but they vanish into the stillness. The crickets begin to call, accompanied by a bush baby.

The vehicles of departing families and staff have long ago left dust clouds behind on the drought-infested road. Tired survivors of the term are nestled away in their homes replaying the events of the day, playing games, or just curling up by a fire and catching up on their reading. I can almost smell the rainclouds closing in.

Jason and I are alone in the dark. He finally breaks the silence. "I always wanted to do this without getting a demerit for it. You were beautiful today."

"Bruce is coming this week," I say without hesitation. "He's been given an early honorable discharge. Tonight I want to say goodbye to you in a way we won't regret."

Again the silence lingers. Five minutes. Ten.

Finally Jason eases himself off the railing he's been resting against. He draws up to his full height. I step back from the railing as well and try to see his eyes in the dim light of the lone bulb near the chaplain's office.

"Thanks for being honest with me. Thanks for not running. Thanks for giving me a friendship I'll never forget." He looks away at a bat swooping through the shadows at the edges of the basketball court. "I would love to meet Bruce and find out what kind of man is lucky enough to have you for a lifetime. God gave us this time for healing. While the healing isn't over yet, at least it's begun." He turns toward me. "Please let me walk you home one last time. I promise I won't make things awkward for you in the future. I just needed to hear you say that I'm still okay."

We hug and we cry, but it's like a brother and sister letting go. The walk home is slow and meandering, as if we don't want it to end. At the door, we pray for each other and give one final hug.

I shut the door and lean against it, sobbing. Goodbyes are never easy.

One minute later, as I'm sliding to the floor, I hear the terrible snarl of the leopard and Jason's scream of terror.

Without hesitation, I roll away from the door and crawl toward the fireplace. I reach for the machete panga I keep for chopping firewood. As quick as I can manage, I leap to the doorway and fling it open. There's nothing but night—and the hiss of a nearby snake.

Then I hear Jason's yell. He's down the driveway fighting off the hungry cat. I run out in my socks and hardly notice the sharp gravel digging into the soles of my feet. I hear the struggle and my screams join in the deathly tussle.

Jason lies prone under the leopard's attacking fangs and claws. As lights on neighboring houses flip on, I reach the scene screaming and swing the panga down onto the back of the black cat. The leopard turns to focus its wrath and vengeance on me.

I hear Jason yelling, "No, Katie, run!"

But it's too late. I'm committed. The cat howls in agony from my stabs and slashes, but it musters up its weight to knock me to the ground. I use a rollaway technique Bruce taught me in martial arts and keep swinging the panga. The sharp blade connects and sticks. The cat is so strong that, when it pulls away, my weapon goes with it.

Right at that moment, the moon makes its appearance. I barely make out the handle plunged deep in the leopard's shoulder. Its golden eyes and glistening fangs are a terrible sight, its guttural howl a terror to my ears and heart.

Jason lies still just behind the cat, and when it turns toward him I reach down to grab a handful of gravel and launch it as strongly as I can. The strike gets the attention of the cat and it begins to prowl in my direction.

The panga hampers the cat significantly. I back away slowly to draw him away from Jason. However, the animal sees that I have no weapon left. My backward movement suggests fear and gives the beast courage to resume its attack.

One of the neighborhood German Shepherds runs quickly across the lawn to charge the leopard. As the leopard turns to face its new attacker, I lunge forward and jam the panga in deeper. The leopard catches my elbow with its fangs. Both of us scream in pain as we fall to the ground.

And then it's all over. Whether it's the dog, the panga, or an act of God, the life goes out of that cat and it lies still beneath me. I stagger over to Jason just as someone runs up and catches hold of me.

The next thing I know it's day and the face of a Kenyan nurse is looking down on me. "Jambo, Mrs. Southerland. So, you have delivered us of the Kijabe leopard. It is good that you will live to tell your children about it."

I only have one thing on my mind. "How is Jason? Dr. Miller?"

The nurse smiles. "Thanks to you, he is alive. His condition is quite serious. He has been taken to Nairobi for emergency surgery. I think that he will be taken back to the United States to complete his recovery."

"Can I see him?"

She smiles again. "You must first recover. There are serious injuries to your arm and leg. Also, you have a visitor."

I close my eyes and wait for the upcoming lecture from Andrea. I can almost preach it to myself word for word.

Instead a man's voice speaks over the top of my head. "So I come halfway across the world and my wife tries to kill herself."

Bruce has to physically restrain me as I attempt to get off the bed and launch myself at him. He pushes my shoulders back into the bed and kisses me passionately. The intense pain in my leg and arm finally force me to surface for air.

The love of my life's expression is a mix of joy and concern. He speaks quietly as I hook my left hand around his neck. "Are you sure you're okay, Katie? First a hyena, and now a leopard. The authorities are going to send you home so they can keep some of their wildlife for tourists like me."

The next four days in the Kijabe hospital are uncomfortable but bearable. Bruce moves into my place and spends most of his free time playing guard at the door of my hospital room. Members from both the missionary and national community drop by to see me. Many never believed the Kijabe leopard even existed. Miriam hovers outside the door and takes advantage of slack times to come in, thank me, and pray for me. She tells her story to Bruce in bits and pieces.

"I have to apologize to you," he says to me with wide eyes. "When you used to read me those journal entries about the girl in the cow skin and the leopard, about all the strange adventures you had, I was skeptical. It's amazing to see this all for myself. You're more amazing than I thought."

A week after the encounter with the leopard, I move back into my own place. Bruce becomes my personal nursemaid and Andrea is a frequent drop-in. As is Miriam.

Bruce has been busy even when he hasn't been visiting me in the hospital. He and Andrea exchanged my double bed for a queen size. With the extra-large mattress, there's barely any room to squeeze by the walls. The dresser now sits in the hall, making it tough to walk through. The closet and dresser are overstuffed now that Bruce has brought along his stuff. Life is a little cramped with two of us in an apartment built for one.

Two days later, as I lie on the couch stretching and watching Bruce make some of his special waffles, he turns to me and asks, "Do you remember being at the farmhouse after you jumped through that window to save my life? How I had to serve you day and night while you recovered?"

During that wonderful time on our honeymoon nine months ago, I was wrapped in bandages. Like now, I was lying near a cozy fire. Like now, I was alone with my husband. Life is good. Wherever Bruce and I are together, I am home.

Andrea brings the news that Jason is indeed being flown back to California. He's going to require extensive surgery and rehabilitation. She also brings back a few words from Jason, but first she makes sure Bruce is preoccupied with someone at the door.

She leans over me and whispers, "Dr. Miller says he's glad you got to say goodbye. Since you saved his life, he knows you meant it. He says that you shouldn't forget the widow's house. He also says that he's glad you have Bruce. You're a little too wild for him."

I smile on the inside but can't keep it to myself. God was good in giving us that last farewell.

Andrea pokes my shoulder. "Katie, what's going on? What are you smiling about?"

Finally Bruce walks over. "What's the matter? Did the cat get your tongue?"

The picture forming in my mind makes me smile even wider.

CHAPTER FORTY-NINE

Bruce finally coaxes me to 'fess up. I tell him. "I was thinking of you knee-deep in cow dung, making mud loaves for this house we're going to build."

The image is too much for a clean freak medic like Bruce, and we engage in stimulating interaction on what we will and won't do together after promises have been made.

The nerve damage in my right arm turns out to be more extensive than I imagine. The medical staff consult with Bruce and suggest that we head back to the States to get some plastic surgery and other repair work done. For now, I'll have to wear a sling and be honest with Bruce about my physical challenges.

However, I have a promise to fulfill for the old widow we helped on our piki safari. I also have a full term left as a staff member in which to continue building my relationship with Shelly. Bruce needs to experience the school I love. And I have so many places I want to experience with my husband. There are so many reasons not to go.

Bruce and I spend several days, between interruptions, sorting through our options. He finally consents to help me with the widow's home as long as I let him and others do the physical work. I'm supposed to be getting as much rest as possible. Bruce changes my dressings each day and assesses the healing.

We finally decide that we will spend a week during the August break building the home, take another week down in Mombasa, and then start preparing for the upcoming staff orientation. Bruce will spend any spare time he has getting his class prep done. If at any time my leg or arm gets infected, or shows significant complications, we will abandon our quest and head back to the States. Since neither of us really has a home base, we'll negotiate that when the time comes.

It takes a day and a half of emailing and calling to gather a crew of nine staff and five kids who are willing to commit to five days of building the house for the grandmother and her five grandchildren. Community outreach is a normal part of the Rift culture, so this project is a natural for those who don't already have plans. Jim and Les secure the supplies and contact local pastors who might be able to provide other volunteers to help. Andrea joins me in planning the food selection and preparation.

For some reason, nightmares, which include the snapping jaws of hyenas and the snarling howls of a leopard, increase in the next days. Bruce spends time focusing on the wounds to my body and spirit. I'm determined not to break my promise despite what it's costing me. I still struggle with the issue of being good, even if it isn't good for me.

In the morning, we finally load up the pickup, a van, and a Land Rover. The clouds roll over Kijabe and begin to release the rain everyone has been praying for. I have a hard time believing that this is a day of blessing as the drivers decide we should postpone our departure for another day. The reason is soon obvious, as rivers stream down the mountain and into every roadway and crevice on campus.

Bruce and I cuddle in front of the fire and enjoy the coziness of finally being alone. The pounding on our corrugated tin roof is deafening at times, but it sure helps bring back some memories—and it helps to create new ones.

On Wednesday morning, a break in the rain permits the crew to head out. The rain is lighter to the west where we'll be going.

Two of the teen guys who were on the piki safari decide to ride their bikes again, despite the ominous weather around us. Andrea has agreed to help build on the condition that these guys teach her how to ride their motorcycles.

Our convoy is led by Jim and Les driving a fully loaded pickup and trailer with a huge blue tarp over the supplies. The van is packed with backpacks and food. The Land Rover has gifts, tools, extra water, and petrol. Jim has recruited two Kenyans from the community to give us instruction and lend their experience. They know how to work with stone blocks and mbate roofing.

As we head out of the gates, Miriam stands near the church driveway with a panga in one hand and a rooster head in the other. Andrea is driving and I have her slow down.

Miriam walks over with her trophy. She pushes the rooster head toward my window and shouts, "We have killed two. There is only one to go."

I explain where we're going and assure her that I'll see her when I return. She's still waving that head in triumph as we pull around the corner and lose her from view.

Although we spoke briefly about what will happen on this trip, I take the time again to explain the situation regarding the grandmother and her five children. Despite his dislike of unsanitary conditions, Bruce's life in the military has prepared him for pretty much anything. Still, he's happy to hear we will be working with stone and wood and cement instead of cow dung and mud. The coming of the rain might actually be a benefit as it will mean hauling water a shorter distance.

The direct route, with only one stop, lasts three hours. The rain eases up as we continue west, just as we'd been told. Despite the sprinkling, when we pull into the village we are welcomed by a group of at least one hundred people. The church elders are there along with the five children who lead a colorful song and dance as we disembark. One of the church elders mentions to me that the song was written by the people in thanks to God for sending his deliverer. I'm happy to hear of their praise until he mentions further that they're saying I am the deliverer.

When all the singing and dancing and greeting finishes. I ask for a chance to speak. I preach my very first sermon, speaking about the true deliverer who saved us from an enemy far more dangerous than a hyena. When the people ask questions about my recent injuries and discover that I have also dispatched a leopard, they burst into song again and I have to turn over the speaking to an elder far more eloquent than I.

The rest of the crew unloads the supplies and sets up their tents. Bruce helps Jim and Les and the boys anchor two large grey tarps to cover the work area. The effect is something similar to a Barnum and Bailey circus. The crowds increase and it's almost impossible to limit the number of volunteers wanting to pitch in. It's also impossible to publicly set out our food, so we have to send our workers into tents in pairs so they can help themselves to what we brought.

Our major impediment is a lack of tools. With everyone wanting a turn with the shovels and the wheelbarrows, the men manage a good pace. The foundation of the new house is framed and poured before night steals our chance to work anymore. In fact, we finish smoothing out the concrete with the help of the pickup's headlights. Most of the people have gone home so as not to tempt the hyenas to return.

One of the elders tells me, before he leaves, that some of the men were actually debating about staying through the night so they can watch me take out another hyena. When others argued that I was obviously too wounded to fight a whole pack, it seemed to convince the crowd not to press their fortunes.

Bruce and I sleep on a three-inch foam mattress, but with my injuries I'm as uncomfortable as I've ever been. Taking my sling off for the night may not be the wisest move, but I do it anyway. Sleep is minimal and the dawn seems to take forever to come. Every sound in the night heightens my senses. A good wind whips up and makes the tarps flap for several hours without stopping. With my restlessness, Bruce doesn't get too much sleep either.

In the middle of the night I realize that I'm straining to hear the sounds of hyenas or other night hunters. The pressure of people's expectations wraps around my chest like a straightjacket. In the middle of this turmoil, a quiet whisper settles in my heart again: "There is only one Savior and it isn't you."

Sleep still doesn't come, but I can feel my muscles ease up and my breathing settle. A wave of peace washes over my mind. The quiet focuses me on the incredible itchiness I feel around the edges of the scabs on my arm and leg. I want to scratch, but I don't want to disturb Bruce any more than I already have.

Once my dressings are changed in the morning, and I have a sponge bath to take the edge off the grunge feeling, I join Andrea and a few others as they lay out breakfast—bread and jam, a fruit salad, corn flakes, and some juice boxes. Fortunately, we have a bit extra for some of the local workers who returned early to get in on the project.

While the rest of the crew sets the cinder blocks for the walls, Pastor Mandigo accompanies Andrea and me into a nearby town to pick up a few cases of Coke for all the workers. A good warm Coke is the traditional thirst-quencher during breaks here. The pastor finds a duka shop that not only sells Coke but also the sweet mandazi doughnuts everyone loves. We make the shop owner very happy by buying up all his stock.

By the time we return and unload the cokes and mandazis, the wall of the home is already two feet high. With so many willing hands, this project looks like it's going to get done in just three days. Even the weather is cooperating.

The five children who will be living in this space help me distribute treats and sweets whenever breaks come. The youngest one, Lidia, is fascinated by my bandages and finds a way to stay close to me through most of the lunch break. She has a smile which can melt the hardest heart. It doesn't take much to melt me.

In the early afternoon, the clouds part for a few hours and the tarps serve to provide good shade for those who are sweating below. I catch myself watching Bruce laughing and joking with both the teens and the national workers as he sets the pace.

By the time the afternoon chai break rolls around, I can tell that everyone is pretty fatigued. We call a halt to the labor and the pastors take some time to share a word and lead us in some energetic singing. This seems to revive everyone a little.

That evening, the village invites us all to a feast complete with roast goat. Although I can't join in the dancing, I enjoy the impromptu skit that the villagers put on about the woman who killed off a whole pack of hyenas and saved the world. Each of the widow's five grandchildren come forward to present gifts to us. It's the kind of night on which dreams are made.

When Bruce takes off his artificial leg, the children are stunned. He's comfortable with who he is and my love and respect for this man, who has given up so much to commit himself to me, expands. While my sleep isn't much better that night, the rest is.

By the time we finish breakfast on the third day, the rains begin to pelt down on our tarps. The limited workspace means that only a few extra volunteers can keep working without getting drenched. Jim and Les release the extra workers and invite them to come back when the rains diminish. That afternoon, we nail down the mbate iron sheets onto the rafters. Once the sheets are in place, I walk through the structure. It's a four-room house with one room for the grandmother, one for the girls, one for the boys, and one for a living room. The outhouse and kitchen will be built in a traditional style outside the living quarters. Those tasks will be completed by volunteers from the village. Our work is almost done.

The construction workers we brought with us install iron bars on the open spaces designed to be windows. Andrea and two of the teen girls set curtains in place. Jim and Les and Bruce work on getting a wooden door fitted.

In the last good light of day, everyone poses for pictures with the widow and her grandchildren in front of the new house. We pray, thanking God for his goodness in providing this place. I give Lidia her last sweet of the day and she shyly hugs my good arm before waving goodbye and ducking into her new home.

Most of the equipment has been packed away as the project comes to a completion. When the sun rises, we dismantle the rest of the camp, with the tarps and tents coming down last. Breakfast is served out of the van and we say our final goodbyes. The church elders each give a lengthy thank you. The widow claps and smiles and encourages the children as they give us all a round of hugs.

We're just getting into our vehicles when a young man runs down the road in our direction, screaming. People begin running and yelling. Some begin banging on our doors, wanting to be let in.

One of the elders walks quickly toward us and starts waving. "Quick, you must go."

CHAPTER FIFTY

Bruce squints in the direction the elder came from. "Look, it's a mob!"

The church elder urges us to go quickly, then hurries off into the bush. I see the grandmother and her five children huddled inside their new home. It's clear that this new place will be the target of the approaching group.

I open the side door of the van and announce, "We can't leave! The house will be torched."

Bruce looks at me as if I'm out of my mind. "Katie, just move over and let them squeeze in. We have to get out of here."

I can almost see his brain estimating how long it will take for the group of forty or fifty panga-waving attackers to cover the last two hundred yards.

My mind races into overdrive as I grab my cellphone. I scroll through my contacts just as the first rock hits the roof of the van. Andrea screams and lurches the van forward.

"Stop!" I yell.

Andrea stomps on the brake and I smash into the back of her seat with Bruce right beside me. One of the teen guys up front nearly hits the windshield with his head.

I'm in significant pain as I step out of the van. Crashing into the seat has opened a wound in my elbow. A red stain begins to spread on the white sling.

The pickup and van are already several hundred yards down the road waiting for us. Les is leaning out the driver's window, waving and yelling for us to hurry.

I do what I have to do. I walk toward the mob.

The sight of a single white woman approaching doesn't seem to impact them at all. The fact that I have one arm in a sling doesn't help. I look around and

Bruce is scrambling out of the van with a tire iron. This seems to both distract and enrage them. More rocks hurl down on the van.

"Stop!" I look back at Bruce. "Get back in the van!"

Studying the mob, I discern who the leader is: a young man about thirty years of age. I take a chance and point at him and yell. "The Minister of Security, Timothy Kamau, would like to speak to you." I hold out the cellphone.

The leader hesitates and stops fifteen feet away from me. Since only the front members of the mob hear me, it takes a while before the group envelopes me like an amoeba and quietens down. They wait for their leader.

He yells to make sure all his group can hear. "This lame colonialist says she is talking with the Minister of Security." He waves his panga high in the air and directs his speech to someone in the group. "Jackson, come here."

A young man about the same age as the leader steps forward. The leader addresses him again. "Jackson, Timothy Kamau is your uncle. You know his voice. Speak to him. If this is a trick to make fools of us, then these people will be part of the headlines tomorrow."

The stall has given me enough time to punch in the number that Valerie's aunt called her from. I'm living on hope at the moment. I try to stall a little longer before handing over the phone.

For the sake of the person answering, I declare my identity to the mob. "My name is Dr. Katrina Southerland. I was born in this country, not as a colonialist but as a daughter who loves this land and its people."

Several of the group begin to yell in anger at my words. I wave them down until their leader signals them into silence.

"The Kamaus are my friends, as you will see," I continue. More protests. More silencing from the leader. "I know you are wanting justice to be done. You need to talk to the man who can help you. Look around you."

I beckon to the old widow who's peeking out her doorway.

"We have come as friends to help an old grandmother and five orphans she is trying to feed. If you know her, you know that she has nothing. We have only come to help an old woman and some orphans."

The leader steps forward. "We have heard that you are building a police post in this village and that we will be left without protection when the elections come."

"Come and see," I say. "It is only the home for a grandmother and her orphans."

The leader examines me up and down. It makes me uncomfortable.

"What is the cause of your wounds?" he asks.

I look down at the significant red patch that has developed at my elbow. "I had to fight a leopard."

"What happened to the leopard?"

"I killed it."

He seems skeptical. "But you are a woman!"

He circles me and repeats his crude looks.

I stare at him until he looks me in the eyes. "I have also fought and killed a hyena in this very place."

Jackson steps closer. "You are the one that slays the devils of the night?"

Those who are within hearing range chatter excitedly.

I don't say anything else. I walk through the crowd in the direction of the widow and the five children who are cowering just outside the door of the new home.

The leader walks beside me and motions people out of our way. When we get near the home, the widow and children scamper around the back.

The leader and the man he called Jackson both join me as we step into the four-roomed home. They look around briefly and then emerge back to face down the crowd.

"It is as the doctor has said," the leader shouts. "A home. We will talk to the Minister about the need for security. We will talk inside. Jackson will convince his uncle that we are in need of help as well."

There is general bedlam for a moment until the leader waves down the group.

Jackson takes my cellphone and walks into one of the bedrooms. I can hear him speaking energetically for several minutes before he walks out into the living room again.

"It is my mother's sister," Jackson says, "but her husband is there talking to someone else. My aunt confirms that you are their friend. She will intercede on our behalf. My uncle will not argue with her."

Jackson hands me the phone so I can talk to his aunt. He and his leader leave to lead their people back home in triumph. Somehow they are heroes.

Valerie's aunt confirms that I'm safe and reminds me to stop by their home three days from now. I hear Valerie yelling in the background: "Wear the black dress!"

Our group gathers around the widow's home and thanks God again for his protection. We leave the grateful family before any other excitement can develop. The local pastors have promised they will look after the other needs of the family, and we trust them.

If the discussion in the other vehicles is anything like the chatter in our van, it's no wonder the trip home seems quick. I just witnessed something as miraculous as the parting of the Red Sea.

Bruce is ready to take the next plane home. He's seen and heard enough to last a lifetime. I never considered how my man would feel because he couldn't protect me. I haven't learned the right times to be afraid.

Bruce replaces my dressing and makes sure the bleeding has stopped. By the time we reach home, the sun is setting again and another day is done. I sleep really well in my own bed, even with Bruce there.

On Saturday night, we prepare to leave for Nairobi to visit the Kamaus. Due to the danger of the roads, we'll stay overnight at the mission guesthouse, attend the Nairobi church next door, and then take the train down to Mombasa in the evening.

The news announces that several rallies are being held during the day, but security is tight and the massive gatherings seem to be going well. I call Valerie and she assures me that the evening's plan is still on. As she prepares to say goodbye, she says one more time, "Don't forget to wear the black dress."

I dismiss her suggestion. The outfit doesn't seem to fit in this culture, and it will show off my wounds. But surely Valerie knows what's appropriate here. I finally break down and show it to Bruce. He wants to see it modeled. His whistle tells me all I need to know.

My husband steps up behind me while I stand in front of the full-length mirror. He gently puts his hands on my shoulders.

"Katie, I think this dress is for my eyes only. Keep it for Mombasa next week. You can show Valerie your wounds if she wonders why. Let me try and limit these bandage dressings as much as possible. You get enough attention already wherever you go."

The evening with the Kamaus prove to be a great time. The meal is first-class. I'm comfortable in the lengthy mid-calf ensemble Bruce brought for me in his luggage. The cherry red blouse and white skirt aren't exactly what I would have picked for myself, but the outfit suits the occasion and looks good on me.

Since Bruce worked in the Special Forces, and knows a thing or two about security issues in foreign countries, he and Timothy Kamau have some great man-to-man time. I spend time with Valerie and her aunt, discussing much more important issues like changing fashions, significant women in our world, the problem of living in fear during uncertain times, the men in our lives, and family.

When we settle in for coffee and cheesecake, the discussion turns to the mob we faced, then the hyena, and finally the leopard. Mr. Kamau comes alive as I describe each incident as briefly as possible. He chuckles as his imagination rolls, then lets it go into a full-out belly laugh.

The Minister of Security's wife touches my knee. "I haven't seen him laugh like this in many years. It is good that you are here."

Around ten o'clock, the minister is interrupted in the middle of one of his stories by his ringtone. He leaves the room and returns ten minutes later with grave concern on his face.

"I'm afraid I must attend to an urgent matter. Thank you for coming." He shakes our hands and gives his wife a hug. "I have arranged for you to have a security escort. The streets in the past hour are no longer safe. You will need to leave now in case things become worse. These elections make everyone so emotional."

With that, he turns and leaves.

A few minutes later, two young officers introduce themselves and escort us to our car. One of them announces that he'll drive us; we'll need to take a few diversions on the way to the guesthouse. Bruce and I are asked to sit in the back, to stay low, and to hang on.

It doesn't take more than a minute of digging my nails into Bruce's leg to realize that I'm in for a ride of terror. My heart beats way too fast. My eyes open too wide. It feels like we've been thrown inside a safari rally car determined to break every speed record on the planet. The flicker of fires erupt ahead. Our tires screech as we swerve without warning into a side street. A rock bounces off the passenger door panel with a loud thud. I scream and Bruce pulls me down over his lap.

The loud chatter in the officer's radio only adds to the chaos as we drive only a few yards from the vehicle in front of us. The flashing lights on the car ahead blind me and it seems impossible that our driver can see enough to anticipate the next swerve. The high-pitched siren hurts my ears and I try to put my wrists over my ears and hang on at the same time.

Bruce places his body protectively over me. Another rock bounces lightly off the roof. At one point, my lungs feel like they're on fire and I gasp for air like a swimmer too long underwater. Suffocating, hyperventilating, not daring to breathe. Back and forth I go. Then the car jerks to a stop and the ride is over.

The officer throws the keys to Bruce as we sit up, stunned, in the back seat. The driver dodges around a flower garden and slips into the passenger side of the lead vehicle. In a moment, the vehicle with the flashing lights and piercing siren is gone. The guard clangs the iron gates behind the departing car and slides the bolts into place.

The missionary host of the guesthouse taps on our window before I return to a state of calm awareness.

Bruce rolls down his window. "Jambo! Habari? How are you?"

A little while later, Bruce sets the luggage down in our room. The guesthouse is strangely quiet. This doesn't feel like the city I knew and loved as a child. I find myself in the fetal position on the twin-sized bed as Bruce takes a shower down the hall. I'm unnerved and don't want to be alone. I walk out into the hallway to the shower room and slump down with my back against the wall. That probably isn't the best move, since I'm still wearing the new white skirt Bruce brought for me. I pull up my knees and try to arrange the skirt as modestly as possible. The cool floor feels good against my bare feet. Sweat soaks through the armpits of my cherry red blouse. Any relief is welcome, and for now this hallway floor is all I have.

That's where Shelly finds me. When she spots me, she bounces down the hall like a tigger and envelopes me in a huge hug.

"Wow, you know how to arrive in style," she says. "My mom thought it might be a terrorist attack or something. My brother and I hid under the bed until Dad told us it was only you. What's happening? You look like you just hunted down another hyena."

When Bruce emerges in his shorts and muscle shirt, Shelly and I are still sitting in the hall. I try to explain the ride of terror I just experienced. This man I've committed myself to is easy on the eyes and I find myself speechless looking at him with new appreciation.

Shelly elbows me slightly. "You've got a ring, Aunt Katie," she whispers.

Bruce has never met Shelly and a smirk eases onto his face. He deliberately bends down and kisses me on the lips. Shelly gasps and elbows me harder.

Bruce winks at me and walks down the hall to our room. He looks back purposefully. "You know where to find me, good-looking."

Before Shelly is totally disillusioned with my constant flirtation and fixation on different men, I break the news. "That's the man who gave me the ring. I've got a license for that kiss."

Of course, after that the curious teen wants to know all the details about how we met, when Bruce arrived in Kenya, and what we're going to do over the next month until school starts again. I give her the short version, then hug her goodbye. My heart is starting to race for a different reason than some wild ride around Nairobi.

As I turn the knob on our room door, anticipating what's on the other side, the blast of an explosion knocks me off my feet and into the wall.

CHAPTER FIFTY-ONE

Light disintegrates. Blackness swallows me. The throbbing pounding in the back of my head keeps me aware that I'm alive. Nothing is broken, but I choke on waves of dust streaming over me. For the second time in the same night, I hear sirens blaring into my eardrums.

I crawl to where I think my room is. I pull my blouse up to cover my nose and mouth and try to cough out the dust. Flashlight beams shine on me. Someone finds me. I'm physically dragged outside into the cool fresh night air and dumped on the wet grass. Then I'm abandoned as my rescuer goes back for more.

Another flashlight beam eventually discovers me and I'm helped up and walked to a center where I wipe my face and get a cool drink to bathe my throat. The headlights of several cars light up the area. Two ambulances and several police cars block the parking lot.

The grit is in my teeth and hair and throughout my clothing. My skirt and blouse are ruined. One of the ladies in the house brings me her husband's t-shirt since several buttons ripped off my blouse. Another young woman brings me her jean skirt to replace my torn white one. I pull the t-shirt overtop and hold the jean skirt until I find a place to change.

My first attempt at words come out as a whisper: "Bruce. Where's my husband, Bruce?"

Of course, no one knows who Bruce is. They don't even know me. Several ladies try to keep me seated, telling me that everything is being done to find people inside. They suggest that I take some time to clean off my face and hands. I don't want to leave yet.

Twenty minutes pass with no word about Bruce, and I cannot restrain myself any longer. While the ladies are distracted by someone else in need, I drift away back into the darkness where flashlights sweep back and forth across the carnage. I can tell that the structural integrity of the building doesn't seem to be badly compromised. Only the small back section where Bruce and I were staying seems to have suffered obvious damage. I hand bottled water to one of the searchers and reach for his flashlight. He doesn't object and leaves to sit down for a break.

Working my way through the wreckage to where Bruce was doesn't take long. The only problem is he isn't there. As I comb through the debris, all I find is his artificial leg. I carry it out with me and walk to the front gate. An idea parachutes into my mind as I pray in desperation.

I approach one of the guards. "Did anyone get taken to hospital?"

"Only two people."

"Was one of them a white man, a mzungu?"

"Ndio. Yes, Memsep. His leg was blown off." His eyes grow wide when I pull Bruce's artificial leg from behind my back.

I race over to one of the police officers with the leg and tell him I need to get the leg to a man who was just taken to the hospital. He grabs one of the ambulance attendants to explain the situation. They push me into the back of the ambulance and, with sirens blaring, I endure another helter skelter ride through the city.

The first hospital doesn't have Bruce, so we jump back into the ambulance and drive to a second hospital.

When I walk into the emergency ward, accompanied by the ambulance attendant and the police officer, I'm grabbed and almost put onto a gurney before I can explain what's happening. I forgot what a mess I must look like. As I hold up the prosthetic limb and try to explain that I'm looking for a mzungu who lost his leg, smiles emerge onto the faces of the medical staff.

"Yes, the man is with the doctors," says one of the nurses. "I will take you there, but you must sit in a wheelchair."

Within five minutes I'm being wheeled into a room where Bruce lies flat on his back talking to two doctors. I wave the limb as I come through the door.

Bruce smiles. "Why am I not surprised! Doctors, this is the woman I was worried about. My wife. And this is the leg I was trying to tell you about."

It's ten in the morning before we're finally released. I was able to take a shower, endure a checkup, and explain my story a dozen times. I'm given yet another t-shirt, yellow, and a green skirt that had been left in the hospital's lost and found. It's a bit roomy, but I cinch the covering into place with a safety pin.

Bruce walks out on two legs. He has on some oversized black jeans and a Boston Celtics sweatshirt. We catch a taxi back to the guesthouse and wind our way through a city which seems to be just as choked with traffic as always. It is as if nothing has happened.

At the guesthouse, we're welcomed with open celebration and a lot of laughs when we tell our story. Apparently Bruce had just slipped off his prosthetic limb and climbed into bed when the hot water tank next to our room exploded. He wasn't seriously hurt but he was knocked unconscious by a collapsing wall. When the searchers discovered his unresponsive body in the rubble, with only one leg, they rushed him into the ambulance.

The group of missionaries, including Shelly's family, gather around us and thank God for his deliverance. Most of them are having to make other arrangements for accommodations, but they seem to take the inconvenience in stride. They're grateful that no one died.

Fortunately, we had only taken one suitcase of clothing into the guesthouse so all our things are still protected in the car outside. I slip into a polka dot ensemble that slides just slightly above my knees. It's meant for Bruce on our first night in Mombasa, but he doesn't mind getting his surprise early.

Bruce and I wait for the arrival of Jeff Sanderson, another Rift staff member returning to Kenya fresh from spending three months in Connecticut with his father, who'd had a heart attack. At five o'clock, a taxi pulls into the swept-up parking lot and Jeff, a lanky young man with rust-colored locks and dark-rimmed glasses, retrieves five duffle bags from the trunk and piles them next to our car. We exchange greetings and then hand him the keys. He motions for us to get in, and soon we're bound for the train station. On the way, he quizzes me on a few of the details from the last term. He welcomes Bruce to the staff, gets an update on the political situation, inquires as to when we'll be back from Mombasa, and offers to pick us up.

By 5:30, we're working our way through a mob of people making their way through the Nairobi train station. Across the street, we see the old U.S. embassy, which was once bombed by Osama bin Ladin. Bruce played a key role in the elimination of that terrorist, but I also know that I'll never find out what that role might be.

The heat is sufficient enough that sweat trickles down my back. Nairobi is unusually muggy for this time of year. The atmosphere feels close and the odor of hundreds of fellow travelers prods my feeling of claustrophobia. Bruce finds a small area against the back wall and uses our luggage to create a little space for me.

Unfortunately, the skirt is a bit too short to sit comfortably and I don't want to get it dirty by sitting on anything around. With the drought conditions, the wind has blown layer after layer of thick red dust onto every surface. Even the withering Calla lilies look like they're almost pink.

My white blouse is starting to feel soaked and I'm sure it will be stained by the time I change again.

We soon board the train, and I'm drained. Without sufficient sleep the past few days, and considering the emotional cost of almost losing Bruce, my spirit is taxed to its limit.

Bruce and I share a two-berth airless compartment and I can't wait for the train to get moving. The train leaves almost right on time, at 7:00—one of the few things you can count on. As the train moves, I stick my head out the raised window like a dog hanging out from a car. The *clickety-clack* and gentle rocking of the train take me back to my girlhood days when our family of five traveled this way to the coast once each year.

I'm so caught up in my childhood memories that I jump when Bruce puts his hands around my waist and gives me a love squeeze. I hit my head on the window frame, but it's nothing serious. I him say something about taking pictures of children outside but don't think too much about it until twenty minutes later when I pull back inside and notice that I'm still alone.

I hope we can get in on the first dinner seating, so I head out to look for my husband. One of the washrooms is empty. When the other door opens, an old Kikuyu gentleman steps out. I continue my search, in case Bruce had to use the toilets in another car.

While on my way back past our compartment, as I'm reaching the dining car, I find Bruce sitting in handcuffs with a young police officer.

Bruce smiles and holds up his hands. "I guess you're not the only one who knows how to get into trouble."

CHAPTER FIFTY-TWO

I greet the police officer in Swahili, immediately assuming that he'll be looking for a bribe for some infraction. I want to establish that we aren't tourists with a load of cash we want to contribute to whatever dream he has for his future.

I ignore Bruce and talk in Swahili about the officer's family, his home, his country's beauty, and my birth and family life here. Anything I think of to prove my establishment here. When I discover that he had once been to Kijabe's hospital for a health problem, and when I find out his family is from Eldoret, I draw as many connections as possible. When some rapport has been established, I talk about Bruce. How excited he's been to come to the place of my birth. We were even married here in the valley at Mayer's Ranch. After more than twenty minutes of discussion, I finally ask what he's done. Apparently Bruce leaned out the open door to take a picture of children running alongside the moving train. This is a serious violation, as the sign clearly states. I don't argue, but thank the officer for his considerate vigilance in keeping the passengers safe. I suggest that perhaps Bruce is a little dazed from a blast we were in during the night. This opens the door to more storytelling. Bruce gets uncomfortable with the length of time these negotiations are taking.

Finally, the young policeman broaches the subject of what comes next. "I have arrested your husband and he will be taken off at the next stop and sent to prison."

"My husband is truly sorry that he broke the law without knowing. He's also a security officer and is used to keeping the laws."

"It will cost a lot of money to be released from prison." He looks at me to see if I understand his intention.

J.A. TAYLOR

I do. "There is a lot of confusion in this country right now, with the elections coming. Last night we had dinner at the home of the Minister of Security, Mr. Kamau. He gave us an escort to our rooms for the evening. I think he would be disappointed to receive a call hearing about our situation."

The policeman looks visibly disturbed. "You are friends with Mr. Kamau?"

I take out my cellphone and scroll down until I have the Kamaus' number. This is the second time I've used this ploy to get out of trouble. I hold the cellphone up so the young man can see it in the dim light. "See, here is his home number. I will call him right now and you can speak to him and tell him what you're doing with his friend."

He takes the phone and examines the number closely. Finally he hands it back. "That will not be necessary. Since you have admitted your husband's guilt, and since he is new to this country, I will forgive him this once. You must warn him that the laws of this country must be obeyed."

With that pronouncement, the young man takes a key from his shirt pocket, unlocks the handcuffs, shakes my hand, and bids us farewell. Bruce hasn't said a word for the whole forty-five-minute exchange.

We make our way back to our compartment. Ten minutes later, the train makes its first stop of the night. Bruce doesn't even suggest taking a picture, and he definitely doesn't leave our room.

Once the train continues on its way, we're able to get in on the second seating for dinner. Bruce takes my hand and prays a long sweet grace of appreciation for God's mercy in giving him a wife who's familiar enough with trouble that she can get into it *and* out of it. After dinner, Bruce demonstrates his appreciation of all I've done to get him out of his foolishness.

As we approach the Tsavo River railway bridge, a full moon shows itself through the clouds above the plains and I remind Bruce about the photographs in my great-grandfather's album. There is one picture of a man named Lieutenant Colonel John Henry Patterson holding two lion skins.

Bruce leans out the window with me. "You mean the famous man-eaters of Tsavo? The ones on display in that Chicago museum?"

"Right! Patterson says those two lions killed up to 135 of his Indian workers during nine months in 1898. The workers did everything to protect themselves, but the lions still got through to drag the men out of their tents. Hundreds of workers ran away and the bridge seemed like it would never get built."

"For once, no one in your family was in the middle of the trouble," Bruce says.

I give him a good thwack across the back and enjoyed his responding grunt. "How do you think my grandfather got those pictures? He was heading up to join Mr. Patterson for Christmas." I shiver as Bruce's back massage turns pleasurable. "He arrived in mid-December, just after the first lion was killed. They went hunting for the second lion and it charged them. The lion was shot five times and only crippled." I reach back and move his hand to a more tender spot. "The gun was empty, but the lion wasn't dead yet. It got up and charged again. It was my grandfather who handed Mr. Patterson the gun whose final three shots finished off that lion. At least, that's what our family history says."

Bruce turns me around and looks at me with a smirk. "I'm just glad old Mr. Patterson took care of those man-eaters. Otherwise I'm sure you'd find a way to get us face to face with them all over again."

I thwack him another good one in the back.

Once we've crossed the Tsavo Bridge and are about to move away from the window, three distinct shots break the still air. The most incredible screeching sound pierces the night as Bruce and I are thrown into a heap on the floor.

CHAPTER FIFTY-THREE

The train's braking action is effective and we're trapped in a vacuum of stillness. Bruce pulls me up to stand with him. For a minute, we hear nothing. Finally, we hear people outside lowering their windows to see what's happening. A large group of individuals near the front of the train move in the dim light of the moon dodging in and out of cloud cover.

When an urgent knock sounds on the door, Bruce steps in front of me, and waits.

"It is Samson. I am the policeman who arrested you. Hurry, you must come quickly."

Bruce leaves me, walks to the door, and opens it.

The policeman talks quickly. "We have been stopped by shiftas, Somali bandits. They are down here escaping the famine. They will be looking for tourists to help them out. You must come up to the roof and lie down quietly until they pass."

I grab Bruce's arm. "I'm not going on the roof in a dress. Can't we hide in the washroom?"

Samson looks at Bruce and motions. "We need to go now. Put your things under the bed. They will search everywhere if they know you are here. Hurry."

The young policeman leads us out the back of our car to a ladder on the far side from the shiftas. Bruce urges me up until I'm over the top and flat on my belly. The three of us lie there, as still as roadkill. The roof still holds the heat of the day and I continually shift back and forth to manage my discomfort. I have ruined another outfit.

After ten minutes, the voices grow louder below us. There are occasional arguments as travelers are probed for donations to the cause. An hour later, the bandits must be satisfied because the train lurches forward.

I want to scream and get off the roof, but the policeman tells Bruce to stay still. The bandits are checking to see if anyone is hiding on the roof. We travel a good mile or two before he finally puts his head up and looks around. The threat seems to have disappeared.

With the train picking up speed to make up for lost time, the car we're on rocks vigorously. Samson tugs on Bruce and urges us both to make our way to the ladder and back down into the compartment. Bruce grabs me by the arm and tugs me toward the edge of the speeding train.

The moon emerges in all its glory and the shadowed scrub brush along the tracks seem to fly by. My stomach lurches at the thought of trying to release my hold on this roof and go over the side, especially with only one good arm to work with.

The young Kenyan slips over the side and disappears. Bruce nudges me in that direction. I hold on tight. I try to look into his face but he's shadowed and focused on getting me to the ladder. I pray and try hard to trust. I've been in worse situations than this.

When a hand grabs hold of my ankle, I squeal in surprise. Bruce grabs my shoulders, tells me to relax, and let Samson put my foot on the ladder. I try to ignore what's happening with my dress and blouse as it bunches up under me on the filthy train car.

I take a deep breath and slide over the edge.

I'm still shaking as we pull into the stretch run into Mombasa. The heat and humidity are oppressive. Bruce and I change into shorts and t-shirts after our ordeal on the roof. Samson leaves us immediately after our descent to check on the condition of the other passengers who didn't have the chance to climb onto the roof. We don't see him again, even after we leave the train and make our way through the crushing crowds that move us steadily out the exits.

The taxi driver who wins our bartering rights drives a beat-up old white Subaru. The car is a veteran of these roads, as I realize from the scrapes and creases in the body and serious dints in the rusty rims.

The inside of his cab captures the town perfectly. The stuffing sneaks out of the seams of several seats. Muslim prayer beads hang on the mirror with a chain that holds a crucifix. Pictures of four children are taped to the top of his cracked windscreen. The mixed aromas of curry, cinnamon, and cloves seem to saturate the interior so as to disguise the smell of dead fish, raw sewage, and rotting food that drifts in from the surrounding area.

As we move faster through the streets and closer to the ferry, I imagine again the smell of the sea, the coconuts, and the coffee from the men with the big brass pots. The incense wafts around my nostrils.

The driver slows at the ferry to pay our fare and let us barter for a newspaper cone filled with cashews. Bruce buys a few oranges to slake his thirst. He looks out at the busy harbor and smiles like a little boy who's gotten his own way.

We're here for our second honeymoon, just ten months after our first.

My black dress serves its purpose well. It's like magic. Several male tourists express too much interest as we stand in the buffet line, but Bruce hovers protectively to make sure we get a back table in the shadows. I am well romanced afterward.

On my first morning in Mombasa, I get up early and slip out of bed without waking Bruce. I slip into my one-piece bathing suit and go for a dip in the pool. My disability keeps me from doing my usual laps.

Boys on the beach call, luring early birds to buy their wares, or take a tour, or just spend some time haggling. The translucent sea is a mirror broken by shadowed whitecaps in the first wisps of dawn's light. Silhouetted boatmen pole their way between bobbing dhows at anchor. A solitary tourist stands in the receding tide, perhaps caught in the ambivalence of awaiting the glories of a new sunrise and wishing the new day won't come, for this may be his last day in Africa.

The stillness of the morning draws out a single hawk which glides over broad, white sandy beaches on the slightest of breezes. A pinkened cloud tornadoes across the pale blue sky as other clouds display their bipolar natures, half-dark, half-white.

I pull myself out of the pool and stop on the edge of the sand. Coconut palms stand like stately courtiers welcoming the sovereign light. The glow of buildings dull and wink out as their efforts become redundant. The footprints of a jogger slowly fill with water, leaving no traces of the day's pioneer.

I close my eyes and listen. The lapping of wavelets against boats. The shrill whistle of a guard greeting the jogger. The laughter of the boatmen casting his nets and probing the sandbar for shells. The calls of children racing across the sand, not wanting to waste a second, or any of the energy they've saved up for these moments. The first bird calls... *tee-wee, tee-wee... chir, chir, chee.*

Cats stretch, calico, tabbies, blacks, greys, endless felines preparing for a day of scavenging, begging and guarding against the hoteliers' nightmare: rats.

Indigo butterflies, splashed joyfully with yellow highlights, valiantly flap their way through lush tropical gardens. Monkeys begin their invasion, along with baboons. The baboons charge yellow trash bins and rip at plants and coconuts. The monkeys claim rooftops and scale the ceiling beams to spy out unsuspecting sunbathers and breakfasters making an early appearance. The watchman, with his wrist-rocket slingshot, hasn't arrived yet, so they are bold and daring in their snatches. Soon their day will revert to hide-and-seek, coordinated distraction, and stealth attacks.

The heat begins its healing work, like an expert masseuse as it seeps into the muscles and bones of row after row of bronzing subjects. Books are common fare among the older gatherers. The younger expend their energy in the pool, creating underwater worlds and games with newfound friends who share the same wonders of life and liberty. Hawkers prepare their wares, aggressively flogging camel rides, ebony keychains, bracelets, carvings, shells, brightly patterned Kitange cloths, glass-bottomed boat rides, and an assortments of trinkets, crafts, and services.

Bruce joins me for breakfast and then stretches out by the pool to read. He definitely could use a tan. But several young women walking by still give his muscular features an extra-long look. I move my bench closer to stake my claim.

The pace is slow. The life is easy. The clock ticks by all too quickly between dawns, meals, dusks, and a nightlife that uncorks the dormant energy of the day just done. Endings come too quickly.

A rainbow of colors shine against brilliant white sand flowing into beige shallows, aquamarine channels, and indigo deeps, all punctuated by ceaseless whitecaps under the sweeping canvas of the purest cloudless blue sky. Greens dance their own kaleidoscopic tale of lushness. Emeralds and jades, aquamarines and limes.

The day before we return to Kijabe, a couple of young girls grasp each other as their parents try to separate them. Last hugs. Eyes lock. Arms embrace in a death clinch. Pieces of their hearts tear and remain behind as their bodies are pried apart. Loss overwhelms the excitement of their upcoming adventures. Their clouded eyes release showers over quivering cheeks and chins. The soulmates' fingers unhook, sobs escaping in words of protest. Last looks. Last waves. Last glimpses.

My book is soaked before I realize I'm crying all over it. The feeling of those two young girls is all too familiar.

CHAPTER FIFTY-FOUR

The pounding on the door must be a mistake. Darkness still wraps its warm comfort around Bruce and me as we wake from our slumber, still wrapped securely in each other's arms.

Bruce tosses the blankets, slips on his robe, and hops quickly on his good leg to the door. The phone begins to ring. Bruce flips on the light and does a shoulder-check to see that I'm modestly snuggled under the blankets. The phone keeps ringing.

I reach out and answer it as Bruce unlocks the security latch. The call is from the front desk warning that a U.S. Navy officer is coming to our room over a security matter. Apparently Bruce has verified the knocker and he motions me to move into the washroom. I scoot as quickly as I can, scooping up one of Bruce's t-shirts along the way.

With the door shut, I can't understand the conversation happening in the hallway outside our room, but it doesn't last long. Soon Bruce is knocking softly on the bathroom door.

After ensuring that he's alone, I open the door for him. He moves in quickly and embraces me. I bury my face into his broad chest and wait for the news.

"We have to leave."

I pull back and look into his face. "What did you say?"

"We have to leave," Bruce repeats. "We've got five minutes to get down to the lobby."

I can't fathom why. "What did we do?"

Bruce is already reaching for his suitcase. "We didn't do anything. There's been an attempted coup and U.S. personnel have been told to evacuate. They've got a Navy helicopter waiting down on the beach. They're going to take us to an aircraft carrier just offshore."

I pull on the t-shirt and walk out after my husband. "Surely Mr. Kamau can take care of things. Nairobi's eight hours away. No one's going to bother us here. I'll phone him."

Bruce looks patiently into my eyes. "This is an order, Katie. This isn't an option."

I'm not ready to give in yet. "But you're retired. You don't have to take orders anymore."

Bruce secures his leg and begins to slip into his best grey dress slacks. "I don't retire for another year. Remember, I'm on a leave of absence. We have to go."

He doesn't even look back at me.

I rip off his t-shirt, throw it at him, and grab my black dress from off the hanger. He doesn't even notice. He needs to listen to me. "You can go. I'll stay until I can get back to the school."

Bruce buttons up a sky-blue, short-sleeved dress shirt. He doesn't say a word.

I try again. "They need me for next term. I need to see Andrea and Shelly. I promised."

"You've got two minutes to get dressed, if you don't want to go as you are," he threatens.

"I'm invoking my Canadian citizenship. You can't just kidnap Canadian citizens."

Bruce walks over to me, sees the black dress in my hands, and starts a tug of war over it. A solid rapping on the door makes us pause.

Bruce finally gives up and walks to my closet. With careful grace, he slides a pair of white capris and a colorful flowered blouse off their hangers and tosses them in my direction.

"Katie," he says sternly, "I promise I'll explain everything on the way. Rebel forces are already in Mombasa. We don't have time to waste. Whether or not you want me now, I am going to protect you, whatever it takes."

I comply, and slip into my clothes as quickly as I can. Bruce bundles up most of our clothing and belongings into two suitcases and slips on his shoes. I step into a pair of flip-flops, grab my toiletry bag, and follow him out into the hall. The Navy officer directs a sailor to take the bags from Bruce and we all move silently down the hall as two hotel residents stand in their doorway with questioning looks on their faces.

As we pass the second hotel resident, a young European woman about my age, I can't stop myself. "It's just a coup."

Bruce squeezes my arm, but it's too late. The young woman runs back into her room, screaming to someone about the coup. As I near the stairs, the other resident, also a European, moves quickly down the hallway pounding on doors and yelling in his best German.

We're through the lobby and heading out onto the beach before I look back. All the lights on our floor are on and noises of considerable distress float across the swimming pool in our direction.

I kick off my flip-flops and scoop them up. The sand feels barely cool under my feet, the warm breeze rustling through the palm trees and across my face. More lights flicker on. Bruce grabs my hand and tugs me across the moonlit white sand. This is the most romantic I've ever seen this place.

The Navy helicopter is whirling loudly a few hundred yards down the beach, and many of the hotel lights have switched on. Residents perch on their balconies watching. Four Navy SEALS stand alert and on guard as hotel security gathers in a bunch with their clubs poised against the unknown intruders.

Bruce almost hurls me into the loading bay of the chopper. I scramble up and into the arms of another SEAL who fastens me into a harness. Another good pair of capris ruined.

Bruce is soon seated next to me in his own harness. This isn't the sendoff I envisioned from our second honeymoon.

We lift off within a minute. As we dip away from the beach, a fully lit compound reveals dozens of people already gathered on the beach. I pity the staff having to deal with the panicking tourists.

Once we're securely airborne, the officer secures the exit and makes his way over to crouch near us.

"Commander," he says, addressing Bruce. "We are now getting intelligence that there are disturbances in the highlands, near the school you were stationed at. An evacuation order will soon be issued for those still onsite."

"Plan A is always to evacuate over the Tanzanian border," I say over the drone of the engine. "Do you know if that's what they'll be doing?"

The officer ponders his response a moment. "Ma'am, my goal is to get you safely back home so you can testify."

Without thinking, I reach for his collar. Bruce's hand grabs mine and twists me away before I have time to react. I'm louder than necessary. "I am not going home."

I'm sure my look could have burned a hole through Bruce.

"Let me work this out," he says as he unhooks his harness and motions to the officer.

Images of my first trip away from the land of my birth sweep over me. I can see that sixteen-year-old girl giving one last wave as the plane leaps off the tarmac in Nairobi. I see her frantically writing in her journals, trying to capture every thought and adventure of her final days. I see her skipping and playing and laughing with her African friends and schoolmates.

The drill is straightforward. Numbness, life out of control, denial. When my feelings emerge again, there will be anger and fear. I will understand the feeling of a t-shirt caught in a dryer cycle that just won't stop. Wherever I land, Bruce will be there. Unless, of course, the Navy takes him away again and leaves me all alone.

I can't leave Andrea. Not again. And Shelly. I promised to help her. And all those kids who really don't understand what kind of a world we live in. Someone has to tell them. It will be chaos—and then, maybe one day, even wonderful.

These wonderful world-changers need to know that God will never abandon them in their transitions. There will be others, somewhere, ready to meet them and care for them. The planes they sit in will one day land. Another home will be waiting. Brothers and sisters who share their faith will embrace them. Then, like me, they can reach back and find someone else to help. Someone else to encourage. Someone else to walk toward healing with.

Without a doubt, the deeper pains helped to hollow out the hidden crevices of my heart and make me a deeper, more empathetic person. My pattern of leaving has built character in me I can't fathom or deny. At each juncture, I've learned the secret of desperate dependence on God and interdependence on others. I've seen the world through new eyes and a new heart. The pain may never fully leave, and healing may never fully come, but I guess that's what heaven's for.

Bruce slips back down beside me. I barely see his face through my tears. He takes my hand and speaks clearly. "The RCMP and FBI have been working together on all these people with the golden rings who've been dying all around you. They think you and I may know something about a black king and queen who have been trafficking young girls. I have no idea what they're talking about, but I'm afraid to ask if you do."

I rest my head on his shoulder. "Where are they taking us?"

He squeezes my arm to reassure me. "Right now we're landing on an aircraft carrier and staying there until the security situation onshore is determined."

I raise my head and look at Bruce as the helicopter begins its decent. "Where to after that?"

"I don't care. As long as we're together."

I search his eyes and see the truth of his words. "Then I don't care either. As long as I'm with you, I'm home."

Read the Blog Series: Walking Your Son into Manhood.

From the moment the first man walked out of Eden and looked at his new reality the weight of his future threatened to crush him. He sauntered out of paradise with a fear he had never known before – a fear that somehow the future of his offspring depended on the effort he put out to keep things right in a world going wrong. Fathers in the 21st century feel the tension still. It's as if the well-being of the world depends on our ability to prepare the men coming after us – our sons and grandsons.

The *Walking Your Son Into Manhood* blog series is designed to assist fathers on the suspension bridge of change to adjust from their comfortable position of leading in the front, where they alone set the pace and example, to a relationship where they can support their sons with encouragement from close behind.

With J.A. Taylor's advice, you'll learn how to help your son:
• build a sense of confidence and accomplishment.
• create positive connections with solid adults.
• live with a positive purpose.
Visit jackataylor.com to follow along.